THE PATH TO MISERY

Book I in the Hallowed Treasures Saga

VICTORIA STEELE LOGUE

RAVENLORE

Victorialogue.com

Published in the United States by Ravenlore,
an imprint of Low Country Press

ISBN 978-0-9883044-5-1
eBook ISBN 978-0-9883044-6-8

Cover art copyright ©2016 by David Hayworth
Cover design, map and heraldic crests by David Hayworth

Printed in the United States of America

10 9 8 7 6 5 4 3 2 1

Dedication

To my own Princess, Mary Griffin Logue.
From a castle bed to fairy dusters,
you have always been the jewel in my crown.
And to my Muse. Thank you for your Divine inspiration.

Western Kingdoms

Northern Waste

Kamartha

Kaumari

Naphtali

jungnay *

Dziron

Sea of
Blood

kamea

Devastation
of Pelf

Aden

ponike

buta *

N

W E

S

Anoon Ocean

EASTERN KINGDOMS

NORTHERN WASTE

muezi-barafu

sigwald★

SIMOON

goshen★

NAPHTALI

SHEBA

ZION

★jazeel

prychew

ANNEWVEN

◆kamea

arbenth◆

stonehelm

ADEN

FAVONIA

seemu★

★ponike

ADAMAH

DYFED

TARSHISH

portuma

cartessos

THE THIRTEEN HALLOWED TREASURES

The quest central to this saga centers on recovering the Thirteen Treasures of the Thirteen Kingdoms. These hallowed treasures come from a Welsh tradition dating to the 15th-16th century, which lists these treasures as:

I. White Hilt: The Sword of Rhydderch the Generous
or *Dyrnwyn: Gleddyf Rhydderch Hael*
If a wellborn man drew it himself, it burst into flame from its hilt to its tip.

II. The Hamper of Gwyddno Long-Shank
or **Mwys Gwyddno Garanir**
It is said that one could put food for one man into the basket and when it opened, for one hundred men could be found within.

III. The Horn of Bran
or *Corn Bran Galed O'R Gogledd*
It was said that whatever drink one might wish for could found in this horn. It is also rumored that Merlin obtained the horn, which had been cut from the head of a satyr.

IV. The Chariot of Morgan the Wealthy
or *Car Morgan Mwynfawr*
Once in the chariot, a man could wish to be a certain place and thus get there quickly.

V. The Halter of Clydno Eiddyn
or *Cebyster Clydno Eiddyn*
When attached to the foot of the bed, this halter would be filled with whichever horse one wished for.

VI. The Knife of Llawfrodded the Horseman
or *Cyllel Llawfrodded Farchog*
This one knife would carve enough food to allow twenty-four men to eat at table.

VII. The Cauldron of Dyrnwch the Giant
or *Pair Dyrnwch Gawr*
The cauldron would boil food for brave men only; never boiling for cowards

VIII. The Whetstone of Tudwal Tudglyd
or *Hogalen Tudwal Tudglydd*
If this stone was used by a brave man to sharpen his sword, and he drew blood with it, that person would die. No harm would come to the opponent from a coward's sharpened with it.

IX. The Coat of Padarn Red-Coat
or *Pais Padarn Beisrydd*
If worn by a well-born man, it would fit; if not, it would not go in him.

X. The Crock and Dish of Rhyngenydd the Cleric
or *Gren A Desgyll Rhyngenydd Ysgolhaig*
Whatever food might be wished for would appear in the crock and dish.

XI. Mantle of Arthur
or *Len Arthyr Yng Nghernyw*
The cloak has the ability to make the wearer invisible.

XII. The Chessboard of Gwenddolau, son of Ceidio
or *Gwyddbwyll Gwendolau ap Ceidio*
Made of silver and gold, the chessboard was said to possess mystical powers and would continue to play by itself once set up.

XIII. The Ring of Eluned
or *Eluned's Ring and Stone*
When it is placed on one's finger, with the stone inside the hand and closed upon the stone, the wearer is invisible.

Following the this book, you will find information on each of the Thirteen Kingdoms, a pronunciation guide, as well as lists of the days of the week and months of the year.

THE PATH TO MISERY
Book I in the Hallowed Treasures Saga

"And for a long time yet, led by some wondrous power, I am fated to journey hand in hand with my strange heroes and to survey the surging immensity of life, to survey it through the laughter that all can see and through the tears unseen and unknown by anyone."

-Nicolai Gogol
Dead Souls

PROLOGUE

"The most difficult path to tread
is the way that leads to one's own soul."

-Geillis Saille
The Ghost of Loss

Eleven years ago . . .
Perched atop her golden ball, Eluned made a great show out of searching for a four-leafed clover amidst the brilliant green patch that grew profusely in one of the castle's many courtyards. She found herself smiling, her cheeks flushing as she pondered the mischief she might achieve before they realized she was missing yet again. Keeping a surreptitious eye on her ladies-in-waiting, she rolled backwards a little ways to see if they noticed her movement.

It was one of those breathtaking days late in the month of Saitheh when the air is crisp but warm in the sun, the sky is a brilliant azure, and all the colors, scents, and sounds seem more palpable than usual. The three women were so deeply engrossed in their gossip that the seven-year-old princess decided she would either have to start screaming, or perhaps throw her ball at them to get them to notice her. Perfect. But just in case, she slowly rolled backwards a few feet closer to the edge of the forest.

Still nothing. It was as if they had forgotten she even existed. You would think they would learn! On the other hand, they had yet to get in trouble because she hadn't tattled on them and what was the harm, really? She always let them find her when she was ready.

Sliding off her ball, she picked it up and gave it a forceful toss into the woods. She saw the faint glint of gold as it hit the pine needles and began to roll gently downwards towards her favorite glade. The Princess liked this particular spot because she was able to scramble up the large parapet of granite that stood watch over the small clearing. Standing atop the giant boulder, she felt adventurous and more importantly, free. Even at her youthful age she felt trapped by the bounds of her father's kingdom. Alone in this little glen, she could be anything she wanted—an elf, a faery, a mermaid; better still (and this would horrify her mother) a knight, a pirate, or a wizard.

Eluned followed her golden ball downhill, footsteps nearly silent on the pine straw. She had just stepped onto the velvety moss that marked the transition from the forest into the clearing when she heard the bell-like chime of her ball as it made contact with the granite. Striding into the flower-filled glade, she was just in time to see her ball bounce off the rock and roll backwards into the center of a ring of toadstools.

Her mouth parted in awe. A faery ring! The Princess felt her eyes well with tears of happiness. Eluned had always known this was a special spot and now she was convinced it was enchanted. Joining her ball in the center of the ring, she pulled it into her lap and rested her chin on its polished surface, eyes closed as she basked in her secret knowledge, pondering faeries with delight.

Suddenly she felt the coal black hairs on the back of her neck prickle and she was overwhelmed with the sense of being watched. She slowly opened her eyes to find herself staring into a pair the same shade of sea green as her own. Except these were in the face of a bizarre little creature that looked a bit like a fox, but with coarse grey fur and really long and twitchy ears.

Eluned scrambled to her feet, but more in amazement than fear. What on earth was this creature? It continued to stare at her so she finally just asked. "What are you?"

The creature had smiled, and caught off guard, she laughed at its sharp-edged and skewed teeth. By the time she left the glade more than an hour later, the Princess and the Bandersnatch (for that is what the creature called itself) had become fast friends.

10th Neeon

WAITING FOR THE PRINCESS TO ARRIVE in their little clearing was something Jabberwock the Bandersnatch, who had named himself for a beloved ancient poem, had done many times during the past eleven years. Rarely did Eluned reach the glade before he did. He could probably count the times on the claws of his front left paw. But that was no doubt because her various tutors, and most lately, Brother Columcille, tended to keep her at her lessons until the very last moment.

Jabberwock often bided his time by pondering time while waiting for Eluned. It was something he liked to engage in as time remained to him a perpetual mystery—a concept that he persistently tried to grasp and which, just as his long, sharp, curved nails scratched its surface, would slip inexplicably and inexorably from his clasp. He, himself, had been around for a very long time—centuries. And while he knew he was capable of being killed, he had long since forgotten whether his kind were immortal, or if they had an actual life span. To his knowledge, he was the only remaining Bandersnatch in existence.

But this chilly, and somewhat breezy winter's day in early Neeon was an exception as it was the last time for perhaps as many as three years that the Princess and her mentor would meet here. And while they usually met within the castle during the Kingdom of Zion's cold winter months, they agreed for old time's sake that they must meet in the clearing one last time.

So rather than ponder time (because tomorrow they would begin the journey for which the Princess had been longing since she was a child), he just listened. Perhaps Omni, his god, would try to speak to him one more time. A whisper of affirmation in the icy wind would suffice. He wasn't asking for much. And he did listen for a time, but soon his mind drifted back to the Princess.

Eleven years, he sighed. It had been eleven years since he had first become acquainted with Eluned. He had known about the young Princess since her birth, and had been requested to keep an eye on her by her great grandmother, the former Queen Fuchsia.

When he had arrived in Zion eleven years ago, it had been many years since he had been at Castle Mykerinos. He remembered that he had been worried that his reception there might be a tad on the frosty side, as frigid as the wind that now ruffled his fur. And it had been until he had a chance to speak with King Seraphim and outline his strategy. The King had grudgingly acquiesced and plans were set in process.

And so it was that on that beautiful day in the balmy month of Saitheh eleven years ago he had found the clearing where, Eluned's ladies-in-waiting informed him, she escaped to every chance she got. As a matter of fact, one of the ladies said with a twinkle in her eye, on orders from the King they had taken to ignoring her for a few minutes just so she could experience that thrill of escape. Obviously things would have been handled differently had she not always headed for the glade with the granite boulder.

Scrambling up the humongous rock was rather more difficult than he liked, but once settled atop it he had a perfect view of the grass and flower filled glen. When a golden ball suddenly appeared at the edge of the woods, he wasn't unnerved, having been warned in advance of its arrival. As a matter of fact, he tried to maintain a neutral expression in case the Princess spotted him instantly.

The glimmering sphere had rolled silently across a carpet of moss softer and more richly green than the velvet cloak that swung from the Queen's ivory shoulders, before reaching the grass and bouncing, with a gentle ding, against the wonderful tabernacle of granite upon which he perched. The plaything then ricocheted backwards and quivered to a halt precisely in the center of a faery ring of toadstools.

And what could be more perfect for a child than to have her golden ball enchanted by faeries, Jabberwock remembered thinking at the time.

This was how the Bandersnatch met the young Princess. Eluned sat in the center of the faery ring, golden ball clasped in silky, plumpish, childish hands. Her eyes had been closed, and Jabberwock sensed she was imagining herself as a faery. He had to bite his cheek to prevent himself from smiling. And that was when she had felt his eyes upon her. He watched as her thick-lashed eyes had trembled open, and soon he was staring into a pair of sea green eyes every bit as deep and unfathomable as his own.

One day she would learn that Jabberwock had chameleon eyes that seemed to change with his thoughts, often reflecting his surroundings—the crystal clear water of a spring, the royal purple of violets, the ashy grey of a stormy sky—but on this day she just assumed he had the same unusual eye color as she did.

Rising to her feet, Eluned's full lips had parted in surprise but not fear. The Princess was too self-contained, too independent to feel fear. Impatience she felt deeply and often, but as protected as she was in her father's kingdom, she had as yet no reason to experience fear. When she was older, she would yearn to discover all emotions but at the tender age of seven she did not realize there were a multitude, a legion of emotions eager to clasp and caress, touch and tear, at her heart.

"What are you?" she had finally spoken, and her voice had fallen like the song of a nightingale upon Jabberwock's pointed

and rather large ears. Jabbberwock had smiled, revealing a for-
midable number of sharp and profoundly crooked teeth.

The Princess had laughed and recited a line from a book of
nearly forgotten faery tales that her great grandmother had left
behind in the castle, "My, what big teeth you have, Grandma."

"A curse are these teeth," he had replied in a voice as unexpectedly deep and rich as fresh-tilled earth. The Princess
smiled at him and he noted that she was firmly planted in the
awkward tooth stage sporting a combination of baby teeth and
permanent teeth. But they were clearly going to be straight
and lovely.

"No more a curse than my being a princess." Eluned had
slapped her golden ball for emphasis.

"A curse being a princess?" Jabberwock had asked.

My parents never let me do anything," she had complained. "It seems like I always have someone watching my
every move."

"Indeed." he had looked amused. "You seem to be alone
now."

Eluned had snorted then blushed, because her mother had
told her that was very un-princess-like. "Oh, they'll be here
shortly."

Jabberwock happened to know that it hurt King Seraphim
and Queen Ceridwen deeply that their only child champed
constantly at the bit of royalty. Though naught but a fledgling,
she was clearly ready to take on the world; and the walls that
surrounded her father's kingdom were to her the walls of a
cage.

"She is much too impatient," the Queen had said, placing
her long and fragile hand over her heart.

"Must be from your side of the family." The King had
frowned at his wife, but there had been a sparkle of mischief in
his eyes for he knew full well it was his own grandmother reflected in his daughter's beautiful face. And Queen Fuchsia was
the reason that Jabberwock had returned to Castle Mykerinos.

The Bandersnatch had smiled again. "Do you escape your ladies on a regular basis?" he had asked.

"I . . ." she had replied, clearly trying to come up with a reason for being alone. Her lower lip caught between pearly white teeth, she hesitated for a second before the Bandersnatch had rescued her from a lie.

"So, you do elude them often?"

"They're so boring. They never let me do anything. They're always afraid."

"Afraid?"

"Because I'm a Princess and they think that I'm going to hurt myself and they'll be to blame." She had flushed in indignation, and roses bloomed on her ivory cheeks. "I see only the fear in their eyes."

"Fear is what you see? Are you sure?"

"I," she had stuttered. "What else could it be?"

"But if they are afraid of your harming yourself, would they not follow you directly?"

"They're so busy talking that they never see me leave."

"Or, perchance, they've been instructed to allow you a little freedom?"

Eluned's eyes widened as the truth dawned on her. Of course! She blushed again. And all this time she had thought she was getting away with something. She wanted to pout but that was apparently unseemly for a princess, as well.

"Do you not have any companions your age?" the Bandersnatch interrupted her thoughts. "What about the Prince, Uriel?"

"Him! He won't even deign to meet me, and all the children of my father's lords are much older than I."

"I am sorry to hear you have no companions. It must be difficult."

"Honestly, I don't mind at all. I am very content to spend my time alone."

"I would be more than happy to spend some time with you," Jabberwock offered. "Do you like faery tales?"

"I love stories! I read whenever I have the chance. Will you tell me one?" Her pale green eyes were alight with anticipation.

"Have a seat," Jabberwock had invited her, indicating the faery ring. The Princess had crossed her legs and once again rested her chin upon the golden ball in her lap. The sun reflected a delightful gold onto her complexion; Jabberwock had given a quick lap to his bristly grey fur before settling down, forepaws crossed.

"Do you suppose there really were dragons once?" Eluned had asked hopefully as Jabberwock finished his tale. She had leaned toward him in expectation, carelessly imprisoning a tendril of hair behind her ear.

"There are too many stories about the creatures for dragons not to have existed at some point. Don't you agree?"

"And unicorns?"

"And mermaids, gryphons, wyverns and phoenixes."

"Is that why so many kingdoms use them as their sigils? What a wonderful time that must have been."

"It's easy to mourn the past," Jabberwock had sighed.

"I know. What has passed is past," Eluned had sulked, slapping the golden ball again for emphasis. "I do know it's true but I see a long, boring life stretched ahead of me. I want . . ."

"Knights in shining armor, dragons, unicorns and mermaids?"

"Yes," she had nodded emphatically, raven curls bouncing around her shoulders.

"These creatures can disguise themselves," he had warned. "Beware or you may miss them."

"You think so?"

"I know so."

She had mused on this, simultaneously wondering where the faeries went during the day. She was sure they were nocturnal. She liked that word. Nocturnal. She had tried it, aloud.

"Oh, definitely nocturnal," Jabberwock agreed.

"So, how will my knight in shining armor disguise himself?"

Jabberwock had revealed his ragged teeth in a grin so broad it split his face. His eyes, reflecting the deeper green of the forest before him, caught the sunlight and refracted into a thousand spikes of shimmering light. It was like the sun breaking from behind a cloud and setting a cool green pool ablaze with fire.

"I think you know." She had stated almost wonderingly.

"Let's just say that I have a vague idea."

"More than vague."

Jabberwock had continued to grin; then he stretched, skinny little rear end and bushy bottle brush tail raised high in the air. "I believe it is time for your lessons with Brother Cuthbert, is it not?"

Eluned had sighed, but she stood and stretched as well, for the first time wondering how the Bandersnatch seemed to know so much about her. He had obviously been right about her ladies-in-waiting because they still had yet to appear. This meeting, like so much of her life, had been planned. Fortunately, she liked the little Bandersnatch. "Will I see you again, Jabberwock the Bandersnatch?" she had giggled. Such a funny name!

"I should hope so," he had replied.

And so she had, Jabberwock remembered. And now he continued to bide his time—awaiting the arrival of the Princess Eluned, just as he had nearly every day for the past eleven years. Time had changed things, he mused. Golden balls had been tossed (though not indefinitely, he hoped) aside for better, if not bigger, things for far and perhaps lost horizons. The wise (but mad, he mused) John Ruskin had said, "You may chisel a boy into shape, but you cannot hammer a girl into anything. She grows as a flower does."

Jabberwock's rose was beginning to bloom—an exotic blossom existing on the edge of a most common forest—and one that he would soon introduce to the world outside the walls of Castle Mykerinos.

He was startled from his reverie by the sound of her voice calling his name, huskier now at the age of seventeen. Gone was the angelic nightingale. Here now, rushing into the glade as if it might disappear before her liquid eyes was the impetuous lark. And he knew in less than twenty-four hours the door to her gilded cage would finally swing open.

Part One

1ˢᵗ Hetal

"Now you're sure this is going to work?" King Uriel and Jabberwock the Bandersnatch were standing next to each other, surveying a map spread out upon the table in front of them. Well, actually, the king was standing upon the tiled floor; Jabberwock was poised on the table itself.

"Of course," the Bandersnatch replied.

"Well, if it doesn't," Uriel groused, "then there is absolutely no way in the universe she'll marry me, despite the fact we're betrothed."

"Uriel, I have known Eluned for eleven years; seen and conversed with her nearly every day for the past eleven years, I might add. We agreed when you were a mere child that refusing to meet her would alone instill you with some mystery. Not actually showing up for the betrothal ceremony just sealed that. I know the Princess. She thrives on adventure, the enigmatic. If she meets you when you're not 'you,' she's guaranteed to fall in love with you, just as we have always planned.

"Guaranteed, hmm? I don't actually see how you can guarantee something like that. And if you mess this up for me, I may never forgive you. I'll take your word for it now, but if it ever seems as if it's not going to happen, our course of action will have to change."

Jabberwock rolled his eyes and bared his crooked teeth. "Eluned's eighteenth birthday is just a months away . . ."

"Fine, fine," Uriel grimaced, "let's get on with it." He hated the thought of living in doubt, and living in the hope that the plan would work, but at this point it was the only option.

"Now this is what I need you to do . . ."

THE SUN WAS BREAKING OVER THE HORIZON when the tip-tap of Jabberwock's claws could be heard leaving Uriel's palace behind. After years in the making, it seemed as if all their planning might finally come to fruition. The real question was, of course, would the Princess actually fall in love with Uriel or was she, perhaps, hiding facets of her self from the Bandersnatch? It was never beyond reason that a monkey wrench might be thrown into their plans; but should that happen could they overcome it? In his heart, Jabberwock knew that love would win but what or who might intercede in the meantime?

If the Bandersnatch had learned anything in his eternity of a lifetime, he had learned that you could not completely predict the future. Free will, importunate circumstance . . . hang it all, what had it been called in the distant past? Chaos theory? It reigned freely, much to his disgust.

Wasn't he a living testament to chaos theory? Sure, at this point, all had gone according to plan, but the Princess was still confined to her father's kingdom.

Uriel, a trifle older than the Princess, had already escaped the bounds of his kingdom. His father died when he was thirteen and he had reigned with the help of his Protectors until he was eighteen. Fortunately, during those five years, Uriel, with the aid of Jabberwock, had remained stalwart in his convictions and had not been taken advantage of by his father's lords and counselors. Although, Jabberwock reminded himself, there had been rumblings from other kingdoms, particularly from the Kingdom of Adamah, which bordered Uriel's Kingdom of Aden to the southeast. Those threats had died an abrupt and mysterious death as far as Uriel and Jabberwock were concerned. They felt in their bones that a larger threat was looming on the horizon.

So, Uriel had spent the past three years visiting the Thirteen Kingdoms and continuing to educate himself, both politically and in the art of war. Though personally he despised the thought of battle. Why couldn't people just discuss things rationally; work things out that way? The traveling had done him a world of good, and he felt he had a pretty clear view of where loyalties lay with the various rulers.

Certainly the Kingdom of Zion, ruled by Eluned's father and mother, was his greatest ally. The fact that he had been betrothed to their daughter at such a young age and the recent "official" betrothal ceremony (which he had missed on purpose) were both testament to the fact that the alliance was still strong. But, who else could they count on if it came to war? The Kingdoms of Sheba, Favonia and Dyfed were also part of the Triquetra Alliance. But, the Kingdoms of Naphtali and Tarshish were apparently remaining neutral until pushed one way or the other. Unfortunately, the Awen Alliance, headed by King Arawn of Annewven and King Hamartia and Queen Foehn of Simoon along with King Hevel of Adamah were as strongly united as his kingdom with Zion and Dyfed, and not only did they wish to greatly increase the size of their kingdoms, but they had managed to pull the rulers of Dziron and Kamartha into their evil schemes. How long would it be before they started attacking the Triquetra-aligned kingdoms at their borders? Regardless of the politics, Uriel had come to realize at twenty-one, that Eluned was the one for him despite the fact that his father's wishes to make a powerful alliance with King Seraphim had at first made him resent the Princess. Regular reports over the years from Eluned's tutors and Jabberwock, had allowed him to fall slowly in love with her. Those feelings had made it easy for Jabberwock to talk the King into missing their betrothal ceremony, not to mention his spurning actually meeting her. So Eluned thought Uriel a milksop, so much the better.

Jabberwock recalled the final moments of his visit with Uriel. The Princess still had no idea why he really disappeared for a couple of months every year. He claimed vacation, maintaining old ties, and that sort of thing and she believed him. And a good thing too.

The previous year he had been at Castle Bennu in Ponike, Uriel's capitol, for the King's twenty-first birthday. He wasn't sure how the Kingdom of Aden had ended up with the Mantle of Arthur. No doubt a bride from Annewven had brought it over the mountains in a past too dim for mortals to remember. He knew with absolute conviction that there was absolutely no way it had knowingly left that ever-evil kingdom. It was too great a treasure. One of the Thirteen Hallowed Treasures, for that matter. The treasures, once confined to Annewven, were now scattered to the four winds. Jabberwock suspected that the majority remained in Annewven and Simoon, which had been linked for as long as he could remember—centuries and centuries.

On his twenty-first birthday, Uriel had finally been able to open the ironbound and incredibly plain chest that had belonged to his father. He had imagined that it would contain family papers and maybe a last letter from his father reminding him of his duties as king (and of his love for his only son). But what he had found when the chest creaked open was a slightly moth-eaten woolen cloak of an indeterminate color. Perhaps it had once been grey? As he had pulled it from the chest, the odor of cedar and sandalwood followed. He had held it up, questioningly, to Jabberwock.

"Put it on," the Bandersnatch had commanded. Uriel had swung the soft wool around his shoulders.

"Fasten it." An ornate breastpin of gold fashioned in the

shape of a phoenix, the sigil of his kingdom, was attached to the cloak. Uriel had done as he was told.

"Now look in the mirror." Uriel had turned to face the long mirror that was suspended from the molding that topped the marble wall in his father's former bedchamber. The new king had yet to feel comfortable enough to take over the royal compartments—still too many memories of his mother who had preceded his father in death by a year; Uriel was sure that his father's death a year later was in part due to the loss of his beloved wife. Uriel had stared into the mirror for several minutes.

"What do you see?" the Bandersnatch had finally barked.

"Nothing."

"Nothing?"

"Is it . . .?" Uriel hadn't been able to go on. He swallowed hard, and tried again. "Is it the Mantle of Arthur?"

"Indeed."

Uriel had chuckled, ruefully. "Oh how I could have used this in the past three years! Talk about being a fly on the wall!"

"Well, it's not too late," Jabberwock had replied. "I have a strong feeling you will be needing it in the not-too-distant future."

Uriel had raised an eyebrow, "This is going to be more of a quest than a journey, I suspect."

Jabberwock only smiled mysteriously in reply, and had suggested that the King return the cloak to its chest until he set out for the predetermined rendezvous point.

This very morning before he'd departed Castle Bennu, Jabberwock had reminded the King, "Please do not forget the cloak! I imagine it will come in handy in more ways than one. I have no doubt the King Seraphim will be presenting Eluned with her treasure before we leave tomorrow. Unfortunately, she will have to discover what it does on her own."

Uriel had raised an eyebrow, yet again, but this time more

sardonically as if he had little faith in that ever coming to pass.

"You're still underestimating her!" Jabberwock had laughed.

"I know, I know." He conceded, shaking his head. "Where's my faith? I want to believe, and I do understand that we will be married regardless. I would just prefer that she love rather than tolerate me."

The Princess. Jabberwock had felt his spirits beginning to lift while thinking of Uriel. But Eluned. His mood suddenly plummeted. She was perfect for Uriel. They complemented each other beautifully. They hadn't even met yet, and they were both fighting their eventual union—Eluned resenting her marriage being arranged for her; Uriel dreading a marriage founded on resentment. And notwithstanding his eleven years of work with her, he had been unable to do anything with that will of hers. That strong will. Sometimes she did things just to irritate him. He knew it but could do nothing about it. And though he hated to admit it, he wasn't perfect. There, he thought it.

"I'm not perfect!" He shouted to the barren hayfields on either side of him. He felt a slight weight lift from his heart. "I'm not PERFECT!" There. Well, he could just do the best he could do, by Omni. He was just Its pawn after all. Okay, he thought as he looked heavenward, maybe that was a bit harsh. But the truth remained, he could only do the best he could do.

"And that's all I expect." The words weren't as much heard as felt.

"Yes, and we both know what happens to those like me."

Silence. A chill breeze laden with the scent of impending rain ruffled his wiry gray fur.

10ᵀᴴ Neeon

The Princess Eluned stared out the leaded glass of her bed-room window, high in the turret of the southeast tower of Castle Mykerinos. She could just see the snow-capped peaks of the mountains over the palace's walls. Tomorrow, she shivered, she might be lodging beneath their slopes.

The following day she would celebrate her eighteenth birthday, and she didn't even know what to expect on the day's dawning. Yet, the Princess had felt that her anticipation of the event was nearly more than she could bear because of what the date promised—freedom. It was less than twelve hours until dawn, and officially her birthday, and the wait seemed inter-minable.

Jabberwock had hinted that she would experience another world—a world that reflected fear and worry in his glass-like eyes. But if that were so then why was he so determined to show it to her? Surely her father's kingdom, outside the castle walls, would have been enough to satisfy her curiosity?

Yet the Bandersnatch knew her better than she knew her-self; at least, that was how she felt most of the time. Eluned sighed again. She must trust him completely. If it hadn't been for the strange little creature she would soon be married off to King Uriel and she would have to spend the rest of her life bound within the walls of yet another castle. And, she doubted she'd find a friend comparable to Jabberwock in its woods.

Stretching, she vacated her window seat, unconsciously smoothing the pleats of her soft flannel skirt. Catching a glimpse of huge eyes and creased brow in the gilt-framed mirror that took up significant space on the wall opposite the window, Eluned stopped to compose herself. She looked almost frantic. Two spots of color burned along her cheekbones, distressingly vibrant on skin as white as fine alabaster.

Hair as dark as obsidian had escaped from the black velvet ribbon that unsuccessfully attempted to control locks savage with curls. She hadn't helped it any by pulling at it in her anxious state. Her eyes were wide with fear, as well, as if she were afraid she might miss something.

Untying the black velvet ribbon, Eluned took a deep breath and closed her eyes. The Princess exhaled slowly and concentrated on a few more deep breaths, just as Brother Columcille had taught her in order to calm herself down. "Omni within," she thought, inhaling slowly, "Omni without." Her heart rate began to level off. Much better.

Eluned surveyed herself once more. Definitely much better. Definitely. Her dark hair curled, wild and barbaric, around her face. She liked it like that although her mother absolutely despised it. It made her feel untamed and gypsy-like, primitive and savage. She wanted to strip down and dance nearly naked around a fire. She wanted to meet an equally exotic man. On the beach. The waves pounding the shore matching the pounding of her heart as he took her in her arms . . . Once again, her heart caught in her throat. She wanted too much. She knew it. A fine spray of tears misted from the ocean of her eyes. It was hopeless, she thought, biting her full lower lip. Her expectations for the rest of her life were too high. And, tomorrow would never come.

Returning to her the window seat, Eluned once again regarded the mountains that formed the eastern boundary of her father's kingdom. The snow that capped the Mountains of Misericord's western slopes was beginning to glow a pale orange as the rays of the setting sun reflected off the crystalline surface.

The dinner bell rang, and the Princess stood, sighing. It would be her final meal with her parents for perhaps three years. And while she was desperate to be on her way, she felt an obligation to be on her best behavior for this combination bon voyage and prevenient birthday feast.

WHEN SHE RETURNED TO HER ROOM HOURS LATER, it was with a heavier heart. The meal had turned out to be as bittersweet as she had feared as her parents tried to make light of her leaving. Yet the weight of their trepidation was palpable, and she found herself constantly biting her tongue in effort to refrain from speculating about what she might encounter beyond the castle's walls.

THE PRINCESS WAS ALREADY UP THAT MORNING as the day dawned pink, orange and purple around the mountains to the east. Eluned had barely slept that night, tossing and turning as her mind raced. The only thing the Bandersnatch had admitted is that they would lodge the first night in Roodspire, which was southeast of Castle Mykerinos.

Eluned finally crawled out of bed, and was in her window seat, goose down comforter wrapped around her slender shoulders, to watch the sky lighten from velvety black to deep purple and blue. Eluned waited with trepidation and anticipation for the appearance of the sun. She longed to feel its warmth against her face; to finally experience the freedom it would bring as it summoned the new day. And that made her wonder where she and the Bandersnatch would travel to first. Some place warm, she hoped, for she lived in a mostly cold land and was born in an always cold and snowy month. She hated being cold, and during the long winters it sometimes seemed as if the sun had deserted her father's kingdom permanently.

The sun crested behind the mountains reflecting shimmery gold light into her eyes. She blinked, lifting her face to the perceived warmth, and shivered with delight, throwing the comforter onto the floor. She always made her bed but never again, not here, anyway!

She bit her lip. On second thought, was that really the impression she wanted to leave behind. She bent over and picked up the crumpled rose-pink duvet, placing it back on her bed and smoothing it out. She even picked up her pillow, re-plumped it, and reclined her stuffed unicorn against it. She was going to miss her little Eira. There had been countless times in the past eighteen years when she had hugged the stuffed animal to her chest as she fell asleep; she had cried many tears into its soft fabric as well, but she was afraid that carrying it with her would be yet another sign of her immaturity, something of which she was constantly aware.

It was time to pack. The Princess had saved this final act of preparation for the very last moment because Jabberwock had told her she could bring little more than what she was wearing. A medium-sized tapestry bag would have to suffice for she did not want to overburden Hayduke, her beloved mule. He would be carrying the majority of their things—blankets, some food, clothes, cooking gear, and so on, and she couldn't bear the thought of him struggling under undue weight.

Gazing, reflectively, into the depths of her closet, she wondered what to bring. They would just have to go someplace warm. That was all there was to it. She couldn't possibly carry all the clothes she would need to keep warm. Eluned decided she would wear her wool cloak to begin with, and toss it whenever they reached the warm place. The islands, most definitely, she decided. She would ask him to take her to the Favonian Islands.

White, then. The choice of color wasn't difficult. Until she turned eighteen, she was required to wear white in the spring and summer, black in the fall and winter. Now, she neither wanted nor needed a brightly colored frock. She just wanted to be gone. So, she would pack white, wear black. Long skirts and dresses were all that were worn by women in her father's kingdom. The Princess had often pondered what it would be like to wear pants. She wondered now what people wore in the Favonian Islands, what kind of clothes they wore in the world they would be exploring. Would she stand out? Would people look at her and laugh? Would it be obvious that she had led an amazingly sheltered life?

Shaking her head as if to clear the cobwebs that were obscuring her thoughts, she donned her favorite blouse and skirt, and reined in her hair with a lace ribbon after braiding it loosely. Sprawled coltish on the floor, she pulled on thick wool socks. Shoes were tossed overhead and on to the marble floor behind her as she scoured the armoire for appropriate footwear. Ah! She pulled soft leather boots over delicately arched feet and lean calves. Pearl stud earrings completed her travel outfit. That and the little suede pouch she always wore around her neck.

Nightshirt, toothbrush and other necessary items were tossed into the tapestry satchel on which virgins and unicorns danced through an enchanted forest. She was ready to go. She was shaking. Her heart felt as if it were racing. When would the Bandersnatch be announced? Where in creation was he?

Pacing the pink marble floor, picking up her shoes and tossing them back into the wardrobe, and simultaneously kicking throw rugs impatiently aside as they got in her way, she wondered if she could stand waiting another minute, even another second.

A gentle knock at her door. Her heart stopped.

It was her mother. Tears coursed down her cheeks. The Princess, uncharacteristically, threw herself into her mother's arms.

"I wish you didn't feel as if you must embark on this . . . this folly," her mother whispered, holding her only child close to her breaking heart.

"Mother we've discussed this oh so many times," Eluned said, patiently. "Please don't try to stop me. Not now! Not so close . . ."

She heard the commotion downstairs and stiffened. Jabberwock must have arrived. Her mother slowly distanced herself from her daughter and, almost as an afterthought, kissed Eluned gently on the lips.

"I know I haven't told you often enough," she sighed, patting the tears from her cheeks with a silk handkerchief, "but I love you, desperately."

Tears made a journey of their own down the rose-dappled cheeks of the Princess. "I will miss you, Mother," she whispered. "Both you and Father, but mostly you." Grabbing her colorful valise, the Princess flew out of her room and down the winding stairs, not daring to look back at her chamber, her mother standing there in tears. She didn't want to stay. She must get away. She must! She felt as if her entire life depended on it.

But, it wasn't going to be quite that easy. At the bottom of the stairs, the King, and Brother Columcille and the Bandersnatch watched her descent.

"A word before you leave," her father said, quietly. His eyes, a slightly deeper shade of green than her own, were brighter than usual.

"Yes, Papa." The King led the way to the sitting room and they settled themselves. The Princess was anxious to leave, but it was clear that her father was not in a hurry. She grudgingly accepted a cup of coffee and allowed the maidservant to stir some cream into the porcelain mug decorated with the Kingdom's heraldic symbol, a golden Gryphon on a field of black. She stared into the tawny liquid and waited for her father to say whatever it was he felt he had to say, mentally rolling her eyes.

"I am not really sure how to begin," he started, cleared his throat. "I would imagine that you are aware that your mother and I are not thrilled with the prospect of this so-called, uh, journey." He was silent a moment, heaved a sigh and began again, "But, Brother Columcille and Jabberwock, here, have convinced us that it is of utmost importance that you be allowed this chance; that it is essential to your growth in The Way, among other things. And so, you shall go. BUT, and this is a very strong and absolutely essential "But." You must be back at this castle by your twenty-first birthday. You will marry King Uriel. The date has been set and will not be moved. Do you understand?"

Eluned's eyes echoed with mutiny, but she inclined her head and murmured, "Yes, Sir."

As soon as they'd finished their coffee (although the Princess managed only a few sips), the King and Brother Columcille stood. Eluned hoisted the tapestry bag onto her shoulder and began moving toward the exit that would take them across the courtyard, through the battlements and over the drawbridge. From there they would take the wide, white track that would lead them through the village of Goshen that sprawled around the castle's walls and along the banks of the River Musk, and on to Roodspire.

At the drawbridge the King embraced his daughter before pressing a small package into her left hand. Despite her nearly frantic need to begin the journey, Eluned found tears springing once again to her eyes.

"Don't worry, Papa," she said. "I will return when I am supposed to do so, and I promise to write."

11ᵀᴴ Neeon

"So, what did he give you?" Jabberwock indicated the clumsily wrapped package that peeked from the top of Eluned's satchel where she had tossed it in her haste to hit the road. She had been so eager to begin that she'd held onto the tapestry bag rather than attach it to Hayduke's packsaddle.

They were walking, had been walking in silence for more than four hours, side by side, down the great road that led out of King Seraphim's castle. They had passed through the town of Goshen and followed the track through the largely cultivated lands that surrounded it. Mostly groves and groves of fruit trees—plums, pears and cherries—that in a few months would be covered with a faeryland of blossoms. They had long since left behind the castle with its black banners twitching slowly in the slight breeze. It had disappeared from view completely as she and Jabberwock entered the foothills that rolled in muted tones of brown and gold into the mountains beyond. Hayduke had followed contentedly behind them attached to the lead secured around Eluned's wrist.

Jabberwock had been content to leave the Princess to her thoughts, but he considered that it was now time for her to find out what her father had given her. It was now well past lunch

time but she seemed so intent on putting miles between herself
and her home of eighteen years that he had chosen to remain
silent.

The Princess stopped suddenly, dropped her satchel on
the hard pack, pulled off her leather gloves, and ripped and
shredded the gossamer tissue of the package her father had
pressed into her hand as she fled her home of eighteen years.

Her fingers, stiff from the cold, fumbled at the lid. Throwing her head back, she took a deep breath and tried again. She
could already feel the tears stinging behind her eyes. Why did
she have to cry so much? The ornate ring and stone nestled on
a bed of purple velvet inside the box broke the dam. She could
barely see the ring's design through her flood of tears. She
swiped them angrily away so that she could study the contents
of the small container. Like her valise, the golden ring abounded in mythical creatures, albeit miniscule: a knight battled a
dragon, lovely maiden at its clawed and horny feet; a beautiful
virgin (for only virgins can see unicorns) embraced the one-
horned creature beneath the mourning boughs of a weeping
willow; and, what was this? The Bandersnatch? Sitting upon a
rock in the middle of a forest in discussion with a young princess with what was apparently a golden ball clutched to her flat
chest?

She looked at Jabberwock in awe. He looked rather nonplussed, himself. Maybe puzzled was a better word.

"Are you not going to read the note?" he asked, impatiently. She picked up the box at her feet, retrieved the thrice-folded
parchment.

My dearest daughter,
It breaks my aging heart to see you leave these walls
to seek the mostly cruel wonders of the outside world.
I have long teased your mother, and in your presence,
that you get your ways—passion deeply felt and hun-
ger for adventure—from her side of the family. But that

has never been true. I have always known well from whence come those generally unacceptable characteristics. My grandmother fled these very walls in the company of your little pet, leaving her husband and son to fend for themselves. I had this very special ring (it has been in the family for centuries) engraved especially for you. A plain gold band didn't seem appropriate. I am sure Omni won't mind. Be careful my darling, and remember that we love you, as your mother no doubt told you, desperately.

Your loving Papa

Eluned's head was reeling. Her great-grandmother (she'd heard the whispers—it was a forbidden subject in the castle) had known the Bandersnatch, had headed off on a similar adventure?

"What, where, wh…?" she sputtered.

"Pull yourself together," Jabberwock replied, crossly. Count on the king to be the first one to throw a monkey wrench into his journey, although no doubt she had a right to know.

The Princess closed her eyes and took a deep, almost imperial, breath. And, raising her head on its long, delicate neck she peered, aristocratically, down at the Bandersnatch. "I think you have some explaining to do." A storm raged in her regal eyes, pearly teeth clutched sovereign lower lip in suppressed wrath.

She plopped herself down in the middle of the road, and crossed her legs, waiting. Hayduke, given a brief respite, wandered to the side of the road and began cropping at the withered grass there.

"Well, we're off to a mighty good start," Jabberwock drawled.

The Princess stared at him, perplexed. Where had that come from? Her lips thinned and lightning flashed in her eyes. "Cut the crap," she returned, tartly, proud of herself for remembering the phrase. She had read the line in a book she had discovered hidden underneath the boards in the storage space beneath the window seat in her bedroom. The frontispiece had been inscribed in her great-grandmother's flowing script:

This book is the property of Queen Fuchsia of Zion

It was a script that did not look dissimilar to her father's. Eluned had read that book, and the few others stored there, a dozen times since she had discovered their hidden spot. She had found it while looking for her own secret hiding place. They were books of adventure and romance, of mythical beasts and fearsome dragons and knights in shining armor, although one, her favorite, had been about someone called a gunslinger. They had always filled her with excitement and longing. The books spoke of other worlds and other ways of living. At any rate, her reply was enough to catch the Bandersnatch off guard.

"Where did you learn that?"

The Princess had the grace to blush before admitting that she had found some of Queen Fuchsia's books in her bedroom.

"And read them more than once apparently?"

She nodded.

He surveyed her for a second, with an odd expression on his furry face, and then sighed, and lowered himself to the pavement, front legs crossed before him.

"Are you ready?" Eluned asked, honeyed voice dripping with sarcasm.

"Quite so, your highness," Jabberwock replied, his own eyes sparking with annoyance. "We'll be lucky if we make to-night's lodgings," he muttered under his breath.

"What?"

The Bandersnatch scratched, absently, behind his long, pointed ear. The left one. The Princess was growing impatient and frustrated. If she didn't need Jabberwock to make it wherever it was they were going, she'd leave him right now.

"It was long ago and far away," the Bandersnatch began his tale.

"And the world was younger than today . . ." Eluned interrupted. She had heard him start more than one faery tale this way.

Jabberwock glared at her. "Would you like me to recount the story or not?"

The Princess sighed and rolled her eyes. "Pray, please continue, kind sir."

"Patience is definitely not one of your virtues, my dear." The Bandersnatch grinned (or was he growling?).

Eluned studied the scuffed toes of her boots, concentrated on stilling her wildly beating heart. Did it really matter that she was following in her great-grandmother's footsteps? And what about her great-grandmother's great-grandmother? Had she, too, skipped along this wide, white track, Jabberwock at her young side? She was her parents' only child. What did that mean for the Kingdom of Zion? If she had to marry Uriel, then who would rule Zion when her father and mother were gone? Would the two kingdoms join or would they rule them jointly? Would she be able to produce another heir to the throne, or thrones, for that matter? She was actually the current heir to the throne. Queen Eluned. Why was nothing ever simple? This was an aspect of her adventures that she had never considered; that would now constantly tickle at the back of her mind.

"But I'm young," she whispered to the Bandersnatch. "There's lots of time, right?"

"Plenty of time," he replied. "Do you still want to hear about your great-grandmother?"

"Of course." She stood up, stretching, tugging at the mule's lead. "But we shouldn't be wasting time sitting here." She looked at him as if it had all been his idea. "You can tell me while we're walking. If we don't get a move on, we might not make tonight's lodgings."

Jabberwock was forced to suppress a smile. Had he really expected her to grow up overnight? He was just happy she was a quick learner.

"Oh, and what's this?" She had slipped the golden ring onto the ring finger of her right hand where it seemed to fit perfectly. But, as she returned the note to the box, she noticed the stone again. The Princess carefully picked it up and studied the gently glowing gem. "Moonstone?"

"I believe so," Jabberwock agreed. The stone had the pearly luminescence of a full moon. Mysteries and their answers seemed to swim in its depths. Despite the fact it was no bigger than the smallest coin of the realm, it was nearly hypnotizing. Jabberwock cleared his throat.

"Why did he give me this?" Eluned's brow creased in perplexity.

"Try asking Omni."

"In other words, you don't know."

"I didn't say that."

"So you do know," she stamped her foot. He simply gazed unwaveringly into her eyes. She sighed. "But you're not going to tell me." Eluned withdrew from beneath her blouse the small, suede pouch she wore around her neck, and slipped the stone inside to join her good luck charm, a small heart-shaped piece of amethyst, which was also her birthstone, and her betrothal ring from Uriel, a delicately woven band of rose gold knot work with hands embracing a diamond heart. It would be more than a week before she thought of it again.

Eluned slung her bag over her shoulder and was soon ambling down the road, Hayduke trotting behind her, every step bringing her closer to the mountains in the east. Behind her right shoulder, the sun slowly burned its way toward the horizon.

"QUEEN FUCHSIA WAS FROM THE FERTILE LANDS north of the Devastation of Pelf."

"You mean the Kingdom of Kamartha?"

"Yes, but that is hard to admit now. Of course, it wasn't quite so corrupt back then. Anyway, that is where I met her . . ."

"Am I like her?"

"She is the reason I am here now."

"What do you mean?"

"Let me finish my story. When she reached her eighteenth birthday, she was sent to your great-grandfather's . . ."

"King Seraphim?" Her father had been named for him.

"Yes . . . your great-grandfather's kingdom to be his bride. I attempted, through cajolery, even bribery, to inveigle her to disappear. I knew that what she was doing was not right for her, that she was marrying the king through a misguided sense of honor and responsibility. I knew, even then, that it would all come to a bad end, that at the very least, it would leave her name tarnished and battered, never to be spoken in her land or any other.

"But she married the king with much pageantry, pomp and fanfare, not to mention a touch of theatrics and more than a little bit of grandeur, glitter and gaudiness."

"You're alliterative today," she smiled. "So, it was garish, huh?"

"Definitely so, as if to rub my nose in it all."

"But you knew her too well."

"Goes without saying, my dear. By the end of the year, young Fuchsia was expecting her first child . . ."

"King Simeon."

"Yes," the Bandersnatch sighed. He would never get accustomed to Eluned's constant interruptions. "And chomping at the bit the whole while. The child was barely weaned before Fuchsia was beseeching me to rescue her, to 'take her away from it all.' You two are so alike."

The Princess laughed, a pleasant sound like the comfortable burbling of a brook, "She didn't last very long, did she?"

"Fortunately, she did manage to accomplish the one adjunct expected of her—she bore the king an heir, a male heir, which definitely improved her situation."

"You mean it didn't matter so much if she took off?"

"It was a great embarrassment to the king, of course, but the onus for the debacle . . . "

"I hate that word!"

"Debacle?"

"Onus. Would it bother you if I asked you not to use it again?"

"What?" He sputtered. Trust Eluned to disrupt a story by objecting to the use of a word, a rather common one at that.

"It's just that that word gives me the creeps."

"The creeps?"

"You know very well what I mean. Can't you use burden instead?"

"Then I will rephrase the entire sentence. After all, my dear Princess, I am your servant."

"My friend. Not my servant. You'd make a lousy servant. You can't button buttons or bring me breakfast in bed. You can't even make a bed."

"A figure of speech, that's all. What I meant was that your wish is my command, so to speak. Does that make you happy? Don't take things so literally—it could get you into serious trouble."

"Anyway, who was the burden on?"

"Fuchsia's family were blamed for her indiscretion . . ."

"That's a nice way of putting it!"

"If they hadn't lived already beyond Naphtali near the Devastation, there would have been serious repercussions. But it was a great distance from Zion, so all contact with the Kingdom of Kamartha was dropped."

Eluned shuddered. "Will we pass through The Devastation on our journey?"

"No one passes through The Devastation. You know that."

"But you can do all kinds of magical things."

"Limited telepathy and the ability to speak are about the extent of my so-called magical powers."

"You're immortal," she said.

Jabberwock looked at her, oddly. "That hardly makes me a ledgerdemainist, a thaumaturge, a magus."

"Great," sighed Eluned, "I'm on the adventure of a lifetime with a four-legged thesaurus."

"Besides," the Bandersnatch sniffed, feigning hurt, "The Devastation is to the west, beyond the Plains of Naphtali and the Sea of Blood. We're currently traveling east. The sun is directly to our backs. You know that, as well."

Eluned felt the hairs rise at the back of her neck. She had often wheedled her nurse into telling her stories of the Sea of Blood upon whose shores the Aberrations of The Devastation dwelt. Absolutely nothing existed in The Devastation, the former Kingdom of Pelf, she'd been told. Not even the most loathsome, abominable and vile creatures that inhabited the areas adjacent to the Sea of Blood. "It's probably just as well," she whispered, eyes wide with fear. "I am not sure I want that much adventure."

"I ventured that way, myself, once, but that's another story and we'll have plenty of time for stories but right now I would like to finish the story I began hours ago."

"It hasn't been hours. You certainly love to pout!"

"No more than you, my dear."

"Yes, but I am a Princess. It just seems a bit unseemly for a Bandersnatch."

"And how would you know what is seemly for a Bandersnatch and what is not? I don't have to remind you that I am the only Bandersnatch in existence. I make my own rules. I determine my own actions."

"Yeah, yeah, heard it all before." Eluned laughed and bent down to ruffle his coarse fur, paused to scratch behind his long ears. "You're absolutely right! So, you and Fuchsia departed the Kingdom of Zion, sneaking out in the dead of night?"

"It was dawn, and I dislike the word, sneak, but yes, that's what we did."

"I'm surprised my father let me go with you, then."

"So am I. I am actually quite amazed that Brother Cuthbert and I were able to convince him of the necessity of your leaving."

"Cuthbert? I was seven!"

Yes, but I knew I needed to ask years in advance, so that when your eighteenth birthday finally approached, it wouldn't catch your parents off guard. Anyway, when we had first arrived in Zion, Fuchsia and I parted ways at the forest."

"And she'd visit you there during the day?"

"Never as often as you and I met."

"But she did when she was young, did she not? When you lived in the Wilds of Discord?"

"Yes, that's true. We're about three miles from our lodgings."

"That gives you another hour to finish the story."

"You've made me lose my train of thought," Jabberwock groused. "All these interruptions."

"Complain, complain, complain."

He sighed. "We maintained our relationship through the birth of her son and his weaning, and then began making plans to leave. She wanted to head back toward Kamartha, and we eventually arrived in Kaumari." The Bandersnatch paused sure that Eluned would interrupt. After all, Kaumari was notorious, often compared to Hollywood, which had replaced Rome in notoriety before its decadences caused its eradication by the powers in control at the time. But that was ages ago. She disappointed him. "There, Fuchsia became quite the star on The Masala," he continued.

"Star?" The Princess was perplexed. A star? On The Masala? Did they go to another galaxy?

Jabberwock began to chortle in his wheezy, rasping way.

"What? What?" Eluned was blushing. "All right. I give up. I've heard of Kaumari but The Masala? A star? What are you talking about?"

"Basically, Fuchsia became an actress, not unlike the mummers that perform at the castle. The Masala is the district in Kaumari where the actors and actresses perform. When you have a successful career in the theater, you become a star."

Eluned was horrified at the thought of her great-grandmother sinking so low as to perform for money, but was intrigued by the concept of becoming a star. It sounded so brilliant. "Why is someone called a star?"

"I don't know. Perhaps because they are self-luminous or maybe because they are full of hot air. Or, perhaps, because they are the featured performer and their name was once marked with an asterisk."

"Maybe it's because an excellent performance is rewarded with a star," Eluned mused, "or maybe, it's because . . ."

"Does it really matter?" It was Jabberwock's turn to interrupt. "Suffice to say that she did become a star. Not surprising, really, she always had a flair for the dramatic."

"Did you really save her from a dragon?"

"Where did you hear that?"

"I heard talk. Besides, what about the faery tale you told me on the first day we met?"

"Gossiping, you mean. It wasn't an actual dragon. It was an Aberration, a nameless monstrosity from the borders of The Devastation, seeking fresh meat. It had wandered too far into the Wilds."

"She was outside the castle walls?"

"She never obeyed her parents."

How romantic, Eluned sighed. For years and years she had been longing for similar adventures. Perhaps, at last . . .

"Are we on our way to meet her?" The Princess asked. "I can't wait!"

"Darling, your grasp of geography is dismaying, and I know better. Please use that pretty little head instead of just your emotions!" Then the Bandersnatch added, gently, "Fuchsia died the day I met you."

Eluned's face fell, tears once again pricked her eyes. She had already developed a strong bond of feeling, of kinship, even love for this woman, a woman so like herself. "So why are you doing this again?"

"Because when you were born, we both agreed that you would have the same opportunities that she had had, but that you wouldn't have to make the same mistake that she had made."

"You mean marrying against her will?"

"She didn't want you to marry and give birth to a child that you would never see again. You are so much like her, even when you were young I could tell. I suppose that is what eventually killed her—not being able to watch her son grow, marry, have his own children and grandchildren. She didn't want you to have to make the same, horrible choice."

They hiked on in silence.

"THANK YOU," ELUNED BROKE THE SILENCE, half an hour and a hundred yards from their lodgings later.

"For what?" Jabberwock's eyes reflected the serious sea green of Eluned's own.

"For rescuing me from the dragon."

11ᵀᴴ Neeon

After finding someone to care for Hayduke in the stables at the inn in Roodspire, they headed toward the open doors of their lodgings. The entrance of the Princess and her Bandersnatch silenced the raucous laughter and loud talk. Eluned surveyed the dim, smoky room with curiosity and was delighted. The rough hewn plank tables and benches and the even more roughly hewn men and women that occupied them brought a secret smile to her lips not dissimilar to that of the Mona Lisa. This is life, she thought. The air reeked of tobacco, wood smoke and human sweat. Eluned inhaled, deeply entranced.

Jabberwock, on the other hand, was regretting his decision to stay here. We should have camped beneath the stars, he thought, observing the shocked faces of the inn's customers. As he was wondering whether or not there would be any trouble, the innkeeper, a tall, thin man reminiscent of a great blue heron with his bushy black eyebrows, scruffy white beard and long, thin and pointed nose, rushed forward with his bright-eyed robin of a wife.

Eluned wondered if the innkeeper's wife would awake her the following morning with an "ain't you 'shamed you sleepy head?" Jabberwock had often said that very thing when, during the past decade, she had nodded off over their lessons. Learning about ancient rhymes and faery tales and other literature as she grew older had been among her favorite lessons with the Bandersnatch.

"Princess," the innkeeper croaked, and then cleared his throat. "Princess, welcome." He glanced down at Jabberwock and back at the Princess, yellow eyes twitching, nervously. "Norm'ly we doesn't allow pets, yer Highness, but," he glanced back down at the Bandersnatch and mumbled something.

"Oh, dear, dear, don't worry," the innkeeper's wife twittered when she saw the lightning flash of anger in the eyes of the Princess, "o'course yer pet kin sleep wit yer. Boris, shame on yer," she nudged her husband with a plump little hand. "Yer fergettin' yerself and yer manners. Show'm t'ther room. More'n likely ther want'a be freshnin' up afore supp."

With little more than a backward glance at Eluned and the Bandersnatch, Boris led the couple through the still silent crowd and up the stairs at the far side of the big room. As they ascended, the talk and laughter began again, quietly at first then rising until the din was so loud, the Princess couldn't hear herself think.

"Why didn't you say anything?" The Princess asked as she shut the door behind them. The thick walls and the heavy wooden door shut out most of the noise.

"What? And be thrown in with the horses and mules for sure!" Jabberwock scolded her. "That is, if they didn't throw me on that spit and burn me alive, and you, too, for that matter. Just because you're a princess doesn't mean you can't be a witch. Burned at the stake we'd be and no one would ever say a word! No. Sometimes it is better to keep your mouth shut."

Eluned paled and turned to assess the room. "Is this their best?" she asked, shocked. Touching the thin, straw mattress, her face blanched even further. She looked as if she expected to be attacked by bed bugs. Wiping her hand on the soft, gray wool of her cloak, Eluned spied a pitcher and washbowl on a rickety table against the wall, and hurried over to it to wash her hands. The soap smelled strongly of lye.

"Enjoy it," he said, his eyes snapping with amusement, "tomorrow we sleep on the ground."

"The ground?" She was horrified.

"You wanted the adventure. I never said you would get luxury accommodations."

"I think that I would rather sleep on the ground than in that bed."

"Well, don't tell the innkeeper that. You'll insult him." As if on cue, there was a knock at the door. Eluned jumped, guiltily. But it was just Boris's wife (Zelda, she introduced herself) wanting to know if they wished to supp in "ther room."

"Yes, if you don't mind," Eluned said, remembering the silence and the curious, bordering on rude, stares of the country folk downstairs.

"Ale er wine?"

"Wine, please." Zelda bustled off. Eluned had another moment's misgivings when she suddenly imagined Zelda arriving with a platter full of plump and juicy worms. Her fears were unfounded, though, for the innkeeper's wife soon returned with two heavy pottery bowls: one filled with thick, savory stew, the other with some scraps of meat. There were also steaming, fresh-from-the-oven bread, sweet, creamy butter and an earthen jug filled with cool, spiced, red wine. The Princess hadn't realized how hungry she was until the food was set before her. As a matter of fact, now that she thought about it, she had been so eager that morning to leave her prison of eighteen years behind (a castle, she reminded herself and felt a momentary guilty twinge about her devastated parents), that she had thought of doing nothing but putting one foot in front of the other for so long that not only had she forgotten to eat, breakfast or lunch, but she had had to be reminded about the gift she clasped in her hand.

"You're salivating," the Bandersnatch remarked when Zelda had left them to their meal.

A pretty pink tongue was directed at Jabberwock, "Phooey on you," she replied, spooning the rich broth into her mouth before she realized that Jabberwock was left with the bowl of scraps. Feeling guilty, she offered him some of her stew. He had definitely been accustomed to much better fare at the castle.

The Bandersnatch sighed, "Quite all right, my dear. It is my fault for choosing to stay here. In the future, we'll try to be better prepared. Besides, I've existed on raw meat more than once in the past."

DAWN WAS STRETCHING HER GOLDEN LIMBS when Jabberwock awakened the Princess. "Oh, I slept terribly," she complained.

"You don't have to tell me," snarled the Bandersnatch. "I had to listen to the rustle of straw as you tossed and turned all night."

Eluned padded over to the washbasin and splashed cold water on her puffy face. "I feel like I slept in the dragon's lair last night." She poked, tenderly, at the tired flesh beneath her eyes. "I must look like a dragon," she croaked and bared her teeth at Jabberwock.

"Sorry, my dear, but I am afraid you couldn't even frighten a mouse. You always look beautiful. It doesn't seem to matter whether you are mad or sad, tired or even sick."

"Well, thank you," she pulled a wide-toothed comb through her tangled curls. "I'd hate to meet my knight in shining armor and look like a fiend."

"Not to worry," Jabberwock yawned, waiting for the Princess to get dressed and idly wishing he could see the expression on the face of the first man to see her undressed. Uriel, preferably. She was something to behold.

"You're holding out on me," she said, with a laugh. "You know who my prince charming is, don't you?"

"I mean only that when you finally meet him, he will be enraptured despite your appearance."

Eluned studied him for a moment, comb raised halfway to her head. Her eyes narrowed for a moment. "I assume that's all I am going to get out of you?"

His eyes broadened in mock innocence, as opaque as the dark wool of her long skirt. "All I can say is that you'll know him when you meet him." At least, he hoped so.

"Hmmpf," she snorted, tossing her comb into her satchel. She opened the creaky wooden door of their chamber. They tiptoed downstairs, but Zelda was already up and insisted on pressing a mug of hot coffee into Eluned's fragile hand. Her long fingers curled around the cup, thankfully, as they were already numb with the cold. The Princess sipped greedily at the strong brew, relishing the sensation of the hot liquid as it slid down her throat and began to thaw her insides. She usually preferred it with cream but heat was priority and it wasn't long before the warmth in her belly started to spread to her extremities.

Biscuits, warm with melted butter and thick honey, were wrapped in a red-checked cloth and shoved into her tapestry bag. The two backed out of the inn's massive front door, which had been standing open the previous evening in order to dissipate not only body heat but body odor. This morning, only Eluned's eagerness to be on the road gave her the strength to shove the door open with her back (although she would pay for that later with a bruised shoulder blade). With the Princess stating the necessary goodbyes and thank-yous to the hovering Zelda, they exited the inn.

A waiting stable hand presented the Princess with Hayduke's lead and scampered back to the barn as they turned toward the road.

"Be yer sure yer dersn't be wantin' bread an' cheese fer yer lunch?" Zelda chirped as they walked away.

"No, thank you, we've made plans," Jabberwock called back, leaving the poor woman leaning against the doorjamb, mouth agape.

Eluned sent him a reproving look but was soon choking back the laughter that threatened to explode from her throat.

It was her turn to be eyed, sternly, and she tried to apologize. "I guess I . . ."

"Don't worry about it," he said, "we're both tired, and," he grumbled, "we have a hell of a long way to go today."

"Hell?" The Princess raised an eyebrow in feigned shock.

"You're a bad influence, my dear."

She leaned down to kiss the soft hair on top of Jabberwock's small and round skull. "But you love me anyway, right?"

He rolled his marble eyes. "Indubitably. It looks as if we're in for a storm." He changed the subject.

Eluned watched the roiling, boiling clouds gathering over the snowy peaks to the east—the Mountains of Misericord. The jagged mountains were soon hidden beneath a cinereous, churning mass of clouds. She looked, worriedly, at the Bandersnatch. They, well she, at least, were not prepared to travel in the rain.

As they stepped onto the wide white track that led toward the mountains in the east, Eluned shuddered as the wind picked up, and buttoned her wool cloak. Head forward and bowed against the wind, she tromped, determinedly, ahead. Jabberwock and Hayduke had to trot to keep up with her, and it wasn't long before the creaking sign that marked the entrance to The Golden Gryphon Inn was far behind them.

THE HILLS HAD CLOSED IN AROUND THEM, many of them topped with barrows and standing stones, when the first drop of rain landed with a splat on the top of Eluned's head. She was surprised by its warmth and reached up to touch the sphere of precipitation that was now trickling through her hair to her scalp. It didn't feel right. It had too much texture for water. And not only that, it was warm! When had rain, except maybe in the desert, or perhaps, the most tropical of climates like the Favonian Islands (well, she could hope) been warm? She withdrew her hand and stared in horror at her fingers. Blood! She lifted her face to the skies as if she expected to see ruby red clouds raining garnets of blood. She saw nothing but the ashy clouds above her; felt the warm, unpleasant smack of another drop against her forehead. She wiped it away in disgust and turned to see Jabberwock watching her, eyes mirroring her fear and repulsion. His hairy brow wrinkled in perplexity.

A large drop splattered his moist, black nose, and he shook his head, spraying droplets of blood all over the white roadbed. Eluned began to moan and picked up her pace in an effort to avoid the rain. Poor Hayduke stumbled after her, trying to keep up. But, the faster she ran, the harder it fell. The soft clay of the road was soon a sticky red paste. Blood dripped from the Princess's ebony curls and slowly soaked her shoulders and insinuated its way inside her wool cloak, staining the collar of her white blouse.

As suddenly as she started running, she stopped and dropped the mule's lead. Eyes rolling, wildly, she searched for cover. Panting, the Bandersnatch finally caught up with her.

"What is wrong with you?" he gasped, scrawny chest heaving.

Eluned stared down at him as if she were talking to a madman. His gray fur was matted with blood. Even his eyes reflected the bright, dark red that coated the landscape with its evil smell.

"Take a deep breath," he ordered, "and calm down."

The thick, metallic smell was asphyxiating. Gagging, she continued to search for cover, mumbling, "no, no, no."

"What the hell is wrong with you?" Jabberwock barked, frustration and fear echoing in the rising octaves of his doggish voice. His precious princess was losing it in front of his very eyes, and he had no clue as to why the rain had prompted this insane behavior.

She was now mumbling, "blood, blood, blood," while simultaneously scrubbing the slimy liquid from her carnelian lips with a blood-smeared fist.

The short, bristly hairs on the neck of the Bandersnatch stood at attention. Ears pricked and alert, tail ready to march, he carefully eyed the hills around them. A phantom was at work. A Wight, a creature of the barrows, home to the dead, had spotted the Princess and was spinning its evil web . . .

Out of the corner of his eye, Jabberwock saw a flash of gray wool and mud-stained suede as the Princess suddenly turned and sprinted up the hill. His eyes widened in terror when he saw where she was heading. A door had opened in the barrow where heretofore none had existed. And Eluned was running toward it as fast as her lithe young legs could carry her. Using all the power available to him, Jabberwock screamed with his mind, "STOP!"

The Princess reacted as if struck by lightning. Hands to head, and back arched, she briefly resembled a bow before her feet began to slip from beneath her and she rolled, ungracefully, back down the wet, grassy slope.

Eluned had barely reached the bottom before she began scrambling back up the hill again. Pupils large, lids heavy, she looked drugged, or perhaps hypnotized. With only a modicum of regret, Jabberwock sank his razor sharp teeth into Eluned's hand as it sought purchase in the slippery turf of the slope.

She screamed in pain, but her eyes cleared and she looked in disbelief at her friend. Blood was trickling from his narrow jaw but he retained his grip until he was sure the Wight had lost its grasp on the mind of the Princess.

Eluned looked around her in dismay. The door in the barrow had disappeared, and the blood was gone, replaced by a cold drizzle. Tears slowly cleansed the mud and grass from her face. Unconsciously, she wrapped a linen handkerchief around her wounded hand.

"A Barrow Wight," Jabberwock explained as they stumbled the last few feet to the road.

"A . . .?" she whispered, face pale with shock.

"An apparition," he muttered, "the putrid, dripping eidolon of unwholesome revelation."

"Eidolon?"

"H.P. Lovecraft."

Eluned buried her face in her hands, shuddering. "There was blood . . . everywhere. It was raining blood. I was walking in a stream of blood. The hills were red with blood . . . blood . . . blood." Her hand ached terribly, and she was shivering with shock and cold. The Princess began to cry again. "I'm sorry," she managed when the sobs had finally subsided, "I just didn't expect our journey would be so . . . so . . . uncomfortable."

"I always told you that you were too much of a romantic," Jabberwock chided her, but kindly. "If you can hold out another half hour or so, we'll reach the last inn before the mountains. We'll call it an early day. You need rest and warmth . . ."

"Mulled wine," she interrupted.

"Exactly," he agreed, picking up Hayduke's tether with his teeth and urging him back onto the road.

"Warmth," she continued. "The islands. Heat. Sun. Sand. Blue Skies." The last mile disappeared beneath her feet as she chanted a mantra of and for comfort.

They finally reached a crossroads. Straight ahead, the Mountains of Misericord towered above them so high Eluned could see only the lower slopes, shrouded as the mountains were in billowing robes of cloud. An ancient sign creaked and twisted in the breeze. The archaic lettering, a remnant of the Great Demesne, was weathered beyond legibility. Tracing the indentations with a finger yellow with the cold, Eluned discovered the track led north to Muskroe and south to Seagirt. She looked at the Bandersnatch, eyebrow raised. Would they be heading north or south or would they continue their journey to the east?

"We'll be traveling to the east, my dear," he answered her unspoken question.

"The desert?" she asked, hopefully. Didn't the Desert of Serket lie beneath the eastern slopes of the Mountains of Misericord in the Kingdom of Sheba?

"Don't get too excited," Jabberwock smiled. "It's a high desert." He inclined his head toward the road straight before them. Soon, just around the curve of a hillock, an inn came into view. The slate roof was covered with mosses and lichens creating the effect of a natural patchwork quilt. Smoke curled from the chimney, dipped and swirled with the currents of air before settling on a path to the heavens. Golden light brightened the windows and beckoned the cold and weary travellers. With a sigh and a groan, the Princess and the Bandersnatch set their stiff muscles in motion, leather soles and sharp claws slapping and tapping the cobbled path to the door. The mule trailed behind, glancing longingly at the thick, rich grass that carpeted the dooryard of the inn.

Before they climbed the few shallow steps to the door, Eluned tied Hayduke, albeit awkwardly thanks to her wounded hand, to the hitching post at the bottom of the stairs.

Except for the crackling of the fire, the inn was blessedly silent. It was also empty.

"Hello!" Eluned called, shutting the heavy oak door on the cold air outside. "Hello?" She tried again, making her way over to the fire.

Silence, and more silence. Eluned and the Bandersnatch shared an uneasy glance.

"I'm not sure I like this." Jabberwock whispered.

"You don't think it's deserted?" The Princess looked over her shoulder, nervously.

"There's no telling . . ." A door slammed somewhere above them and they both jumped. Eluned shrieked. She clapped her bandaged hand over her mouth in case another scream should try to erupt. Her eyes rolled, wildly, in their sockets, for the second time that day. The throbbing in her hand reminded her of what had happened the last time she lost control. Closing her eyes, she took a deep, calming, breath.

"'Ello!" Basso profundo. "'Ello? Body dere?"

"Hello," Eluned squeaked, cleared her throat and tried again, "Hello! Yes!" What sounded like an elephant was lumbering down the stairs.

The largest man she had ever seen appeared at the bottom of the staircase. He had to be at least eight feet tall, Eluned estimated. But he wasn't just tall. He was large. Not fat, exactly, but he appeared to be carrying a couple hundred pounds of muscle on his barrel-chested torso, alone. He had to weigh at least a quarter of a ton, she thought as she unashamedly gawked. Thick, shiny (he was clean, that was a plus!) and straight blue-black hair framed a face as broad as Dziron. Dark, slanted eyes, a squat nose, and a full, smiling mouth seemed somehow out of place on this giant.

"Yes, can I 'elp you? Yes?" His hair, poorly cut (as if someone had stuck a bowl on his head and chopped around it), swung around his face as his head bobbed up and down. He was making Jabberwock dizzy.

"We need." Eluned stopped. She didn't know what she wanted more—mulled wine, hot food or a warm bath and bed.

"Yes?" the giant asked.

"We need a room and food and bath and wine and," she bit her full lower lip, thinking, "and shelter for Hayduke, I mean, our mule."

Their host was staring at the Bandersnatch, wonder in his oblique eyes. "You," he addressed Jabberwock, "You da Dhami Dhole."

"Historically speaking," the Bandersnatch sighed, and then smiled, wickedly, "and you must be the Dzu-tch."

The giant bellowed laughter. "Teoleticary speakin', yes. I eight-feet tarr. I eat beef."

"Damidole? Dzu? Dzu?" Eluned stuttered.

"I get wine," their host left the room, chuckling.

"Explain." The Princess ordered.

"I hate it when you get imperious," Jabberwock kvetched, but he was actually enjoying himself.

"Explain, please," Eluned amended, sitting on a bench in front of the snapping fire. "He recognized you. What's a dami-dole? What's a dzu, a dzu-whatever you said? How did he know you could talk?"

"Are you quite finished?"

Eluned rolled her eyes.

"It's Dhami, d-h-a-m-i, Dhole, d-h-o-l-e."

"Yes, so?"

"A dhami is a sorcerer or necromancer."

"A ledgerdemainist, thaumaturge or magus?" Her look was penetrating. If Jabberwock had been capable of blushing, he would have done so.

"I told you the truth. So I'm a living legend, what can I say?"

"I still don't understand," she pressed him. "What's a dhole?"

Jabberwock muttered something unintelligible.

"What did you say?"

"I said a dhole is a doglike mammal."

"A calnivole, too, no?" Their host rejoined them with a steaming jug of mulled wine and two, thick, clay goblets. He poured for himself and the Princess.

"Where I come flom," he said, "Dhami Dhole myfrical cleatures wif many powers. Didn't know Dhami Dhole stirr exist."

"Like telepathy and prescience?" Eluned asked the Dzu-tch.

"Yes, terepafy. Know future, too. Tought Dhami Dhole ting of past. Can't berieve Dhami Dhole 'ere, 'fole my eyes."

"Wait a second," she stopped him. "Did you say creatures? Plural?"

"Prural, yes," the giant agreed.

"I have reason to believe I am the only Bandersnatch in existence," Jabberwock sniffed.

"Bandelsnac?" It was the giant's turn to be confused.

"That's Bandersnatch, you oaf." Jabberwock was miffed. It was important that the Princess never doubted his word.

"Jabberwock the Bandersnatch," the Princess indicated the grouchy Dhami Dhole. "I am the Princess Eluned of Zion."

"Bonpo," he introduced himself, extending a hand the size of a ham hock. Eluned clasped it, tentatively, but Bonpo was surprisingly gentle.

"So," she eyed the Bandersnatch, "I thought you were immortal?"

"Unless killed," he replied. "I don't die of old age."

"Kind of like a tortoise, huh?" the Princess offered.

"I suppose that's an apt enough comparison," Jabberwock agreed.

"Are you sure you're the only Bandersnatch in existence?" she pressed him.

"Vely rikery," Bonpo said, "In Dziron, onry myf, regend."

"Which reminds me," Eluned turned to Bonpo, "What's a Dzu-whatever Jabberwock said?"

"It is Yeti," the giant explained.

"Yeti?" Eluned was still confused.

"The abominable snowman," Jabberwock helped him out. "A creature about eight feet tall that eats cattle."

"Abomneral snowman!" Bonpo's laughter clapped like thunder. "Vely good, vely good!"

Eluned was edging away from the laughing giant. "Sounds like a pretty good description to me."

"Eat cow, not 'uman," he was still laughing.

"So why did you leave the Peaks of Vulpecula?" Jabberwock asked.

"Too cold," Bonpo replied.

Eluned shivered, but she was no longer listening. Vulpecula. Didn't that have something to do with the word, fox? "Why Vulpecula?" Eluned asked just as Jabberwock was opening his mouth to ask another question.

"Vely qrick, dis woman," Bonpo's face was flushed with admiration.

"What else is hiding up there in those mountains?" She asked the Bandersnatch. "Dragons, unicorns?"

"Too cold," Bonpo explained.

"I heard you," she snapped.

"I meant too cold for dragon." Bonpo seemed unaffected by her ill humor.

"Oh." Eluned blushed. "I apologize. It's all so much to take in. An Abominable Snowman in my father's kingdom."

Bonpo sailed off into gales of laughter. Jabberwock was grinning, too, in his usual way—teeth bared, tongue lolling.

"No need 'porogize," Bonpo smiled. "'E know I 'ere."

Eluned shivered and moved closer to the fire. Bonpo refilled her cup with hot wine and stood.

"I fix 'ot baf, den see to mule." He shambled back up stairs, steps creaking loudly beneath his weight. In the ensuing silence, they could hear his continued chuckles muffled by the sound of splashing water as he filled a tub for the Princess.

"How come there are no more Bandersnatches?" She sipped the soothing, deep red liquid. Somehow she just couldn't compare it to the similarly colored liquid that had nearly made her lose her mind only hours earlier.

"Genocide. About five hundred years ago, we were considered warlocks. We were hunted down with dogs," he spat the latter word, "spitted and burned."

A cold chill insinuated its way once more through her

body. She shook her head in denial. She didn't even want to imagine. "No wonder you despise dogs," she said quietly. "Were you the only Bandersnatch to escape?"

"No, there were others. We scattered to the four winds."

"I assume you can reproduce."

"Most certainly, but only if we have a mate."

"You didn't have a mate?"

"I did."

Eluned's heart sank. She wasn't sure she wanted to hear what he was about to say.

"She was killed when we crossed The Devastation of Pelf."

"You crossed The Devastation! I thought, I thought . . ."

"Thought it was impossible?"

"Yes."

"Very nearly. But there is life there, the most repulsive," he shuddered. "Lovecraft, himself, would be hard put to describe the terrors, the monstrosities in that wasteland."

"Lovecraft again! I don't understand."

"I couldn't save her," his voice cracked. Nearly five hundred years later and it was still like it happened yesterday. "The monster was hiding beneath the sands. Its fiendish claw tore into her flesh." He stopped and took a deep breath. "Suffice to say that Kamali did not suffer long, but I carry the anguish of that moment for eternity."

The Princess was stunned into silence, even forgetting Lovecraft for the time being. The tears stung her eyes. She had been meeting with Jabberwock almost daily for eleven years and she had never had the slightest clue. As he might put it, she had had neither inkling nor intimation, nor even an indication that he had once loved some one as she might never even hope to love.

The Yeti was pounding down the stairs. She wondered how long the staircase would last beneath his weight.

Jabberwock stared, morosely, into the fire remembering a time more than half a millennium earlier when love was life;

and life was a hidden, verdant valley in the Peaks of Vulpecula. A time when there was little to fear; when the Janawar (for Bandersnatch is what the Jabberwock chose to call himself in his new life) coexisted peacefully with the yeti, yak and snow leopards; where lotus bloomed in cerulean pools and snow never fell; and why was a question that did not require discussion.

Eluned quietly stood, leaving Jabberwock to his memories and tears and still-aching heart. Bonpo whispered directions to the bathroom and she did her best to climb the stairs silently.

Easing her sore body into the hot, scented water, the Princess inhaled the fragrance of honeysuckle and roses, and slowly her muscles began to relax. But, her mind was racing. Nothing is ever as simple as it seems, and this seemed to particularly apply to her at this point. Had she really been so self-centered that she had never pressed Jabberwock on his past? Why had it taken her eleven years to find out about her great-grandmother? Kamali? How long had she been taking things at face value? She was beginning to scare herself. Eluned vowed to look more deeply—at herself, the Bandersnatch, at everyone and everything she came in contact with. Surely the climate was not the only reason Bonpo had ventured here from Dziron. This was a cold land, too. The Mountains of Misericord towered above the inn and brought snow and storms nearly three seasons out of four. Surely if he had desired a temperate climate he would have journeyed farther south. There were many warmer lands in the south—the Desert of Tarshish, the Favonian Islands, the Kingdom of Adamah, to name just a few.

She resolved to question him further after her bath. Jabberwock, too, for that matter. She sipped at her wine as she contemplated the events of the past two days. So much beyond the realm of her experience had already happened. What had she gotten herself into?

12ᵀᴴ NEEON

"What's the real reason you left Dziron?" Eluned asked, testing her coffee with a tentative tongue. It was still too hot. She set it gently back in her saucer and looked Bonpo in the eyes.

"I terr you, too cold." He couldn't meet her eyes.

"It's not that much warmer here," she insisted. "There has to be another reason." Jabberwock was watching her with wonder.

She waited for Bonpo to answer, unbuttoning her skirt to relieve the pressure on her overfull belly. Bonpo had filled her with an exquisite soup of stuffed dumplings along with rice and stir-fried vegetables, lemon mousse and shortbread. She tried her coffee again. Almost.

Bonpo sighed and his chair protested, loudly, as he resettled his weight. "I no know how say dis."

"You killed someone." The Bandersnatch stated it for him. The Princess was startled.

"Really?"

"Dhami Dhole know all," Bonpo acknowledged.

Her eyes searched the Yeti's face. Fire burned along the high cheekbones, the dark, tilted eyes danced across the table searching for distraction, anything but the face of the beautiful Princess.

"Well," Eluned asked, "are you going to tell us why? Obviously, it's not something you're proud of. Was it self-defense? You must have had a good reason. You don't strike me as the murdering type."

"No. Not kirrer. Ret me exprain. I kirr not fah me. I kirr fah sao."

"Sao?" Eluned asked.

"Snow leopard," Jabberwock defined.

"You killed a snow leopard? I don't understand."

"No. No kirr sao. Kirr fah sao."

"You killed a man? Or another animal?"

"Man. Sao arlmos extinck. Dis man, 'e poacher. 'E kirr many sao. Mus stop."

"So you just killed him?"

"I cause avaranche so 'e die."

Eluned laughed. "I'm sorry. It's not funny, but it is. Sounds like justifiable homicide to me."

"The 'he needed killin' defense'? I wish I had had Bonpo around five hundred years ago," Jabberwock groused. "We could have used his help when we were being exterminated by the Dzironi."

"No. You no unnerstan. Never right take rife."

The Princess was silent a moment, reconsidering. "You're right, but I still don't understand why you had to leave."

"Big mistake kirr dis man. Big man, big name. Search party t'reaten udder Dzu-tch. I tol' reave."

"The other yeti ran you off!" Eluned was aghast. "How could they do that to you? Wouldn't it have been easier to hide out for awhile?"

"You no unnerstan. I bleak ancien' raw. No bring 'tention, danger, to 'ome of yeti. I know dis yet I kirr man anyway."

"You should have broken his neck and carried him to a lower elevation," the Bandersnatch said, coldly. "At least that way he would have been found right away and perhaps you would not have been suspected. Certainly it would have kept away the search parties."

"Yes, better sorution," Bonpo concurred, "but I did not want touch dis man."

"We learn from our mistakes," Jabberwock chided the giant.

Bonpo laughed. Eluned was glad the yeti had a good sense of humor. She glared at the Bandersnatch. Why was he being so contemptible?

"Is it always this empty?" She indicated the inn's dining area.

"Vely quiet 'cep on res' days."

"Rest days? Yes, I guess that makes sense. It has been very relaxing," she yawned, "and the wine, the food, and the company have been outstanding."

"Yes, thank you," Jabberwock said. He needed to pull himself together. The Yeti had stirred up bad memories.

"You mos' welcome. I have queshuns fah you, but dey wait 'tir morning. I show you your rooms."

"Please." Eluned stood and stretched. "I am exhausted." She arched an eyebrow at the Bandersnatch. I'll talk to you later, her look plainly said.

Once more they ascended the creaking stairway. The room Bonpo opened for her impressed the Princess. She took in the large feather bed with its fluffy down comforter and the cheery fire in the fireplace and felt her lids growing heavier. Bonpo produced a flask from his vast pockets and set a snifter of brandy warming on her bedside table. She idly wondered if she had not actually died earlier that day and this was heaven.

As his back retreated down the hallway, Jabberwock tagging along at his heels, she called, "You'll probably have to wake me in the morning, Jabberwock."

"Oh, I wake," Bonpo offered. "What time you want get up?"

"At dawn," the Bandersnatch answered. "We stopped short today. We have lots of time to make up."

"Why are we in such a hurry?" Eluned asked.

"Tell her," Jabberwock ordered the yeti.

"If you no closs mountains nex' few days, you be trap in Snow of Misely."

"Snow of Misery?" Eluned repeated.

"Yes, rate winter snowstorm come same time each year." Bonpo explained.

"Satisfied?" Jabberwock asked.

Lacking a better retort, Eluned extended her tongue, "Phooey on you." What was his problem, anyway?

But, in the morning, Bonpo didn't ask any questions. Eluned wondered if they had had further conversation that night—in Jabberwock's room or down by the fire or even somewhere else. Certainly, it seemed as if the two shared a deeper connection than one could see on the surface. She wondered what they had talked about while she was drowsily sipping her brandy and enjoying her own fire, daydreams and warm comforter. She had thought she would read for a few minutes as she had discovered a thin volume of poetry on the mantelshelf, but she couldn't seem to keep her eyes focused on the words. She had even wondered, though idly, whether Bonpo had helped her drowsiness along . . . a little secret something slipped into the flask? But, of course, she was extraordinarily exhausted—both physically and emotionally. Either way, it didn't take her long to slip off to a most restorative and dreamless sleep.

When Jabberwock awakened her at the crack of dawn the next morning, she was sound asleep and it took her more than a few minutes to fully awaken. But, once she did, she felt re-energized. She did regret sliding out of bed. The fire had died out during the night and the room had grown chilly.

She debated re-igniting the fire but decided against it because by the time it actually had any effect on the room, she'd probably be a mile or so down the road.

As she dressed, she began to regret her decision to bring only warm-weather clothes. Instead of gaining the warmth she desired, she seemed to be losing it. And, it appeared that there would not be an opportune moment any time in the near future to not only wash her clothes, but to allow them to dry. Only two days into the trip, and she was ending each night completely exhausted! And now there were intimations of being trapped in the Snow of Misery. That was definitely a feeling she wanted to avoid at all costs. Misery. Even saying the word made her feel miserable!

Instead of donning the flannel blouse she had worn the previous day, she opted to layer. She just couldn't bear the thought of putting on that blood-smeared blouse despite the fact she could only barely discern a grass-stain or two (at the most) on the front of it. But she had felt that blood soak through her collar. It had seemed so real at the time.

She put on a couple of lighter blouses and her wool skirt (again) before plaiting her hair, surveying the room (she had even somewhat made her bed) and treading lightly downstairs.

Bonpo (Bless his heart!) was ready with a hot, but not too hot, cup of coffee and cream. She sipped it, eagerly, relishing the sensation of the hot liquid as it made its way down her throat and warmed her belly. The Yeti then set a plate of fresh-from-the-oven turnovers in front of her. She watched, nearly mesmerized as the steam wafted from them. Finally, she picked one up and tasted it and she remembered Jabberwock harassing her about the food the night before last. She could feel herself salivating even as she took a bite. Apple, flaky, cinnamon . . . mmm. She nearly shuddered. Too bad Bonpo had a job; she'd hire him as her personal cook.

As Eluned enjoyed her breakfast, Jabberwock sat grimly on the bench opposite her. She purposefully ignored him. She had had a wonderful night's sleep; she was not about to let him disrupt her digestion with his grumpiness. She thoroughly enjoyed her turnover and coffee and decided that she wouldn't even ruin things by talking about serious matters. She made small talk with Bonpo and left Jabberwock to his own ruminations.

"What's your problem, anyway?" Eluned asked when the inn had disappeared from view. She already missed the comfort and company it had offered. Hayduke plodded complacently behind them—the lead no longer necessary.

"Problem?" he asked.

"You seem to be suffering from a bad attitude," she complained.

"So, you've discovered another side of me."

"I don't mind seeing yet another side of you, but if I were acting the way you are you would want to know what is wrong with me."

He was silent for a moment. "That's true," he admitted. "I owe you an explanation although I am surprised that you don't have the faintest idea."

"Actually, I do. I'm sure it has to do with meeting Bonpo and provoking memories of the past. How come you never told me about Kamali?" her voice rose, accusingly, "and the destruction of your kind, the flight out of Dziron, the horrors of The Devastation?"

"It is a long story and to be perfectly honest there hasn't been a time in the past eleven years that I felt you were mature enough to understand my past nor handle its ramifications."

"I think I am ready now."

"I concur."

They continued to walk in silence while Jabberwock gathered his thoughts.

"Mine is a long and sad tale said the Mouse," Jabberwock

began by quoting Lewis Carroll, then replied to himself, "It is a long tail, certainly, said Alice, but why do you call it sad?"

The Princess held her tongue. The Bandersnatch was trying to explain, even if it did seem a most unusual way.

"My given name is Hiurau," he continued, sighing, "and I was born of the Janawar in the Vale Vixen." The silence continued for another ten minutes before Jabberwock spoke again, changing the course of his focus. "When Kamali died, I spent the next three hundred years trying to find a reason to continue to live. I became involved in mysticism, cabalism, shamanism. You name it. I studied it. Magi abounded and I drowned myself in their teachings. But I could never seem to fill that empty space in my heart. Yet, I continued to read and read and read . . . anything about any subject . . ." he paused again, remembering.

"And one day," he continued after a minute or so, "I picked up a very old children's book by one of the Ancients—Lewis Carroll. But that wasn't really his name. It was Dodgson, Charles Dodgson." He stopped, abruptly, and the Princess almost spoke but thought better of it. His story was coming out, as twisted and irrelevant as it might seem.

"Through the Looking Glass was the name of the book," he continued. There was a poem in it." He cleared his throat and recited in a voice scratchy with emotion:

> "'Twas brillig, and the slithy toves
> Did gyre and gimble in the wabe:
> All mimsy were the borogroves,
> And the mome raths outgrabe.
>
> 'Beware the Jabberwock, my son!
> The jaws that bite, the claws that catch!
> Beware the Jubjub bird, and shun
> The frumious Bandersnatch!'

He took his vorpal sword in hand:

Long time the manxome foe he sought—
So rested he by the Tumtum tree,
And stood awhile in thought.

And, as in uffish thought he stood,
The Jabberwock, with eyes of flame,
Came whiffling through the tulgey wood,
And burbled as it came!

One, two! One, two! And through and through
The vorpal blade went snicker-snack!
He left it dead, and with its head
He went galumphing back.

'And hast thou slain the Jabberwock?
Come to my arms, my beamish boy!
O frabjous day! Callooh! Callay!
He chortled in his joy.

"'Twas brillig, and the slithy toves
Did gyre and gimble in the wabe:
All mimsy were the borogroves,
And the mome raths outgrabe."

THE TEARS RAN DOWN ELUNED'S FACE in a steady stream. Oh, her poor Jabberwock, she thought, his family, his friends, his people, well, his Janawar, so cruelly hunted down and slain. It was too much for her to bear. How could humans be so inhumane? She often wondered if Omni had created humans imperfectly on purpose. Perhaps It had still to perfect creating. Maybe next time around humans wouldn't be so cruel, selfish, greedy . . . It seemed that humans always worked to destroy themselves. They'd come pretty close more than a millennium ago.

The Oral spoke of a great battle, the Har Megiddo, to be fought by the forces of good against evil. She had no idea where those forces were to come from. She wondered, particularly, about the great warrior who was prophesied to lead the forces of good. She knew of no man worthy in this world, although admittedly she knew very little of the world outside of Zion other than what she was taught by her teachers, Jabberwock and Brother Columcille.

She took a deep breath. She was allowing her mind to wander. Anything but dealing with the problem at her feet. Impulsively, she knelt upon the rocky track and hugged the small mammal to her. For hundreds of years he had wandered this world, and perhaps, others, searching for a reason. How had his travels brought him to her? Were they really so important? There had to be a larger purpose.

"There is, but do not ask me what it is," he said, once again reading her mind.

"Why? Because you don't know or because you cannot tell me?"

"I'm just a pawn . . ."

"Is that what life is?" She was indignant. "Some cosmic chess game? Omni making move after move. Is It playing against something, someone? Or is It just amused by the consequences of Its actions?"

A delighted grin parted Jabberwock's grim muzzle. "Whoa, whoa, slow down. I spoke rashly. I should have said, 'I am a willing pawn.' Don't forget free will. I only meant sometimes when we are open to Its will, we must follow a path we do not necessarily wish to travel, be led in a direction we may not necessarily wish to go. But, I am happy to say that there appears to be hope for you yet, my dear. Hope for you, hope for this world and perhaps others."

"In other words, ours is not to ask but rather to do."

"You betchum, Red Rider."

"You say the oddest things. Who is Lovecraft?"

"Another writer."

"One who has seen the horrors of the soul?" It was a statement. She wondered if Lovecraft had seen the execrations of the Devastation. If the Bandersnatch could find entrance to other worlds, surely others could as well. How many worlds were there?"

"If not here, perhaps in another world," Jabberwock said, musingly.

"So, the only reason the Janawar were destroyed is because the Dzironi were afraid of your magic?"

"Humans need very little reason to commit genocide. Have you heard of the Gaeans?"

"The goddess worshippers?"

"They were very nearly wiped out several hundred years ago."

"But they were strong."

"Tenacious."

"Always religion," Eluned sighed. "Always over which God to worship and how. And power. Who can be dominated. Possession. Greed. Men." She glared at him.

The Janawar are not human and therefore are not guilty of human weaknesses. We lived in peace, always . . ." he trailed off, remembering what prompted the discussion.

"I'm so sorry," she hugged his tiny head. "It just makes me so tired. So tired."

"There are many out there who wish to save the world."

"I don't pretend to think that I am the one. To be perfectly honest, I'm not even sure it's possible."

"That's entirely up to You-Know-Who."

"If It is there. Sometimes I wonder."

"Breaking Faith, Princess? I am shocked." But his tone of voice said otherwise.

"Father would kill me."

"And it would break your mother's heart."

"Well, they need not worry. Faith is there more often than not. When I argue with myself I always find Omni in the end."

Omni, as It was crudely and commonly called, was derived from the fact that It, the Supreme Being, was omnipotent, omnipresent and omniscient, or so it was said. A trinity of powers for the three-in-one.

"Do you?" he asked.

"What do you mean?"

"What do you mean?" Jabberwock pressed her.

"Omni," she faltered. What did she mean? How do you explain faith? Eluned looked at Jabberwock, oddly. "Why are you doing this to me?"

"What?" he asked, all innocence.

"Don't give me that. You know exactly what I mean."

"You are absolutely positive, in your heart of hearts, that there is a Divine Being?"

She pondered for a moment before nodding her head, vigorously. "Yes, Jabb, I'm sure of it. A God. A supreme being. I guess . . . I guess I just wonder why?"

"Why?"

"What is this being's purpose for us?"

"Purpose? Other than to love It, love one another? That's not enough?"

"No. There has to be more."

"Spoken like a true teenager. Perhaps there is no other purpose."

"Don't say that. It's unconscionable."

"Why is that?" Jabberwock continued to prod.

"Because I cannot believe we were put here as some experiment or some vast diversion . . . "

"Ah, the cosmic chess game again . . . a satire, tragedy, melodrama."

"Satire," she sighed. "No, I cannot believe that."

"And once again I ask, is love not enough?" They reached a steep stretch in the road where it climbed out of a switchback. The Princess felt the muscles in her calves and thighs tighten; the exertion stole her breath. She was going to be sore tonight. It wasn't even lunchtime yet, and she wasn't sure how high the Misrule Pass was, but she knew they had a lot of climbing left to do before they reached it. On that thought, she began to look forward to lunch—just a moment to sit down, catch her breath.

She was on the adventure of a lifetime, but would she find any answers? After all, what on earth did she know about love? How could she know if love was the answer to her questions? Yet another question she couldn't answer. Best now just to clear her mind, and question Jabberwock more thoroughly later when she could breathe again.

13TH NEEON

The last of the logs had died down to coals. Next to him, wrapped around his small body for the meager warmth it provided, the Princess slept soundly. She slumbered peacefully, the sleep of innocence, youth and exhaustion. But not so for the Bandersnatch. He was far removed from the campsite clearing. The Vale Vixen bloomed lushly around him. He inhaled the scent of tropical flowers, hummed to the symphony of birdsong and falling water, the sweet music of Kamali's laughter; and remembered a day when immortality and the immensity of time were something to look forward to. For eternity was not questioned in paradise. It simply was.

Since the slaughter, he had worried the question of time like a bone, gnawing it incessantly, unable to break through to the marrow. He and Kamali had once spent a perpetuity staring into each other's bottomless eyes. There he had known heaven, the answer to life and life everlasting. The glyphs of all great questions spiraled and danced, revolved and whorled in the depths of Kamali's eyes, and Hiurau had no need to ask for explanations. He had known.

Then: The slaughter. It had changed all that. As they fled heaven, their haven, like Adam and Eve exiled from the Garden of Eden, all knowledge disappeared. Survival. That was all that mattered. All unknowing they had entered Gehenna—the Devastation—and suddenly Hiurau was plunged into his own private Hell.

How long had he been alive? How many years had he spent in the bliss of Vale Vixen? Had he ever been a child? Surely? He could no longer remember. Time after the slaughter had been counted, painfully, second by second. Eternity measured by the slow burn of the sun across the sky, the cold light of the moon that gleamed off his silver fur. Sometimes he wondered if he even slept but he knew that he must for surely the nightmares that ravaged his mind only snaked their way into his unconsciousness when he closed his eyes? And, the serpent, his nightmare, was time.

And once again, he meditated on time. Time flies when you're having fun, he thought for what had to be the zillionth time. Time is a great healer. What time is it? We have plenty of time. The hour is late. Time is short. Ahead of time, behind the times, good times, bad times and in the fullness of time. Long time, no see, and so on and so forth, ad infinitum.

The world abounds with timely idioms inextricably linked to the fabric of our lives, he mused. The moon had phases, and so, therefore, did the earth. Seasons changed, tides changed—everything broke down into smaller and smaller increments. Even time. The nanosecond! Why on earth (or in the universe) was there an all-consuming need to measure something by one-billionth of a second? The thought of that alone was enough to age you, Jabberwock considered with a fierce grin. Nothing, it seemed, could exist in perpetuity. Everything, even the very earth, aged. Except for himself. It was as if he had reached maturity, found his mate, and time had spun out forever leaving him trapped within it never to age again. Perhaps that was why he and Kamali had never felt the need to reproduce. It was essentially unnecessary, and they had yet to reach a point in which they wished to share their happiness.

He sighed, and Eluned stirred. He had long ago come to terms with time. At least, that it was a matter that needed to be dealt with. His views on it varied constantly. One day, he was perfectly at peace with the concept of a non-spatial continuum; the next, silently raging over the need for it; the next, pondering the apparently irreversible succession of events from past to present to future that marked his time. He wished he could freeze Eluned's time, suspend her in ageless innocence—virginal, naïve, guileless. An Angel. But he could no more stop her from aging than he could prevent her from having her heart broken or from recognizing her purpose in life. For, contrary to their earlier discussion, he did have an inkling, although it was still true that he was a pawn, albeit a willing and important pawn, in the great and secret show.

Freewill not withstanding, much was preordained. From the rise and death of prophets, false and true, to the tossing of a golden ball (not maliciously) into a forest where it rolled silently across a carpet of moss softer and more richly green than the velvet cloak that swung from the ivory shoulders of a certain queen, and across the moss and into a clearing filled with flowers where it bounced with a gentle ding against a wonderful tabernacle of granite and quivered to a halt precisely in the center of a fairy ring of toadstools.

Perhaps he should close his eyes and attempt some semblance of slumber, but he feared the flickering figures that would play upon the screen of his eyelids. Since the previous eve when suddenly reminded of the atrocities of the Devastation—first the Barrow Wight, then the Dzu-tch, Bonpo—he had been unable to banish them from his thoughts.

Indescribably horrible—the suppurating flesh, the oozing craters of their eyes, craggy teeth in the lipless caverns of their mouths and the odor, fetid, rotting, putrid as if they were actively decaying. He shuddered. Would he ever forget? Was he supposed to? He felt a hand heavy against his ribs and his heart stopped for a moment before he realized it was only the Princess, comforting him even while she slept.

He wished he could delay the trip. They would make it through the pass in a matter of days. And then their trip would truly begin and it wouldn't be long before the Princess learned how harshly cruel life could be.

Jabberwock was moving in his sleep, skinny legs jerking and muffled squeals issuing from his chest. Once again, Eluned put out a hand to calm him, but this time she awakened completely. The nightmares again. He seemed to experience them almost daily.

A log in the fire popped and Eluned froze. Surely it would have died out by now? She had already been dreading getting it going again. She sat up and looked around and her movement awakened Jabberwock.

"What is it?" he grumbled. A twig snapped in the woods behind them and Jabberwock and Eluned scrambled to their feet, hearts pounding.

"Who's there?" She squeaked. A monstrous hand pushed aside the branches of a fir that stood at the edge of the small clearing they had camped in. A giant body followed it, ducking under some of the higher branches.

"Bonpo!" The Princess wasn't sure whether to laugh or cry. "You scared me to death."

"I solly," he dumped an armload of logs next to the fire. Da fire was out. You want me . . ."

"To explain just exactly what you're doing here?" Jabberwock interrupted, sarcastically, but there was a peculiar glint in his eye.

A huge grin split Bonpo's face. "What? You 'af to ask?"

Jabberwock rolled his eyes and flopped back down on the fir needles. "So, what's for breakfast?"

Bonpo chuckled and turned to his huge pack. "What? What?" Eluned asked in frustration. "Why do I always feel like

I am not even present when you two are having a conversation? Would you care to explain to me why you're here?" She glared at Bonpo's wide back as he measured some coffee into a pot. He turned and settled the pot firmly into the coals before answering.

"I rearize when you arrive dat I was meant to be wif you," he said, simply. "O'course, Jab have dat feerin' too."

"Why?"

"I know no leason. Jus know it meant to be."

She looked to Jabberwock for further explanation. He only stared back, unblinking, eyes reflecting the oranges and yellows of the jumping flames between them.

"Omni." A statement.

"Likely as not." His skinny rear ascended as he stretched. Absolutely no doubt as to why they called that particular stretch "downward dog," she mused. He shuffled off into the woods as Bonpo was removing a heavy black frying pan from his pack. The woods beckoned to her as well. She couldn't complain about having him with them on their journey, she thought, crouching behind the ubiquitous fir, certainly they would be much safer and she was far from an experienced cook!

As she stepped back into the clearing, Bonpo was expertly cracking some eggs into the pan alongside some bacon that was already beginning sizzle. Her stomach twisted in on itself and she realized that the few bites of bread she managed to swallow before slipping off into an exhausted sleep the previous evening had done nothing to nourish her fatigued body.

There was no cream for the coffee (guess he couldn't carry every possible concession in his pack) but it tasted marvelous anyway. Of course, hunger was a great spice, and the eggs, bacon and some of the leftover bread toasted in the bacon grease, renewed her energy, considerably. Yes, it was definitely going to be an advantage having Bonpo along, especially considering their former breakfast prospects had been only the leftover bread and water as their rations were limited to what Hayduke could carry and Eluned prepare.

THE CLEARING THEY SPENT THE NIGHT IN had long ago been leveled out as a camping spot for those traveling across the mountains. They hadn't hiked but a hundred yards down the road before they began to ascend once again. They spent the next few hours in silence. It would be nearly noon before they made it to the pass, and nightfall before they reached the campsite halfway along the pass.

IT WASN'T TRUE, but it had seemed that every yard they ascended the temperature had dropped a degree. Okay, the Princess corrected herself—maybe half a degree. But, it had definitely gotten colder the higher they climbed toward the pass. At one point, Eluned had begged to stop, and pulling her blood-stained (all right, it was grass-stained) blouse from her tapestry bag, donned its soft and warm flannel over her two cotton blouses. Hmmm . . . maybe she should put on her cotton skirt, as well; but then what would she have to keep her warm between stopping for the night and getting the fire going? Sigh.

Bonpo waited patiently, but Jabberwock looked disgusted at the waste of time, though his anger stemmed from the dropping temperatures rather than from her procrastination.

Even with stopping for a cold lunch of leftover bacon and eggs between rapidly staling bread, and the Princess adding more layers to her frigid body, not to mention those "necessary breaks" and the not-so-necessary, "I can't walk another step," they made pretty good time, and arrived at the pass campsite a good hour before sundown.

All Eluned wanted to do was sit, but she gritted her teeth and wandered into the woods to gather some blow downs to keep the fire going. She had no doubt that Bonpo would have it started and roaring by the time she returned. Well, she rationalized, not only am I cold (she couldn't even feel her fingers), but I am not accustomed to this type of walking. Gee, Jabb had four legs to walk on and she couldn't imagine Bonpo ever getting tired. Besides, they both seemed acclimated to high altitudes. As far as she was concerned, it felt as if her feet were trying to push their way through the soles of her boots. But heaven, and Omni, forbid that she be thought of as weak! She was just as capable. She just didn't have as many miles on her yet.

She stumbled back to the campsite with an armload of wood and Bonpo nodded approvingly as he lifted it from her outstretched arms. She wanted to stick her tongue out at Jabberwock as if to say, "See, this isn't a waste of your time." But, she knew that was a juvenile reaction and that she really needed to refrain from doing that again, if possible. She was growing up, after all. Eighteen years old. She relished that thought for a moment. Eighteen years old and on the journey of a lifetime. She tried not to feel too smug.

As she huddled by the fire (She had been correct. Bonpo had managed to get the fire going, and she was now enjoying its warmth.), Eluned couldn't keep her mind from drifting to that knight-in-shining-armor, the Prince Charming Jabberwock had hinted at. Her exhaustion led her mind in directions she preferred it not go. Like: what would he look like, this man who was to sweep her off her feet? She tried to imagine. She wasn't really sure what kind of hero she was looking for, but she knew that as soon as she saw him she would know. Her knees would go weak. Her breath would be taken away. Eye color, height, hair—well, she had nothing to which she could compare those features. She would just know.

She guessed it was bizarre if she actually thought about it, and she was thinking about it despite part of her mind telling herself not to do so, but she had never found any man within her father's small realm attractive. Not even any of the traveling minstrels, many of who had tried to woo her. They always struck her as somewhat disreputable.

She was distracted by the thought of home and she stood up to see if she could still see the castle from this point on the pass but there were too many trees blocking the view, not to mention clouds and miles.

Had she known that even on the best of days she wouldn't have been able to spot the walls of her father's castle from this viewpoint, she might not have looked harder every time a view presented itself. Or, had she known that from this particular vantage point, she was taking not only her last, but most comprehensive view of her father's kingdom, she might have paused a moment longer. But that was yet another piece of knowledge about which she would remain blissfully ignorant.

Anyway, she thought, as she returned to the fire disappointed but not knowing why (she didn't recognize homesickness because she had never left home before), she was beginning to wonder if attractive and exciting men existed solely in the few novels belonging to Queen Fuchsia that she had chanced upon and devoured time and time again.

Certainly they weren't in her father's kingdom, or at least what she had seen of it. And believe me, she thought, I have looked more than once. Tantalizing smells were beginning to issue forth from the cook pot over the fire and she was easily distracted.

ONCE AGAIN BONPO WORKED HIS CULINARY MAGIC. No actual meat this time other than some salt pork, but the beans tasted as good as any gourmet meal. How did it come to be that she was always so hungry by the end of the day? How was it that thoughts of food and filling her belly could surpass thoughts of men? Who would believe it? On the other hand, as she was drifting off to sleep, snuggled warmly in her wool blankets, she couldn't help thinking of soft lips pressed to hers, yielding warmly, and sparking a fire in the depths of her belly. With a nearly inaudible moan, she drifted off to sleep.

WHEN SHE AWAKENED THE NEXT MORNING, she was surprised to find a coating of frost covering her blanket and the ground. She glanced up at the sky and shuddered. If she were right there would be snow before the day was out. As if in response to that thought, one delicate, but icy flake promptly landed on her nose. Her first impulse was to snuggle back beneath the blankets. That or cry. But after all, she was the one who couldn't wait to leave her father's kingdom behind. Gritting her teeth once again, she eased her way out of the blankets and was soon shivering despite her cloak, two cotton blouses as well as one of flannel, and both her cotton and wool skirts. Brrr . . . when would Bonpo ever have that coffee ready?

Rationally, she knew that once they started walking, her body would begin to warm up, but she was too cold to think rationally. And, if the cold wasn't bad enough, a fine mist of snowflakes had begun to fall. If they didn't get moving soon, she would be soaked from the sticky flakes. Her toes and fingers and nose already felt frozen. Eluned sniffed and began to stamp her feet. She needed to make a trip into the woods but the thought of raising her skirts even a fraction of an inch deterred her. Not that she actually had much of a choice. She grimaced, eying the woods in disgust, before she looked longingly back at the fire that was roaring happily away once again thanks to Bonpo's ministrations. Hayduke was blissfully unaware of her dilemma. His head was down and he was cheerfully munching away on the hay Bonpo had laid at his feet. Jabberwock was sitting beside the fire, and apparently care free as he seemed to be watching her quandary with great amusement. She glared at him and he barked with laughter.

"Valdaree, valdara, valdaree, valdara ha ha ha ha ha," he started singing. If looks could kill, Jabberwock would have been silenced immediately. As it was, Bonpo, missing entirely the fact that the Bandersnatch was pestering the Princess, took up the song as well:

"A knapsack on my back," he sang, lustily, in his rich bass. The Princess shrieked and stomped off into the woods. "What?" he asked Jabberwock, much taken aback by Eluned's response. "What I do?"

"Not a thing," he was assured. "Not a thing."

To give the Princess some credit, she returned to the fire seemingly embarrassed. "I am sorry for my outburst," she apologized, formally. "I don't know what got into me." And I don't know why Jabberwock has become so short-tempered with me, she wondered. But, if she had really thought about it, she would have realized that both Jabberwock and Bonpo were as uncomfortable as she was with the dropping temperatures. The flakes were beginning to fall more quickly, and they all continued to glance at the sky as they gulped their hot coffee and bolted down some oatmeal. They left their camp barely an hour after first awakening and not a one gave it a second glance when it disappeared from sight as they turned the bend in the trail.

THE SNOW WAS FALLING SO THICKLY that the trio could barely see a few yards ahead of themselves. Because Bonpo's stride was so long, Eluned was leading and both Jabberwock and Bonpo nearly fell on top of her when she tripped over a root hidden by the snow and tumbled head first into the snow along the path. The curse she bellowed would have sent the Queen into paroxysms of dismay.

Jabberwock was dumbfounded, but only because the Princess had obviously spent more time with the castle's various servants (Who would have cursed like that? The stable hands? The domestics?) than she had let on. Bonpo was so caught off guard that he brayed laughter, the tenor of which extracted a reciprocal bray from the usually oblivious Hayduke.

Eluned righted herself, brushed as much of the wet snow off her clothing as possible and continued to march. But it wasn't just the cold that made her cheeks red. Every time Bonpo snorted with laughter (it took a good mile and a steady ascent to calm down his hysterics the first time), the hue in her cheeks would deepen. They hadn't stopped for lunch yet, and she wasn't sure she could make it the rest of the day. Not only was she frozen and tired, but she had also humiliated herself, and that, along with the fall, had taken a lot out of her.

As a matter of fact, when it came time to stop for lunch, Eluned started shivering so quickly that Jabberwock suggested marching rations. Despite the fact she was tired of walking, she wanted to stop even less. The Princess gratefully accepted the pemmican Bonpo offered her and gnawed on it as they continued their climb to the next campsite. She was sure they would arrive early. They had been walking steadily all day.

IT MUST HAVE BEEN THE SNOW, but about the time they figured they should be reaching the campsite, they could find nothing that resembled a flat spot with a permanent fire ring. Six pairs of eyes squinted through the falling snow and bluish light over the course of the next few miles, seeking anything that even slightly resembled a spot to camp. They had long since given up on finding the actual site, and Eluned was at the brink of despair—her feet were throbbing and cold, her nose ran constantly and was chapped, as were her lips and cheeks, and she couldn't remember the last time she had felt her finger tips. Where, oh where was the site? And precluding the actual site, why, oh why couldn't they find at least a halfway flat spot in which to camp for the evening?

The bluish light was beginning to fade to gray and still the snow came tumbling down. Eluned was the first to voice their fears, although she tried to make it sound lighthearted, "This must be the Snow of Misery," she laughed, or was it a sob? "Because I sure am miserable."

"I imagine this is the prelude," Jabberwock answered. "If this were the actual storm, we wouldn't even be able to walk." Bonpo grunted his agreement. This snow was bad, but it was a spring shower compared to the hurricane that was the Snow of Misery, which had been very aptly named.

"What happens if we get caught in the storm?" Eluned asked, quietly. Neither Bonpo nor Jabberwock responded. How to tell her it meant certain death? Not only because of the amount of snow that would be dumped on the mountains and block the pass from either side, but also because they were carrying only a few days' rations—enough to get them comfortably down the eastern side of the range and to the village that sat on its lower slopes. Presuming they could build themselves some sort of shelter to last them until the worst of the snow melted, they would run out of food, even if they rationed it, long before that happened. The Snow of Misery could easily keep the passes blocked for up to a month, depending on how much snow fell. They would be lucky if they made it a week if they were unfortunate enough to be trapped. At that moment, Jabberwock could not think of a more dismal death.

Eluned had begun to moan softly, as if every step brought her insufferable pain. No doubt her feet were nearing frostbite in the relatively thin-soled suede boots she had chosen to wear. If Jabberwock had thought about it, he would have made sure she was better outfitted for the trip. He had known they would be crossing these mountains, and yet he hadn't thought of warning her about either the potential for severe cold nor the fact that if she weren't used to it, the hiking might cause her feet to feel as if they were being struck continuously with a rod of iron.

It hadn't occurred to him because he always trotted around on four legs. He eyed her, guiltily, and started looking harder for a spot to camp. Obviously, they had passed the site. "All right," he barked, "I give up. Let's just camp in the middle of the trail!"

Bonpo and Eluned stopped so suddenly that Jabberwock ran into the giant's left leg; it was like running into a tree trunk.

Bonpo didn't waste any time. Setting down his load of food and blanket, he tromped off into the woods to gather wood for a fire. Unlike the previous day when she had to force herself into the woods to gather wood, this time she took off quickly after Bonpo. The idea of standing still for even one minute in the constantly falling snow made her shiver uncontrollably. So, despite her throbbing feet, she scavenged with Bonpo, pawing away snow and numbly picking up fallen branches.

Back on the trail, Jabberwock was leading Hayduke around and around in increasingly tighter circles in an effort to get as firm a base as possible for the fire. He sighed. At least they wouldn't have to worry about setting the woods on fire. Bonpo returned with wood, and with what seemed like magic, soon had a fire blazing. Eluned followed shortly with more wood and began pacing the perimeter of the blaze, passing behind Bonpo and Jabberwock as she made her circuit. In some ways, she was afraid to stop, fearful that her body temperature would drop too much if she stilled herself for even a second. Eventually, exhaustion won out and she wrapped herself in a blanket, and sat as close to the fire as she dared.

Using snow for water, Bonpo elected to make a soup for dinner. The more hot liquid he could get into the Princess, the better off she would be, he decided.

All things considered, it didn't take long for the soup—just a matter of rehydrating the vegetables and meat—to cook. And, during that time, Bonpo and Eluned made several more forays into the woods to gather an overnight and morning supply of wood. Once they had savored every last drop, Bonpo pulled out a tarp and rigged them a covered space close to the fire. They had to suffer the occasional blast of wind blown smoke, but at least they were free of the falling snow. Although Jabberwock worried whether the tarp would withstand a night's worth of the precipitation.

Bonpo saw him eyeing the roof of the tent, and offered to occasionally wipe it clear during the night should the tarp begin to sag. There was a collective sigh of relief from both Jabberwock and Eluned; the latter snuggling down into her blankets and drifting off to sleep to the sounds of the crackling fire, the murmured conversation between her two companions, and the soft sound of Hayduke's breathing. Oddly enough, she felt content.

16TH NEEON

Cluned awoke the next morning to Bonpo's hearty guffaw. It seemed to echo through the snow-covered world. The fire was still blazing merrily or so she assumed; at least it looked as if had been tended throughout the night. She could see wisps of steam emanating from the spout of the coffee. The Princess craned her neck and could see an azure sky through the boughs of fir above, and the sunlight reflected off every icicle and was mirrored by every particle of snow. It was chilly, yes, but it felt more invigorating than the previous day, which had been a miserable and mind-numbing cold.

"Good morning," boomed Bonpo, happily.

"It certainly appears to be," she replied with a radiant smile. Jabberwock and Bonpo couldn't help beaming back.

"Yesterday, it seemed like the end of the world," she reflected as she crawled from beneath the tarp, and then stood, releasing herself to one of her patented feline stretches. "Today, it feels like we have been given the hope of a new life."

"Sounds like a Paschal sermon," Jabberwock chuckled.

"Well, I guess death and resurrection are a constant in this world," she mused, sipping the coffee Bonpo had handed her. "From death comes life."

"I'm pleasantly surprised. Apparently you were paying attention in Chapel," the Bandersnatch teased her.

"Not enough in all likelihood," she frowned. "My mind seems to get stuck on the 'dying to self' bit."

"Give yourself time," Jabberwock counseled, gently, "You are only eighteen, after all. And isn't that part of the point of this trip? To experience life? To grow?"

The Princess smiled a bit self-deprecatingly. He was, of course, always right.

IN SPITE OF THE HORROR OF YESTERDAY'S HIKE and even the physical pain involved, not to mention the thought of each step taking her closer to the desert she so desperately desired, Eluned was reluctant to leave the hastily made, but sun painted, camp behind. And, of course, her feet were still aching terribly. If they already hurt this bad, she grimaced, how would they feel by the end of the day?

But a mile or so down the trail, which was taking forever because they had to slog through a couple of feet of snow, the pain began to fade. Or maybe it was just because she had to be so vigilant over every step she took. Until she stepped, she couldn't see or feel what her foot was landing on and she didn't want to take another tumble. It helped that Bonpo was leading. His height and weight significantly reduced the trouble she had to go through. But, his stride was much bigger than hers. About the time Eluned's pain began to recede (to be taken up by the dull ache of frozen digits), Jabberwock suggested to Bonpo that he try a sliding step so that he would clear more snow.

Yikes! Eluned glanced guiltily at the Bandersnatch. She had been so caught up in keeping up with Bonpo and making sure she didn't fall that she had entirely forgotten Jabberwock. The snow was nearly as deep as he was tall. Poor little guy!

"Why don't we put Hayduke behind Bonpo? Between the two, they could really stamp down the snow," she suggested.

"Excerrent idea," Bonpo said.

Before they finished the next mile, they happened on the final Misrule Pass campsite.

"By Omni!" Eluned cried in awe. "I thought I walked my feet off yesterday. I can't believe that we not only passed the second site but got this close to the last."

"It does seem nearly miraculous," Jabberwock observed. "That means we hiked . . ."

"Nealy tirty mire," Bonpo interrupted.

"Not bad for a beginner!" Jabberwock grinned at Eluned.

"You know, I don't know why this is just occurring to me, but is there any particular reason we aren't riding horses? I mean with horses and a pack mule, I might still be able to feel my feet. I mean, just for example."

"A horse couldn't take Bonpo's weight," Jabberwock stated.

"Yeah, but we didn't know he would be traveling with us. Or did we?" she peered down, accusingly at the Bandersnatch.

"No, that was definitely kismet."

"Well, I don't know about you, but I vote that when we reach Sheba we invest in a horse for my use. You can ride with me, Jabb. Bonpo walks twice as fast as we do, anyway."

Bonpo grunted and shrugged his shoulders, "Fine by me."

"You're right," Jabberwock agreed. "I'm afraid that I just don't think along those lines, but it makes sense."

"Well, we can't stay here despite how tired we are," Eluned glanced around the snow-covered campsite. "It's just too early in the day, and there would be all that extra work maintaining a fire. I say it's better to go on and see how close we can get to the first campsite down from the pass. The sooner we get to Mjijangwa, the better!"

ONCE AGAIN, THE TRIO PUSHED ON to near dark and stumbled into their last campsite before reaching the trade town at the base of the mountains nigh on exhaustion. Even Bonpo was moving slower than usual. A half-hearted fire, which mostly smoked because of the wet wood, did little to push back the darkness and it seemed an eternity before the water boiled for tea. Cold beans were reheated to lukewarm and eaten mechanically.

The wind that night seemed adept at ferreting out any chink in the armor of her blankets. The three of them tossed and turned as if even in their troubled sleep they fought to keep warm. The usually placid Hayduke seemed to twitch continually with the cold. It was a miserable night, and Eluned checked the sky numerous times as the stars arced their way through the bowl of heaven. This was worse than the night she had waited for dawn to arrive so that she could begin this hellish journey. Her worry and discomfort made it harder for her to doze off and it was with great relief that she saw the lightening of the sky.

Apparently, Bonpo and Jabberwock had had just as bad a night. All awoke grouchy, and instead of the beatific faces of the previous day, three faces scowled into the barely flickering flames of the fire as they once again awaited boiling water.

"Darn it! It is so true," Eluned groused as she huffed off into the woods. "A watched pot NEVER boils."

As THEY STARTED OUT ON THEIR FINAL DESCENT toward the high desert border town of Mjijangwa, no one ventured to break the thick silence. Even the birds opted not to sing until the glowering and exhausted trio was out of range.

Finally, about noonday, they had dropped enough in elevation that most of the snow had disappeared, laying mostly in the crevices of rocks or in shadows not yet touched by the sun. Despite their fatigue, they began to feel a glimmer of hope. Mjijangwa didn't seem such an impossibility. Perhaps they would sleep in beds and eat at table that night! As if on cue, they rounded another switchback to find a sign bearing the sigil of Sheba, a red hawk on green, informing them they had now entered the land ruled by King Adeyemi and his queen, Yobachi.

"O come, thou Key of David, come," Eluned began in her clear contralto. Bonpo and Jabberwock joined in, bass and tenor. "And open wide our heavenly home; Make safe the way that leads on high, and close the path to misery."

"Can I hear an 'amen'?" Eluned asked when the last note faded.

"AMEN!" Jabberwock and Bonpo replied, heartily.

THE LIGHT WAS RAPIDLY FADING as they left the track that led them over the mountains for the wider road that led into the small desert outpost of Mjijangwa. They had taken the quickest route through the mountains rather than the wider and better-traveled trade route in an effort to keep the Princess safe. The further they traveled away from the Kingdom of Zion without the whereabouts of Eluned being known, the safer they would be.

She had been so protected during her childhood that very few were aware of her appearance other than the fact that she was rumored to be quite beautiful.

Jabberwock glanced at her out of the corner of his eyes. Yes, definitely still beautiful but the reddened and chapped cheeks, constantly dripping nose and shuffling walk would, at first, earn her nothing more than a passing glance from the ill-mannered types they were likely to find in this trade station.

But once she'd had a bath and warmed up . . . he sighed, loudly, and Bonpo and Eluned, each ruminating on their own worries, sighed in response.

As they approached the inn, they saw the torches being lit to ward off the coming darkness. Their pace picked up a bit, and as the last torch was ignited it was as if the sun's fading red light was snuffed out as surely as a candle.

They hobbled the last fifty yards to the inn in darkness and the dim light provided by the torches. Soon the moon would be up and the sandy soil would reflect some of its light back toward it, but as yet they could keep their eyes only on the beckoning flames.

Eluned shivered suddenly as the thought crossed her mind: come toward the light. Images of death and destruction and the gaping mouth of hell rose unbidden in her imagination, and she shivered again.

"Are you all right," Jabberwock asked, his forehead creased in worry.

"It's nothing," she assured him. "A rabbit just ran over my grave."

"You do realize I'll be unable to speak publicly while we're here," he whispered as they neared the steps.

"Again?"

"Too dangerous."

She cursed under her breath. Hopefully, between herself and Bonpo, they would be able to speak to the proprietor. She would try the common tongue first because her Sheban was rusty. If she were lucky, whomever they needed to arrange rooms with would speak the common tongue. After all, it bordered Sheba and this was an inn on the western trade route.

Bonpo handed off Hayduke to a stable hand as they approached the inn's front steps.

Eluned glanced up as she mounted the stairs and saw the first star of the evening shimmer into view. "Star light, star bright," she began to whisper.

"Planet," Jabberwock coughed as they crossed the porch to the wide door of the inn.

"So much for luck," the Princess sighed.

Bonpo heaved open the heavy door and they stepped into a wide hallway that led to a larger room with a fire roaring in a huge stone fireplace and well-worn tables scattered about the room. Three men with weather beaten faces sat at one of the tables nursing their ales or wines or whiskeys. They barely looked up as the odd trio entered.

A single man sat at a smaller table on the far side of the room, close to the fire and staring into the wildly dancing flames. If he noticed them, he didn't show it.

Eluned looked around with trepidation. Certainly she hadn't been expecting a warm reception like the one she'd received the first night of her trip at the Golden Gryphon. Not that she'd noticed any gold at that particular inn anywhere but in the badly peeling paint that highlighted the mythic creature on the inn's sign, she mused. Nor was this quite as bad as the fear she felt upon first entering the Crossroads Inn. How imaginative, Bonpo, she chided him in her head, you couldn't come up with something better than crossroads? But this utter indifference?

"'Ello?" Bonpo suddenly shouted, voice booming. One of the men at the nearer table jumped and sloshed his ale. His two friends began ribbing him for it, but continued to disregard Eluned and her companions.

A door opened behind him, and a cranky looking man with a shock of black hair, bangs tumbling into his eyes but the rest pulled away from his face with a dirty piece of cord, stepped into the room wiping his hands on an even dirtier towel.

He grunted something that could have meant "what the hell do you want?" but neither Eluned nor Bonpo recognized the language, only the intonation.

"We need a couple of rooms," Eluned began in the Common Tongue.

The man stared at her uncomprehendingly.

She tried again in her native Zionese, and when that failed, then in her broken Sheban. But he continued to shake his head. Her Adenese was much better and she attempted that.

He said something in his language and it was Eluned's turn to shake her head in incomprehension. She looked to Bonpo and he tried his Dzironese.

Still nothing. Damn, Eluned found herself cursing under her breath yet again, what language did this fellow speak and what the hell was he doing working at a trade route inn if he didn't speak the Common Tongue? Royalty and those who worked in trade were expected to know the Common Tongue, she brooded as the silence descended once again. She couldn't believe that this man didn't understand any of the languages that either she or Bonpo spoke.

Jabberwock looked amazingly unperturbed.

"Excuse me," she spoke to the three men at the table, but they just shrugged their shoulders and looked down at the table. She wanted to cry. All she wanted was a clean room, a bath and some real food and she might start feeling human again, but instead she was stuck with someone who obviously worked in the kitchen and hadn't dealt much with travellers.

She turned toward the man who was still gazing unseeingly into the fire. He seemed unaware of what was going on. She took a deep breath and began to walk toward him.

"Excuse me," she said when she was a few feet away.

Reluctantly, he pulled his gaze away from the fire. He raised his eyebrows.

"Do you speak Zionese?" He nodded in reply, and she nearly wept in relief. She had to bite her lower lip to stop the flood that threatened to issue forth from her tear ducts.

"You don't, perchance, also speak whatever language this fellow is speaking?" she asked, indicating the cook or dishwasher or whatever he was.

"Annewvenese?" he finally spoke, standing. The hood that had been covering his head slipped away, and she was pleasantly surprised to find a nice looking young man staring down at her with clear hazel eyes.

"Is that what it is?" she found herself blushing, much to her chagrin. The way he was looking at her made her feel very uncomfortable. He was tall, more than six feet, she was sure of it. His hair tumbled to his shoulders in dark brown waves and there was a mysterious glint in his eyes she couldn't identify. She wasn't sure, because of his facial hair, but was that a dimple at the corner of his mouth? He seemed to be studying her with secret amusement.

"Yes, Annewvenese," he confirmed.

"Could you please help us? We need a couple of rooms and," she stuttered to a halt as she saw the muscles of his jaw clench. "What?"

"A couple of rooms?"

She was confused. "One for myself and one for Bonpo. I don't understand?"

"That's not your husband?"

"Hus…?" she nearly guffawed, but clapped a hand over her mouth, coughing instead.

"A guide then?" But he said it in such an insinuating tone that she found her self outraged when she finally realized what he was implying. Cheeks flaming and fists clenched, she wanted to stomp off and sleep on the porch. She didn't have to put up with that! She was a Princess! But, one of the reasons she was on this so-called adventure was to live life like a "real" person. Closing her eyes, she took a deep breath.

Exhaling, she said, quietly but coldly, "My guide, yes, and cook. And bodyguard," she added, arching an eyebrow.

He laughed out loud at that, but added, "so, you're travelling alone, so to speak, with a guide who doesn't speak anything but Dzironese and Zionese?"

Eluned looked down at the snow-stained and soaking tips of her suede boots. The truth was, she had thought the Bandersnatch would be responsible for all that. She supposed that in the eyes of a stranger, their little trio seemed particularly odd.

Thank Omni for Bonpo; the thought chilled her to the bone. If it hadn't been for the giant, she would appear to be insane journeying alone in this day and age with nothing but a small and wiry "dog" to protect her.

There was no way to explain her situation to him without telling him the truth. Or, alternately, without coming up with a cover story first. Blast that little Bandersnatch for not thinking about this ahead of time. She glanced over at him and was shocked to see him with a smirk on his face. Her eyes widened.

"You little jerk," she started to say, but then realized her mistake. "Oh, I'm sorry," she continued, bending over to pat the top of his head.

Then to the man she still hoped would help them, "I thought my dog," a sliding glance at Jabberwock, and she was happy to note the disappearance of the smirk, "was crouching to relieve himself."

"He's not house-broken?"

"Oh, yes, quite, but we've had such an exhausting trip over the mountains, I thought he might have forgotten himself."

"You came over the mountains?"

"Yes, and the last two days in nothing but snow and cold." She suddenly swayed and the young man reached out a hand to steady her.

"Are you all right?" he asked, worriedly.

"Just oh so very tired," she said as the exhaustion of the past few days finally caught up with her.

Bonpo pulled up a chair and gently pushed her into it.

The scullion, if that's what he was, said something unintelligible.

The young man answered in the same language. The scullion disappeared behind another door.

Eluned gazed at the young man, hopefully.

"He's gone to get you keys for your room," he said, flatly. Eluned pushed herself out of the chair and stood up, extending her hand.

"I'm Eluned," she said as he took her small hand into his grasp. "And I thank you from the bottom of my heart."

"Gwrhyr," he said, squeezing her hand, gently. "And I intend to discuss this more tomorrow. Understood?" His hazel eyes, looking more blue than green, bored into hers.

"I promise," she said, collapsing back into the chair.

The scullion returned with the keys and Gwrhyr instructed him to have meals sent up to their rooms and a warm bath drawn for the woman.

"And make sure they are not disturbed before noon," he added.

18ᴛʜ Neeon

Out of habit, Eluned awoke early the following morning. But, when she saw the dull grey light, she rolled away from the window pulling the comforter over her head. She had no idea what time it was, but it not only seemed early, it looked cold outside. It didn't take her long to doze off again.

When she wakened again a few hours later, the light hadn't changed. Pulling the comforter around her for warmth, she crossed the narrow space to the window and peered out. The sky was steel grey with low-hanging clouds. She put her hand to the leaded glass of the window, and pulled it back quickly as if stung.

Starting to shiver, she groaned. There was no way she was going to head out on a day like this – cold and grey and threatening snow. Eluned hoped she could talk Jabb into staying one more night. So much for her dreams of the desert. She wondered if there were any other clothes available in this town. Hers were filthy and she couldn't bear the thought of putting them back on.

The Princess scanned the room, looking for the pile of dirty clothes she had so unceremoniously tossed on the floor the previous night. They were nowhere in sight. Her brow creased in perplexity. Had she really slept so hard that she hadn't heard Bonpo, or someone else, for that matter, enter her room to gather them up to wash?

Or, she sat down on her bed with dawning realization. Had they even been here when she returned from her bath? Of course, that was it. Bonpo or a servant had entered her room while she was immersed in her hot tub, soaking away the miles and the cold.

Eluned remembered thinking as she finally pulled herself out of the rapidly cooling water, that she had soaked in all the warmth and transferred her cold to the water. Even her marrow finally felt warm. And, she recalled, she had pretty much run straight to her room from the bath, diving into bed and scrambling beneath the covers before she had a chance to get cold again.

But that still didn't solve her problem. What clothes was she supposed to change into?

The Princess peeked out into the upper hallway. It was empty. She tiptoed down the hall to the next room where Bonpo and Jabb were staying. She knocked, somewhat timidly, on the door. Listening intently for sounds of movement or even snoring, she was disappointed to hear absolute silence.

The feather comforter still clutched around her thin shoulders like a royal robe, she stamped her foot in irritation. She was hungry. Starving, actually, as she had fallen asleep before she had a chance to eat.

"Damn it," she said aloud, heading toward the staircase that would lead her down to the kitchens and great room. As she reached the foot of the stairs, she could hear voices and when she turned the corner into the great room, she saw Bonpo, Jabberwock and Gwrhyr sitting comfortably around a small table and talking animatedly.

Bonpo saw her first and stood up so fast he knocked his chair over with a crash.

"Plincess!" he blurted.

Eluned's eyes flashed in anger, and Gwrhyr gave her a calculating look. She decided to ignore it, but she wasn't about to forget that she'd heard Jabberwock's voice. He had told her it was too dangerous to speak here. She would definitely be speaking to him about that. But at the moment, there were more important things to worry about.

"Where the hell are my clothes?"

"Dey are being creaned," Bonpo said, apologetically. "I tought dey dry by now, but too corl dry fast."

"Is there anything else in this god forsaken place that I can wear? This is a trade route. Surely someone sells clothing."

"I imagine that something can be pulled together," Gwrhyr spoke.

The Princess was torn. On the one hand, she was really angry that this man had so easily wormed his way into Jabberwock's good graces, so much so that the Bandersnatch was speaking. Yet, she really preferred not to spend the rest of the day stuck in her room because she was wearing only a nightgown. Once again, it looked like she was going to have to be indebted to him, a complete stranger and Omni knew what else. He could be a horse thief, for all she knew; and besides, she found not being able to be self-sufficient truly irritating.

Eluned blushed, more in anger than humiliation, "Would you mind going with Bonpo to find me something? Unfortunately, I can't exactly wander around like this."

The Princess felt her cheeks coloring again as Gwrhyr made a point of scanning her from the top of her bare head to the tips of her bare toes.

"I kind of like it," he grinned in such a way that her blush deepened a shade or two. Tears pricked her eyes at the humiliation. If she had been looked at that way in Zion, her father would have punished the malefactor.

"Thank you," she managed to choke as Bonpo and Gwrhyr left the inn to search the town for clothes. Pulling out a chair, she said, "Is there anyway I can get something warm to drink around here?" while staring accusingly at Jabberwock.

He had the good grace to look chastened, but nodded at the hand bell that rested on the table. "Just ring that, and someone will be here shortly."

True to his word, a youth arrived from the direction of the kitchen.

"Can I get you something miss?" he asked in Sheban.

Eluned almost cried in relief. "Yes, please," she said in his language but with a heavy Zionese accent. "Coffee, please? And something to eat?"

"Yes, miss," he said, staring at her as if she were a vision.

"Thank you," she prompted. He reddened and backed toward the kitchen.

"I'll be right back, miss."

"Thank you," she said, again, turning to look with amusement at Jabberwock when the boy had disappeared back into the kitchen.

The Princess shook her head, "You'd think he'd never seen a female."

"Oh I would guarantee he's never seen a female as beautiful as you. He probably thinks you're an angel."

Eluned laughed, but then remembered she was angry with the Bandersnatch. "Did I hear you talking with Gwrhyr?" her tone was a reprimand.

"I apologize for not being able to discuss this with you, first, but Bonpo and I were negotiating with the man. We feel it would be really helpful if we paid him to serve us for as long as necessary."

"Serve us? How?"

"Not only is he fluent in many languages," Jabberwock explained, "but he knows horses and pack animals, and it would definitely look better for you to be travelling with at least one more person. Although, I cannot believe I didn't think to hire a maidservant to travel with us. We are really going to have to come up with a cover story until we can hire a female to travel with us."

"Does he know who I am?"

"Well, thanks to Bonpo's little slip, I would imagine he has a few questions. It is up to you to decide whether to entrust him with that information."

The door to the kitchen opened again, and the young scullion entered carrying a tray laden with coffee, cream and a typically Sheban breakfast – thick creamy yogurt, brown sugar, dried fruit and nuts.

The Princess felt her stomach clench at the sight of it. She had had no idea that she would spend so much time during this journey nearly faint with hunger. She set about eating the meal slowly, though, so that her empty stomach wouldn't rebel.

Once the boy was gone and she had managed a few, bless-edly warm, sips of coffee and stirred some of the sugar, fruits and nuts into her yogurt, she began to ponder whether or not to let Gwrhyr know the identity of her father.

"Do you think he'll try to take advantage of us if he knows?" she asked.

"Take advantage? How?"

"Well, we don't know what kind of person he really is. Just because he has been helpful doesn't mean that he doesn't have some sort of ulterior motive," she responded.

"A good point," Jabberwock mused, "but I tend to believe him."

"Believe him?"

"His story."

"What's his story?" she asked, dubiously.

"Ask him your self," he retorted as footsteps could be heard approaching the dining room. She turned to look over her shoulder as Gwrhyr and Bonpo appeared.

"I solly," Bonpo said, depositing a parcel in her lap, "onry fine men crove."

Eluned stared at him in incomprehension.

"He means that we found only clothing suitable for males," Gwrhyr interpreted.

An expression that was a cross between consternation and intense curiosity crossed the Eluned's face. Clothing for a man, huh? She had never had a chance to wear pants. And you never knew when the opportunity might arise again. The Princess found herself smiling despite herself. As a disguise, well, who would think to look for a princess in pants?

"Thank you," she said, standing up. "If you'll excuse me, I'll go get dressed." She readjusted the comforter and walked toward the stairs. The impression was regal, to say the least. You almost didn't have to imagine the tiara perched atop her shining black curls.

"If you're trying to hide a Princess," Gwrhyr addressed Jabberwock with a crooked grin and raised eyebrow, "you might want to teach her how to act less uppity."

Bonpo flushed. If only he hadn't called her Princess. It didn't matter now, but it could be dangerous at some point.

There was a mischievous sparkle in Jabberwock's eyes as he watched the Princess leave the room. She was definitely going to have to let Gwrhyr in on the truth. Not only did she think that he already suspected, but it would also more than likely be advantageous to them all if she allowed him to possess that knowledge.

THE PRINCESS RETURNED TO HER ROOM, which was still just as chilly as when she'd left it, and ripped open the package Bonpo had dropped in her lap. Her anticipatory smile widened as she withdrew a pair of leather pants, a rough spun wool sweater and a leather jerkin.

The comforter slid to the floor as she pulled her nightgown over her head and hastily replaced it with the sweater, lacking any small clothes over which to layer it. Those were being washed, as well. Sitting down on the bed, she pulled the close-fitting pants over her feet and up, fastening them with the leather laces that crisscrossed up the front. She pulled the jerkin on over the sweater, fastening its toggle buttons, wishing she had a mirror in which to appraise this new look.

Bonpo had taught her the trick of sleeping with her socks rather than in them so that she would wake up to warm and dry socks in the morning, and she searched under the sheets for her only pair. It was then that she realized that she should have asked Bonpo and Gwrhyr to purchase her another pair or two. But that hadn't occurred to her anymore than remembering to bring more than one pair on the journey to begin with. Her nose wrinkled at the smell as she pulled her only pair on yet again. She was definitely going to have to venture out with Bonpo or Gwrhyr to find some more socks! These were not only in desperate need of washing but they had worn dangerously thin in the heels and the toes, and she really couldn't continue to go around bare foot.

After pulling her boots on over her pants, she suddenly experienced a moment of trepidation. The Princess had never dressed as men dress in her entire life; her parents would have never allowed it. She felt not a little guilt as she strode over to the door. What if she looked like a fool? What would she do if they all burst out laughing when she returned to the great room?

She took a deep breath, shot an arrow prayer toward Omni and opened the door.

"There's only one way to find out," she muttered under her breath as she started down the stairs.

BUT SHE SAW NOTHING BUT APPRECIATION in the faces that turned her way when she entered the room. A variety of expressions, actually, now that she was closer. Jabberwock, as always, managed to look both approving and mysterious at the same time. There was always a lot going on in that tiny little head of his.

Bonpo looked both surprised and proud. He had done well at guessing her size.

Gwrhyr wore the oddest expression. Eluned could have sworn there was a small flame of desire burning within his eyes, but he somehow seemed bored or even disinterested, as if it was beneath him to desire her? She wasn't sure, but his reaction intrigued her.

Despite the look on his face, he said, "You wear men's clothing very well."

"Thank you kind sir," she responded with a tinge of sarcasm. He grimaced, but stood up and pulled out a seat for her.

Sliding into the chair, she once again surveyed the faces around the table, and for the first time the full realization that she was surrounded completely by males hit her. Albeit one of the males was a Bandersnatch, Janawar or dhami dhole, depending on which appellation one preferred; and another was a giant Dzironian or what had Jabberwock called him? A dzutch?

Finally, she looked at Gwrhyr. His hazel eyes looked teal today and were boring into her own. She held his gaze, studying him. He was the wild card. Or was he? Had he been thrown into this odd mix just as Bonpo had? Had Omni set her up with this unusual trio for a reason? And why was she the only female?

"Jabberwock tells me he asked you to help us out as we continue our journey," she said.

"That's true," his gaze shifted to the foxlike mammal.

"And?" She prompted.

"And?" he repeated.

"Have you agreed?" The telltale crease of irritation appeared between her brows.

Bonpo and Jabberwock turned toward him in anticipation of his response.

"Well, I must admit, it's truly tempting, and possibly a lot more exciting than my current option," he began.

"Which is?" Eluned interrupted.

"Hooking up with the next caravan that passes through..."

"And that would be mostly likely what this time of year?" It was the Bandersnatch's turn to interject.

"Most likely coal from Annewven heading north toward Muskroe," Gwrhyr answered, not sounding particularly thrilled by the prospect.

"Oooo coal," Eluned couldn't keep the sarcasm from her voice. There was just something about him that grated on her nerves. "That sounds so exciting!"

"Oh, and you think traveling with an arrogant wench such as yourself would be preferable?" Gwrhyr drawled, leaning toward the Princess menacingly.

"Wench!" Eluned shouted, leaning toward him and grabbing his short beard in her fist and twisting it. "How dare you speak to me thus? By Omni, I would rather walk every step of the way than . . ."

Gwrhyr grabbed the curls on either side of her head and pulled her face closer. Eluned's eyes sparkled, dangerously. But before the palm she was raising could reach its mark, Gwrhyr kissed the Princess soundly on the mouth before letting her go and pushing his chair away from her.

Eluned jumped up, tears springing to her eyes from both fury and shock. "You can't do that!" she screamed, launching herself toward him like a catamount defending its territory.

But he easily seized her fragile wrists in a steely grip, and before she knew what was happening, he'd knocked her feet from beneath her and she landed hard on the dirty flagstones that tiled the great room's floor.

The tears that now overflowed her lids were from pain and humiliation. She had never been treated like this before in her life! Who, or better, what, did this man think she was? Women had never been misused this way in her father's kingdom.

"Women?" a quiet voice in her head asked, "or was King

Seraphim's daughter an exception?" The room around her blurred as she picked herself up and dusted herself off. Bonpo already had Gwrhyr's neck in a vise-like grip, and Jabberwock was noisily telling him to let go and for every body to just calm down. But, the Princess was a thousand miles away.

As she slumped back into her chair, she tried to remember how things were in and around the castle, but she had been so protected, so coddled. Everyone had always known where she was, and while their tongues might occasionally slip around her, their tempers seldom did.

The tears spilled down her cheeks as she stared down at her hands. But, she admitted to herself, there had been those rare occasions when she had dashed into the kitchen for a snack just as a scullery maid was receiving the back of the cook's hand to her face; or wandered into the stables just as a stable boy was fielding off the angry blows of the ferrier. She supposed if she thought about it, she could raise dozens of such memories. But they had been, she hiccoughed, servants.

"No," her conscience scolded her, "they had been humans." And why should Gwrhyr expect her to be any different than any other woman he'd encountered in his life? After all, she really was just some strange 'wench' who had appeared out of the blue demanding all manner of assistance from him. Her eyes began to clear and she noticed that Gwrhyr was holding out a handkerchief. She accepted it with a murmured thank you and wiped her face.

"I'm sorry," he apologized. "That was completely out of line."

"No, I probably deserved it," Eluned sighed. She stood up, "Will you take a walk with me? There are probably some things I need to tell you before you can make a decision. Besides, I need some socks."

"Socks?"

"Obviously, I'm not used to packing for myself," she said,

self-deprecatingly. "I neglected to bring more than the pair I was wearing when I set out on this journey."

AS THEY TOOK THE LAST STEP FROM THE PORCH of the inn onto the hard pack in front of it, Eluned's foot slipped on a small patch of ice and she began to go down, wheeling her arms as she tried to regain her balance. But, once again, Gwrhyr proved how necessary he was by catching her around the waist with his left arm and steadying her.

Up until that point, Eluned had forgotten the kiss. Feeling the warmth of his arm around her waist, dangerously close to her left breast, brought it all back in a rush, and she stiffly removed herself, saying brusquely, "Thanks, I'm fine now."

Gwrhyr glanced at her knowingly and with a glint of amusement in his eyes. "That way," he pointed to the left. "I'm sure they'll be able to provide us with socks in the same place we bought the clothes."

Eluned felt her cheeks redden yet again. Oh if there was only something she could do to turn off that response. Why couldn't she keep her face neutral when something embarrassed or angered her? Always the telltale blushing.

They lapsed into silence as their feet crunched their way down the small dirt street lined with rough, dog-trot-style buildings. Despite the wool sweater and leather jerkin, Eluned shivered as wind sought access through even the tiniest opening in her clothing.

As they neared a building that looked just like all the others, Gwrhyr lightly touched her arm and pointed. She nodded, sniffing (damn the cold, she thought, it always set her nose to leaking like a faucet), and headed toward the few steps that ascended to its porch. She held tightly to the railing this time to keep Gwrhyr from having to grab her again.

They entered into the dimly lit room, eyes widening as they attempted to adjust to the dim light. Gwrhyr spoke quietly with the proprietor who called roughly for his wife. She entered the room and asked the Princess to remove her boots. Quickly sizing up her feet, she indicated that she could have several pairs of newly knitted wool socks by the following morning.

Gwrhyr assured the couple that tomorrow was fine, asking them to deliver the socks to the Inn as early as possible, and paying for them in advance.

Eluned found herself grudgingly respecting the stranger's talents. Other than his occasional antagonism toward her, he seemed capable of doing just about anything. But why was it she kept envisioning herself slapping him across the face? There was just something about him that really rubbed her the wrong way. He just seemed so damned self-assured. 'So?' she argued with herself, 'what was wrong with that?' 'Because,' she continued the argument raging in her head, 'if he were high born, she might be able to dismiss it, but on a peasant it didn't sit as well.' Her better self was shocked. 'Do the circumstances of his birth determine his abilities?' She felt the heat rising to her cheeks. Would she ever win that battle with herself? Did the fact that she was the only child of parents with so-called royal blood really make any difference? Well, she sighed to herself, if she allowed him to continue the journey with them, she might just find out.

And it seemed, from the continuous little problems they had faced once they were no longer in her father's kingdom, that his services just might be invaluable.

The Princess took a deep breath and forced herself to speak once they were back in the soft grey light of the overcast day. "Obviously, you've realized that I'm not behaving like a so called 'normal' person," she began. Gwrhyr lifted an eyebrow in conjunction with his signature lopsided grin.

Eluned responded with her signature reddening of the cheeks.

"Princess Eluned," Gwrhyr said, significantly.

"That obvious, huh?"

"Well, there is undoubtedly, hmmm, how do I say this, a distinction to the way you behave."

"Probably the biggest understatement of the year," she couldn't help from laughing. He joined her, but encouraged her, saying:

"Oh, I have no doubt that it will pass in time. You seem to be a quick learner."

"Do you really think so? I've never been beyond the castle walls . . . I didn't realize there was so much to learn about," she paused, searching for words.

"Us peasants?" He filled in for her.

"No," she blushed again, "I didn't mean that. Really, I didn't realize there was so much to learn about life. I never knew just how protected I was. I thought I knew so much because of all the books I've read . . ." she trailed off.

"Not exactly the same thing as reality, is it?"

"Over romanticized, I'd say. And I fell for it. That's the truly sad part."

"And yet you made it over the Mountains of Misericord during a snowstorm. No, you shouldn't chastise yourself too harshly."

She was silent for a while. It was hard to explain, briefly, just why she, the daughter of a king, was on this journey. She wasn't sure she understood the reason herself.

"Give it time," he assured her, seemingly reading her mind. "It won't be long before you understand a lot more than you do now."

She looked at him, oddly, "You're right, I don't understand. I don't even know why I am on this journey yet it seems so clear to you . . ."

"No, actually, it isn't. But, I do know that it is in the journey, hmmm, how does that old proverb go? 'The journey is the reward.'"

"Or, 'The journey of a thousand miles begins with one step . . ."

"Yes, something like that. 'We shall not cease from exploration and the end of all our exploring will be to arrive where we started and know the place for the first time.'"

Eluned gaped at him. "How did a, uh, you come to learn poetry? Particularly one of the Ancients?"

"Oh, I'm full of surprises," he laughed, "and I've been on my own for quite a while. I've often thought of myself as a sponge, soaking up every bit of knowledge that came my way."

The Princess could only shake her head in wonder, and murmur, "'What we call the beginning is often the end and to make an end is to make a beginning. The end is where we start from.'"

"Little Gidding is one of my favorites," Gwrhyr mused, "although I'm also partial to Ash Wednesday."

WHEN THEY WERE ENSCONCED ONCE MORE before the inn's roaring fire, Eluned sighed and rang the bell for the server. She needed something to take the chill off her bones, not to mention a bit of time to process the enigma Gwrhyr seemed to be.

"Were you successful?" Jabberwock asked.

"Hmmm? Oh, yes," Eluned replied, "the socks will be here in the morning." She eyed the Bandersnatch for a moment. "That's okay, isn't it? I mean, you weren't intending to head out today, were you?" she concluded, shivering for emphasis.

The boy appeared and as much as she wanted mulled wine, she still needed all her senses. "Tea," she ordered, and looked around. "Anyone else need anything?"

"Tea's fine," Gwrhyr said, reluctantly. He'd obviously been hoping for a bit of mulled wine or ale, himself.

"No, no, we can spend another night here," Jabberwock answered her question. After a brief pause, he prompted, "And . . ."

Both the Princess and Gwrhyr looked at him blankly.

"I thought you were going to discuss whether Gwrhyr was to continue the journey with us." He sounded irritated.

They all looked at Gwrhyr expectantly. Gwrhyr's eyes lingered on Eluned's, and she found herself remembering, once again, the pressure of his lips against hers. Damn it, she thought, why did that have to be my first kiss? Damn him. He's nice enough, just not what I imagined . . ."

Gwrhyr interrupted the beginning of her usual fantasy. "Oh, all right," he began, begrudgingly, "seeing as how you all so obviously need my help . . ." He saw the flare of anger in Eluned's eyes and couldn't keep from allowing himself a small grin. She was so damn easy to manipulate. "I'll come along with you. For a little while, at least. Until it's clear you're well on your way," he added, sternly.

"Well on our way?" Eluned asked.

"I'm sure you will reach a point in which you will feel confident to proceed on your own."

Eluned felt a flutter of fear. Why now, suddenly, was she afraid to be on her own?

Only Jabberwock seemed to sense the truth; that Gwrhyr was trying to boost Eluned's self-confidence. He had no doubt, considering the flame of ardor that had been ignited in Gwrhyr's eyes, that the young man would be around perhaps longer than even the Princess desired.

The boy arrived with the tea and Eluned waited impatiently for it to steep, checking it every couple of seconds. Finally, she pulled the tea strainer from the steaming water and dumped in a teaspoonful of sugar. As she waited for the liquid to cool enough to be drinkable, the rest of the day seemed to stretch interminably in front of her.

Funny, she mused, just over twenty-four hours ago she was longing for a break. Now, an entire day stretched in front of her, and she wasn't sure how to amuse herself in this strange town without books or games or people. She sighed, loudly.

"What's wrong?" Gwrhyr asked.

"I'm not sure."

"Well, if you need something to do, you could always write your parents and let them know that the trip is proceeding nicely," Jabberwock offered.

"I imagine that they are worried about you," Gwrhyr added. "Have you written since you left?"

"No," she admitted. "Do you keep in touch with your parents?"

"My parents are no longer of this world, but when they were alive, I always kept them informed of my whereabouts."

"Hmpff," she grunted. "I'm an adult now. They need to learn to live without me."

Shaking his head in disbelief, Gwrhyr pushed his chair back from the table. Had she been looking at him instead of lifting her mug of tea, she might have caught the flash of disappointment in his eyes. He had finished his tea just as she was picking hers up for the first sip, and he and Bonpo headed out to arrange rides for the following day and supplies for as much as a week.

The Princess slumped down in her chair as soon as they left and looked morosely at Jabberwock.

"Don't say a word," he said, recognizing that look. How many times had he seen it during the past eleven years? Too many to count. 'Bored as a board?' he had teased her. "Well, if you're not going to write your parents, there is a small room down the hall to the right that has a number of books, worn but legible."

"Praise be to Omni," Eluned straightened, looking curiously down the hall.

"Go ahead," Jabb encouraged, "take your tea and go peruse the offerings."

She smiled at him, thankfully. "I'll be back. I'd love to curl up by the fire with something short and light. I promise I'll write Mother and Papa before we leave." She paused for a moment, considering the masculine atmosphere that so deeply penetrated the inn that it nearly exuded from the walls. "If I can find a light romance . . . or poetry," she said as she wandered off. "Anything but war stories," was the last the Bandersnatch heard before she was out of range.

18TH NEEON

It was a small and narrow room but two floor-to-ceiling windows on the far wall shed enough light, dim and grey though it was on this particular day, that Eluned could easily read the titles on the books that lined the built-in shelves on both sides. In front of each window was an ancient and ragged armchair with a small table set between them.

As she had worried, most of the volumes were trash, if a book could be considered trash. Boring manuals, encyclopedias and almanacs seemed to make up most of what was available. But, here and there a work of fiction could be found. Eluned was beginning to feel frustrated and hopeless as title after title sent a shudder of dullness down her spine.

She was nearing the end of the second shelf when a narrow book, nearly hidden betwixt a thick and extremely boring tome entitled Coal: Sources, Mining and Safety by Dornick Purine and an almanac that was nearly fifty years old, caught her eye.

Thirteen Royal Treasures the spine read. And, being a princess, Eluned couldn't help but pull the book from the shelf. The ancient red leather was cracked and the title, apparently Thirteen Royal Treasures of The Thirteen Kingdoms, had been imprinted in gold at some point but not much but the impression was left as the gold had mostly flaked away.

She moved as close to the windows as she could get, seeking more light. Setting her mug down on the small table, she stood with her back to the window and the book held above her head for maximum light. She could see the faint remains of an imprint of the author's name. She could barely make it out. She squinted her eyes and turned the book various ways to see if the light was better. It looked like, but she couldn't swear to it, Pryderi Gruffyd.

'Looking at the title page might be a good idea,' she reminded herself. She carefully opened the delicate text fearing the pages would be as fragile as the cover. The musty smell of old and yellowed paper drifted up to her nose and she inhaled of it deeply . . . there was something almost sacred about the smell of an old book; it was akin, in her mind, to the incense they used in church.

She glanced eagerly at the title page. Yes. She had been right. Pryderi Gruffyd. Much better than Dornick Purine, she snickered. The name definitely sounded like someone who would know what they were talking about.

She turned the brittle page to the table of contents, which promised an introduction followed by thirteen short chapters (one for each treasure, she presumed). "White Hilt: The Sword of Rhydderch the Generous," the title of the first chapter read. The second chapter was entitled, "The Hamper of Gwyddno Garanir." She scanned the titles of the next few chapters.

"So very intriguing," she murmured, picking up her tea and heading back to the great room and its roaring fire.

"Find something?" Jabberwock opened one eye as Eluned joined him in front of the fireplace. He was curled in front of the fire, napping contentedly.

"I hope so," she replied, pulling a chair closer to the fire so that she could prop her feet up on the raised hearth. After settling her self comfortably in the chair, she continued, "It's called Thirteen Royal Treasures of The Thirteen Kingdoms."

Jabberwock's head rose in a flash, pointy ears alert and twitching. "What did you say?"

"I said Thirteen Royal Treasures of The Thirteen King- doms. Why?" she eyed him in wonder.

"Hmmm," he said, musingly. "I haven't thought of those in years." But inwardly his mind was reeling. Omni was surely at work again. Once Eluned read that book, once she learned of the thirteen hallowed treasures, there was no doubt in his mind that they would become her grail. And, how well would her ring be described?

Eluned was staring at him. "What? What are the thirteen royal treasures?"

"Best you read the book," he stated, simply, and pretended to return to his napping, resituating himself and curling up more tightly before the fire.

Eluned frowned, but opened the book to the introduc- tion. It wasn't her nature to read introductions; she wanted to skip right to the first chapter, diving in, headfirst. But, her new, more mature self (she had the grace to roll her eyes at that), felt she needed to take things more slowly, savor the moment, so to speak.

After several paragraphs, way more than necessary as far as she was concerned, Pryderi Gruffyd finally began to write about why he had written the book and what it was about – the thirteen treasures. According to Gruffyd, the thirteen trea- sures, sometimes with one or two added on, but essentially thirteen, had been collected by a certain wizard named Myrd- din or Merlin, who had taken them under his protection. But thousands of years had passed since that time and the trea- sures had been retrieved only once, but rather than being used for good, their purpose, they had been used for great evil and millions had died. Each time they'd been gathered together, for good or for evil, they had always wound up once again dispersed. To this day, still hidden or scattered to the four winds, no one knew the fate of each and every treasure though some were known to be in certain kingdoms. What was rumored though, what the legend seemed to be, Gruffyd wrote, was that once collected together again, a righteous and good man might bring peace to the world. The inverse was also true: if collected by a selfish and malevolent man, great evil could be wrought.

"Really?" The Princess blurted and Jabberwock snorted in surprise, quickly turning the sound into a prolonged snore so that the Princess would think he was asleep.

Now deeply captivated, Eluned turned to the first chapter – White Hilt: The Sword of Rhydderch the Generous. Below that, it read, "Dyrnwyn: Gleddyf Rhydderch Hael."

All right, she mused, that must be some ancient language. The only word I get out of that is 'Rhydderch' and that is obviously a name. She soon discovered that if the sword, White Hilt, was drawn by a wellborn and virtuous man, it would burst into flame from its hilt to its tip.

"That could come in handy in battle," she murmured aloud. But, it appeared there wasn't much to say and extremely little known about the treasures. Everything seemed to be mostly speculation on Gruffyd's part.

The next treasure was "The Hamper of Gwyddno Garanir," otherwise known as Mwys Gwyddno Garanir or The Hamper of Gwyddno Long-Shank. Why did that remind her of food more than someone who was long legged? Her stomach rumbled. Maybe that was why, she snickered to herself. She looked around. Not a soul but herself and Jabb. Because the day was so overcast, she couldn't even estimate the time of day.

Finally deciding to wait a while longer, she settled down to discover more about this hamper. Great, her stomach grumbled again. Not only did "Long-shank" remind her of food but also the hamper turned out to be a picnic hamper that if one put only enough food for one man into the basket, food for one hundred men could be withdrawn from it.

Eluned groaned, and the Bandersnatch stirred and mumbled, "What is it?"

"I'm hungry and I have no idea how close it is to a regular eating time. My whole day is off keel because I slept so late," she grumbled.

"No one forced you to sleep late."

"I know it," she snapped. "But it was so ugly outside there seemed no reason to get out of bed."

"But, you're right," he said, stretching, "I do believe it is heading toward that time. I will go and round up Bonpo and Gwrhyr."

"Wow, I am beginning to suspect he paid you to be a part of our little coterie."

"You're just jealous," he groused as he pattered off, bottle-brush tail twitching irritably.

The Princess smiled, indulgently, at his retreating backside, and returned to the book and the third treasure. Simple enough. The Horn of Bran or "Corn Bran Gogledd." She didn't know what 'Gogledd' meant, but the other two words were easy enough to figure out.

The Horn appeared to be a good match for the Hamper as it promised its possessor whatever drink he might wish for.

"That would have certainly come in handy during the past week," she murmured, and jumped as a heavy chair scraped the floor next to her.

"What would have come in handy?" Gwrhyr asked, eyeing the book.

"How did you get here so quickly?"

"I was already on my way in. What would have come in handy?"

"The Horn of Bran," she stated, waiting for the look that

would say, 'tell me more, tell me more.' As always, he disappointed her.

"Ah, yes, the Horn of Bran," he said, surveying the room, which was, not surprisingly, devoid of any servants. "That would come in very handy at the moment."

Eluned's mouth dropped open. She snapped it shut, quickly, before he could make some nasty comment about her catching flies, and sputtered, "By Omni, is there any thing you don't know?"

"Well, if you must know, I'm not well versed in the propagation of tropical fruits."

The Princess wanted to wipe the annoying grin off his face. "But you excel at growing fruits in a temperate zone?" Eluned asked, sarcastically.

"If I do say so myself," he returned, smugly.

Closing her eyes, she gritted her teeth. That tactic obviously wasn't working. Maybe if she ignored him he would go away. She opened the book to the next chapter—nothing better than getting lost in treasure. The Chariot of Morgan the Wealthy was the next treasure in the book. Eluned read silently for a few minutes, Gwrhyr sitting peaceably by her side, apparently enjoying the warmth of the fire and the entertainment provided by the dancing flames.

Car Morgan Mwynfawr, she read, is one of the more fantastic of the treasures. It is said that once in the chariot, a man could wish to be a certain place and thus get there quickly. Eluned dared a glance at Gwrhyr. She wouldn't mind possessing that chariot just about now. The Princess wasn't sure exactly where she'd wish to be but it sure wouldn't be here, sitting next to this obnoxious man. And, it would definitely be some place warm. The Favonian Islands were beckoning, and she felt a smile beginning. She sighed, audibly, picturing sand and palm trees, not that she had ever actually seen them in person. Eluned felt the sun warm on her face, a cool drink in her hand.

And then she imagined a gorgeous man at her side, stroking the black curls away from her face as the breeze tossed them into her eyes.

"That must be quite some treasure," Gwrhyr interrupted her thoughts. Instead of answering him (she didn't want to ruin the moment; her imaginary lover was turning her face towards his), she handed him the book.

He scanned the title and first few paragraphs quickly. "So where are you?"

Eluned kept her eyes closed. She didn't want to see him, but murmured, "The Favonian Islands."

"Well, I hope you're sheltered," he said, "because with that skin you'd burn in a flash."

"Thanks," she said, disgustedly. "Do you not even have one molecule of romance in you?" And with that, she snatched the book from his hand, stood abruptly and went to find Jabberwock.

He watched her departure in dismay.

"I JUST DON'T KNOW IF I CAN DO IT," she told the Bandersnatch, who was still discussing travel details with Bonpo in the stable. "That man drives me insane. He is such a know-it-all. The smug, self-serving, son of . . ."

"Be careful," Jabberwock interrupted, "the things that annoy you about him just might be aspects of your self."

"What?" she gasped, flabbergasted. All she wanted was a little sympathy and here he was getting all psychoanalytical on her.

"I only meant that maybe you should reflect on the things about Gwrhyr that drive you crazy, and come to terms with why that might be so. I wouldn't be surprised if he feels the same way about you."

"That I'm a smug, self-serving . . ."

"Know-it-all. Yes."

"Hmpff," she snorted, tossing her curls. But, as she turned away from Jabberwock, muttering "traitor" under her breath, her brain was already elsewhere. She walked slowly back toward the inn's entrance. So this journey she was on, she mused, thinking back on her earlier conversation with Gwrhyr, was to be as much a journey inward as outward, it seemed. Of course, what did she expect? Eluned had known the Bandersnatch long enough to know that all her lessons with him over the years had had a spiritual, if not moral, emphasis. Even the very first time they had met, he had entertained her with a fairy tale about a princess who stood up for someone who was different and in doing so won a friend who later saved her life.

The door to the inn opened just as she was reaching for the handle, and she jumped back, startled.

"Sorry," Gwrhyr apologized, "I was just coming to let you all know that they're ready to serve us supper."

"Bonpo and Jabb are still in the stable," she said, gesturing over her shoulder, embarrassed to look at his face.

"Thanks," he murmured, and stepped past her, heading in that direction.

The Princess was glad to be away from him. Despite the fact she had been traveling with a giant for days, she kept forgetting how tall Gwrhyr was. She barely reached five feet, two inches, which made him nearly a foot taller than she, and somehow she found that much more intimidating than Bonpo's eight feet. But once you got past Bonpo's size, he was as sweet as a kitten. Gwrhyr, on the other hand . . . Once again she remembered the press of his lips against hers. Eluned was glad the dark entry hid her deeply flaming cheeks. She would hate for anyone to see her blushing yet again.

Taking a deep breath, then another, she settled herself before she entering the great room. A table had been set for the four of them. (They set a place for Jabb? Of course, he had sat all day in the great room with various combinations of their party or alone; surely no one had missed his nearly constant yapping.) And it was clear they were the only occupants of the inn that night. It was still early in the year for trade route travel—many places were still snowed in.

By the time the other three had arrived, she had already poured herself some wine from the pottery decanter on the table and was gratefully taking a long sip.

Gwrhyr took the seat across from her, whether to keep an eye on her or to ensure that he wasn't sitting next to her, she couldn't quite determine. He quickly filled his own goblet, raised it briefly, if somewhat mockingly, toward the Princess, and swallowed half the contents.

The Princess hid her smile behind her own goblet, and picked up the book again, while she waited for the food to arrive.

The Halter of Clydno Eiddyn, she read, alternately known as "Cebyster Clydno Eiddyn," Cebyster meaning halter, no doubt. She soon discovered that when the halter was attached to the foot of the bed (Of its owner, presumably? Gruffyd was so damned nebulous.), that is, once attached to the correct bed, belonging, no doubt, to a righteous man, Eluned guessed, the halter would be filled with whichever horse was wished for.

An awesome treasure, she mused, but she was still bothered by the bed. What if you were traveling and sleeping in a different bed every night? Surely it didn't have to be a particular bed, which could be long gone by now? Or maybe it mattered only who was sleeping in the bed, as long as it was an actual bed? She wondered where these treasures now resided. She pictured the halter, leather cracked and dry, silver ornaments tarnished to an ebony black, lying in some abandoned corner of a stable; tossed unknowingly atop moth-eaten saddle blankets still reeking of ancient horse sweat, broken stirrups, and other pieces of tack no longer needed by their owners.

The Princess suddenly felt an overwhelming need to run

out to the stable and tear it apart, just in case the halter was here. She had half-risen in her chair before she decided she was being ridiculous. She sat back down, blushing, as three sets of eyes surveyed her, questioningly.

Gwrhyr held out his hand for the book, briefly scanned the page, nodded and handed it back to her.

"I've already searched here," he stated, flatly.

Eluned's eyes widened a bit, but she was already getting used to his ability to read her like a book. Instead, she raised her eyebrows.

"Once you know about the treasures," Gwrhyr continued, "it's hard not to keep an eye out for them everywhere you go." He paused. "Well, for some, that is. I would hate to make that a generalization."

"So, that's the fifth treasure," Jabberwock interjected, "only eight more to go." Eluned turned the page.

"The knife of Llawfrodded the Horseman," she read aloud and paused. No one objected, rather they watched her expectantly, almost as if it were a great treat to be read to about something that at least Jabberwock and Gwrhyr seemed already familiar with.

"Do you know the thirteen treasures, too?" she couldn't help asking Bonpo.

He nodded, slowly, as if embarrassed. "All dzu-tch know."

"Why am I not surprised?" The Princess shook her head, but she was no longer nonplussed by the fact that the entire party seemed to know about something legendary that somehow had escaped her extensive education.

"Cyllel Llawfrodded Farenog," she read, wondering, not for the first time, if she was even beginning to pronounce these strange words correctly. "It says this knife can carve enough food to allow twenty-four men to eat at table." She wondered, idly, if "at table" was meant literally as she had recently used a knife while camping, both around a campfire and in a tent; if not, then the owner was out of luck. She suspected, though, that it was just an archaic turn of phrase—one that she had become familiar with after reading her great grandmother's books. "Interesting," she murmured, before turning the page.

"The Cauldron of Dyrnwch the Giant," she said, nailing Bonpo with a penetrating stare. His booming laugh nearly shook the table.

"Pair Dyrnwch Gawr," Jabb said loudly enough to be heard over the giant's laughter, "yes indeed, that would be delightful on both accounts. But, hopefully, we'll happen upon that particular treasure. It would be nice to have an assured method of cooking with us."

"You're making the assumption we are all brave. What if one of us is a coward?"

"Speak for yourself," Gwrhyr teased.

"Well, I wasn't exactly brave when attacked by the barrow wight," she admitted.

"My dear," Jabberwock said, gently, "I would say in the long run you handled it all quite well."

"Yes," Bonpo seconded. "You even out da nex' day, at dawn."

"I think you woke me up at dawn, but yes, we did leave. I'm still not sure that qualifies as being brave, but I appreciate that you think so. Of course, at this stage of the journey it's all a moot point because we don't own Dyrnwch's cauldron and we have nothing to boil in it to test whether or not it even will boil. Speaking of which, do all the treasures revolve around food? If the next one has to with cooking, drinking or eating, I might swoon from hunger."

But, at that instant, the kitchen door swung open and the scullion appeared carrying a huge tray. The aroma wafting from it caused Eluned's stomach to groan in anticipation. Cumin, curry, cinnamon and other spices emanated from the platters being set on the table. Flat breads, couscous, vegetables

and meats swimming in tantalizing sauces . . . she found herself forcibly holding her palms in her lap until everything had
been set on the table.

"Omni, bless this food to our bodies and our bodies to
your service," she said, quickly.

"Amen!" They shouted in acclamation. Despite her hunger, Eluned scooped some of the food onto a plate for Jabberwock before serving herself.

"Thank you," he said.

"Despite your brilliance," she ribbed him, "there are some
drawbacks to not having opposable thumbs."

"Indubitably," he laughed, and lowered his head, deftly
skewering a piece of meat on his sharp canines.

"By Omni, I am too full," The Princess declared a quarter of
an hour later. "But it was so good. I couldn't stop myself."

"If you rike," Bonpo said, preparing to push away from the
table, "I go kitchen; find out 'ow to make."

"Oh Bonpo, would you? I would love to have this again.
And we'll be in Sheba for a little while?" Sheba was a narrow but long, from north to south, kingdom. She still wasn't
quite sure which way they were heading: northeast to Simoon,
southeast to Annewven or straight south through Sheba to Baharimoto where they could take a ship to the Favonian Islands;
her personal choice no matter what Gwrhyr thought of her
skin.

"A few days," Gwrhyr said, dashing all her hopes.

"Simoon or Annewven?" She asked, disappointedly, as
Bonpo headed for the kitchen.

"Annewven," Gwrhyr and Jabb answered simultaneously.

She dredged her memory for any knowledge she might
have of the place, but she was so logy from the meal that all she
could manage was the name of the country's king, Arawn.

"Arawn," she yawned, covering her mouth belatedly. "Is

there a queen?" And, for some reason, as she said that, she shivered.

"Cold?" Gwrhyr asked, unbelievingly.

"A rabbit ran over my grave," she responded before noticing he was already a thousand miles away.

Gwrhyr was thinking that the room seemed quite comfortable to him. 'Or, maybe,' his mind jumped, 'the wine's making me warm,' he looked up at Jabberwock, guiltily, wondering if he'd had too much to drink. He caught the Bandersnatch staring at him, crystal eyes gleaming in such a way that Gwrhyr could read his thoughts. "Ok," he directed his thoughts toward Jabberwock, "maybe the Princess is making me warm."

Jabberwock chuckled and turned to answer Eluned, who had been watching the silent exchange with amusement.

"You two seemed to have bonded," she said in a tone dripping with honey, but they both heard the sting beneath it.

"Sometimes you just feel a connection to people," Jabberwock explained, lamely.

"No one has answered my question."

"No," Jabberwock continued, hurriedly, "Arawn is not married."

"He's relatively young though, isn't he?" she asked.

"He can't be twice your age," Jabberwock said.

"Thirty-three, I believe," Gwrhyr stated.

"That seems old to me," Eluned grimaced, thinking, 'he's definitely out.' "So why are we going there?"

Jabberwock, who had been relieved to perceive Eluned's previous thought, stuttered, "Uh, because . . ."

"Oh, just tell her." Gwrhyr said.

"Fine," he pouted. "Because that is where all thirteen treasures were once gathered, and King Arawn is rumored to have three of them, more than any other kingdom."

"Really?" And then her eyes narrowed, and she demanded, accusingly, "You didn't plant this book in the library, did you?" She picked up the book lying next to her goblet.

"Surprisingly not," Jabberwock admitted. "I wish I had thought of it, but I guess Omni has it all under Its control, as per usual."

"You're saying this is an Omnincident?" she asked, using the slang for an Omni-inspired coincidence.

"I'm saying that I did not put it there."

"You?" It was more of an order than a question.

"No, your highness," Gwrhyr simpered, sarcastically.

"I'm doing it again?"

"Yes."

The Princess wasn't sure if she was ever going to not be able to act like royalty, particularly when she was suspicious or angry or embarrassed or . . . she slumped down in her chair. "I'm sorry," she said it so quietly that Gwrhyr leaned forward.

"Excuse me?"

"I'm sorry," she said it louder, cheeks flaming. And apparently Gwrhyr wasn't going to let her forget she was a princess. To change the subject and distract herself, she opened the book to the next treasure. The Whetstone of Tudwal Tudglyd, it proclaimed. She glanced up to see her companions watching her, expectantly. Gwrhyr poured some more wine into her goblet and then topped his own off with the remainder.

"Hogalen, etc.," she said, grudgingly. Why couldn't they let her finish the book in peace?

"At least it's not about food," Gwrhyr grinned.

She couldn't help but laugh. "True and for the opposite reason now." As they no doubt knew its magic, she scanned through the text and discovered that if this particular whetstone was used by a brave man (always a brave or righteous man, she thought, sourly. Surely, a woman could use it, too.), to sharpen his sword, then if he drew blood with it, that person would die.

"Youch," she interjected, "what if you accidentally nicked someone with it?"

"Good point," Gwrhyr murmured. He hadn't actually considered that before.

"Doesn't that just sound like an ancient love story," Eluned continued after a sip of wine, which was relaxing her tongue. "I mean, I can see it now, the brave knight finally rescues his damsel in distress and in the process of killing the dragon, the tip of the blade pierces the skin of her chest and . . ." She glanced up and saw Gwrhyr observing her, intently. She bit her lip and bent to the book again. It was clear from the glint in his eyes that he was remembering the kiss or at least fantasizing about the next one. "Oh what a surprise," she continued, sardonically, trying to change the tone, "a coward won't hurt his opponent at all."

"Maybe that's the key," Gwrhyr ventured, "maybe it has to be your foe."

"But what if they don't know they're not your foe?"

"Huh?"

"I mean, what if you think it's someone who likes you but they really hate you?" Eluned attempted to explain what she meant.

"Or someone who hates you but in reality, is enamored of you?"

"Something like that."

"Well, if it's magic involved or Omni, for that matter, then I am sure the truth will be known," Jabberwock intervened.

"It is only with the heart that one can see wisely," Gwrhyr began.

"What is essential is invisible to the eyes," Eluned finished.

"Exactly," Jabberwock agreed. "Next treasure?"

"The Coat of Padarn Red-Coat," Eluned read. "Now that's redundant. I assume it's the magic red coat he's named for. Pais Padarn Beisrydd. It says it will fit a well-born man. That seems rather pointless to me. Who cares if it fits, well-born or not?"

"I have to admit," Gwrhyr said, agreeably, "I always wondered about that one, myself."

"Number Ten. The Crock and Dish of Rhyhgenydd the Cleric."

"Gren A Desgyl Rhyhgenydd Ysgolhaig," Jabberwock said, apparently fluent in the ancient tongue.

"Uh, yeah," Eluned giggled. "Seems rather pointless, again, for a cleric to have both a crock and a dish, one; and two, that whatever might be wished for would appear in them. Uh, lead us not into temptation, right?"

"Really," Gwrhyr guffawed, "he could become quite a glutton!" The scullion appeared to clear away the dishes and Gwrhyr ordered a flagon of mulled wine. Eluned wondered, briefly, if he were trying to intoxicate her but Jabb didn't flinch so she let it go. She was actually beginning to enjoy this. Sad that they both had to have wine to lighten up, Eluned thought, but 'c'est la guerre,' as that old maxim went.

"The Mantle of Arthur is the eleventh treasure," she read. "Llen Arthyr yng Nghernyw. I know I pronounced that wrong. But, this one is really worthwhile. The cloak has the ability to make the wearer invisible. That could come in really handy."

"Oh yeah," Gwrhyr seconded.

"Oh yeah?" Eluned insinuated.

"What? I only meant that there are times one might benefit from being a ghost, so to speak. Politically speaking. Only a vulgar person would use such a cloak to spy on a woman. I would never ... "

"We believe you," Jabberwock chuckled. "I believe the Princess is harassing you."

"Guilty as charged," she claimed, laughter tinkling like bells. The scullion arrived with the wine and filled their goblets with the steaming, fragrant liquid before setting down the pitcher he was pouring from.

"Just two more," Gwrhyr said, standing up. Let's go over to the fireplace to enjoy this.

"Yes, m'lord," Eluned giggled, bowing.

"Very funny," Gwrhyr shook his head, but he couldn't help grinning. Bonpo, returning from the kitchen, drew a bench over to the fireplace.

Settled in front of the cheerfully snapping flames, Eluned once more found her spot in the book. "The Chessboard of Gwenddolau, son of Ceidio," she began, taking a tentative sip of the wine. Perfect. Cinnamon, orange and cloves wafted in her face and she inhaled the scent, deeply. "Mmmm, I love the way this smells."

She informed Bonpo, Jabberwock and Gwrhyr, though she knew they were well aware, that this particular chessboard was said to possess mystical powers and would continue to play by itself once set up. "That's an odd one," she commented, "but intriguing."

"I would guess that the opponents choose silver or gold ahead of play to determine the outcome of something," Gwrhyr proposed.

"Likely. Very likely. I can see no other practical use." She had tried to say it seriously and profoundly, but Eluned worried that she might have slurred a word or two. Thank God there was only one more treasure. It was probably time for her to be settling down for the night.

She could almost feel a palpable tension in the air as she named the final treasure. "Eluned's ring and stone." She stopped. Her heart had speeded up considerably. Gwrhyr and Jabberwock seemed to be studying her intently but she couldn't fathom the expressions on their faces.

"That's my name," was all she could manage, but she was staring at the ornately carved band around her right ring finger.

"And?" Gwrhyr finally growled, impatiently.

"When it is placed on one's finger, with the stone inside the hand and closed upon the stone, the wearer is invisible." They could barely hear her above the crackling of the flames. She groped for the leather pouch about her neck. Was the stone a milky white moonstone, she wondered? If she pulled it out of the bag and clutched it in her hand, would she disappear? Was it even possible?

"What?" Gwrhyr asked.

"Do you want to try?" Jabberwock asked. "You're safe with us."

"Safe. This isn't a question of safe. You've known all along haven't you?" she accused the Bandersnatch. "You knew the moment my father pressed the box into my hand, perhaps even before." Jabberwock shifted uncomfortably under the intensity of her gaze.

"I didn't think the time was appropriate to discuss it."

Eluned tried to think back to the moment she had unwrapped the package to discover the ring and stone inside. It is true that her head had been reeling, and that typically, she had been weeping and antagonistic. Her father had mentioned Omni. Jabberwock, she remembered, had admitted he knew something. But following her little temper tantrum they had begun to walk again, and then she had been lost in Jabb's story of her great-grandmother. So, the question was: Did she want to try it with Jabberwock or did she prefer to be alone? She stared into the depths of her mulled wine, hoping for an answer. She looked up to find three sets of eyes watching her.

"All right," she sighed, "I'll try it here." There wasn't a mirror in her room, anyway. She took a swig from her wine and pushed back her chair. She didn't have to stand up but it seemed more dramatic. She opened the pouch around her neck and shook out the moonstone into the palm of her right hand. Taking a deep breath, she closed her fingers around the stone.

As far as she was concerned everything seemed the same. "Well?" she asked.

"It works," Jabberwock responded.

Eluned suddenly had the evil impulse to do something to Gwrhyr, like pull his chair out from beneath him, but she was sure he weighed too much and he seemed, thanks to the wine, pretty firmly seated. She could twist his beard or pull his hair but that seemed too childish. She really wanted to get him back for that kiss, but it was going to take more planning. She unclenched her hand, slowly reappearing to those in front of her.

"Wow," Bonpo managed.

"Truly impressive," Gwrhyr said, clapping, but it somehow managed to sound mocking when he did it. She'd be angry but at the moment she just felt tired.

"I'm tired," she groused, slumping into her chair. Her eyes seemed to have a hard time focusing on the goblet in front of her. She concentrated and managed to pick it up, she hoped, in a smooth sort of way.

"Perhaps it's time for bed," Jabberwock suggested. He had an uncanny feeling that Gwrhyr would be more than happy to help her finish the pitcher of mulled wine. But, he wanted to start out at least relatively early in the morning.

"Hmmm?" the Princess looked up. Her eyelids were beginning to droop.

"Yes, definitely time for bed," the Bandersnatch stated, firmly. "Early start tomorrow. Bonpo, can you escort the Princess to her room?"

As Eluned stood, and swayed, Bonpo firmly gripped her shoulder and guided her in the direction of the stairs.

Gwrhyr grunted, "Goodnight Princess," as he poured himself another glass of wine and silently cursed Jabberwock. Another goblet-full and Eluned might have willingly sought his kisses, he thought, glowering at their retreating backs. After draining his goblet in a single swallow, he pushed back his chair and reluctantly headed toward his room.

19TH NEEON

The fragrant smell of coffee woke her early the next morning. And a good thing too, she grimaced. Her eyes felt like they were sealed shut and her head was full of cotton balls.

"Good mornin', Leened," Bonpo bellowed.

"By Omni," Eluned winced, "Please don't shout."

"I solly," he tried to whisper and failed miserably. Even his whispers were loud.

"Just leave the coffee and go," she groaned and tried to sit up. The room spun, crazily, and for a second she thought she might throw up. She closed her eyes and waited for the dizziness to dissipate. It didn't take long, but the dull thudding continued in her head. "By Omni," she groaned again. "What possessed me to drink so much last night?"

"Uh," Bonpo began.

"Rhetorical, Bonpo."

"Oh. I go get you someting fah dat 'eadache."

"Good idea."

"Drink coffee."

"Yes sir." She took a small sip as Bonpo left the room, and waited for her stomach to protest. It didn't, so she swallowed some more. Bonpo had opted for strong and black rather than her normal heavily-creamed. And she was thankful for his wisdom. She was beginning to feel a bit better already. She sipped in silence for a while, listening, eyes half-closed, for the heavy tread that would signal Bonpo's return. Until she took the pain killer, she wasn't even going to try to get ready for the day.

When he arrived, she gladly swallowed the pills. "Thank you, Bonpo, and please, next time, if it looks like I'm over indulging, just take the wine away from me. Even if you have to hold me down."

Bonpo chuckled, "Yes, Plincess, but dis good lesson, no?"

"A very good lesson. And a terrible way to start the next leg of our journey."

"You tink you can eat someting?"

"Hmmm," Eluned pondered. What sounded appetizing? "You don't suppose I could get some scrambled eggs with cheese and bacon, do you?"

"I go tell cook."

"Thanks, Bonpo. I'll get dressed and be down shortly."

A PLATE FULL OF EGGS AND BACON along with a couple of huge biscuits awaited her when she arrived downstairs. The biscuits dripped with butter and practically melted in her mouth.

"These are so good," Eluned said around a mouthful. "Tell the cook he outdid himself."

"Tank you," Bonpo replied.

"You made these?"

Bonpo grinned, hugely.

"Wow. I am so very glad you decided to join us."

"Tank you. Anyting else you need? No? Ok, I go pack food now."

With her stomach full, and now completely caffeinated, Eluned felt better equipped to take on another day of travel. And at least this time they'd be riding horses. She ventured outside to discover which horse had been chosen for her mount.

She heard Jabb and Gwrhyr in the stable and headed that way, inhaling deeply the varied odors—fresh straw, leather, soap, even the horses themselves—that combined to make the unique perfume of the barn.

"Good morning Princess," Gwrhyr eyed her. She didn't look like she was suffering too much from the mulled wine.

"How are you feeling?" Jabberwock chose to be blunt.

"I'm fine, thank you," she said, primly. If Gwrhyr hadn't been standing there, she might have told Jabberwock exactly how she felt, but she wasn't about to let Gwrhyr know she'd awakened with a hangover. "Bonpo made me the most wonderful breakfast. I'm so glad he decided to come with us."

"Indeed," the Bandersnatch agreed.

"Which is my horse?" Two horses stood saddled and ready for the road with bulging saddlebags—a buckskin and a chestnut. There was also Hayduke, though he was still in the barn. He would no doubt carry Jabberwock along with some of the provisions. Either Gwrhyr or Bonpo had fashioned a "saddle" for Jabberwock out of a basket. It sat on the ground at her feet awaiting the mule's arrival. A small cushion had been fitted in the bottom of the basket to make his ride more comfortable.

Gwrhyr handed her the reins of the buckskin. "This is Honeysuckle. I wasn't sure how much riding experience you have, but she's gentle and very capable."

Eluned stroked the soft velvet of Honeysuckle's muzzle. "She's beautiful. Who are you riding?"

Gwrhyr started to lead the chestnut stallion out of the barn. "This is Heiduc," he said over his shoulder.

Eluned followed with Honeysuckle. "Hayduke, Heiduke, Hoduke," she sang under her breath.

"What?" Gwrhyr asked.

Eluned giggled. "I think I'll call my horse 'Hoduke.'"

"Whatever for?"

"Well there's a Hayduke and a Heiduc."

Gwrhyr didn't look amused, and the Princess buried her face in Honeysuckle's mane as she fought the impulse to stick her tongue out at the old grump. Did he not have a sense of humor?

She prepared to wait for Bonpo, but he emerged from the inn with several large bags containing their food and beverages as well as cooking equipment.

Gwrhyr handed her Heiduc's reins, "Hold him while I go get the mule." Eluned clenched her fists, angrily. How dare he order her around!

"Save the anger for later," Gwrhyr said as he saw the warning flash in Eluned's eyes. "We still have a number of things to do before we can get out of here." And before she could respond, he brushed past her and into the barn.

"Men," she whispered, fiercely to Honeysuckle. "You can't live with them and you can't kill them." Heiduc whickered, softly. "Not you," she informed him, "you're not human, thank Omni."

Gwrhyr soon returned with Hayduke, Jabberwock trotting alongside them. Bonpo began to load the food and his gear onto the sturdy mammal.

"Don't go getting all softhearted on us," Jabberwock ordered her when he saw the Princess bite her lip with worry. "He's carried a lot more as well as a lot heavier loads."

"You don't feel bad when you make a horse carry your weight, do you?" Gwrhyr asked.

"No," she admitted, but then she didn't weigh as much as some people, she thought, eyeing Gwrhyr's tall but slender frame. He still probably weighed nearly twice what she did. Well, at least they'd be eating the food everyday so the load would get continually lighter until they had to restock.

Gwrhyr disappeared into the inn and soon returned with the remainder of their gear, including a few tents and blankets. He strapped their bedrolls behind the saddles and stuffed their more personal items into the already full saddlebags of the horses and handed the rest to Bonpo to strap on the mule.

"Are you sure we don't need two mules?" Eluned asked.

"Hayduke will be fine," Jabberwock assured her.

"All right," Eluned sighed, "I believe you." But she would be keeping a sharp eye on the mule, just in case.

"So," Gwrhyr asked as Bonpo finished, "anyone need to use the facilities before we head off?" All heads turned in her direction and she found herself blushing. Damn, it had been bad enough having to wander off into the woods with Bonpo and Jabberwock around, but now they were heading off into the high desert and she had Gwrhyr to deal with. Somehow a "Bandersnatch" and an "abominable snowman" didn't seem as hard to be yourself in front of as a man; particularly a man that had kissed her against her wishes and might do so again given the chance. "Damn, damn, damn," she muttered to herself as she stamped back into the inn. "What have I gotten myself into?"

IT WASN'T LONG BEFORE HONEYSUCKLE'S STEADY GAIT began to cause her head to throb to its steady clip clop. She could use some more of Bonpo's magic pills, but she'd have to allow Gwrhyr to draw ahead and ask on the sly. She wasn't about to let him know she had a hangover.

She reined the buckskin in, and then pretended it was her hair that also needed reining in. "Go on," she waved to Gwrhyr when he realized she'd stopped. "It won't take me long. I can catch up." He saw her scrabbling through her saddlebag as Bonpo came up alongside her.

"Go head," Bonpo encouraged, and he took Hayduke's lead from the giant and continued down the road, slowly. He didn't know what was up, but clearly the Princess didn't want him there.

Eluned signaled that her head was hurting again. Within

seconds, Bonpo had pulled a couple of pills from his voluminous pockets and dropped them in her open palm. Eluned quickly dry-swallowed them while securing her curls with the ribbon pulled from her saddlebag. In less than a minute the Princess and Bonpo were on the way again.

They continued on in silence once Bonpo and Eluned had caught up, each immersed in their own thoughts. Gwrhyr was pondering various approaches to gaining Eluned's favor; Jabberwock was wondering how long he could put off the inevitable meeting with King Arawn; Bonpo was wondering when they'd stop for lunch and making calculations on how much food to prepare; and Eluned was regretting not bringing along a handmaid—someone to stand guard for her while dressing or doing her business, so to speak. She suddenly had a terrifying thought that had her heart plunging to her knees—they had been traveling only a little over a week. It wouldn't be long before that so called "time of the month." It hadn't even occurred to her to pack the necessary items for that. "Omni have mercy," she groaned quietly to herself.

"Excuse me," she said, loudly, interrupting their contemplation. "I'm assuming that because we've brought along provisions for a week that means we won't reach another town until then?"

"That's right," Gwrhyr responded. "There is a small outpost at the Annewven border crossing, but I know from experience that we don't want to stay there."

"Why?" Eluned couldn't imagine what could be worse than sleeping on the ground during a snowstorm.

"Let's just say that even if I told them you were my wife, the men that frequent the outpost might not, hmmm, how do I say this? Umm, they might expect me to share the wealth, so to speak."

Eluned was horrified. "Share?"

"Share was a nice way of putting it," Gwrhyr admitted.

"You mean force," she said.

"I'm afraid so," Gwrhyr agreed.

"So what you really mean is that they'd rape me?" The Princess pressed him.

"Beyond a shadow of a doubt," Gwrhyr stated.

"Is there any way we can avoid crossing the border there?" she asked, hopefully.

"Yes, and that's why it's going to take us a week to get to Arawn's castle, Pwyll, and the town of Prythew that surrounds it." He tried to assure her. "We're going to have to take a slight detour south and cross the River Mab at the southern ford. There's just too few of us to defend ourselves at the outpost."

"You mean it would only be you and Bonpo against who-ever's there?" She was amazed that such behavior was toler-ated. Her father would never allow it.

"Yes, and really, at this point, we don't want to draw any unnecessary notice," Jabberwock added. "Bonpo was exiled from a kingdom in the Awen Alliance, and he considers Zion one of his enemies."

"What about you, Gwrhyr? Where are you from?" Eluned asked.

"I'm from Aden."

"And they're in the Triquetra Alliance, not Awen," she stated.

"So, obviously we're on pretty shaky ground," Gwrhyr con-cluded.

"What's our excuse for being in Annewven other than wanting to find the treasures?" Eluned wondered aloud. "And, which of the treasures is King Arawn supposed to have?"

"The chessboard, the chariot, and the halter," Gwrhyr an-swered. "Jabb thinks that we need to pretend that we're inter-ested in emigrating to Annewven."

"Whatever for?" The Princess frowned in confusion.

"Therein lies the rub, my dear." Jabberwock sighed.

"In other words," Eluned said, "we need to come up with a reason."

"Da soona, da betta," Bonpo agreed.

"All right. I'll do that, or at least try to." The quartet lapsed into silence again, lulled into a deeper concentration by the steady hoof beats of the animals and the occasional call of a desert bird or the slithering scuttle of a lizard. Eluned pulled the hood of the jerkin over her head as her ears began to ache from the intermittent sharp breeze. Why on earth would I want to emigrate to Annewven, she thought. And if they were just "emigrating" then how was she going to meet King Arawn? If the kingdom had once been home to the Thirteen Treasures, then surely Arawn was still in possession of at least one of them. Something about Arawn tickled the edge of her memory, but slithered away as quickly as the desert's lizards.

She sighed and returned to the current problem. The emigration story might work only until they arrived in Prythew. But what then? No. She had to come up with something better. Eluned was still deep in thought when they stopped for lunch, silently debating the merits of the plan that was beginning to unfold like a blossom in her mind.

"You're certainly quiet," Gwrhyr said to her as he helped her dismount Honeysuckle.

"I've been thinking," she explained.

"Clearly," Gwrhyr agreed.

"And I'm not sure that using emigration as an excuse is such a good idea," she noted.

Bonpo looked up with interest from where he was pulling the makings for sandwiches from one of the many containers Hayduke was lugging.

"And what, might I ask, is your idea?" Jabberwock said from his perch atop the mule. Eluned lifted him down and went to sit on one of the boulders that sat alongside the road, apparently moved there when the route was cleared.

"We're going to Annewven, and more importantly to Pry-thew, to see if we can find, or at least find out about, any of the lost treasures, right?"

"Yes," Jabberwock acknowledged.

"Well, if we say we wish to emigrate, we'll probably just get handed off to some minor bureaucrat and that will, as they say, be the end of it."

"She's got a point," Gwrhyr said.

"I think we should stick to as much of the truth as possible. What if we enter the kingdom saying that I am the daughter of King Seraphim of Zion and that I have run away and that I am seeking asylum in Arawn's kingdom?"

Jabberwock, Bonpo and Gwrhyr stared at her, open-mouthed.

"What?" She asked as the silence lengthened. "Is it a bad idea or had you not yet realized that I have my moments of genius?"

"I implessed," said Bonpo, simply, and returned to making sandwiches.

"I think it could work," said Gwrhyr. "Certainly it would play to his ego. He'd welcome us . . . well, the Princess anyway, with open arms."

"All of us, if I insisted I needed my traveling companions with me—the people who helped me get away from the suffo-cating grasp of my father and mother," the Princess continued.

"That sounded all too real," Jabberwock commented drily.

"Well, yes, in part," she agreed.

"So, what or who are Bonpo and I to you?" Gwrhyr asked.

"I still say we stick close to the truth. Jabberwock and I hired him on as cook and bodyguard before crossing the mountains; and we hired you on in Mjijangwa for your invalu-able skills."

"Fair enough." Gwrhyr nodded. "It certainly would keep us from mixing our stories. What do you think, Jabb?"

The Princess studied Gwrhyr for a moment. He had certainly become familiar with Jabberwock very quickly. Or was he that way with everyone?

"I think she's right," Jabberwock was thoughtful. "I think if we run into anyone after crossing the border, we'll be taken straight to the castle."

"The question is," the Princess added, "will Arawn be interested in giving me asylum?"

"Oh for many reasons," Gwrhyr almost growled, "not the least being that he may want you for his own perverted pleasures."

"Perverted pleasures?" Eluned repeated.

"Oh, don't worry," Gwrhyr quickly backtracked, "I'm sure he's not as debauched as the rumors say he is."

"Oh wonderful," Eluned groaned. "That makes me feel a lot better."

"Food leady," Bonpo interrupted them.

THE REST OF THE AFTERNOON was spent in silence. Eluned tried to press Gwrhyr on what he had meant by 'Arawn's perversities', but he refused to talk about it.

"In truth, I know only gossip, and I hate to slander him before I know the reality," is all he would say.

Eluned subsided once again into the solitude of her thoughts, contemplating without enthusiasm the high desert rolling out before her. Had it not been yet another gray day, the muted red and brown tones of the desert might have garnered her attention. As it was, the overcast sky further faded the colors, and the landscape appeared only haggard and sickly.

Toward late afternoon, the wind began to pick up and Eluned pulled her cloak out of her saddlebag and wrapped it snugly about her, pulling its hood over the hood of the jerkin.

"You look like a turtle withdrawing into its shell," Gwrhyr remarked.

"The wind is piercing," she complained.

"Yes, tink maybe it brow in corld flont," Bonpo said. "Maybe brow dese clouds away."

"Yes, I imagine we'll be able to see the stars tonight," Jabberwock agreed.

"If it gets colder, I'll be too covered in blankets to see much of anything," Eluned groused.

"I build big fire. Make you warm," Bonpo assured her.

"Thank you, Bonpo." Eluned smiled at him. He really was a lifesaver.

19ᵀᴴ Neeon

That evening the quartet detoured off the main road, travelling nearly half a mile down a dry wash until they found a suitable camping spot. The flat area was high enough above the wash to keep them safe should the wind, that was now gusting more often than not, blow in a storm rather than clear the sky. Eluned found a flat spot between two boulders that was relatively protected from the wind in which to set up her tent.

Once everything was set to her satisfaction, she went in search of wood to feed what she hoped would soon be a blazing fire. Eluned stacked a pile of downed branches and twigs from the cottonwoods, creosote bushes and ponderosa pines that grew sparsely alongside the wash next to the fire ring Bonpo was building before returning to her tent to warm up again.

Within a quarter of an hour, Bonpo hailed her with the news that the fire was well underway. She joined him and Jabberwock by the fireside and watched as Bonpo set about preparing the evening meal.

"Where's Gwrhyr?" Eluned suddenly realized he was missing. She'd spent so many evenings camping alongside Bonpo and Jabberwock, that she'd forgotten for a moment their party contained a fourth.

"Taking care of the horses," Jabberwock explained.

"Oh. Right." Obviously Honeysuckle, Heiduc and Hayduke needed to be settled for the night.

"Don't worry," Jabberwock assured her, "they'll be well protected."

"Are there catamounts?"

"Fire wirr keep away," Bonpo reassured.

She had no choice but to trust them. Besides, she couldn't exactly fit Honeysuckle in her tent.

Because of the biting wind, Bonpo readied a hearty stew for their supper and Eluned found her stomach once again growling in anticipation. She spent a lot of time hungry these days, she continued to marvel. While she was waiting for the stew to cook, she nibbled on a leftover biscuit and gazed longingly into the pot in which the wine was just beginning to simmer in its spices.

Gwrhyr joined them just as Bonpo was ladling the wine into their mugs.

"Your timing is impeccable," she noted, drily.

"I do seem to have the touch, don't I? Mind if I share that log with you?" As it was the only place to sit, other than the ground, Eluned was forced to move over to provide Gwrhyr with room. It was a tight fit, and Gwrhyr didn't seem to mind the fact that he was practically sitting on top of her.

If she could have done so without seeming rude, the Princess would have gladly moved to the ground. She had the feeling Gwrhyr was taking special pains to make her feel uncomfortable and she was determined not to let him know that she'd rather sit next to a catamount or a venomous desert snake than rub elbows with the likes of him. She could swear she saw glints of amusement in both Jabberwock's and Bonpo's eyes and it made her grouchy. Once again she longed for the company of a woman, someone with whom she could commiserate. She avoided Gwrhyr's eyes. She really didn't want to know what they might be saying.

The only advantages to his sitting so close, she consoled herself, were that he blocked some of the wind and provided some body heat.

THE STEW WAS, NOT SURPRISINGLY, WONDERFUL and the four of them managed to have a rather stimulating conversation revolving around philosophy and religion and politics without anyone getting their feelings hurt. Eluned's knowledge of the politics of any but her father's kingdom was slim, and she listened with enthusiasm to their discussion of the various machinations of kings and queens, and who was allied to whom and who was so far neutral and who they might side with if the growing rumor of war ever came to fruition.

The Princess was dismayed by the fact that there were indeed grumblings from a number of kingdoms, and that a war was even a possibility. She knew there were always small rebellions going on in individual kingdoms, particularly those who weren't allied to Zion. And she had heard that there were occasional skirmishes along borders, particularly along Adamah and Tarshish or Dyfed; and Simoon and Sheba.

What she didn't understand is why she had been so sheltered? Surely as the only child of the king and the future wife of a king (whether she liked it or not), she should have been schooled in the world's political situation. Well, she was determined to learn now.

"I understand that Annewven was once home to all thirteen treasures," she said, "but doesn't it seem risky to ask for asylum from my father's enemy?"

"Risky, yes," Jabberwock agreed, "but it will make it all the more likely that Arawn will take us in, which will gain us even more access to his secrets."

"Secrets? So this isn't just about the treasures? It sounds like spying. Is that what you're doing, Jabberwock? Spying for my father? Has this been the plan all along? Is that what you are, Gwrhyr, a spy?"

"I wouldn't go so far as to say I'm a spy, but yes, we've agreed that while searching for the treasures, it wouldn't be bad to kill two birds with one stone, so to speak."

"Where'd you say you were from? Aden?" The kingdom to the southwest of her father's and an ally. And, she grimaced, her future home. She had only three more years of freedom.

"Correct."

"Did Uriel ask you to spy for him?" Eluned demanded.

Gwrhyr looked taken aback. "No, absolutely not. But when the chance came along to join the hunt for the treasures, it seemed a perfect opportunity."

"To kill two birds with one stone?" She gazed deeply into his eyes attempting to detect whether or not he lied.

"Yes," Gwrhyr admitted.

"And it would help you gain in Uriel's favor if you could report any findings to him?" She pressed.

"It couldn't hurt," he agreed.

"Or, perhaps, bring him back a treasure or two," she continued.

"Obviously it would be nice if all the treasures were in the allied kingdoms of Zion and Aden," Gwrhyr said.

"True, it would definitely be to our advantage," Jabberwock affirmed.

"What did the book say?" The Princess tried to remember. "That if a righteous man gathered all the treasures he could bring peace to the world?"

"Something along those lines," Gwrhyr agreed. At least, that's what he'd been taught.

"What about a righteous woman?" Eluned frowned. "Besides, who'd claim to possess them all even if we did find them? My father? Uriel? That doesn't sound fair to me. Besides, they could be anywhere. Well, all but the one we do know about." She twisted the ring on her finger. "That still leaves twelve treasures to find. It seems an impossible task."

"It is rumored that King Uriel actually possesses one of the treasures as well," Jabberwock informed her.

"Really," Eluned looked surprised and turned to Gwrhyr. "Is that true? Have you heard that rumor?"

"I have heard that the Mantle of Arthur is in the possession of the royal family," he replied.

"Hmmm," Eluned mused on this for a moment. "That seems more than coincidence."

"What is?" Bonpo asked.

"That both I and the man I am betrothed to are heritors of not only two of the thirteen treasures, but the two that allow one to become invisible."

"Yes, definitely an Omnincidence," Jabberwock agreed.

"So the spying is incidental, but you were planning to hunt for the treasures as part of the journey?" The Princess continued to press the Bandersnatch.

"Let's just say that I hoped that it would happen," Jabberwock admitted.

"No. I want to know. Is this a call from Omni or something you and Brother Columcille planned?" Eluned leaned forward to look into Jabberwock's eyes.

"You know it is Omni directing my footsteps, my dear." He didn't flinch from her gaze.

"Yes, I did think so, but I'd begun to wonder. Yet the Omnincidences have been too many—Bonpo, Gwrhyr, the book, among others—that I couldn't believe I wasn't part of some larger plan," she mused.

"Me?" Gwrhyr asked.

"Yes, the fact that you were right there in that inn, the only one to speak for us, having all the skills we needed to continue our journey. That couldn't have been a coincidence, could it?" She turned her scrutiny to him.

"True," he considered this for a moment. "It does seem ordained."

"Now, if Omni could just drop a maidservant or some other suitable female," she stressed the word, "companion into our camp."

"I agree," said Jabberwock, "It will appear unseemly for you to arrive at Arawn's court in the company of two men." Eluned stifled a yawn. "I'm sorry," she apologized.

"It get rate. You need sreep." Bonpo said.

"I agree." She stood up. "I think I'll get ready for bed. Where are the horses?"

"Why?" Gwrhyr looked puzzled.

"I want to say goodnight to Hayduke and Honeysuckle."

Gwrhyr stared at her, dumbfounded. "You want to say goodnight to your mule and a horse?"

"Not just any mule and horse. My mule and horse. Hayduke and Honeysuckle. I brought them a treat," she reached into her pocket and pulled out a handful of sugar cubes. "And I'll even give one to Heiduc."

"That's very generous," he said, but it was clear he was laughing at her.

"I don't understand why being kind to animals, particularly those who are serving us, is so humorous?" The Princess frowned at him.

"Were you kind to your servants?" Gwrhyr asked.

"I like to think so," she replied.

Gwrhyr glanced at Jabberwock, apparently for confirmation.

"I've never heard otherwise," Jabberwock allowed. "Eluned is well loved by the people who know her."

"So, I must be the exception," he teased her.

"Ha! Very funny. You intentionally harass me," she clenched her fists. She wanted to rap him on top of his annoying head. "When you're not trying to drive me crazy, I like you just fine."

"I don't try to drive you crazy," he began.

"True, you don't try, you succeed," she interrupted.

"I was trying to say that if you think I'm harassing you intentionally," Gwrhyr tried again, "then why do you react?"

"So you do intentionally harass me?" Her eyes narrowed as her frown deepened.

"Not as often as you seem to think I do," he insisted. "You're just overly sensitive."

That was too much. "Well, fine then. I'll just ignore you from now on," she turned quickly and stomped off.

"Where you go?" Bonpo shouted after her.

"I can find the horses on my own," she sounded petulant. Once again, she wanted to cry. Why did Gwrhyr always make her lose her temper? Why couldn't she, as he'd suggested, just not react? Were all men as infuriating as he was? She hoped not. If so, her chances of finding love seemed dismal.

She stumbled on, sight blurred by the tears she was trying to hold back. "Hayduke," she called, "Honeysuckle, Heiduc."

Forty feet ahead, two lights flickered about six feet or so above the ground. Eluned stopped. Were they eyes? The wind had stopped and the stars and a waxing moon, nearly full, helped illuminate the slick rock landscape. The eyes, if that's what they were, continued to glow steadily.

Her first thought was, 'Why did Gwrhyr hobble the horses so far from camp?' Then she realized that despite what she thought of him, he wasn't actually that cruel or stupid. The horse must be large for its eyes to be that far off the ground; perhaps Heiduc had gotten loose.

"Heiduc?" she questioned, taking a few steps toward the eyes, which were still all she could see. Eluned was nearly entranced by the way they seemed to glow more than the light of the moon warranted. It was unearthly. As she moved closer, the shape of a head and the body of a horse became more defined. But it couldn't be Heiduc, she realized, because it was clear that this horse was black not chestnut.

And it was sleeker with a long, flowing mane, and now that she was closer, she realized its eyes were literally luminescent. The golden eyes on the stallion were surreal. She found she couldn't look away. Her hand seemed to dip of its own accord into her pocket and remove a couple of sugar cubes. Eluned extended her flattened palm toward the horse never breaking contact with its eyes.

The horse very gently lipped the cubes from her palm and whickered a thank you. Or did it whicker? Eluned was suddenly absolutely sure that it had been a verbal 'thank you' she had heard. But had it actually been verbal or had it been telepathic, the way Jabberwock could speak to her occasionally?

'Whom do you belong to and what are you doing here?' she thought, stroking the velvet of its muzzle.

"Follow me and you shall soon discover the why,' a voice as soft as satin answered in her mind. She felt the hairs on the nape of her neck prickle and her knees weaken. She slumped against the horse because it was the only thing to support her. Either she was losing her mind or this huge, incredibly beautiful creature with the hypnotic eyes was speaking to her. In which case, it couldn't be a real horse, could it? In many ways he seemed real. He was solid. The Princess could not only touch him but she could feel the difference between the velvety softness of his muzzle and the coarseness of his mane. It had eaten the sugar cubes. She had felt the warmth of its breath. Yet, it could speak to her and its eyes were hypnotic in their effulgence.

"Follow me," he repeated.

"Who are you?" she asked as the horse turned slowly away from her. "What are you?"

"You must trust me." He had stopped next to some tumbled boulders. "Climb on," he ordered.

Despite the fact she was afraid, she was also intrigued. His intentions apparently were not to harm her. There was something else going on and the only way to find out what that might be was to do as he commanded. Soon she was balanced, albeit precariously, atop the largest rock. From there she was able to scramble onto the stallion's strong back, grasping his mane to prevent her from sliding off.

The horse began to move smoothly but quickly back toward the wash, its lantern-like eyes lighting the way. Eluned caught flickering glimpses of slick rock, ponderosa pines, mesquite and cacti and then cottonwood as they reached the dry watercourse. She spotted the flash of a white tail as they startled a cottontail rabbit nibbling on a small shrub. Its wild-eyed look as it leapt away was not dissimilar from hers. As they descended into the gully, the horse veered to the right and soon they were heading south down the wash.

Eluned was silent as she tried to come to grips with what she was doing. It was just now occurring to her that Jabberwock and Bonpo and perhaps even Gwrhyr were probably wondering what had happened to her or would be soon.

Had the stallion left any prints? Would they think she had wandered off into the darkness of the desert and lost her way? Until they had dropped down into the watercourse, she had been able to see where the light of their campfire pierced the darkness. The horse began to move faster, preternaturally gliding above the sand and gravel of the wash. It was almost supernatural, she realized, as if it were galloping on air.

And that, of course, explained everything. This wasn't a horse but something else. A ghostly version of a horse, perhaps? Or was it a phantom or a faery? She wasn't sure and the further they moved away from camp, the more anxious she grew. Where were they going? Would it return her to the camp? What if it left her in the desert never to be seen again?

"Trust me," the voice coaxed once again.

"I want to trust you but I know so little. Do you have a name? Is this really happening? Maybe I slipped and fell back there and hit my head and I'm lying unconscious on the desert floor and having an amazingly realistic dream. I'm no longer sure I can tell the difference between what's real and what's not."

"And what is real?" Eluned felt the amusement in its question.

"Actual rather than imaginary."

"You are neither dreaming nor imagining this."

"So you are real?"

"Can you not feel me, see me, hear me, touch me?"

Indeed she could. The Princess could even smell his musky animal scent, practically taste the cool night air scented with sage and other desert plants. She lifted her eyes to the night sky where the stars glittered coldly. She was able to pick out constellations she recognized. Yes, this is definitely happening, she thought. Eluned could pinch herself to further reassure herself, but realized that it was unnecessary.

So, destination unknown, she tried to settle down and enjoy the ride. And just think of the story she'd be able to tell, she smiled.

The horse seemed appeased by her decision to fully trust him. "You may call me Aeron," he said. "Now hold on tightly, I am going to run at full speed now."

Fly would have been a more appropriate verb, Eluned thought as they sped down the wash. The wind rushed past her cheeks and she had to close her eyes to prevent them from tearing. Leaning down as close to Aeron's neck as his gait permitted, she hung on for dear life.

Nearly half an hour later, Aeron began to slow down. As he slowed to a trot, Eluned was able to lift her head and survey the surroundings. A trail on the left ascended upward through cottonwoods and Aeron turned into it and began the short climb. Soon they began descending as they approached an oasis of giant fan palms.

The trees towered over them, their crowns of fronds whispering in the night breeze. Beneath their unkempt and shaggy skirts, she could hear small creatures—black widow spiders, lizards, snakes, rodents and other desert creatures—skittering and slithering away from their approach. Aeron halted in the center of the grove and the Princess slid from his back. Her legs protested. She was unused to so many hours spent across a horse's back.

It was dark beneath the palms but once again Aeron's eyes helped illumine the night. Through the gaps in the tall trees, milky white moonlight puddled the ground. She could almost see the pupfish swimming in the quiet pools that winked here and there around the oasis. Even the emerald grass contributed to the mood of enchantment as it fluttered in the wind. It was as if Pan were nearby rendering a hauntingly primal tune on his pipes.

"This way," Aeron directed and she followed him toward another towering stand of palms almost completely denuded of thatch. The powdery sand of the oasis clung to her boots painting them white.

Aeron led her down a trail nestled amongst these trees. The path was littered with the debris of discarded fronds and their footsteps crunched as they followed the trail through the grove dotted with smaller trees and shrubs. A final curve brought them out of the stand of trees and onto the shore of a lakelet encircled by more palms. The moon reflected in its still waters shimmered like pearl and Eluned's hand unconsciously clutched the small leather pouch that contained her moonstone.

It was exquisitely beautiful. Magical even. And it wasn't until her breath rushed from her throat in a loud sigh that she realized she'd been holding it.

"I'm speechless," she whispered as she continued to gaze around her in awe.

Aeron whickered his pleasure at her reaction and asked, "Do you not wish to know why I brought you here?"

The Princess turned to him in amazement, "You mean

there is another reason? I mean, other than that this is the most amazing place I've ever seen. I could stay here forever." It was like her own private paradise and maybe as close as she'd ever get to the Favonian Islands, particularly if Gwrhyr and the Bandersnatch had their way.

Aeron nodded toward the lake and Eluned studied it but saw nothing but its mirror-like surface shimmering in the moonlight. And then she noticed a curious movement towards the middle. The water began to roil as if something were moving just below the surface. Soon it began to glow and Eluned felt her heart begin to race in anticipation of discovering what was causing the light and motion. The air fairly crackled with expectancy.

The Princess jumped when Aeron said, "See that punt there beneath the palms?"

Her eyes searched the shadows to the right and then she did see, in the dappled moonlight that had camouflaged it beneath the trees, a small, flat-bottomed boat.

"Yes?"

"Take it out on the lagoon." Aeron instructed her.

"You mean," she pointed toward the center of the lake where the water continued to bubble and burn with an eerie incandescence.

Aeron nodded. And, with her heart in her throat, Eluned walked over to the punt and dragged it halfway into the water. She tossed her cloak on the ground and removing her boots and socks and rolling up her leather pants, she pushed the boat the rest of the way into the lagoon and stepped inside. Lying on the bottom of the boat was a small oar. Eluned seated herself and began to paddle slowly out to the middle.

Her heart continued to thunder in her chest as she approached the disturbance in the center of the lake. This was all way beyond her limited experience. Aeron definitely seemed a benevolent spirit and she did trust him, but she could not even begin to fathom what might possibly happen when she reached the centermost part of the lake.

But, as she drew closer, the water quieted although something continued to glow just below the surface. She drew up alongside and attempted to peer beneath the surface. This close to the source of the light, the waters of the lake were nearly translucent. She gasped when she saw what floated less than a foot below the rippling waves of the lake. Not only was it floating, which struck her as impossible, but also the object was responsible for the blaze that was setting the waters aflame.

It was a sword, and it pulsed just below the ripples caused by the presence of the punt. Eluned looked back to the shore where Aeron was watching her.

"Retrieve it," his voice echoed in her head. Pushing the sleeve of her sweater up past her elbow, she slowly lowered her hand into the water. The Princess was startled by the cold; because of the radiance emanating from the sword, she expected the water to be warm, at least. Her hand slid easily around the white and gold hilt, and she began to withdraw it from the lake. The sword was heavy but seemed to glide smoothly from the water as she pulled it up. As she held it up to the moonlight, blue fire seemed to race along its blade down over the guard and into her hand and wrist—a not unpleasant tingling sensation darted up her arm and she experienced a sense of strength and purpose.

The beauty of the sword awed her. Twin dragons of gold climbed the mother-of-pearl inset in the handle and twined around the guard, each side ending with a dragon's head whose ruby eyes seemed to spark fire. The pommel was encrusted with jacinth, topaz and diamonds and the blade continued to shine with an eerie blue incandescence. Eluned could see upon the blade ancient runes but could not make out their meaning. She would have to ask Jabberwock.

The Princess was loath to set the sword down in the bottom of the punt but she couldn't paddle one-handed. And, she was afraid if she set it on her lap, it might slide off and sink into the depths of the lake never to be seen again. Reluctantly she set it on the floor of the hull and gripped it firmly between her feet. Then, she began the return trip to shore.

"IT'S BEAUTIFUL, AND I HAVE TO ADMIT it feels somehow right in my hand, but I don't understand," Eluned told Aeron once she had pulled the punt back up on shore and nestled it amidst the shaggy thatch of the palms.

Aeron, who was standing beside her, said, "Yours is not to understand. Just remain open to what may happen and be ready."

"Ready for what?"

"That I cannot tell you." His thought was uncompromising.

"Can't or won't?" When he didn't answer, she groused, "You know, you'd get along really well with Jabberwock."

The whicker of amusement again.

"Well, can you tell me this, is this the sword I think it must be?"

"And what would that be?"

"Dyrnwyn, I think. White Hilt, the sword of Rhydderch."

"And why do you think it is Dyrnwyn?" he asked as Eluned pulled on her socks and boots and donned her cloak.

"Because," she said, unrolling the sleeve of her sweater, which had managed to get damp anyway, "we're on a quest for the thirteen hallowed treasures and I already possess one of them, and I can think of no other reason why. I just read the book, which seems to have fallen into my hands by Omni's grace, yesterday. And I found out last night that this ring," she held out her hand, "and the moonstone in this pouch," she pulled the leather thong that held it from beneath her sweater, "can make me invisible. It's one of the thirteen treasures and it just seems highly unlikely that you should appear and lead me to this sword unless it is THE sword, and yet another treasure."

"But why would you be chosen to find the sword and not a man?"

"Like Bonpo or Gwrhyr?" He was silent and she puzzled over that for a moment. Why indeed? She had no fighting skills other than the minimum of instruction in self-defense. Was it because of her royal blood? But again, why her and not Uriel or Arawn or someone from the other ten kingdoms? Eluned was from what was considered one of the "good" kingdoms, as was Gwrhyr, who she still secretly suspected of being an agent for Uriel, keeping tabs on his future bride, maybe? But that didn't make sense, she shook her head, he'd kissed her! Surely he wouldn't kiss his master's betrothed? She'd worry about that later. As for being from a peace-seeking kingdom, maybe Omni wanted the treasures returned to the peaceful kingdoms? "I honestly don't know," she finally admitted. "But I am deeply honored, and I hope I can live up to whatever is expected of me."

"Then perhaps it is time to return. I have no doubt your friends have noticed that you are missing." Using the boat as a mounting block, Eluned once more climbed upon Aeron's back.

WITH THE SWORD CLASPED FIRMLY against her chest, Eluned used what little strength was left in her legs to hold herself on as Aeron trotted back through the oasis and back to the trail that led to the wash. Once in the gully, Aeron was once again able to use his full speed to propel them back toward camp. Eluned was now able to lean forward and use her body to protect the sword while holding on to Aeron's mane with both hands.

About a mile distant from where the quartet had sheltered for the night, Aeron slowed to a walk and finally stopped. "I'm afraid I can take you no further," he said.

Eluned groaned and slid from his back. She understood

but it would have been so much easier to explain had Aeron been with her. Were they really going to believe that a horse that could speak had taken her to an oasis where she had pulled Dyrnwyn from a lake? Of course, she did have the sword so she had to have found it someway, right?

"You will be fine," Aeron promised.

The Princess felt a pang as he turned to disappear back down the watercourse. "Thank you," she said, tears pricking her eyes, "I will never forget your kindness. I don't know how I was chosen or why but I thank Omni that you were selected to take me to the sword."

"It has been my honor," Aeron said with sincerity, and then he was gone as mysteriously as he had appeared.

Eluned took a deep breath and began the trek back to camp, cradling Dyrnwyn in her arms like a precious child. "I'll have to find a scabbard for you as soon as possible," she promised it. The moon was hanging lower in the sky and she no longer had Aeron's lantern eyes to light her way but the sandy wash stood out from the slick rock on either side.

The Princess hadn't walked a quarter of a mile when she heard a deep voice bellowing her name.

"Bonpo," she yelled but her throat emitted no more than a squeak and tears were suddenly spilling from her eyes. She cleared her throat and tried again, "Bonpo!" For some reason, upon hearing the gentle giant call her name she felt she was returning home. Eluned could no longer remember what Gwrhyr had done to cause her angry retreat.

"Leened!" She heard Bonpo whoop in relief. Within minutes they had reached each other in the wash. "Tank Omni," he said. He scooped her up into his arms. He looked so happy to have found her that Eluned began to sob and apologize.

"I'm so sorry. I'll tell you the whole story, but I'm so tired I just want to get back to camp first."

"We be dere no time." And true to his word Bonpo jogged the last three-quarters of a mile back to camp and they were there in minutes. "Found her!" he yelled as they made the final approach to camp. Eluned bit her tongue to keep from correcting him. Technically, she'd never been lost; had been within a mile of the camp when she heard his call. But if he needed to feel like her savior, she was happy to let that happen.

Jabberwock's normally deep voice had risen an octave or two as he trotted up to them, "Where in Omni's name have you been? I've been worried sick."

"It's a long story. Can I please have some wine?"

"I don't know whether to be angry or relieved," Gwrhyr stormed, then his eyes widened. "Where did you find that?"

It was then Jabberwock and Bonpo noticed what she had clasped to her chest.

"Is dat?" Bonpo stuttered.

Jabberwock just shook his head in wonder, his glassy eyes catching the fiery hue of the dragons' ruby eyes, "I should have known there was mischief afoot. The way your footprints just disappeared . . ."

"Please," she tried again, "it's been a long day . . . I just want to sit down, some wine . . ."

"I get wine," Bonpo hurried toward the stash of food and cooking equipment.

Gwrhyr took her arm and propelled her toward the campfire. "May I?" he asked, gesturing to the sword. She was still clenching it tightly to her, and only with reluctance let Gwrhyr pry it from her fingers.

Bonpo handed her a cup of wine and then joined Gwrhyr and Jabberwock, who stood facing her.

The Bandersnatch, voice returned to its normal range, recited:

> "There drew he forth the brand Excalibur,
> And o'er him, drawing it, the winter moon,
> Brightening the skirts of a long cloud, ran forth
> And sparkled keen with frost against the hilt:

For all the haft twinkled with diamond sparks,
Myriads of topaz-lights, and jacinth-work
Of subtlest jewellery."

"My word," Eluned breathed, "that fits it almost perfectly. Of course, it's not Excalibur."

"Well, some say that Dyrnwyn and Excalibur are one and the same," Gwrhyr noted.

"I guess in the long run it doesn't really matter," she sighed.

"So, will you be gracious enough to tell us how you ended up with yet another of the treasures?" Jabberwock asked.

She took a long swallow of wine and moved over, patting the log. "Please join me," she offered. Gwrhyr complied with pleasure, happy to be back in her good graces.

She began with her assumption that the horse she was seeing was Heiduc.

"A pwca," Gwrhyr stated once she'd described the stallion.

"A what?"

"Poo-ka," he said slowly. "It's a solitary faerie. They're shape changers, sometimes a horse, sometimes a rabbit. Usually mischievous but they can also choose to lead one to treasure."

"Fortunately I ran into the latter," Eluned laughed and continued her tale.

"Do you think you could find it again?" Gwrhyr asked when she finished.

"Find what?" She was tired and the question confused her.

"The oasis," he replied.

"Honestly, I don't know. Aeron was running so fast I had to keep my eyes closed. I just know we went south down the wash and the trail to the oasis was on the left, but how far from here? That I couldn't tell you. Why?"

"I would just love to see it," Gwrhyr explained. "But, I imagine that even if you could find the trail, the oasis would no longer be there."

"Really? You think it would disappear like a . . . what is it called?" Her exhaustion was making it difficult to think.

"Mirage?" Jabberwock supplied.

"Yes, mirage," she agreed, taking another sip from her mug.

"Well, we are in the desert," Gwrhyr said.

"But I thought mirages were caused by heat, and it's night time." It's all so confusing, she thought. She was so drained by the adventure and the long day that her thoughts were muddied with exhaustion.

"True, but has anything that happened since you met Aeron struck you as anything other than supernatural?" Gwrhyr asked.

"It has been both super-real and surreal." She turned to Jabberwock, "So, do you know what the runes on the sword say?"

"I'd have to study them," the Bandersnatch replied, "but the legends say that one side of the blade is engraved with the words, 'one edge to defend' and the other side says, 'one edge to defeat'."

"So either way I can't lose, right?" Eluned grinned.

"Why? Are you intending to ride into battle soon?" Gwrhyr laughed.

"Hopefully never," she said, "but it's nice to know that should I ever have to, I have Dyrnwyn to help protect me. Until then, though, I could really use a scabbard. It seems wrong to carry it so exposed."

"Yes," Jabberwock agreed, "it would be nice to find a way to disguise it before we get to Annewven."

Eluned yawned. "I'm so tired. How long till dawn?"

"Few hours yet," Bonpo answered. "You need sreep. Go sraight tent dis time."

"Yes sir," she stood and stretched, before slowly heading that way. Her legs felt like lead.

Gwrhyr, Bonpo and Jabberwock watched her go. The

sword seemed happy to be back in her hand; blue light sparkled along the blade and glowed through her fingers.

Gwrhyr swallowed hard. "Damn," he allowed, "the sword was meant for her hand."

"Jealous?" Jabberwock chuckled.

"A bit."

"I honored," Bonpo stated.

"Yes," Gwrhyr agreed reluctantly as he stood, "me too."

20ᵗ NEEON

The next morning dawned cool but clear, and Jabberwock and Bonpo decided it would be best to let Eluned sleep an extra hour.

But just over half an hour later, Eluned emerged from her tent, dressed for the day and eyes sparkling. The only evidence of the previous night's adventure—the pale purplish smudges beneath her eyes. Those, and the makeshift belt and scabbard she'd fashioned from a piece of rope and one of her blankets.

"Morning Plincess!" Bonpo called, hurrying to the fire to prepare her coffee.

"Good morning!" she replied over her shoulder as she began to disassemble her tent. Gwrhyr looked up from where he'd been carefully lashing his baggage behind Heiduc's saddle. His expression was unfathomable as he studied her for a moment before returning to his chore.

Jabberwock watched the various players in his little drama with a bemused expression. The Princess seemed to be blossoming as if the adventure, itself, were a fertilizer. Unfortunately, her only thorn was Gwrhyr—one minute her friend, the next her enemy. Only time could change that.

Eluned finished her packing and carried her gear over

to the horses. She inhaled deeply and sighed again. "What a glorious day." Everything seemed sharper to her this morning—the scent of the fire, the horses, the plants. Even the earth itself seemed to exude its own perfume. The air was brisk and tingled in her nose. Everything from sound to scent to sight seemed amplified. "Thank you," she said, accepting coffee and a bacon-and-cheese-stuffed biscuit from Bonpo. Yes, she sighed, as the hot liquid washed over her tongue and down her throat, even the coffee tasted better this morning.

WITHIN TWENTY MINUTES THEY WERE READY TO GO, and as they regained the main road, and the miles disappeared beneath their horses' hooves, Eluned continued to find joy in even the tiniest of details—the pale pink fairy duster dancing in the breeze, the happy yellow buds of the prickly pear flowers waiting to burst into bloom, and the clownish gait of the roadrunners chasing after insects and lizards. It was an enchanting day still suffused with the magic of the previous night and Eluned hoped that she would find tomorrow as equally enthralling.

They stopped only a few times during the day and that night camped beneath a trinity of hoodoos. Bonpo prepared a light dinner and Eluned crept off to bed early, lulled to sleep by the comforting sound of the men murmuring by the fire (assuming it was apropos to call Jabb a man), and by the feeling she was being guarded by Omni, itself, disguised as a geologic formation. She slept soundly until Bonpo awakened her at dawn. Fully rested, Eluned felt the day promised to be just as brilliant as the day before as long as Gwrhyr kept his thoughts to himself.

She cast a sidelong glance at him as he mounted Heiduc. He had been oddly quiet this morning and she wasn't sure what she disliked most—his paying her too much attention versus ignoring her completely. Surely he wasn't jealous that she'd found Dyrnwyn, or rather, had been led to it? It certainly wasn't her fault the pwca had chosen to appear to her. As her body adjusted to Honeysuckle's gait, she brooded over Gwrhyr's apparent disinterest. But, the sky was too blue and the landscape too intriguing for her to dwell upon it for long and soon she was enjoying the day and wondering what it might bring.

DURING THEIR LUNCH BREAK, Gwrhyr and Jabberwock agreed that if they pushed on, they might actually be able to make the post road that followed the River Mab southward.

"It will mean riding an hour or two longer before stopping for the night," he warned the Princess.

"That's fine," she assured him. "I'll feel much safer once I know we're heading away from the Outpost instead of toward it."

BUT, WHEN THEY FINALLY REACHED THE ROAD, and began looking for a place to camp for the night, every muscle in her body was aching and she just wanted to get out of the saddle and lie down. Sunset was fast approaching and the land on either side of the road was either too rocky or too swampy for them to camp on. Eluned was getting grouchier by the second, and even the rocks were beginning to look enticing when she suddenly reined in her horse.

"Stop," she ordered. "Listen." They did so grudgingly, looking to her for explanation. "Do you hear that?"

"It sounds like . . ." Gwrhyr began.

"Viorin," Bonpo shouted.

"I was going to say, 'music,'" Gwrhyr added.

"There must be a gypsy camp ahead," Jabberwock said.

"Gypsies," Eluned breathed, eyes lighting up, and energy restored. She'd heard of them but they had not been allowed inside the castle walls, and unlike the servants, she'd been forbidden to have anything to do with them. But she'd listened to many a tale of fortunes being told, palms being read, gambling, dancing and more. "Can we stay with them tonight?"

"It's doubtful they'd allow us in their camp," Gwrhyr said, "but perhaps we can put up our tents nearby." He didn't look thrilled by the prospect.

"Why?" Eluned's voice echoed with disappointment.

"They have unusually strict purity laws," Jabberwock explained. "Some tribes won't have anything to do with us gaje. But, others are more lenient. We'll have to wait and see."

"Gaje?"

"Not gypsy," Bonpo replied.

"Oh." No fair, she wanted to shout. I finally have a chance to meet gypsies and they may not want to have anything to do with us. The group descended into silence as they started up again. Bonpo and Jabberwock were indifferent, but Gwrhyr and Eluned, unaware, prayed opposite prayers. As the road brought them closer to the gypsy camp, the sound of the music continued to swell. Eluned wondered what they were celebrating. Gwrhyr wondered if the noise would keep him up all night.

A final curve in the road brought them within sight of both the camp and the River Mab. A number of wagons were set up in a broad field that ran from the road to the shallow banks of the river. Jabberwock thought the field would probably be under water once the mountain snow melted come spring, but by then the gypsies would have moved on.

A large campfire was blazing in the center of the camp and those gathered round the flames were eating, drinking and listening to the music. A few children wove around the adults, dancing and laughing.

The music halted suddenly, and heads turned their way. The Princess and her entourage had been noted. Before they reached the camp, two men approached them on foot.

Gwrhyr dismounted and handed his reins to Bonpo before advancing toward the men. "Peace be with you," he said as they drew near.

"And with you, also," they responded, eyeing the strange trio behind him.

"We seek your hospitality," he added, knowingly presenting them with the dilemma—refuse hospitality or risk impurity—which side would this gypsy community err on?

"You are more than welcome to join us," the younger man offered. He'd already taken in the odd grouping behind the young man—a giant, a beautiful young woman and a dog. He was willing to risk angering the giant just for a chance to dance with the gaje woman. He wasn't sure he'd ever seen anyone as beautiful. And the young gypsy's heart thumped painfully in his chest, and he felt his cheeks coloring when his words were greeted with a brilliant smile and gushing thanks from Eluned.

Her prayers had been answered; she'd get to spend the night with gypsies after all. Maybe she could find someone to tell her fortune, as well. Nor was she blind enough to her own desires not to notice the effect her words had on the young gypsy. She did miss, though, the sudden clench of Gwrhyr's jaw as he noticed the interplay between the Princess and the Rom.

"I'm Gwrhyr," he introduced himself. "And this is Eluned and Bonpo." Until they knew they were safe, he didn't want to risk losing Jabberwock's advantage.

"I am Moshe," the older man said, "and this is my son, Daniel. Come and join us. We are in the midst of celebrating."

"What are you celebrating?" Eluned asked.

"It is the twelve-month feast for my aunt, Chokhmah," Daniel explained.

"I don't understand."

"It is the anniversary of her husband's death. Today his soul enters heaven and she is no longer in mourning."

"And you celebrate this?"

"Yes, the pomana is essential for the good luck of the family."

"Pomana?"

"The funeral banquet." Daniel smiled up at her, and she found herself grinning back. His dark good looks and sparkling eyes were pulling her in despite herself.

"You will share a dance with me, perhaps?"

"I," she stuttered, "I guess so. I mean I'm not sure if I know your dances. I wouldn't know . . ."

"I will teach," he stated. Gwrhyr, who was leading his horse, ground his teeth. He'd be damned if he let this Daniel usurp all of Eluned's attentions. If she chose to dance tonight, he would find some way to make her dance with him, as well.

THEY WERE WELCOMED INTO THE COMMUNITY with genuine warmth, and not a little curiosity. Clearly, every one was in a good mood. As Bonpo, along with a couple of the gypsy men, went off to see to their horses, Gwrhyr and Eluned were introduced.

But, other than Moshe and Daniel, the only name and face Eluned was able to keep track of was that of Moshe's sister, Chokhmah. She was a striking woman, her dark hair streaked with flashes of silver. But her eyes were the most startling— fringed by long dark lashes, they seemed to glow like sunlit amber.

Eluned was wearing her jerkin and pants and Chokhmah asked her, politely, if she would like to change into something that better befitted the celebration.

"Bonpo has the baggage," she said. "I have a couple of skirts." It was clear from the expression on her face, and the tone of her voice, that the prospect of choosing one of those particular items of clothing wasn't thrilling her. All the women in the camp were dressed so gaily—bright colors and lots of jewelry.

"I am sure we can scrounge up something festive for you

to wear. Let us go see what I have in my wagon." She linked her arm through Eluned's and led her toward a caravan, which had been painted a dark lavender. As they got closer, the Princess found her breath catching in her throat. She had never seen anything so exquisite. The detail on the vardo was amazing—birds and flowers as well as words and symbols vied for space; and each was a piece of artwork unto itself. Ladybirds and butterflies fluttered across the sides of the wagon, and doves and swallows nested beneath the eaves. A cornucopia on the door overflowed with fruits and vegetables, and the pentacle of Solomon stood guard above the entrance.

Chokhmah laughed as she watched Eluned struggling to absorb it all. "It is a lot to take in all at once, I know. Tomorrow, I promise I will explain it all to you. But the banquet is waiting, and I know a certain young man who is dying to dance with you."

"It's so beautiful," Eluned breathed, eyes wide. "Did you do all this yourself?"

"I added some of the paintings but my husband, Yitzak, painted most of it as a wedding gift to me."

"Oh," Eluned replied. She had forgotten the reason for the celebration. But of course, it was because Chokhmah's husband had been dead for a year. Yet she didn't hear any sadness in the woman's voice.

"Do not worry yourself, my dear. I am at peace with his death."

"Was he a lot older than you?" Eluned asked.

"No," Chokhmah said, this time a bit more sadly, "he was only a few years older, but he was sick for a long time before he departed this world."

"I'm so sorry," Eluned said.

"Thank you, dear. But now it is time to celebrate for I no longer must wear black, and Yitzak is now in heaven." And, lifting her purple skirt (obviously one of her favorite colors), she ascended the steps into the vardo.

The wagon was as beautiful on the inside as it was out-side—hand-carved woodwork, tiled floor and etched glass as well as the painted flowers, birds, and more that decorated some of the wood.

Eluned's eyes scoured the caravan's interior compartment while Chokhmah rummaged through her dresser. Not only was the small wagon beautiful, it also felt inviting, homey. A padded bench lined one wall, and a platform that served as a bed was padded by a down mattress and feather-filled duvets. A small stove with a metal stovepipe was set into a tiled area. Eluned could imagine Chokhmah sitting at the small table, sipping her cup of tea as she gazed into the large crystal ball that sat in the center of the table. Next to the crystal ball was a deck of tarot cards, and Eluned wondered if all the women had these divination tools in their vardos.

Chokhmah finally pulled a skirt from the bottom drawer and held it up for Eluned's approval. "I am sure it will fit," she explained, "I, myself, can wear it only over another, longer, skirt or petticoat." The skirt was sewn from panels in various fabrics of forest and olive green—velvet, silk, damask—with a final panel of ecru lace. "It was my grandmother's and she was about your size." It was true that Chokhmah was significantly taller than Eluned, perhaps by as much as half a foot. She was tall and slender and graceful, Eluned thought, just like a wil-low.

"I would be honored to wear it," Eluned accepted the skirt. Chokhmah then handed her a full-sleeved blouse of pale green that had been embroidered in the same colors as the skirt. "Is this the shirt she wore with it?"

"Yes, that does not fit me. The sleeves are too short, but I couldn't bear to part with it. It belongs with the skirt." Eluned let Chokhmah help dress her (old habits die hard) and then let her fix her hair, pulling her ebony curls away from her face with a ribbon of emerald velvet. Chunky earrings of green stone soon adorned her ears, and Eluned stood back for Chokhmah's inspection.

"Festive indeed. Every man will want a dance with you tonight."

Eluned blushed. It was true that the deep green of the clothes seemed to cause her light green eyes to shimmer like opals. But, as much as she wanted to join the festivities outdoors, there was a part of her that would have been just as happy curled up on the bench in Chokhmah's vardo, sipping tea and spending a quiet evening with her new friend. But, this was Chokhmah's day, and every one was waiting. She took a deep breath to steel herself before opening the wagon's door and stepping out.

The first thing she noticed was that a number of people stopped talking and turned to look at her, including Daniel who had been talking with Gwrhyr. He looked clearly appreciative, and she blushed again, but it was the look on Gwrhyr's face that made her stumble to a halt. He looked angry, furious even, and she couldn't even begin to comprehend why. Before she could bring herself to start approaching the campfire again, Gwrhyr turned and disappeared in the crowd. She looked up at Chokhmah to see if she had noticed. She was clearly amused.

"That was interesting," she laughed, but before Eluned had a chance to comment further, Chokhmah's nephew and brother were there and escorting them to a seat near the fire, the violins started up again, and she had barely made herself comfortable before someone was shoving a mug of spiced wine into her hand and shouting, "Baksheesh!"

"Baksheesh," she chimed back, unsure of what she was saying.

"Good fortune to you," Chokhmah interpreted. Eluned took a deep sip, the color once more returning to her cheeks. "Baksheesh to you," she said, clinking her mug with Chokhmah's.

A moment later, plates filled with veal-stuffed pancakes, sautéed mushrooms and nut-filled cookies were thrust into their hands. It was then that Eluned recollected that they had stopped for a quick lunch hours ago and that she was hungrier than she'd realized. It also occurred to her that she had absolutely no idea what their "story" was supposed to be. She looked around for Jabberwock, Gwrhyr or even Bonpo to no avail. How much could, should she tell Chokhmah? The inn had been so empty they hadn't really needed a story, and this was the first time they'd run into anyone since they'd left. Should she go with the 'seeking asylum' story? She knew it was only a matter of time before she was asked.

She had just taken her first bite of pancake, when Chokhmah said, "So, tell me Eluned, where are you and your friends bound? The Favonian Isles?"

Eluned finished chewing and swallowed, then took another sip of wine for good measure before answering. "Actually, we're on our way to Prythew."

"Really?" Chokhmah's brow wrinkled in consternation. "What business do you have in kingdom of the Crimson King?"

"Crimson King?"

"He is everything that is prikaza about the color red."

"I don't understand."

"Evil. Bad luck. He is Beelzebub, himself."

"I didn't know that," she stuttered, and feeling somewhat guilty for being forced to lie to Chokhmah, she stumbled over what she could remember of the official version of the "seeking asylum" story.

"I can understand why you might want to run away from home. What normal child does not have a taste for adventure? But to seek asylum with your father's enemy, not to mention a man like that, that I do not understand."

It was true, Eluned contemplated. While the story might

play well with Arawn, himself, it was hard to understand why she might voluntarily seek asylum in Annewven other than the fact that as her father's enemy, Arawn was unlikely to send her home. Although he might hold her ransom. Oh, the complications! Neither had she heard that he was evil, although she guessed that if she thought about it, there was probably more than one reason he was an enemy of Zion.

Her instincts told her she should trust Chokhmah and tell her the entire truth, but loyalty to Jabberwock, Bonpo and Gwrhyr prevented her from speaking. What should she do?

She was saved from making a decision, though. Daniel had come to claim his dance. With a mumbled apology to Chokhmah, she took his hand and followed him to the circle of dancers.

The next few hours were spent dancing with occasional breaks for another mug of spiced wine. She danced with Daniel and numerous other gypsy men, enjoying the perfervid music and the men's adoration. Every song seemed more and more boisterous, and she was beginning to regret that last mug of wine when Gwrhyr stepped in.

Despite the music, he slowed the pace. He still looked grim, and he frowned when he looked into her unfocused eyes. "I believe you've reached your limit," he told her, grasping her chin firmly in his hand. "You're going to need some more of Bonpo's magic pills tomorrow."

He knew about the pills! Suddenly she felt very maudlin and tears filled her eyes. "I've made a fool of myself, haven't I?"

"No, you haven't made a fool of yourself. Yet. Princess."

The ground began to undulate beneath her feet and she slumped against Gwrhyr for support.

"As I suspected," he murmured, searching for Chokhmah in the crowd. He finally caught her eye, and motioned to the Princess, who was soaking his linen shirt with her tears.

Chokhmah nodded and pointed toward her vardo.

Gwrhyr hefted Eluned easily into his arms and followed the gypsy woman. By the time he laid her gently on the duvet-covered platform, the Princess was sound asleep.

"She's going to be useless in the morning," Gwrhyr grumbled.

"Had you intended to leave so soon?" Chokhmah asked, reaching up to stroke his beard. She was standing very close to him, and she was still quite attractive, and Gwrhyr found himself responding immediately.

He glanced, guiltily, over his shoulder at the sleeping Princess.

"Worry not. She will sleep for hours. Perhaps we should return to the dance?"

Well, at least the dance is a public place, he told himself as he followed her out. What could happen at the dance?

But, things were slowing down out there. People were still dancing but the songs were growing progressively slower, and bodies were moving progressively closer. It wasn't that he was unwilling to spend the night in Chokhmah's arms; rather, he wanted nothing more. But what if Eluned found out? What would she think of him?

And yet, his desire and pent up frustration were becoming more difficult for him to master. He groaned and Chokhmah pressed her body against his and whispered in his ear, "Believe me when I say that she will never know."

Against his better instincts, he allowed himself to be led back to his tent. As he fumbled with the straps that kept the door closed, he heard a muffled snoring from inside. Who had stumbled into his tent in their drunkenness? He flung open the canvas door to find Jabberwock curled up in his blankets.

"Jabb?" He choked. He wasn't sure whether to be angry or relieved.

"Urr . . . gwr . . .," he snuffled, twitching himself awake.

Gwrhyr bit his lip, and looked with both apology and appeal at Chokhmah. She nodded her head in understanding despite the fact she couldn't quite understand how a dog might interrupt their pleasure. Putting a finger to her lips, she turned and disappeared quietly into the night.

"I'm sorry," Jabb said, now fully awake. "Was there someone with you?"

"Not to worry," he said, crawling into the tent. "It wasn't meant to happen." He sent a silent prayer to Omni for protecting him yet again. "What are you doing in here?"

"I apologize. I had a strong feeling you wouldn't make it back here tonight."

"Well, you can thank the Princess for that. She's sleeping it off in Chokhmah's vardo."

"One too many, I take it?"

"More like two or three."

"Fortunately, she has you to keep an eye on her."

It dawned on him, slowly. "And you to keep an eye on me, mayhap?" The Bandersnatch didn't reply, just watched silently as Gwrhyr stripped off his boots and shirt before arranging the blankets over his tired body. "It doesn't look like we'll be going anywhere tomorrow," he mumbled as he drifted off to sleep. "Once again, thanks to the Princess," were his last words before sleep overtook him.

Jabberwock rolled his eyes before curling up again. There hadn't been a dull moment since the journey began, but Gwrhyr had been correct, despite what he'd said—spending the night with the gypsy would have begat calamitous results. They would both thank him later. Sleep continued to elude him as he contemplated their eventual arrival in Prythew, and what must inevitably happen in the court of the crimson king.

22ND NEEON

The entire camp slept late the following morning. Even the rooster's crowing didn't penetrate their sodden and exhausted sleep. The children had stayed up late, as well, and were also glad to sleep in.

The sun was approaching its midday zenith when the gypsies and their guests finally began to stir. Eluned's groaning pulled Chokhmah from the vivid dream she was having in which mythical creatures battled with each other. She was trying to rescue the unicorn, and it took her mind a while to realize that it was Eluned and not the unicorn that was groaning.

The Princess was pale and perspiring. Chokhmah quickly got up from the bench on which she had slept and was at the young woman's side. "Are you going to be sick?"

She shook her head weakly and groaned, "I don't think so, but my head, the light . . ."

The gypsy closed the curtains and started a pot of water boiling. She then immersed a cloth in cool water and laid it across Eluned's forehead and eyes. The Princess was still pale but the perspiring had passed. When the tea was ready, she had Eluned sit up slowly and take small, slow sips. A half hour later, the color was returning to her cheeks and her stomach was no longer doing somersaults.

She sighed deeply, "For awhile there, I was sure I was going to die." Even the throbbing behind her eyes was receding. "What did you put in the tea?"

"That was a recipe that has been handed down through the generations. Unfortunately, its effectiveness wears off the more it is used. So, it is best not to find yourself in that condition again."

"I should have refused the wine and had water, instead. I was just so hot and thirsty and it tasted so good, and Bonpo wasn't there to stop me."

"Well, lesson learned, hmmm?"

"Yes, indeed." Then she blushed, remembering. "Oh no, did I? I didn't pass out when I was dancing with Gwrhyr, did I?"

"I am afraid so. He brought you here."

The Princess looked mortified. "Anything else?"

"Not really. You were crying."

"Crying?"

"You do not remember why?"

Her memory was foggy. She remembered that he had seemed angry that she was drunk and that she had been embarrassed that she might be making a fool of herself, but other than that . . . She shook her head. "No. No, I just can't remember."

"Well, count yourself lucky. People have done many worse things while intoxicated. And, despite the fact you are a gaje, all the men who danced with you treated you with respect. But, of course," and she smiled, remembering, "you had your handsome friend looking out for you."

"Handsome friend?"

"You do not find Gwrhyr attractive?"

"I hadn't thought about it," she said with annoyance. "He's so . . . I don't know. He always knows just how to drive me insane. I spend more time mad at him than not so I haven't really noticed his looks." She paused. That wasn't completely true. She had noticed, but then he'd angered her, and she'd mostly tried to ignore him since.

"Interesting," the gypsy interrupted her thoughts. "So, he is free territory, so to speak?"

"Free? What? You mean you're interested in him? Aren't you older than he is?"

"What has that got to do with anything? You have so much to learn my dear."

"It's a moot point, anyway. We'll be leaving soon."

"Ah, yes, heading to the court of the Crimson King, I believe."

"True." Eluned blushed again. She had forgotten that the last time she had spoken with Chokhmah, they'd been discussing her reasons for seeking asylum from King Arawn.

"Speaking of which, are you certain it is wise to be entering his kingdom unaccompanied by a lady-in-waiting or at the very least, a maidservant?"

"Actually, we have thought of that and are at a loss as to what to do about it."

Chokhmah eyed her with obvious interest while Eluned pondered once again whether she should share the truth with her. And thinking about the truth reminded her of her sword. Where was it? She rose in panic. She'd left it with Honeysuckle, and therefore, Bonpo, when they entered the camp.

"Forget something?"

"Yes," she said, pressing her hand to her chest in an effort to still her heart.

"Why should I not make us some breakfast while you go assure your friends that you survived the evening and see to whatever is troubling you? But, you must promise to return as soon as possible. Please?"

"Absolutely," the Princess promised, grateful for the reprieve. "I'll be right back."

SHE MADE HER WAY TENTATIVELY through the slowly awakening camp toward the tents of her friends. She prayed that they were already up and about; well, she prayed that Bonpo was up and about. She really didn't want to run into Gwrhyr. Why did she always end up looking like an idiot around him?

Once she got close enough, it was easy to spot Bonpo feeding and watering the horses.

"Good mornin', Leened," he smiled, broadly. "It rooks rike you no need my pills, afta all."

Oh great, she groaned inwardly. Gwrhyr obviously had already spoken to the yeti.

"No, fortunately Chokhmah made me some miracle tea. I feel pretty good, considering." She looked around for her baggage.

"You lookin' for sword?"

"In all the excitement yesterday, I forgot about it," she explained with some embarrassment.

"You no worry. I rook after sword fah you."

"Thank you Bonpo. I don't know what I would do without you," she said, while looking around the camp. "Is Jabberwock around?"

"'E and Gwrhyr went dat way," he said, pointing toward the river.

"Thanks again," she smiled, and headed in that direction. She'd only gone a few yards when the land dipped toward the river flats and she saw Gwrhyr and Jabberwock standing on the banks of the River Mab, apparently in serious discussion. Because of the unobstructed view, they saw her approach and started their return to the camp, meeting her half way.

She ordered herself not to blush as Gwrhyr approached but her body disobeyed her yet again. Her flaming cheeks were duly noted and dutifully ignored.

"Bonpo's magic pills?" Gwrhyr asked.

"Actually, Chokhmah's magic tea."

He raised his eyebrows. "I guess that's not surprising. Gypsies are known for their mastery of herbs and their healing powers."

"That would be another asset," Jabb remarked, seemingly apropos of nothing. Gwrhyr nodded agreement.

"Why do I feel you two are having a separate conversation?" the Princess asked.

"We've been discussing the relative merits of whether to invite the lovely Chokhmah along on our journey," Jabberwock said. Gwrhyr nodded agreement.

Eluned was confounded. Had something happened while she was sleeping off her drunken stupor? And the lovely Chokhmah? She'd noticed immediately that Chokhmah was a strikingly beautiful older woman, but to have that acknowledged by these two males irked her. For some reason she couldn't fathom, it stung. She'd never thought of herself as particularly vain, but then she'd never had competition.

"Eluned?" Jabb prompted.

"Sorry. Thinking. You just caught me off guard, that's all. I came to meet you to see if it would be wise to tell Chokhmah the truth. She doesn't believe our story."

"Wise woman," Gwrhyr approved.

The Princess shot him a glare before continuing, "Anyway, I promised her I'd be right back. She's making us something to eat."

"I believe you can trust her to keep our story confidential," Jabberwock said. "If she knows the truth, it will be easier for her to decide whether or not she wishes to be your attendant, so to speak."

"All right. I'll let you know later how it goes," she said over her shoulder as she hurried back to the lavender vardo.

On the short trip back, she tried to decipher her animosity about the apparent Gwrhyr-Chokhmah connection. She decided in the end that it must simply be her vanity. The Princess had already decided that she liked Chokhmah a lot, and she felt that she could overlook the gypsy's attraction to Gwrhyr. She couldn't be positive that Gwrhyr felt the same because he was adept at finding ways to taunt her. And even if he did desire Chokhmah, was that really any of her business?

Making that decision made her feel more adult and thus more confident. She approached the wagon in higher spirits than she'd left it. The scent of herbs and broth and baking bread wafted from the vardo's open windows and before she reached the top step, Chokhmah was opening the door.

"Oh wonderful," she smiled, "you are back just in time. The soup and the bread are ready." Bowls and plates were already on the table and she quickly ladled the soup into the bowls and cut them some bread.

The soup was very simple, just some diced vegetables and herbs in a clear broth, but it was extremely soothing to her stomach.

"I apologize," she said after eating non-stop for a few minutes, "I hadn't realized how hungry I was. Actually, I seem to be saying that a lot these days. I seem to be either full or starving."

"Well, you are on a journey, right?"

"Yes, well about that . . . can you keep this between us, that is between yourself and me and Gwrhyr, Jabb and Bonpo?"

"Jabb?"

"Jabberwock."

"The dog?"

"Um, well, he's not actually a dog."

Chokhmah raised her eyebrows, questioningly.

"Actually, he is the last, or at least one of the last, Janawar."

"I was under the impression that they had been exterminated."

"Jabb, who was then known as Hiurau, managed to escape with his mate, Kamali."

"I am thinking Kamali did not survive."

"Unfortunately for Jabb. She was killed when they crossed the Devastation."

Chokhmah leaned back on the bench and took a slow sip of her water. "This all sounds so serious."

"It's not that it's so serious, or maybe it is, I don't know. The truth is that I didn't run away, and my father knows that I am on this journey. And my father allowed all this despite the fact he is the King of Zion."

"Ah," Chokhmah nodded, "so why the story about seeking asylum in Arawn's kingdom?"

"Because that is the story we will have to tell him once we finally arrive so that he will agree to let us stay there."

"I do not understand."

"We're actually on more of a quest than a journey."

"A quest? In search of what?" She was leaning toward Eluned now, interest thoroughly piqued.

"We're searching for the Thirteen Treasures of the Thirteen Kingdoms."

"That sounds familiar, but I am sure it is only a myth or a legend."

"I did, as well, until I found that I was already in possession of one of the treasures."

Chokhmah shook her head in disbelief. "But these treasures are said to perform miraculous things."

"Nevertheless, it is true. I can only vouch for one of the treasures, but we have found two. Well, three if you count the one owned by King Uriel."

"Remind me of what they are again."

"Let's see, there are a red coat, a chessboard, a sword, a ring and stone, a mantle, a cauldron, a crock and dish, a halter, a knife, a horn, a hamper, a whetstone, a chariot and hmmm . . . yes, I think that's all."

"That is thirteen. Why do you want to collect them all? It sounds dangerous."

"I imagine it will be dangerous on occasion, and I'm not sure by what means we'll get them all. The legend claims that they are scattered throughout the kingdoms, but that if they are gathered together peace will reign. My father was in possession of my treasure and I was led to the other. It is rumored that Arawn may be in possession of as many as three of the treasures."

"And why do you count King Uriel's treasure?"

"Because I am betrothed to him; we're to be wedded on my twenty-first birthday. Gwrhyr is from that kingdom and claims the King has one of the treasures."

"So between your little troop and King Arawn, you can account for nearly half the treasures."

"Exactly. It doesn't make the quest seem quite so impossible."

"I do not understand why you are telling me all of this."

"Because it appears to be the consensus that we would like you to accompany us on the quest. I know we've just met and barely know you, but our little troop, as you called it, seems to be growing in just that way. We began the journey from Zion with just Jabb and myself. Bonpo joined us after knowing us less than twenty-four hours, and later, we met Gwrhyr and he seemed to be another missing puzzle piece. The only thing we've been missing is the so-called appropriate female to accompany me. As you were wise enough to note immediately," Eluned added.

"This is a lot to process. I need some time to think about this."

"Of course," said Eluned, standing and carrying the dirty dishes to the sink. "Take whatever time you need."

Chokhmah waved her away from washing the dishes. "Go on," she said, "Chores will help me think."

As Eluned left the vardo, Chokhmah was staring pensively out the window.

"So?" Gwrhyr asked, somewhat impatiently. The guys were gathered around a small campfire, apparently eating the last of their lunch.

"Hold your horses, for Omni's sake!" Nothing like Gwrhyr to put a damper on her cheerful mood. "She's thinking about it."

"As I suspected," Jabb replied. "I wouldn't have been able to trust her if she'd hopped directly on the bandwagon, so to speak."

"Well, at least she's thinking about it," Gwrhyr grumbled.

"You seem to have a stake in her answer," Eluned studied him. Maybe the attraction was mutual. That could make things awkward.

"We all do," Gwrhyr replied. "I was worried how King Arawn would treat a princess not only unaccompanied by a maid but who had also spent time alone with males. He might add you to his harem."

"He has a harem?" The Princess was appalled.

"Not officially," Gwrhyr said. "But, I've heard rumors."

Eluned swallowed, hard. Were they being idiots? Were the treasures worth the risk? Their very lives might be at stake.

"We mus' be vely caleful." There was a somber tone in Bonpo's voice, and he couldn't hide the worry in his eyes.

"Great! The more I find out, the worse the King sounds," Eluned fretted. "We're not taking too big a chance are we? You know he has the treasures?"

"I'm positive. He has the chariot, the halter and the chessboard. We just need to figure out how we're going to win, cheat or even steal them from him," Gwrhyr said.

"Steal?" Eluned gulped. So far, getting the treasures had been so easy.

"Not without a no-fail exit plan," Jabberwock added.

"True. We don't want to steal unless we're literally on our way out of Annewven," agreed Gwrhyr.

"Which is only bordered by Sheba, Adamah and Simoon," Eluned said, thinking out loud, "and Simoon and Adamah are part of Awen Alliance along with Annewven, and Sheba seems too darn close even if King Adeyemi is part of the Triquetra Alliance."

"If we could arrange a way to the Favonian Isles," Gwrhyr pondered.

"Well, Queen Miryam is an ally. It could work," agreed Eluned.

"And, she is the sister of my mother," a voice said behind them. They all turned to stare at Chokhmah.

"Miryam was a gypsy?" Eluned asked. Would miracles never cease? Omni's hand seemed omnipresent. She'd always known It was supposed to but to see that continue to occur never ceased to amaze her.

"It was quite the scandal at the time," Jabberwock was saying, and Eluned refocused on the conversation.

"Yes," Chokhmah began, joining Eluned on the bench that had been pulled up to the fire, "King Rangatira was greatly enamored of her, and regardless of the objections of his people and ours, he married her."

"Did they have children?" the Princess asked.

"There's a son," Gwrhyr said, "Prince Mauri."

"Yes," Chokhmah agreed, "but his gypsy blood is his curse. Even though he was careful to marry a woman from a noble Favonian family . . ."

". . . the people are divided over whether he should be allowed to succeed his mother," Gwrhyr finished her sentence.

Chokhmah smiled, "Ahhh . . . politics. Actually, if he had not had the misfortune of being so young when his father died, I think he would be king already."

"Then shouldn't he be your age?" Eluned asked Chokhmah.

"Yes," she agreed, "a little younger, and he, too, has children."

"Twin daughters who are teenagers and a son who is nine-teen or twenty, if I remember correctly," Jabberwock interjected.

"True, but Miryam was always strong-willed. I imagine that she is unwilling to let go of the throne," Chokhmah noted.

"Much to Mauri's chagrin, no doubt!" Gwrhyr laughed. "Depending on when Queen Miryam dies, Mauri may not get to rule as long he'd like."

"So the throne will go to his son?" Eluned asked.

"Yes, if Miryam is dead," Chokhmah explained. "You see our people are matriarchal, but I doubt that Mauri is. The Favonians are most definitely patriarchal. It is good that Miryam rules them with both a strong and gentle hand or there might have been revolt."

"Agreed," said Gwrhyr, "Her army, in particular, loves her. It's my understanding that Mauri has tried to ingratiate himself with his people as much as possible."

"I would not be surprised," said Chokhmah. "He certainly did not inherit any of his mother's gypsy loyalties."

"Chokhmah," Eluned chimed in, "is the reason you're here because you decided to join us?"

"Actually," she said, putting her arm around the Princess, "I came down to ask a few more questions, but hearing Miryam's name as I walked up . . ."

"Too much of an Omnincidence?" Eluned said.

"Exactly," she hugged her. "I still have more questions, though."

"Such as?" Gwrhyr asked.

"Which treasures do you, and King Uriel, have in your possession?"

"Gwrhyr says Uriel has the Mantle of Arthur," Eluned reminded her. Chokhmah raised her eyebrows at Gwrhyr.

"It's true," he explained. "I have it on excellent authority that his father left him the mantle."

"Which does what exactly?" Chokhmah asked.

"Causes the wearer to be invisible," Gwrhyr replied.

"Which I find highly amusing," Eluned giggled.

"Why?" Gwrhyr and Chokhmah asked simultaneously.

"Because I have a ring and moonstone that make me invisible," Eluned explained.

"So?" Gwrhyr looked troubled.

"I don't know, just think of the possibilities. What if both of us are invisible at once? Would we be able to see each other?" Eluned giggled again. "I think I know what I'm wearing on our wedding night." Then she guffawed. "I can just see him searching for me," she doubled over with laughter.

"Well, thank Omni he has another three years in which to wait for you to grow up," Gwrhyr said, jaw clenched.

That sent the Princess off into more gales of laughter. "What do you care?"

"He's my king." Gwrhyr's voice was cold. "Besides, you act as if you're being married to an ugly old man. He's only a few years older than you."

An understanding smile curved Chokhmah's lips. "It is not his age or what he looks like that bothers you, my dear, is it?"

Eluned sobered up. "No, not really. Jabb knows. I just hate being married against my will. Why can't I choose who I get to marry? I hate this outdated betrothal system."

"Well, if it's any consolation," Gwrhyr added, "I happen to know that King Uriel isn't too happy about it either. It wasn't his choice to be betrothed to you."

"What are you, his confessor as well as his spy?" The Princess jumped up and stomped over to him, eyes flashing fire.

"It's none of your business what he is to me," Gwrhyr grabbed her shoulders.

"It's my business who travels with me to Annewven," she yelled.

"Is that a threat?" He growled, face only inches from hers.

"Threat? I can order you not to attend us if I so choose." The Princess glared at him.

"Order? Attend? By Omni, who do you think you are?" Gwrhyr's hazel eyes were the angry blue of a storm-tossed ocean.

"This is my journey and I can decide who I want on it," Eluned spat.

"You can't keep me away from Annewven," Gwrhyr retorted. "The road is open to whoever travels it."

Eluned's hand was reaching toward the dagger in Gwrhyr's belt. Chokhmah smiled at Jabberwock, knowingly, and nodded toward the pair.

"Children! Children!" The Bandersnatch admonished them. They turned to him in surprise. "Stop behaving like toddlers. You both know quite well that King Seraphim and Queen Ceridwen and King Gavreel and Queen Angharad had not only the best interests of their princess and prince in mind when they made the match, but the interests of the Thirteen Kingdoms as well."

"Well, I'm not sure the Devastation of Pelf can count as a Kingdom anymore," the Princess mumbled.

"Which makes uniting the Kingdoms of Zion and Aden even more important," Jabberwock stated. "The kingdoms of Naphtali and Tarshish must become part of the Triquetra Alliance or we risk war with the Awen Alliance."

"And you think that when Zion and Aden are united, it will pull Naphtali and Tarshish from their neutrality?" Eluned asked.

"That is the hope, my child," the Bandersnatch concurred.

"You know you can let go of my shoulders anytime," she told Gwrhyr, giving his shin a light kick.

"Ouch," his hands dropped promptly.

"I'm going to have bruises tomorrow," she complained, returning to the bench. "Hopefully Uriel won't be as abusive as his subjects appear to be," she sniffed, tossing her hair.

Gwrhyr glared at her, and turned to walk down to the river.

"I have a salve that will help that in my wagon," Chokhmah stood. "Why do we not go back there and have some tea?"

"That would be nice. Thanks, Chokhmah," The Princess replied, taking her arm.

"I think Chokhmah is a lot wiser than I had originally calculated," Jabb told Bonpo when the women were out of earshot.

"Vely wise indeed," the giant smiled and started humming happily to himself as he cleaned up lunch.

THE GYPSY AND THE PRINCESS spent the rest of the afternoon in Chokhmah's vardo getting to know each other better.

"What is it?" Chokhmah finally asked as they began their second cup of tea.

"What is what?" Eluned blushed.

"See, you are blushing. I feel as if there is something you want to ask but are hesitant to do so."

"I," she began but stopped.

"You?" Chokhmah prompted her.

The Princess took a deep breath. "I was wondering if you could tell my fortune," she said in a rush.

"Ah," Chokhmah smiled. "Is that all? Of course I am willing, but it is not something to be rushed or taken lightly."

"No?"

"You must meditate on the question you would like to ask. Think about it and perhaps tonight, before we sleep, I will read your cards."

"Really?"

"Of course, my dear. It is what I do."

Eluned surveyed the vardo, and then looked at Chokhmah guiltily.

"Yes?"

"I just realized that it's going to be awfully hard for you to leave this," Eluned said, looking around again.

"Difficult, yes," Chokhmah agreed. "But this also gives me a chance to begin anew. I have to confess that I have spent the past year turned inward. It is time to join the world again."

"What will you do with the vardo?"

"I will leave that up to my brother," she sighed.

Eluned swallowed hard. "Moshe. How is he going to take your leaving?"

"I am certain he will not be pleased."

"I'm sorry."

"Fortunately, I am no longer a maiden, and can resolve my own future." Chokhmah's voice rang with determination.

"Do you ever read cards for yourself?"

"Naturally," she said. "And I had intended to in order to make this decision but Omni stepped in first."

"I've noticed It has a way of doing that."

"Indeed. And before I decide what to take and what to leave behind, I had better go find Moshe." Chokhmah stood up.

"Would you like me to go with you?" Eluned asked, already rising from the bench.

"Yes, that might help my case."

They found Moshe at a makeshift forge hammering a wheel rim against an anvil.

"Preparing to move on? Chokhmah asked, kissing her brother on the cheek.

"Yes, it will not be long before the snowmelt begins. Time to get to higher ground." He looked up and noticed the Princess for the first time and his brow wrinkled in puzzlement. "What is going on?"

"Moshe, I have made a decision," Chokhmah told her brother.

He put down his hammer and stepped away from the forge. "You are leaving with the gajes."

"Yes," she confirmed.

"Daniel suspected as much. Harah," he spat. "Chokhmah, are you sure you want to make this break."

"Moshe, I need a change." There was a slight tone of pleading in her voice. "And, it will give me a chance to see our aunt again."

"Your journey will take you to Favonia?" he asked the Princess.

"Yes, sir," she answered, meekly. "It is our intention to end up in Favonia once we finish our business with King Arawn."

"The Crimson King?" Moshe quickly made the symbol to ward off evil. "What business could you possibly have with him? He is evil incarnate."

"So I keep hearing," Eluned sighed, "but we're on a diplomatic mission and it would be unseemly for a Princess to arrive without a lady-in-waiting."

"A Princess, huh? Who is your father?" Moshe looked doubtful.

"King Seraphim of Zion," Eluned stated.

"Why did you not think of that before you began your journey?" Moshe questioned the Princess.

"The truth is that the purpose of the journey wasn't revealed to me until we were already well into the trip," she admitted.

"I don't understand," he frowned.

"Exactly," she said, attempting to be nonspecific. "I think I wasn't supposed to understand the purpose until later. I was supposed to be ignorant."

"Hmpff," he grunted, "sounds like prattle. Who planned this?"

"My father's advisors, and we have a representative from Aden, as well," she added.

"You might as well save yourself the time," he spoke gruffly. "King Arawn will never give an inch to King Seraphim or any of his allies."

"You are no doubt right, but we have to try." Eluned spoke as if she had no choice in the matter.

"And you are to be the lady-in-waiting?" he turned to Chokhmah.

"It is meant to be," she confirmed.

"You know this for certain?" Moshe's dark brown eyes bored into Chokhmah's.

"Without a doubt," she confirmed again.

"Then there is nothing I can do." He picked up the hammer and returned to the forge, striking the wheel rim a little harder than necessary.

"Should I ask Daniel to take on the vardo?" she asked.

Moshe nodded curtly, jaw clenched. "When do you leave?"

"Tomorrow," the Princess answered.

"Will you return?" he asked Chokhmah.

"I feel that someday I will be back," she said. "I just cannot say when that will be."

"Do not leave without saying farewell." It sounded like an order.

"Of course not," she smiled. Moshe could be brusque, but he was actually very sentimental. He returned to his work. It was clear they had been dismissed.

THE WOMEN WALKED SILENTLY back to Chokhmah's vardo.

"Your father's advisors, hmmm?" the gypsy asked once they were inside.

"I had to say something. There is no way my father would have willingly sent me to Annewven. He probably thinks I'm on my way to the Favonian Isles. He knows how much I've been longing to see them."

"Well, I hope that all of you are correct in thinking that

we can find the treasures and get them out of the kingdom," Chokhmah said.

"So do I. It seems imperative that we do so."

"But that will be only six of the thirteen treasures. Where can the other seven be found?"

"That's an excellent question, Chokhmah. I have absolutely no idea. I've been so focused on Annewven that it hasn't even occurred to me to ask. But, I imagine they are in at least some, if not all, of the other nine kingdoms if Zion possessed one, Aden another and I found one in the Sheban desert. Doesn't seem fair that Arawn has three, but then again, I'm beginning to understand that he's pretty ruthless."

"That leaves Favonia, Tarshish, Dyfed, Simoon, Dziron, Adamah, Kamartha and Naphtali as possibilities," Chokhmah mused.

"I like the way you named our allies first, but what about the Devastation of Pelf?"

"Omni, I hope not." Chokhmah flashed the sign to ward off evil.

"It seems unlikely but then again, there has been nothing about this trip that has been 'likely.'"

"Well, I have no doubt that it will be interesting. I just pray that King Arawn is hospitable."

"So do I."

Chokhmah took a deep breath

"Daniel?" Eluned asked.

"Yes, I need to tell him. But, I need to go alone. He does not seem to be able to think when you are around," she teased. "Why do you not ask our fellow companions to join us for dinner at nightfall?"

"I'm not sure Bonpo will fit in here."

Chokhmah laughed. "True. We will eat outside then. And I will ask Daniel to join us."

"Not Moshe?"

"Why spoil the party? If he and his wife want to join us, they are more than welcome. They know where I live. Chances are they will drop by for a parting drink later."

Eluned grimaced. "I may stick to water."

WHEN CHOKHMAH RETURNED, Eluned was sitting on the bench studying the tarot deck. "The art on these cards is beautiful. Every single one is different."

"Of course. Each one means something unique. So, will the men join us?"

"Men," Eluned snorted. "Yes, but Bonpo says they caught some large catfish, and he is already making a fish pot."

"Wonderful. Then we should go see what we can find to accompany that," Chokhmah said, handing Eluned a basket and some shears. "About a quarter of a mile south there is a lovely meadow where the high desert ends and the forest begins. I know we can find some sorrel there and perhaps some mushrooms in the wood."

ELUNED THOROUGHLY ENJOYED THE WALK, and looked forward to the coming day when they would be riding through hardwood forest on their way to the river crossing. She and Chokhmah collected a basketful of sorrel before heading into the woods to look for early mushrooms. They were in luck. They returned to the camp with a basketful of morels as well as a dozen oyster mushrooms.

While Chokhmah set to work washing and then creaming the sorrel, the Princess washed and sliced the mushrooms and sautéed them in butter. They worked in companionable silence, and the Princess found the process of preparing the fungi not only easy, but also enjoyable. She had never had the chance to cook at home, and on the journey, all her food had been prepared for her as well.

By the time the men arrived (Daniel with a jug of spiced

wine), their contribution was ready, and all enjoyed the hearty meal. Only Daniel would occasionally lapse into silence. It was clear that he wanted to be a part of the group as well. Eluned felt bad for him but knew it was impossible. It was already hard enough to explain their strange assembly, but there was something unique about its make up that would corrupt it by adding another man, particularly a gypsy man. No, you mean yet another man who is interested in you, she corrected herself. She already had to fend off Gwrhyr's attentions, and she really didn't want to have to deal with Daniel as well. Of course, Chokhmah and Gwrhyr could end up together, she thought, studying them over the rim of her mug, in which she'd kept water until the overzealous Daniel had re-filled the half-full mug with wine. They were apparently oblivious of each other at the moment, but should they wind up together that would relieve her of the Gwrhyr problem. But, if Daniel were along, he would have even more time to dote on her. Nope. Definitely not a good idea for him to join them.

Bonpo's booming bass interrupted Eluned's reverie. He was asking Chokhmah if he needed to arrange to get her a horse before they left in the morning.

"No, I have my own horse," she told the giant.

"I'll have Halelu ready for you in the morning," Daniel offered.

"That would be wonderful. Thank you."

"In dat case, I go get leady fah morning." Bonpo stood.

"Bonpo's right," Gwrhyr stood, as well. We need to make it an early night. We really should be out of here first thing tomorrow," he continued, clearly speaking to Eluned. It took all her self-control not to stick her tongue out at him. She was much too old for that now. Instead, she carried dirty dishes into Chokhmah's vardo. She would say good-bye to Daniel in the morning.

ONCE THE DISHES WERE DONE, and the two women were sitting comfortably at the wagon's small table, Chokhmah asked Eluned if she were ready for her reading. The Princess felt the pace of her heart pick up.

"I think so."

"Have you been thinking about your question?"

"Yes," she said, blushing.

Chokhmah raised an eyebrow in amusement, "A certain special someone?"

"No!" she said more loudly than she intended. "No. I mean, I guess I'd like to know if there will be a special someone."

"Well, dear, that goes without saying. I can guarantee you that at some point in your life you will find love."

"I guess what I really want to know is if I will meet the love of my life while on this journey?"

"Ah, yes, that is a little more specific, but I cannot answer yes or no questions; perhaps something more along the lines of: What are the possibilities for meeting the love of my life on this journey? Something like that? Then," after Eluned nodded, Chokhmah picked up the deck of Tarot cards, "first shuffle this deck your self while thinking of your question." Eluned took the cards from her and cut and shuffled them for a minute while meditating on her question. Chokhmah then took the cards and spread them across the table. "I will do what I call my 'Once Upon a Time' reading."

"Once upon a time?"

"Yes, because those who ask this type of question want a faery tale answer." Eluned blushed again. "Do not worry. I understand, and the answer is always much more complex than a yes or no."

"And not all faery tales end well."

"Exactly. So," she began, slipping easily into fortuneteller mode, "I will need you to choose your first card. Choose carefully for this card represents your purest self, your inner child. It is your guide to love." Eluned pointed to a card and Chokhmah placed it face down in the center of the table. "The next card represents the foundation of your love. Consider thoughtfully what is at the heart of your question."

Eluned pondered for a full minute before pointing to another card.

"Good," continued Chokhmah, "you are taking this very seriously." This card was placed slightly on top of and at angle on the left side of the first card. "The third card is the hidden limitations to your relationship. Keep an open and clear mind as you choose it." Eluned's choice was placed opposite the second card in the same position.

"Just four more to go. The fourth card represents the magic key. It will unlock your potential for love and help heal the hidden limitations." The fourth card was placed below the first. "The fifth card is the status of your current love."

"But I don't have a current love."

"Then picture what you wish for in a true love as you choose this card. It will help you to discover how to use your magic key." Eluned closed her eyes for a moment before pointing to a fifth card, which was then placed above the first. "Two more. The sixth card represents the future. What will happen next? Only you can decide. You must envision your desired destination on your journey of love."

Eluned spent a couple of minutes considering Chokhmah's request before choosing. The card was placed to the left of the first three. "The final card is your star wish. This card will inspire and encourage you on your journey of love. Let your hope, your spirits ascend as you choose this card." The last card was placed to the right of the first three and then Chokhmah turned them over.

While the Princess reveled in their beauty (for she couldn't fathom their meaning), the gypsy studied them in context to Eluned's question.

"Is it good or bad?" Eluned finally asked when she couldn't bear the silence any longer.

"Quite good," Chokhmah confirmed. "Let us start with your inner child, in this case, The Fool."

"The Fool! That sounds terrible!"

"Do not be fooled by the name," Chokhmah chuckled. "This card in this position means that you were born with a passionate need to explore the world and to discover the truest expression of your soul. You were sheltered by your parents, and now you must encounter lessons and apparent detours off the beaten path on your quest for individuality." She paused. "You are crying."

"I'm sorry, it all seems so terribly true."

"What did you expect? Of course it is true. You bring this spirit of adventure into all your relationships, but do not fear the challenges and obstacles you will face. Ultimately, you will overcome them."

Eluned shook her head in wonder. "You will have to help me remember all this."

"Would you like to take notes?"

"May I?"

"Absolutely. I have a journal and pen in that drawer there."

Eluned opened the drawer and pulled out a small leather-bound notebook. The cover, the color of lapis lazuli, was embossed with a wave-like design bordered by intertwined birds. A leather cord wrapped around a pewter button decorated with a knot-work pattern held the diary closed. She opened it slowly. The pages were empty. "This?" she asked in disbelief.

"It is lovely, is it not?"

"Stunning."

"It, too, belonged to my grandmother. I am sure she would not mind your taking it. It seems meant for you."

"Thank you," Eluned breathed, returning to the table. She quickly took some notes on the first card. "Thanks, again. I'm ready for the second card."

"The second card is your foundation of love card. It is the Wheel of Fortune."

"That sounds promising."

Chokhmah smiled. "It means that not only must you learn to be in the right place at the right time, but you must be open and receptive to the opportunities that come your way."

"How does one learn to be in the right place at the right time? That sounds impossible."

"But have you not already found that that is true for you? Were you not supposed to be elsewhere when you stayed at The Crossroads Inn and met Bonpo? And did you not push yourself to make it to the Trade Route Inn where you met Gwrhyr?"

"And if I hadn't checked on the horses, I would never have met Aeron and found Dyrnwyn."

"Exactly. What the card is saying is remain open to those feelings because when it comes to love that is very important. On the other hand, it says you must maintain a balance between doing and being. Too much doing can ruin a relationship. Beware of the pitfalls of overindulgence and ungrounded optimism. You must remain centered to build your love a strong and lasting foundation—one built on rock not sand. Always ask yourself: how does my relationship matter to my true self, to my inner child?"

She waited while Eluned scribbled furiously for a moment. "Your third card is the Queen of Cups. She represents the hidden limitations that may stifle your love. I do not sense it in you now, but if you ever close yourself to the ability to believe in higher powers or invisible presences you will find yourself and your soul mate in a state of darkness. If this ever happens you will need to identify the shadows and projections, belief systems and internal dialogues that are producing the unhappiness within you."

"That sounds scary."

"It will be even less so if you work on these things as you

progress through life. The more knowledgeable you are of your self, the stronger you will be; the stronger your relationship will be."

"I'm not sure how to do that."

"Do not worry. I will teach you some ways to dig deeper. We will have time."

"Now we leave the middle," Eluned noted.

"Yes. The next card is your magic key."

"I like the sound of that," the Princess said, eyes alight.

"And your card is the Knight of Swords. It means your magic key is your cheerful innocence combined with your eagerness to learn, grow and evolve your consciousness, which will open more doors as you and your beloved get to know each other more intimately."

"That sounds promising."

"Something or someone should be coming into your life to help guide you—a book or author, a teacher or mentor."

"You, perhaps?"

"It does seem likely, does it not?"

"But that's what the card says, right? You're not adding that?"

"No, of course not. It did not occur to me until you said it."

"Truly amazing."

"Yes, but while it seems quite obvious, it does not mean it is wrong. Things are often not quite as complicated as we may want to make them. One must remain open . . ."

"To the whisper of the wind?"

"Exactly. Tea?"

"Please."

As they waited for the water to boil, Chokhmah explained the fifth card—current love status. "Yes, I know you do not currently have a love, but your card is the Ace of Pentacles. It is offering you the chance to see those around you with whom you have a relationship, or a potential relationship, with a pure vision. Now is a good time to see those you care about and love without judgment, without projecting on them, to see them for who they really are. You may also be given the rare chance to see yourself as others see you. Relationships are an interactive experience and you must be able to walk in the shoes of the ones you love as well as your own."

While Eluned took notes, Chokhmah prepared the tea and brought it to the table.

"This will help you sleep. When we are done, you must be able to sleep on what you have learned so that your mind can absorb it. Also, we must be refreshed for our journey tomorrow."

"Only two more cards, right?"

"Correct. The future and the star wish. Your future card is the Three of Pentacles. It says that your core desire is for a playful yet purposeful connection with your beloved. This card calls you to nurture the relationships that support that aspect of yourself or to create new ones. The work you have been doing to grow will soon bear fruit, and you must clarify to yourself what you will want to achieve in that relationship. This card says that this will be done in a spirit of community and not on your own."

"Hmmmm. Interesting. I guess it makes sense as there are now five of us traveling together, and we are moving toward the bigger community of Arawn's kingdom."

"We will see. And your final card is your star wish, the Five of Wands. You must trust this message about love sent to you by your higher self. You must allow the chaos of the moment to show you its true purpose, which is to bring forth greater freedom and creativity. You must take action at this time even if the action is to surrender. You must move forward without fear of the coming changes. Remain loving to those around you even as you rid yourself of all the things of the past that have held you back. Give birth to the new you."

The Princess sipped her tea silently as Chokhmah readied herself for bed. "I'm not sure that answered my question," she finally spoke. "It was a lot to take in. I . . ."

" . . . need to sleep on it?"

"Yes. I'll do as you suggested. I'll sleep on it. Maybe it will all seem more clear in the morning. I'm really glad now that I took notes."

They finished preparing for sleep in silence, and it wasn't long before the only sound in the small wagon was their even and gentle breathing.

23ᴿᴰ NEEON

The questers had been riding through the hardwood forest for more than an hour when Gwrhyr suddenly turned to look at the Princess. He and Chokhmah had taken the lead and had become immersed in their conversation. Behind them, Bonpo and Jabberwock were chattering away quietly, which meant that the Bandersnatch was doing most of the talking. Eluned brought up the rear, silently reflecting on the previous evening's tarot reading. He frowned and pulled Heiduc aside to wait for her.

She nearly passed him unseen until he cleared his throat, loudly. That shook her from her reverie.

"Wow, I don't think I've ever had the pleasure of your silence quite so long," he teased her as they both knew that wasn't true.

"I have a lot to think about," she replied seriously, refusing to take the bait.

"Such as?"

"Unfortunately, I'm not prepared to discuss it. It involves things I have to come to terms with about myself."

Gwrhyr's brow furrowed. This was a side of the Princess he had yet to see. Not only did she appear honest and reflective, but she was also treating him with respect. He didn't know whether to take comfort in the change or be frightened by it. He noticed that Chokhmah was watching the interchange with approval.

"Well, as long as you're all right, I'll leave you to your thoughts," he said.

"Thank you, Gwrhyr, I appreciate that," she smiled at him and he felt his heart catch in his throat. Before he said something he might later regret, he spurred his horse back to Chokhmah's side.

"What happened after we left last night?" he asked her.

"I did a tarot reading for her," Chokhmah said.

"What did she ask?"

"That I cannot tell you, but I will say that I have never had someone take a reading so seriously in all the years I have been giving them. Perhaps someday she will share it with you."

"Hmmm," he replied, suddenly pensive himself.

Chokhmah breathed deeply. It was mid-morning but the dew still clung to the grass and leaves, and the air still held the familiar scent of damp earth and wet leaves and grass. Before long, the sun would soak up the moisture, and the fragrance would change. She smiled at the thought of the earth changing her perfume as the day progressed. It was as if Gaea, growing bored with one, would exchange it for another. Ever-changing from dawn to dawn, day to day and season to season.

"What?" Gwrhyr asked, noticing her smile.

"Nothing, my dear. Life just amuses me, that is all."

They continued to ride in quietude for another few hours before stopping for lunch in a sunny clearing.

LUNCH OVER, AND NIBBLING ON THE FRUIT Bonpo had bargained for while at the gypsy camp, the troop reclined for awhile enjoying the warm sun on their heads and dozing off their full bellies. They had agreed before they started out that morning that they would only push as far as the river crossing that night so they could spend one last evening on friendly soil before putting their fate in King Arawn's hands.

Eventually, Eluned pulled herself out of her morning daze enough to approach Chokhmah.

"Did you bring your cards with you?"

"But of course, my dear. Why?"

"I was wondering if I might borrow, briefly, the ones from my reading so that I can sketch them into my journal?"

"Certainly, you may," Chokhmah replied, pulling the deck from her traveling bag. Eluned sorted through the deck until she found the seven cards and sat down, supporting her back against a boulder, and began to sketch. Chokhmah took out the slim volume of Thirteen Royal Treasures of The Thirteen Kingdoms by Pryderi Gruffyd that she had borrowed from Eluned and proceeded to peruse the book. (Yes, the Princess had neglected to return it to the inn's meager library as she felt it had been preordained to wind up in her hands.)

Gwrhyr, seeing that the women appeared to be settling in for a spell, pulled a small harp from his pack. Closing his eyes, he began plucking the strings, enjoying the sounds they produced. He had always thought of the harp as the appropriate instrument for travel and adventure.

Eluned looked up from her sketch of "The Fool" for a moment, noting the look of contentment on Gwrhyr's face. She didn't know why she was surprised but she was. The man's talents and knowledge never ceased to amaze her. Maybe it was time she stopped being irritated by it all. What was the point, after all? No one was left unsettled but her. Gwrhyr didn't seem to care that it bothered her. Everyone else seemed to take his abilities for granted. They were about to enter the unknown. They would all have to stick together or risk everything. Did she want to be responsible for being the only member of their group that consistently diverged from the others? The one that caused the most friction?

She shook her head as she returned to her sketching. The tarot was right. It was time for her to make some changes.

Chokhmah watched as the thoughts played across Eluned's face. The hand that the Princess had chosen the previous evening had been more than happenstance. No, Omni was definitely involved. This was going to be an interesting journey.

Gwrhyr played for nearly half an hour before strumming to a stop. Eluned looked up from her drawing. "Why did you stop?"

"You noticed I was playing?"

"Of course I did, silly. It was lovely."

Gwrhyr looked taken aback. He'd actually been surprised that the Princess hadn't made some comment when he started. He'd actually been anticipating it. He wasn't sure about this new Princess. He felt like he was waiting for the other shoe to drop. "Thank you," he stammered.

"How long have you been playing?" she asked.

"Years now. I was taught when I was a child," he admitted.

"I always wanted to learn to play the lute, but my mother insisted on harpsichord. It's beautiful, of course, but you can't exactly carry one around in your bag."

Gwrhyr laughed at the image. "No, I can't see that at all. May I see your drawings?"

Eluned colored, but handed him the journal.

He studied them for a moment before murmuring, "I'm impressed. These are really quite good. I've always wished I could draw. I can see the picture in my head but it refuses to flow from my fingers."

The Princess laughed, but for a change, not derisively. "I have to admit that I enjoy finally finding something you cannot do. I was beginning to think you were perfect, and that seemed impossible."

"Despite what I may have led you to believe, there are many, many things at which I do not excel."

"Name one more."

"I'm a lousy cook."

"Fortunately, we have an excellent cook with us," she smiled at Bonpo.

"Oh yes, and my sewing skills leave a lot to be desired," he added, pointing to a poorly mended tear on his right sleeve.

"Not my forte either."

Chokhmah and Bonpo indicated they were capable at needlework.

"So, what can you do Jabb?" The Princess teased.

"Very amusing, your highness," he groused in his Jabberwock way.

The Princess stood and stretched, "Goodness, the afternoon is wearing on, isn't it? I guess we need to get moving if we want to make it to the river by nightfall. Do you need a trip into the woods before you get in your basket?" she asked the Bandersnatch.

THEY REACHED THE TOLLBOOTH at the river crossing shortly after sunset. Despite the torch, they could barely see the drooping green banner with its red hawk. One of the guards there informed them that river crossings were allowed only between sunrise and sunset, which was what they had expected. They were more than happy to spend one final night in Sheba despite the appearance of the camping spot, which was muddy and trampled and stank of refuse and ordure. Its only saving grace was a large fig tree although it was much too early in the season to enjoy its fruit. Eluned imagined that during the hot summer months it would provide bountiful shade, as well, but in Neeon it offered only tender new leaves.

"I imagine it's just as bad on the other side," Gwrhyr noted, although it was too dark to see across the river to confirm it.

Eluned nodded in agreement and moved closer to the smoke of a campfire that smoldered in the center of the site.

She hoped that it might help to mask the scent. If they were up and out early enough, they might actually make it to Ruisid-ho, which, according to Gwrhyr and Jabberwock, had a small inn. Not that she minded camping or even sharing a tent with Chokhmah. She just knew that after a night in this place, she was going to want a bath whether or not she actually needed one.

As soon as the fire had burned down a bit, Bonpo nestled some fish wrapped in fig leaves within the coals and soon the scent of baking trout filled the air.

Bonpo had been busy since they'd arrived. While they set to work getting the horses tethered and fed, the tents up, and the firewood collected, not only had he caught enough fish to feed them all but he had gathered greens and nuts and even a few mushrooms for a salad.

"I declare Bonpo the fourteenth treasure of the thirteen kingdoms," Eluned said, solemnly dubbing each of his shoulders with her sword, Dyrnwyn. "You are amazing. Thank you."

Bonpo's face turned a lovely shade of crimson. "You vely welcome, Plincess. It is my honor to cook fah you."

Gwrhyr laughed and clapped the giant on the back. "Sir Bonpo, it is."

Once their laughter had died down, Jabberwock brought up the serious subject of the following day. "We need to decide what our story is and be able to stick with it before we cross the River Mab. It is possible we will be asked why we're crossing into Annewven before we leave, but you can be sure they will want to know once we've stepped onto their shore."

"The simpler the better," Eluned reminded them.

"You're running away, but why?" Gwrhyr asked.

"Because I'm tired of being treated like a child?" The Princess offered.

"No." Chokhmah said. "You are in love with Gwrhyr, but cannot marry him because you are betrothed to King Uriel. You were forced to run away."

The Princess looked at her aghast. Even Gwrhyr seemed shocked.

"It might work," the Bandersnatch mused.

"I'm not sure I can convincingly play that part," Eluned gulped.

"But you do not have to do so, my dear," Chokhmah assured her. "The stress of the journey will have broken the romantic impulse that prompted your fleeing your father's kingdom. I would imagine that by the time we arrive in Prythew, your relationship with Gwrhyr will be cordial at best."

"But now that I've run away with him, I can't possibly return to my father," Eluned continued the fabrication. "He'd be furious and humiliated."

"And I can't return to Aden because King Uriel will be enraged with me," Gwrhyr added.

"And Bonpo and I are just the lady-in-waiting and cook who helped her conspire to run away," added Chokhmah.

"And Jabb is my pet," Eluned stated.

"Always the pet," Jabberwock groused.

"It's not my fault you look like a . . ." she began.

"Don't say it," he interrupted. "I'll keep my mouth shut."

"That's difficult to believe," she teased, ruffling the fur on his neck.

"So it's agreed?" Jabberwock asked, ignoring her.

"I jus' da cook." Bonpo played his part with a grin.

"And I came along for propriety's sake and because I would have no longer been welcome in Zion," Chokhmah added.

"And you two can at least act like you like each other?" Jabberwock asked, placing the emphasis on the word, "act."

Eluned closed her eyes and took a deep breath before moving closer to Gwrhyr. "Yes," she said, resting her head against his shoulder, "he's not that bad."

"Thanks," he replied, sarcastically, but he felt a slight thrill run down his spine at the pressure and warmth of her body next to his. It took every ounce of his self-control not to wrap her in his arms.

"So," the Bandersnatch concluded, "we're seeking asylum in Arawn's kingdom because the Princess and Gwrhyr were forced to leave theirs?"

"Why Arawn's? Chokhmah asked. "Why not an ally's? Or, at the very least, a neutral kingdom like Tarshish or Naphtali?"

"Easy," replied the Princess. "Because it is the last place, other than the Devastation of Pelf, that my father would look."

Gwrhyr nodded. "True. Their enmity is well known."

"So, are we ready? This time tomorrow we should be well into Annewven," Jabberwock asked.

Eluned shivered in fear and anticipation.

"You all right?" Gwrhyr asked.

"I'm both looking forward to it and dreading it."

"Don't worry, my love, I'll protect you," he teased, pulling her closer.

"That's what I'm afraid of," she laughed, standing up. She pretended to suppress a yawn. "I'm more tired than I have a right to be. I think I'll call it a night." In truth, she was enjoying the warmth and solidity of Gwrhyr just a little too much. And, she just couldn't bring herself to settle for the first young man she met outside her father's kingdom. Sure, he was solid and intelligent, and, as Chokhmah had noted, not that bad looking, quite handsome, actually. But, she wanted someone exciting. Someone who made her body thrum and her knees go weak the moment she laid eyes on him. Like most young princesses, she wanted love at first sight.

PART TWO

"From there to here, from here to there,
Funny things are everywhere."

-Dr. Seuss
One Fish, Two Fish, Red Fish, Blue Fish

"The rusted chains of prison moons
Are shattered by the sun.
I walk a road, horizons change
The tournament's begun.
The purple piper plays his tune.
The choir softly sing:
Three lullabies in an ancient tongue.
For the court of the crimson king."

-King Crimson
The Court of the Crimson King *from*
In The Court Of The Crimson King

24ᴛʜ Neeon

The inn at Ruisidho was spartan but clean. They had traveled across the river with no more of incidence than raised eyebrows and were in high spirits by the time they reached The Pilgrim's Door late that afternoon.

"Why do you suppose they call it the 'pilgrim's door'?" Eluned wondered aloud. They were gathered around a worn plank table sipping mulled wine from heavy pewter mugs and waiting for their food to be brought to them.

"I believe there is a stone circle in this area," Jabberwock responded after checking to make sure they were alone.

"Really?" Eluned marveled. "I would imagine it has been thousands of years since pilgrims journeyed to a stone circle."

"I believe that circles of stone and oak groves and the like will always have their devotees," Chokhmah said. "And, if I remember correctly, this particular temple boasts an altar adapted from a stone that fell to earth."

"Yes, I remember reading about that site. It's the meteorite that pilgrims travelled, still travel, to see," Gwrhyr added.

"Sounds fascinating," Eluned's eyes were wide. "Stone circles are two a penny, but I've never seen a meteorite. Do you think we'll have time to see it before we continue?"

Bonpo rose from the bench he occupied. "I go find out Leened." He tromped toward the kitchen and Eluned smiled. It was hard to keep the giant away from where food was being prepared. His curiosity for the cultural variations on local foods knew no bounds. No doubt he would come away from the tavern with yet another recipe or two to add to his repertoire.

"What?" She jumped as Gwrhyr snapped his fingers in front of her face.

"I was just saying that with the full moon tonight, we should be able to find it after our meal, but you were obviously a thousand miles away."

"Just wondering what recipes Bonpo will be angling after in the kitchen."

"Recipes?" asked Chokhmah.

"It seems no matter where we go," Eluned explained, "if someone else is preparing the food, then Bonpo leaves with a recipe or two."

"So cooking, as far as he's concerned, is a joy, not a duty?" Chokhmah asked.

"He really is a marvel. I can still taste those apple turnovers he made the morning we left his inn," Eluned reminisced

"Bonpo owned an inn?" Chokhmah asked, surprised.

"Just below the Mountains of Misericord in my father's kingdom. He left it to join us," Eluned informed her.

"You left behind your inn to travel with Eluned and Jabberwock?" Chokhmah asked Bonpo when he returned to the table.

"Fliend take ova fah me. Mole impoltant forrow where Omni read."

"Then this is more than a search for the thirteen treasures?"

"Yes," Jabberwock began but was interrupted by the kitchen door opening. The group waited in silence as platters of rabbit and lentils, leeks in orange sauce, and potatoes and parsnips mashed together were placed on the table, family style. For a few minutes the only sound was that of the group filling their plates. Once the scullions had returned to the kitchen, Jabberwock continued. "I think most of us feel very strongly that this is an Omni-led quest rather than a self-motivated journey."

"That's true now," the Princess reflected, "but I have to admit that when we first started out I was only interested in the adventure."

"And getting away from your parents," Jabberwock reminded her.

Eluned had the grace to blush. "That's true, but I knew I wouldn't experience anything unless I got far enough away from them. It's probably immature and silly but they were suffocating me. I feel sure that when I return, I'll be able to fulfill my duty whether I want to do so or not."

"But of course you will," Chokhmah assured her.

"Did you find out where the stone circle is?" Eluned asked Bonpo.

"Yes. 'Bout two mire sout'east of inn."

"That's not too bad. Who's going?" Silence. The scullions reappeared and removed the dirty plates and empty platters, returning with a lemon tart and coffee.

"Well," Eluned pouted. "I have Dyrnwyn. I can go by myself."

"Don't be silly," Gwrhyr spoke up, "I have no intention of letting you go alone. If we leave soon, we won't have to spend too much time in the dark."

"What about the full moon?" she reminded him.

"Even with the full moon, we're still strangers here and should be careful," he cautioned her.

"We could ride," Eluned offered.

"The horses are already bedded down for the night. I'm sure we'll be fine. Can you be ready in half an hour?"

"I can be ready in fifteen minutes, maybe less," she said.

"Good. Meet you back here then," he stood up.

"I'd better get my cloak from our room," she told Chokhmah, standing up to take her leave as well.

"Do you really think it's wise to allow her to venture out alone with Gwrhyr?" Jabberwock asked Chokhmah once Eluned had left the room, but there was a twinkle in his transparent eyes.

"Crucial, perhaps," she replied. "She needs to strengthen her bond with him before she meets the Crimson King."

"Yes," the sparkle fizzled. "I understand he can be quite charming."

"And, if the charm does not work, there is always his magic," Chokhmah added.

"He's a powerful adversary," Jabberwock agreed. "I hope that we are up to it."

"We do have Omni on our side," she reminded him.

"Then this may be a night of prayer," he said, jumping down from the bench and trotting over to the small fireplace that no longer seemed quite able to warm the room. He stared into the flames as if trying to divine what lay ahead.

Chokhmah stood, and wishing them a good night returned to the room she shared with Eluned, passing the Princess on her way.

"Be careful, my dear," she said. "Stay close to Gwrhyr. He will not let anything happen to you. I look forward to hearing all about it when you return."

"I will be careful, I promise. Besides," she said, patting the homemade sheath at her side, "I have Dyrnwyn with me."

"It is a fearsome weapon?" Chokhmah asked.

"Oh, it is!" Eluned assured her. "What could go wrong?"

"You are tempting fate." Chokhmah was serious. "You must say: Omni willing, nothing will go wrong."

"Omni willing and the moon doth rise, all will be well," Eluned re-stated the prayer.

"Perfect," Chokhmah smiled.

THE SUN WAS BIDDING THE DAY FAREWELL with an extravagant display of vivid pinks, oranges and yellows as Gwrhyr and Eluned set off from the inn.

"Looks as if it will be a beautiful day tomorrow," Gwrhyr remarked.

"But we won't make it to Prythew by tomorrow night, right?"

"No, but likely the day after tomorrow."

The Princess shuddered. "As I said yesterday, I'm both dreading and looking forward to it. I guess the real question is whether or not King Arawn will take us in."

"Oh, I imagine he'll be positively elated at the prospect of harboring the only child of the King of Zion. I'm more worried about how he's going to feel about the man you ran away with, the so-called boyfriend of the Princess Eluned."

"Well, former, technically, by the time we get there."

"Either way it doesn't bode well for my future," he grimaced.

"Why didn't you say something earlier? We need to come up with a different story."

"Or a reason I'm indispensable," he mused.

"Well, you do know King Uriel, another of his enemies. Maybe you can use that somehow?"

"True. That's a definite possibility. Thank Omni I have another couple of days to think about it."

"I'll try to think of something as well," she murmured, beginning to ponder the dilemma. They walked another twenty minutes in companionable silence, each lost in their own thoughts. The dirt roadway was smooth, the air brisk as the sun's warming rays withdrew, and they were able to walk without much concentration on their surroundings.

"Look," Eluned commanded suddenly, stopping midstride and pointing. Gwrhyr startled at the unexpected interruption.

In the near distance, they could see a ring of stones on

the summit of a hillock overlooking a small lake. The pillars of rock were backlit by the setting sun and seemed to glow an eerie orange.

"They almost look as if they're burning," she said, and Gwrhyr couldn't tell if it was fear or awe he heard in her voice.

Picking up their pace, Gwrhyr and Eluned arrived at the top of the hill in another ten minutes. In the now rapidly fading light, the Princess hurried first to see the meteorite. The dark stone stood just over waist high and looked to be nearly as long as she was. Its depth was only a few feet and she could see why the ancients would have seen it as an altar. She wondered if the stone had fallen first, prompting the standing of the nine stones that encircled it or if it had somehow miraculously fallen into the center of the already standing ring. The latter would be the better story, she thought, climbing atop the altar and stretching out. To take ground that was already holy to someone, she thought, and sanctify it with the addition of a meteorite altar, would no doubt seem god ordained.

"What are you doing?" Gwrhyr asked.

"I was just wondering what it would have felt like lying atop the altar and waiting to be sacrificed."

"Sacrificed?"

"Surely something this ancient would have been used sacrificially, don't you think? Particularly when humans were still offered to appease the gods. I find it difficult to believe nothing was ever sacrificed here. The location is so perfect. I can even see the lake glimmering below me. And what is that?" she pushed herself up on her elbows. "Is that an island in the center of the lake?"

"I don't see anything," Gwrhyr said, squinting into the dimness.

Eluned sat up and peered down at the lake. "It must have been my imagination. I don't see it anymore."

Gwrhyr held out his hand, "Here, get down from there. It's beginning to unnerve me."

"I agree," she said, letting him help her down, "that meteor is freezing. It felt as if the cold was seeping into my bones. Besides, the light is getting spookier. I wish the moon would rise faster."

"Have you seen enough?"

"Let me look at the stones a bit closer, then we can re-turn to the inn. I'm not sure I've ever seen any this tall." She walked over to the closest of the nine megaliths and ran her hand across its pitted surface, still somewhat warm from the late afternoon sun. "Imagine hauling these stones all the way up here," she said, moving counter-clockwise to the next stone. "It must have been hard work."

"No doubt. Are you going to touch every stone?"

"There are only seven more," she admonished. She might have only looked at a couple, but the temptation to aggravate him was too strong. "It won't take that long." She had reached the largest stone, the one that directly overlooked the lake, when she was brought to a standstill by a draft that made the curls around her face dance gently. "Do you smell that?"

"What?"

"Come here," she said, pulling him closer to where she stood next to the pillar. "It smells like . . . flowers?"

He inhaled deeply. "I think you're right but where can it be coming from? And I think I hear music." They listened intently for a few seconds.

"A harp?" she suggested.

"Yes, and, perhaps, a lute?"

"It sounds like it's coming from this stone," she said moving toward the back of it. "Gwrhyr?"

"What?" he asked, following her.

"Is that what I think it is?"

"A door?"

"But, it doesn't seem quite real." She reached out her hand to touch it, and it passed through the image. She remembered the door opening in the barrow what now seemed like ages ago and her knees weakened in fear. Gwrhyr caught her before she crumpled onto the grass of the hill.

"Don't worry," he said, holding her tightly to him. "It's not a Barrow Wight. They use fear, not flowers and music."

"Then what is it?" Her heart was beating rapidly, and she was trying not to panic.

He looked through the doorway. "I don't know. There are steps leading downward."

"That doesn't sound good." The music had taken on a lilting and beckoning tone, and it was taking all Gwrhyr's concentration not to step inside the stone and track the melody to its source. "It wants us to follow it," Eluned spoke as if in a trance. Before he could react, she slipped by him and began to move down the stairs.

"Wait," he said, grabbing her arm. "At least let me go first."

The staircase was narrow and appeared to be descending steeply toward the lake. A pale light glimmered at the bottom but it was too dark to light the top of the stairwell. Gwrhyr braced himself, one hand against each wall, just in case he slipped on the treads of the staircase. The walls were slightly damp but seemed to be made of some kind of plaster. The treads of the staircase, on the other hand, had been worn smooth. Or had they?

"I'm stopping," he told Eluned.

"Why?"

"I want to feel the staircase."

"Whatever for?"

"Doesn't it feel wrong somehow?"

"It feels just like the staircase at home. Oh!"

"Exactly," he said, crouching, and running his hand over the tread. "As I thought."

"It's marble."

"Yes. How does polished marble find its way into the inside of a hill?"

"Magic."

"Definitely not the same hands that erected those crude megaliths." He stood and moved downward again. The pull of his curiosity was now stronger than the lure of the music.

They reached the bottom of the staircase and entered a slightly wider hallway. Candles flickered in the crystal sconces on the wall, lighting their way, but they couldn't see an end to the hallway.

"I feel like we're heading toward the center of the earth." Eluned said as another breeze ruffled her curls. "Exotic."

"Exotic?"

"The scent of the breeze. It smells like the hot house where my mother has the flowers for the castle grown." She inhaled again. "Lavender and lilac, roses and peonies and others I can't identify. Intoxicating."

"We must be getting close. The music is louder as well."

They had now walked far enough that they could see that the hallway was coming to an end and another staircase greeted them, waiting to be ascended.

"We must be in the middle of the lake by now," Gwrhyr noted. "Perhaps you saw an island after all."

"Curiouser and curiouser," she murmured a phrase often used by Jabberwock, and began to mount the stairs.

As with the doorway in the standing stone on the hillock, the doorway onto the island also emerged from a lone standing stone. But, unlike on the lonely hilltop, they were greeted warmly as they appeared, squinting as their eyes adjusted to the dancing firelight and numerous torches that lit the area.

Golden goblets encrusted with precious jewels and brimming with wine were thrust into their hands as they were led toward a dais. The men and women surrounding them were breathtakingly beautiful. Hair of burnished gold or polished ebony, tall and slender with fair features on their ageless faces.

Eluned turned to Gwrhyr, eyes wide with wonder, "Who are they?" she breathed.

"I believe they're faeries," he whispered. "I thought they had disappeared forever."

The faeries seated them at a long table that filled the dais, and plates, filled with the choicest fruits and delicacies, were placed before them.

At once, a particularly striking woman clad entirely in green, stood up and raised her chalice. Glimmering on her wrists were armlets of emeralds and opal stones inset into finely wrought gold. Her hair, which was long and perfectly black, shimmered like silk in its glossiness. It was exquisitely braided and tied about with a cord of crimson ribbon.

Eluned had thought her own skin pale but this faery's face was comparable to ivory for its whiteness and her eyes were so bright they sparkled like jewels. It took her a second to realize that her eyes were as black as her hair, like onyx stones. It was then Eluned realized this maiden was no ordinary faery; that she was of some greater enchantment.

Gwrhyr looked entranced by the jewels that adorned the faery's neck, despite the fact the collar of opal stones and emeralds inset into gold was not greatly dissimilar from the woman's armlets. Eluned watched in disbelief as his eyes traveled upward from the necklace and settled, ardently, on her face. She couldn't honestly say she'd ever seen anyone who could be defined as "lovesick," but pearls of perspiration now decorated his brow and his eyes remained riveted to the faery's face.

The woman had begun speaking, and while she was welcoming them both to the island palace of what she called the Shee, it was clear she only had eyes for Gwrhyr.

Following the toast, and Eluned was forced by politeness to drink from the contents of the goblet, the music started up again. A golden-haired male grabbed her hand and pulled her into the dancing ring where faery couples had already begun swirling to the music.

"Is that your queen?" she asked, indicating the woman

who had spoken and who was now dancing with Gwrhyr on the other side of the ring.

"Cuhvetena? No, not our queen although we do live here at her pleasure."

"I don't understand."

"This is her island, her lake. She was here long before we arrived. We obey the laws she has set but they are few. We are governed, internally, by our own queen, Ffion."

"Do mortals find their way here often?"

"Not so oft as they once did."

Eluned nodded and refrained from asking if they found their way off the island, as well. She could no longer see the door in the standing stone. Had they disappeared forever?

It wasn't long before she lost track of time entirely. Between dances she sipped the ambrosial wine and nibbled on exotic fruits and confections. Every dance featured a new partner, although she noted that Cuhvetena danced exclusively with Gwrhyr. They seemed greatly enamored of each other, and despite the wine and the music and the sense of suspended time, the Princess felt a worm of disquiet wriggling its way through her heart.

She might be able to break from the spell that had been cast as soon as they'd found the open door, but could she pull Gwrhyr away as well? And even if she did, would she be able to reopen the door? Perhaps she should slip away by herself. Surely Jabberwock or Chokhmah would know how to free Gwrhyr from the enchantment.

But how to slip away? She hadn't been alone since she arrived. Her feet should be sore, her bladder full, but that wasn't the case in this world. She couldn't feign exhaustion or ask where to relieve herself. There had to be another way.

But, try as she might, she couldn't seem to steer her dancing partners closer to the standing stone nor was she allowed to sit out an entire dance. Her frustration was mounting, and

Gwrhyr continued to dance, oblivious to anything but Cuhvetena.

When the dance ended, she hurried to the dais to soothe her nerves with a gulp of wine. Her hand was shaking so hard that some of the wine sloshed over the rim and onto the brilliant white tablecloth.

The faeries gasped and Ffion looked at her in wonder. "How is it you are not enchanted?"

Eluned stared into space a moment, pondering the question. "I'm not so sure that it is because I was not enchanted but rather that it's worn off somehow. Does that make sense?"

"You must have a strong reason to return."

Eluned thought of Jabberwock, Bonpo and Chokhmah back at The Pilgrim's Door. Surely one of the three was still awake and wondering what had become of her and Gwrhyr. Perhaps they had awakened each other? What would they do? Would they continue the journey without them? But she was meant to help discover the Thirteen Treasures. Why else would Aeron have led her to the sword? The sword! She nearly panicked but lifting the tablecloth, she could see it was still underneath the table where she had hidden it from prying eyes.

She then considered her parents and how grief-stricken they'd be if they never saw her again. Tears smarted in her eyes and trickled down her face. She dissolved into sobs when she realized that meant she would never see them again either. Never to find the treasures! Never to see her parents! She couldn't take it.

It was one thing to be on the journey of a lifetime knowing her parents were waiting patiently for her to return. Quite another to have disappeared completely—never being able to let them know what had happened to her.

The faeries gathered in front of the dais staring at the Princess in awe and whispering amongst themselves. No human had ever cried once they had reached their magical world.

They turned to Cuhvetena to see how she would handle the situation.

Taking Gwrhyr's proffered arm, she let him squire her back to the dais. He still appeared somewhat bewitched, but Cuhvetena's eyes were both focused and knowing.

"I think it is time you tell me why you are here," she commanded, touching Eluned's cheek where the remains of her weeping still shimmered wetly. "These are the first tears I've seen," she paused, trying to remember as she rubbed the salty liquid between forefinger and thumb, "in what might as well be millennia. It has been a very long time since I have crossed over to the other side. Naught but pain and sorrow there."

"We didn't know," the Princess was defensive. "I just wanted to see the meteorite, and then I saw the door in the stone..."

"And by then you had no choice but to follow the music. Yes, I know. I was asking why you are in Ruisidho to begin with. You don't look like a pilgrim to me."

Eluned swallowed hard. How much should she say? "Always best to stick as close to the truth as possible," she heard the voices of both Jabberwock and Chokhmah advise her simultaneously. She almost jumped they seemed so close, but they were only in her mind.

"We are on our way to Prythew."

"And what is in Prythew?"

"King Arawn."

Cuhvetena looked surprised or, at least, Eluned assumed that's what the slight raising of her eyebrows indicated.

"And what does a beautiful young woman like you seek in the Court of the Crimson King?"

It was Eluned's turn to look surprised, and she had a more difficult time hiding it. Cuhvetena laughed, and the sound was so provocative that even the Princess felt chills coursing up her legs. "Just because I choose not to leave this world does not mean I do not keep abreast of what is happening in the other.

You do not strike me as the type of maiden who would seek his consort."

"I, uh, it's so complicated," she looked to Gwrhyr for help but he seemed ignorant of where he was, much less what was going on. Cuhvetena noticed, of course, and with a mumbled word and a quick caress released the young man from his enchantment.

He looked at Eluned's dolorous eyes and tear-stained cheeks and saw the eyes of dozens of faeries, as well as those of Cuhvetena, set expectantly on his face, and he colored. "What did I do this time?" he moaned.

The sound of their laughter blended melodically and Gwrhyr felt his cheeks flame. The Princess finally took pity on him, and hurrying around the table, she stepped off the platform, throwing herself into his arms. "It's good to have you back," she hugged him. "I was beginning to fear I'd never see you again."

"I don't understand."

"Not literally. I meant that you were no longer you. You were off in another world. And the latter I mean literally."

Gwrhyr managed to look even more baffled.

Cuhvetena laughed. "I think she's trying to say that you were completely under my spell, while she somehow managed to cast it off."

"I was trying to explain to her why we were at the stone circle to begin with," she hinted.

His eyes widened as it all came back to him—the stone circle and meteorite, the standing stone with the open door, the music, the stairs and being greeted by the faeries. And then they were drinking and dancing and then it was all a blur until the moment he found himself the object of some joke he could not fathom.

He touched Eluned's cheek where the tears had nearly dried. "So, why were you crying?"

"I was afraid I would never see my parents or Jabberwock or Bonpo or Chokhmah again."

Gwrhyr turned to Cuhvetena. "Was that a possibility?"

"Very possibly. But it had to be more than fear of never again seeing loved ones to break the spell." Eluned looked searchingly at Gwrhyr who in turn noticed the intense curiosity on the faces of the faeries that surrounded them.

"Where is the sword?" he asked the Princess.

"Do you want me to get it?" Her expression conveyed her ambivalence.

"Yes," he assured her. "I believe it will help explain everything."

She returned to the dais and pulled the sword in its makeshift sheath from beneath the table. As the faeries made room for her, she pulled it from the sheath, and was surprised by the collective gasp.

"Dyrnwyn," Cuhvetena breathed. "The sword of Rhydderch. I haven't seen it in many, many years. How did it come to be in your possession?"

"Maybe we should start at the beginning," Gwrhyr suggested.

"Then I'd love to sit down," Eluned said.

"Follow me," commanded Cuhvetena. "We will speak in my chambers. They are much more comfortable and much less crowded. Ffion, Gwyn, you come along as well. Llinos, Cian, bring us refreshment."

Llinos and Cian bowed their acquiescence and hurried off to do Cuhvetena's bidding. The Princess, Gwrhyr, the Faery Queen and Gwyn followed her past the standing stone and into a small cave lit by torches.

A set of stairs hewn from stone brought them into a much wider cavern, also lit by torchlight and candles and a small fire that crackled cheerily in the center of the floor. The smoke from the fire swirled upwards and disappeared through a small hole as it reached the roof of the cave. Ornate tapestries covered the walls and thick carpets, the floors. A number of large cushions were scattered on the rugs around the fire pit and Cuhvetena invited her guests to recline there as they waited for Llinos and Cian.

It did not take long for the pair to return laden with wine as well as with bread, cheese and fruit.

"What's so funny," the Princess began after taking a sip of the ruby red wine, "is that while it feels like this journey began ages ago, in truth Jabberwock and I left my home a mere fortnight ago."

"I agree that this all seems fated somehow," Cuhvetena agreed as Eluned and Gwrhyr finished their story, "but why does the possession of two of the thirteen treasures lead you to believe that you can find the other eleven?"

"Three," Eluned corrected.

"You mentioned only two."

"I have two in my possession—the ring and the sword—but King Uriel is said to have inherited the Mantle of Arthur. Isn't that correct, Gwrhyr?"

"And how do you come by this knowledge," Cuhvetena asked Gwrhyr.

"I am in his employ."

"You're his spy, admit it." Eluned said, lightly punching his arm.

"In a manner of speaking," he allowed.

"And he made you aware of this for what reason?" Cuhvetena pursued.

Gwrhyr looked extremely uncomfortable, but politely refused to answer, explaining that he was allowed to reveal nothing more than that.

"Handsome and mysterious," Cuhvetena teased.

"I apologize but I am bound to say no more," he said.

"And Arawn is said to have how many? Two, three of these treasures?" Cuhvetena mused.

"As many as three," Gwrhyr affirmed. "My information is that he possesses the Chessboard of Gwenddolau and the Chariot of Morgan the Wealthy. And, it is also thought that the Halter of Clydno Eiddyn is somewhere in his kingdom, although it hasn't been seen in a long time."

"And with nearly half the treasures under the sovereignty of the Kingdoms of Zion and Aden, would that be enough to offset the balance of power?"

"That's our hope. There is only one treasure remaining in an allied kingdom. The Coat of Padarn is said to be in Favonia. But, two of the treasures—the crock and the dish and the Knife of Llawfrodded—are in neutral countries. Well, according to our information, anyway. That could give us as many as nine."

"Wait," Eluned interrupted. "What kingdoms?"

"The crock and the dish are said to be in Naphtali," he said.

"And the knife?" Cuhvetena asked.

Gwrhyr swallowed hard. "The Devastation of Pelf."

"The Devastation!" the Princess cried. "How are we going to find the knife in The Devastation?"

"We'll burn that bridge when we get to it." Gwrhyr's voice was grim.

"Don't you mean cross?" Eluned's brow creased in puzzlement.

"It's The Devastation of Pelf," Gwrhyr explained. "It's probably already burned. Either way, mixing our metaphors, so to speak, may be the only way of solving that problem."

"Well, that will be the final treasure we seek, I say," she shuddered.

"No argument here," he agreed. "We still have to relieve Arawn of his three treasures. We have a long way to go."

Eluned sighed, and nodded.

"And where are the other four?" Cuhvetena asked.

"My research says that the whetstone is in Simoon, the Hamper of Gwyddno is in Adamah, the Horn of Bran is in Kamartha, and the cauldron is in Dziron," Gwrhyr answered.

"Scattered around the Thirteen Kingdoms, in other words," Cuhvetena noted.

"Unfortunately, yes," he agreed.

"It would be wonderful to see the Kingdoms reunited in peace." Cuhvetena looked as if she were remembering a time long since lost to history. "And it seems increasingly evident that you are the ones fated to do so or, at least, to help bring it about." She stood up. "I've kept you here long enough. It is time you continue on your journey. I will escort you back to the stone circle."

AS THEY MADE THE SHORT TREK between worlds, Cuhvetena unclasped the opal and emerald necklace from around her neck, and slipped it into the pocket of Gwrhyr's cloak. When Gwrhyr opened his mouth to question her, she put a finger to her lips and whispered, "It may become necessary at some point to use this. You will see."

The door in the stone swung open in silence just as Eluned's foot reached the top step. She stumbled blindly into the sunlight and Gwrhyr caught her from behind as she tripped over a boulder.

"We're definitely back," he laughed, and turned to say farewell to Cuhvetena. But the door had already closed, and it was hard to believe an opening had ever been present.

"I guess we weren't gone as long as I thought," Eluned said. "It's only noon."

"Then if we hurry we might make it back before the others get too worried," he said.

In the bright light of the noonday sun, the path was much clearer and they made it to the bottom of the hill much more quickly than when they had climbed it the previous evening. "We should be there in no time," Eluned said, trying not to skip. She was so glad to be back in her world she almost felt like dancing. Almost.

THEY HAD JUST ROUNDED A CURVE in the road when Gwrhyr abruptly threw his arm out, and Eluned ran into it full force.

"Oompf," she grunted as her abdomen received the brunt of the contact. "Why did you do that?"

"What the . . .?" He was staring at the empty field next to the inn. Except it was no longer empty. Several tents had been set up on its weed-covered surface. A standard emblazoned with King Arawn's coat of arms, with its telltale crimson dragon, stood outside each tent. A light breeze ruffled the banners, and the sun glinted off the bronze finials.

"Is that who I think it is?" Eluned asked.

"I doubt it is the king, himself. Most likely just his men. Looks like we've been sent a welcoming party."

"Word travels fast," she marveled.

"Perhaps we were gone longer than we realized. It was going to take us two more days to get to Prythew. It would have been impossible for Arawn to be notified, and send out a guard to escort us back in a little over a day."

"Maybe the guards at the tollbooth sent a pigeon," Eluned guessed.

"True," Gwrhyr nodded. "That might explain it."

"Jabb must be frantic," the Princess worried.

Gwrhyr took a deep breath. "Well, the only way we'll know is by continuing. You ready?"

The Princess swallowed, hard, her fear of being militarily escorted to the king warring with her need to assure Jabberwock (and Bonpo and Chokhmah) that they were still among the living.

"Yes," she said, steeling herself, "let's get it over with."

BONPO SIGHTED THEM FIRST, his height definitely an advantage in this case. "Leened!" he boomed, raising his arms high over his head and waving. The relief in his voice was evident even from a distance.

Eluned picked up her speed but couldn't quite bring herself to run. Part of her wanted to turn and scamper back to Cuhvetena and the faeries.

The giant was now ambling toward them, taking full advantage of his long gait. Jabberwock, Chokhmah, and several soldiers followed close behind.

"You'd think we'd been gone a year," she grumbled to Gwrhyr. Half a minute later, Bonpo reached them and swept the tiny Princess into his arms. Despite his strength, his hug was gentle, and he returned Eluned to the roadbed unharmed. The Gypsy and the Bandersnatch arrived next. "We have been so worried," she said, embracing Eluned. "We were beginning to think you that you had disappeared forever."

"How long have we been gone?" Gwrhyr asked.

"It has been a week since you left the inn."

"A week?" Eluned's knees went weak with shock and she swayed. Gwrhyr slid an arm about her waist to help support her. "It felt like hours, not days."

"I must admit, I lost all sense of time," Gwrhyr added.

"He was enchanted," Eluned added, as if imparting a great secret.

"You were too," he scolded. "You were the one who thought we'd only been gone overnight, remember?"

"Well," she stamped her foot and pulled away from him, "if it hadn't been for me we would still be there dancing our feet to the bone."

The soldiers had arrived and were watching their bickering with obvious amusement.

"You don't know that," Gwrhyr retorted. "Just because you broke free of the enchantment first, doesn't mean I wouldn't have eventually fought it off myself."

Eluned rolled her eyes. "As I recall, Cuhvetena had to release you from the spell."

"How did you break free?" Chokhmah asked with genuine interest.

"I'm not really sure. I just know I was worried, and then I was afraid I would never see you all or my parents again, and then I started crying."

"Apparently tears are a rare commodity in Faeryland," Gwrhyr's tone was drier than the Devastation of Pelf.

"Whatever," Eluned rolled her eyes again. "It worked, didn't it?"

"Absolutely," he agreed. "I'm just saying that it was an unintentional benefit."

"Fine. Fine," she said around a huge yawn. "Omni but I'm suddenly exhausted. I think the night's catching up with me." One of the soldiers stepped forward and saluted her. "Captain Bleddyn, Your Royal Highness. His Majesty King Arawn has sent us to escort you to Prythew."

"Thank you," she replied and yawned again. "Is it possible for us to begin the journey in the morning after a good night's sleep? Please? You could dispatch a messenger or a pigeon immediately to let him know we will arrive in Prythew the day after tomorrow. Surely a few more hours can hardly matter at this point?"

Captain Bleddyn nodded curtly to the man behind him who in turn headed back toward the camp at a brisk jog. "As you wish, Ma'am," he said turning back to the Princess. "We will be ready to leave at first light."

"Thank you," she inclined her head in acknowledgement. "I think I hear a bed calling my name."

4ᵀᴴ FEHARN

True to his word, Captain Bleddyn had them up and out just as dawn broke the following morning. Fortunately for the Princess and Gwrhyr, in particular, Bonpo had arisen even earlier and prepared them a hearty breakfast.

Eluned had been ravenous when she was awakened in the darkness of pre-dawn. If Chokhmah hadn't assured her that she had been gone for a week, she would have begun to doubt that her trip beneath the lake had ever taken place. Her hunger also helped persuade her. She was no longer sure when they had last eaten, but she had fallen into a deep sleep as soon as she crawled into bed the previous afternoon. She imparted to Chokhmah in more detail what had transpired during their trip to the stone circle and then beneath the mountain while she washed up and changed into her nightgown.

She had no sooner pulled the covers up beneath her chin and closed her eyes before it seemed she was being gently shaken awake.

"But I just went to sleep," she mumbled, trying to turn over.

"No, my dear, the night has passed, and we must be on the road in an hour."

THEY NOW RODE TOWARD PRYTHEW with Captain Bleddyn and two of his soldiers in the lead, and the remainder of his troops taking up the rear guard with the tents and other supplies in tow.

The Princess was thankful that the five of them had been allowed to travel together but other than idle talk they weren't really free to converse with each other. Too many flies on the walls, so to speak, Gwrhyr had noted grimly. She was no longer sure they had their story straight and she'd never had a chance to come up with an alternate that wouldn't leave Gwrhyr at risk.

It all depended on how much autocracy she would be allowed once they arrived. Would she be able to just put her foot down and demand that her retinue was indispensable to her—that they must remain with her? She sighed, deeply. It was in Omni's hands now.

She looked up to find Gwrhyr watching her, his face an impenetrable mask. He edged Heiduc closer and placed his large work-roughened hand over her smaller and paler fist, which was gripping the pommel of her saddle. He gave it a reassuring squeeze and nodded.

She smiled, tentatively. He was right. Everything really was going to work out. It just had to.

ABOUT AN HOUR BEFORE NOON, several of the soldiers, along with a pack mule, trotted ahead and soon disappeared from sight. When they caught up with them about half an hour later, a meal had already been prepared for them.

It was simple—a bean soup garnished with large chunks of ham, bread, cheese, apples—but quite palatable, and within half an hour they were back on the road again.

SOMEHOW, IN THE EXCITEMENT OF THEIR RETURN, the soldiers had failed to notice the makeshift scabbard that bumped clumsily against her leg. She had been in her pants and jerkin when she'd returned from beneath the hill, and no doubt that had been enough of a shock to keep them silent.

That morning she had dressed in her black wool skirt and white flannel blouse again, carefully securing the provisional scabbard with its precious sword against her left hip and thigh, beneath the skirt. Eluned hoped the grey wool cloak helped to disguise it even more. The last thing they needed was for King Arawn to take possession of it. What worried her the most was her scabbard-less sword. It was her wish that when they finally reached Prythew, she would be able to find, or at least have made, a real scabbard. But, she guessed, that would also depend on how much freedom they were allowed.

All she knew for sure is that she was ready to be in one place for a little while. The constant travel and adventure of the past few weeks had left her weary. And what was worse, she had lost an entire week of her life dancing. That was a week that would be forever deducted from her three years of freedom. Eluned sighed, deeply. Would this day never end?

THEY RODE UNTIL SHORTLY AFTER SUNSET, and the soldiers readied dinner by torchlight. The Princess would have preferred to be able to crawl into her tent as soon as possible and hide herself, but they were ordered to sleep beneath the stars so that they might make an earlier start the following morning. Eluned tried to hide her grouchiness as she would now either have to sleep with the sword still attached to her leg or risk being seen removing and reattaching it. Needless to say, she spent an uncomfortable night lying on her back and studying the constellations, sleeping in snatches, waking when her body forbade her to turn over onto her left side. Despite the fact she was left-handed, she knew enough to know that one's sword belonged on the left hip. It never occurred to her that that was also her favorite side to sleep on. She tried at one point to sleep on her right side, but the weight of the sword pressed uncomfortably into her hip and leg. She silently cursed gravity, and waited for the endless night of the seemingly endless day to draw to a close.

Yet, as always, the earth continued to spin on its axis, the moon continued to orbit the earth, and the earth continued its journey around the sun. So eventually another night passed, and as the velvety black sky transmuted into a deep blue, the soldiers began to stir, and after gulping down bitter black coffee and cold biscuits, they were once more on the road.

AS THEY APPROACHED THE CITY, the sandy brown soil around them began to take on an orange-like hue as it made the transition to the red rock the area was famed for. It was a beautiful but forbidding landscape. Huge sections of tilted and striated rock loomed from the earth like great monsters frozen in the process of escaping their earthly bonds.

The walls and towers of the city seemed to float in the far distance in a hazy, reddish mist. Eluned wondered if the red landscape was the reason Arawn was known as the Crimson King. She'd been under the impression it was because he was somehow malevolent but maybe it was more than that. The Princess once again felt her chest constricting in fear. She would soon discover for herself the mystery that was Arawn. Every step brought them closer to Prythew and she found herself praying earnestly for Omni to save her from the time of trial and deliver her from evil.

IN THE END, THEIR ARRIVAL AT THE CASTLE PWYLL was anti-climactic. The red rock had given away to fertile hills and forests bisected by a lovely river and numerous meadows and fields. The castle and its village sat atop an almost monadnock-like mountain that rose from the valley floor and towered above the surrounding area. Crimson dragons on pennants of white fluttered from the castle's walls and its four towers.

They were shuttled directly to their quarters and instructed to be in the dining room at noon, which left them just over an hour to freshen up and rest. As soon as the servant who had escorted them to the room took her leave (the males had been taken separately), Eluned turned to survey her accommodations.

The room was really quite lovely. A canopied bed took up most of one wall. It looked extremely inviting—a lavender silk duvet held a plump down comforter, and numerous pillows in accent colors of sea green and pale pink were scattered against the padded headboard. She wanted to draw the curtains and sleep for the next twelve hours.

Turning away with a sigh, she moved toward the fireplace where a small fire crackled and danced, adding a bit of warmth to the room. Eluned warmed her hands for a moment before crossing to the window. It was tall and narrow with latticed leaded glass. Despite the chill outside, she opened the window to see what view it offered. Below her window, a labyrinth cut from shrubbery could be seen. In its center, she could see a small gazebo surrounded by rose bushes that had been pruned back for winter. She couldn't wait to explore it.

As the castle stood atop the highest point around, Eluned's vantage point was well above the town that crowded against the stronghold's walls. She could see over the ramparts to the outlying farms in the distance and the cloud shrouded mountains beyond them.

Chokhmah joined her at the window. "It is quite striking, is it not?"

"Breathtaking, really. How's your room?" Eluned nodded toward the door to her left.

"A much smaller version of yours," Chokhmah confirmed.

"Servants quarters in other words."

"Indeed. But adequately appointed."

"I'm sorry," the Princess apologized. "I'm sure assumptions were made."

"Exactly as we wished."

"True," Eluned said, "but I still dislike it. Is there a privy?"

"There is an actual bathroom that we share."

"It has a bathtub?"

"Yes, and running water."

"Luxury! Well," Eluned said, closing the window against a nippy breeze, "if we make it through lunch, I hope I can look forward to a hot bath and a long nap this afternoon."

"Agreed," Chokhmah yawned. "I did not sleep well last night, either."

"Should I go ahead and assume we'll be here awhile and unpack?" Eluned asked, crossing to the wardrobe on the other side of her bed.

"If nothing else, it might be nice to hang and air our clothing."

"Or lack thereof," Eluned grumbled pulling the soiled clothing from her bag. Only the green skirt and blouse were still clean although somewhat wrinkled.

She opened the wardrobe and gasped. Three brand new dresses were already hanging within. "I, uh, how? I don't understand." Chokhmah joined her, withdrawing one of the gowns and holding it against the Princess.

"It is your size exactly."

"How could he know?"

"I suspect gold can buy all sorts of information," Chokhmah's mouth twisted in disapproval, "and he has known for more than a week that you were on your way."

"Hmmm. I don't know whether to be flattered or frightened."

"I suspect both," Chokhmah chuckled. "At least we now know that he does not intend to banish or kill us immediately."

"Kill?"

"I am joking. It would be very unwise to kill the daughter of his enemy unless he is already prepared for war. And, I surmise, that his kingdom is not quite at that point yet."

"That's good," Eluned replied, clearly distracted by the

other two gowns. The frock Chokhmah held featured an empire-waisted overdress of deep midnight blue velvet trimmed in gold and an ivory brocade underdress. Ivory silk ribbon laced up the back of the dress as well as the velvet over-sleeves. The front of the dress opened from the waist to reveal the brocade underdress beneath it.

Eluned pulled the second dress from the wardrobe. The three-piece gown featured a double-lined bodice of creamy dupioni silk that shimmered with undertones of blues and greens and laced up the front with ribbons of periwinkle blue.

The full chemise sleeves were the same periwinkle satin as the underskirt and gathered at the wrist with several rows of eggshell lace. Even more lace, intricately woven, adorned the neckline.

"Beautiful," Chokhmah breathed, replacing the blue velvet dress and removing the third gown. While perhaps the simplest of the three, it was also the most striking. It was also velvet, but it was clearly designed to hug every curve on Eluned's small frame. The drop-waist dress featured a deep V at its neckline, and the tight sleeves also fell to a point with a small hole through which she was clearly to slide the middle finger of each hand. The Princess wasn't sure they could make a fabric blacker than the black of this one and the diamonds that embellished the hip-section of the dress glittered like a thousand twinkling stars.

Eluned nearly choked, managing to blush at the same time. "I can't believe this dress is decorated with real diamonds. I'm not sure I'll ever be able to wear it," she indicated the plunging neckline.

"I am sure you will not have a choice," Chokhmah warned her. "I would not be surprised if the king intends to order when and where you shall wear them."

"Really?" She looked mortified.

"Mark my words."

The Princess suddenly turned and dashed into Chokhmah's room, throwing open the much smaller wardrobe. Just one plain dress of greyish-yellow linsey-woolsey hung from the small bar. The thought of seeing her brightly garbed gypsy friend in such drab clothing brought tears to her eyes.

"I am so sorry," she said, wrapping her friend in a heart felt embrace. "If I had known, I would never have begged for you to join us."

"Do not be silly, my dear," Chokhmah said, stroking Eluned's curls. "I knew full well what I was getting myself into. Perhaps we met as friends, but I knew I was taking on the role of servant. And, believe me, my dear, it is only a role to me, no more. And I must play it well."

"I'll make it up to you some day, I promise."

"I am sure you will. But for now, I will let you do your own unpacking while I complete mine. Then we must go to lunch." Eluned returned to her room and discovered that in addition to the dresses there were several pairs of shoes to match them, as well as a couple of long and virginal flannel nightgowns in a small flower print and a soft flannel robe. She threw her dirty things in a pile on the floor in the hope she could later send them to be laundered. What little remained in her bag she put away in the wardrobe and in the bathroom.

Then she took a few minutes to find a spot in which to hide her journal. There was a desk beside the window with a small drawer with a key protruding from its lock. She put the diary in there, turned the key and removed it. The key she put in the small pouch that remained always around her neck.

The next question was even more important. Where in Omni's name was she going to hide the sword?

"Chokhmah!" she called.

"Yes, my dear?" she asked, stepping into the room.

"What are we going to do with this?" Chokhmah studied the sword for a minute. "I think I have an idea. Come." Eluned followed her back into her room.

"In your wardrobe?"

"No, of course not. I was thinking we might be able to slide it behind the armoire. If you could help me pull it out a bit?" The walnut wardrobe sat heavily on the floor and the women worked slowly to inch the heavy piece of furniture away from the wall.

"This is a time when I'd be especially thankful for Bonpo's strength," Eluned grunted. "This isn't going to work," she realized after they'd moved it an inch or so. "The hilt's too big. If anyone comes in the room, they'll be able to see that the wardrobe's sitting several inches away from the wall."

"You are right, of course. I can see that now. Do you suppose they dust the top of it?" They pushed the armoire back against the wall and surveyed it. It was tall, at least six feet, but the top was flat. From the right angle it would be seen easily.

"What about the wardrobe in my room? It's fancier. If the top isn't dusted, maybe the decoration at the top will hide the sword from view."

They hurried into her room and Eluned grabbed the chair that sat at the desk and carried it over to the armoire. Standing on the chair, she was barely tall enough to see the top of the wardrobe. She climbed down. "You look. You're taller," she told Chokhmah.

"Oh look, not only does the carved piece hide the top, but there is a good two inches all around." She dipped her finger over the side and rubbed. She held it up for the Princess to see. It was covered in dust.

Eluned smiled. "Perfect. I'll take the ropes off but I want to leave it wrapped in the blanket," Eluned said. "I don't want to risk it getting scratched."

"I doubt very much that would happen," Chokhmah said, "but I feel safer knowing it is covered."

Eluned handed the blanket-wrapped sword to Chokhmah who lowered it carefully onto the top of the wardrobe before climbing down from the chair.

As Eluned carried the chair back to the desk, there was a brief but loud rap on her door. She jumped in surprise, but Chokhmah was already opening the door. It was Gwrhyr. It was time to head to the dining room.

Bonpo was with him but Jabberwock was not there. Still playing the "dog" she noted to herself. Safer for the moment, she supposed.

"Are you all in the same room?" she asked, thinking of herself and Chokhmah.

"More like soldiers' quarters," Gwrhyr groused.

"Really? Seems like they'd need a room with a bigger bed for Bonpo."

"Dey bling me big matt'ress," he explained.

"Really, it's not that bad. Definitely not as nice as your room, though," Gwrhyr said, looking over her shoulder. Are you ready?"

"Yes," she said, slipping out the door. She decided not to tell him about the gowns. He would find out about them in due time. It occurred to her that though they were eating together now (she assumed because they were about to meet Arawn), that they might not do so in the future if he and Bonpo and Jabb had been placed in quarters rather than in a guest room like hers. They were clearly being put in their places.

But, when they reached the dining room they discovered that not only was King Arawn not there but that it was clearly a servants' area.

The woman who served them was taciturn and clearly disapproving as she served them mutton stew. She left the room as quietly as she had entered it.

"Power play," Gwrhyr said, disguising it with a cough. Everyone nodded agreement, disinclined to speak. Eluned felt as if her every move was being watched. She shivered and reached for the freshly baked bread. It was still steaming as she tore a piece for herself and handed the loaf to Chokhmah. She spooned some of the stew into her mouth. It was actually quite good, but she couldn't bring herself to say so.

THE GROUP LINGERED OUTSIDE THE DOOR to the women's rooms after lunch, drawing as much comfort as possible from being together.

"Do you think we'll ever meet the king?" Eluned asked, still keeping her voice down. She didn't know the castle well enough yet to trust whether or not Arawn could easily have them being spied upon.

"I would think, considering the sleeping arrangements, that you'll be summoned to dinner on your own, first." Gwrhyr said.

Eluned blanched. On her own! "What do I say? I don't know what to do. We never . . ." her voice began rising in panic.

"Calm down, my love," Chokhmah slid her arm around Eluned's shoulders. "We will figure it out."

"But, if say that I ran away with Gwrhyr, won't that put him in danger?"

"Perhaps it's best if we go back to the original story— that you ran away on your own with the help of Jabberwock," Gwrhyr proposed. Maybe Arawn needs to know the truth about the Bandersnatch; that you were so anxious to get away that you didn't think of bringing a human with you."

"True. And that I gathered the rest of you as we traveled because I desperately needed your help?" Eluned added.

"It may still leave us in danger," Gwrhyr scowled, "but at least it is closer to the truth. What do you think Chokhmah?"

"I agree. Of course, at this point he is unlikely to get rid of her maidservant."

"If necessary, I will beg for your lives," Eluned promised. "I can't imagine, though, that in terms of diplomacy, and no matter what his reputation, that King Arawn would risk imprisoning or even executing any of you."

"Let's hope you're right," Gwrhyr grunted, rubbing his neck in anticipation of the noose, or worse, an ax.

"I'll die first," the Princess promised. "I won't let any harm come to you all."

"Tank you, Plincess," Bonpo smiled, giving her shoulder a gentle squeeze. "I tink we need go tell pran to Jabb."

"Good idea. The sooner the better in case he has any objections."

"Well, until I am summoned," Eluned said. "I am going to take a hot bath followed by a nap. I am exhausted."

"Excellent idea," agreed Chokhmah. "We could all probably use a little rest."

AND SUMMONED SHE WAS. Late that afternoon a page knocked on the door and handed Chokhmah a small envelope addressed to the Princess.

Eluned had just awakened and was sitting up in bed, yawning. Chokhmah handed her the vellum envelope sealed with red wax bearing the dragon sigil of Annewven. The Princess read it and snickered.

"What is it, my dear?"

"I'm not sure what I find more amusing in this," and she read: "His Royal Highness King Arawn requests the pleasure of your company at dinner tonight. You will be escorted to the dining room at seven o'clock."

"Amusing?" Chokhmah asked.

"Well, he says 'requests' and then tells me when I will be escorted to the dining room, and it also seems somewhat pompous. I mean, if I don't actually have a choice, why didn't he just tell the page to let me know I'd be having dinner with the king at seven o'clock?"

"Perhaps this is the most polite he could manage to be?"

"Great. And, somehow I get the feeling that I will be the only one of us attending this 'dinner.'"

"Well, my love, better sooner than later. At least we will soon know which way the wind blows."

"True," she sighed. "I guess I need to choose one of his dresses to wear. At least he didn't order me to wear a certain dress. Yet." Eluned slid out of bed and opened the armoire. As the black velvet wasn't even an option, she assessed the relative modesty of the blue velvet versus the periwinkle silk. "I think I'll go with the blue velvet. I'll be the least self conscious wearing it, and I have a feeling I am going to have to have my wits about me."

"Doubtless. Would you like me to help you arrange your hair? It probably needs to be a little more elaborate than your basic pony tail and I imagine it would be expected considering you have a maidservant."

Eluned blushed. Funny, had she brought Chokhmah with her from Zion, she wouldn't give it a second thought. But, the fact that they had met as friends made it difficult for her to treat the gypsy as a servant. Although, in truth, she'd been waiting on her since they first met. But that was different. She looked forward to finding the three treasures and bidding adieu to this place.

THE PRINCESS DIDN'T KNOW WHAT SHE WAS EXPECTING but when she entered the dining room and King Arawn turned to greet her, she felt her her pulse begin to race and the air rushed from her lungs. A lovely blush colored her cheeks.

"Princess Eluned," he said, taking her hand in his and raising it to his lips. The feather touch of his lips against the back of her palm sent a shiver down her spine and she found herself blushing yet again. He led her to her seat, even going so far as to pull out her chair, while she sucked in deep breaths (quietly, she hoped) in an effort to calm down.

After all the terrible things she had heard inferred about this man, not to mention the fact he was thirty-three, she was surprised to find herself attracted to him. It didn't even occur to her that he might think of an eighteen-year-old as a little girl.

She found she couldn't keep her eyes off him. It wasn't that he was tall or overly muscular, which is what she'd always considered perfection, rather he was average height and slender. It was really his face that was so striking. It was framed by long flowing hair the color of burnished copper. She had never seen hair so long. On a man, anyway. And his eyes were huge. Mesmerizing. And the most beautiful bronze she'd ever seen. She could get lost in his eyes. He had an aquiline nose and a mouth that did, indeed, seem cruel in that it turned down naturally and his lips were rather thin.

And, as a server placed crepes bursting with beluga caviar and crème fraîche before them, she found herself struggling for something to say. She took a gulp from the flute of sparkling wine before her—liquid courage.

She need not have worried. Arawn was adept at making small talk and before she knew it, she was finishing her salade frisée and taking her first bite of a roast fillet of beef with black peppercorns surrounded by oil-roasted potatoes and green beans. They were now drinking a red wine the color of rubies and Eluned discovered her tongue was becoming looser by the second. By the time dessert arrived, she could manage only a bite or two of her amaretto soufflé with chocolate sauce. Arawn then suggested they retire to a parlor where they could sit in front of a fire and be more comfortable.

Eluned was more than willing to draw out this visit as long as possible. Despite the abundance of alcohol, the Princess was keenly aware that she couldn't endanger her friends. As Arawn listened, with a polite expression of interest on his striking face, Eluned explained how desperate she had been to get away from home before she was forced to marry King Uriel and how Jabberwock, her tutor for the past eleven years, had helped her to escape, and . . .

"I thought that must be the legendary Bandersnatch. I believe I have heard tales of how he helped your great-grand-mother escape," Arawn interrupted.

"Queen Fuchsia, yes." She had forgotten that particular tie in. Well, that was certainly in their favor. "But, Jabberwock thought my father might look in the direction of Kamartha, for obvious reasons, and so we headed east instead. It wasn't until our first night out that I realized it probably wasn't wise for a single woman, a Princess no less, to be traveling alone with a 'dog.' So, we agreed to start keeping a look out for possible companions, particularly a maid servant."

"So, the giant?"

"Bonpo. He agreed to come along as our porter and cook."

"And the other young man?"

"Gwrhyr has been invaluable because of his knowledge of languages, among other things. Sometimes I think there isn't anything that man doesn't know," she groused.

"So not your secret lover?"

Eluned blushed. Ah, the original story they had told crossing the border. "No. We just wanted to be able to enter Annewven and it sounded like a good way to be granted permission."

Arawn nodded. "And the gypsy?"

"Chokhmah. We happened upon the gypsy camp near the River Mab. Chokhmah is a widow and was willing to become my maidservant."

"And so now I must ask, why here? Why not the Favonian Islands?"

"I was afraid if I ran to an ally, my father would insist that I be returned immediately."

"And what if I ransom you?"

"That's certainly within your purview. I was just trying to buy myself time. I didn't want to be stuck in Zion and then in Aden for the rest of my life. I wanted a chance to explore, to see the world for myself."

Arawn chuckled. "You are most certainly not your run-of-the-mill princess."

"Thank you. I think."

He smiled at her, and she felt her breath catch in her throat again.

"I must take some time to think about all this," he stood. "If you'll excuse me, I will speak to you about this again on the morrow. I have to prepare for a day of meetings beginning first thing in the morning. Feel free to explore the castle."

"Thank you," she breathed, heart thumping madly. The way his mouth had curled at the corner when he said explore made her want to kiss it.

He rang a bell, and a page hurried into the room. He nodded to him and the page bowed.

"Good night, Princess."

"Good night," she replied, unsure whether to call him King Arawn or Arawn or sir or your majesty.

She was deep in thought when she arrived back at her room, and was shocked to find it crowded with her friends. Bonpo sat on the floor in front of the fireplace along with Jabberwock, and Gwrhyr and Chokhmah were sitting in the two armchairs that faced the dancing flames.

Eluned gaped at the group, hand still on the handle of the door. "What the . . ." She had been so looking forward to returning to her room so she could slide into bed and replay the evening in her mind.

Instead, her friends were looking at her expectantly.

"Well?" Gwrhyr finally prompted. "Are you going to tell us what happened?" He stood up, indicating his chair before crossing to the desk and carrying its chair over to sit on. And, of course, he placed it right next to her chair, she noticed.

Eluned begrudgingly walked over to the armchair and threw herself into it. What had she expected, really? Of course they were curious about their fate. Why wouldn't they be?

"I'm not sure where to begin," she groused. The alcohol was making her drowsy although she hadn't had quite enough to make her sloppy. She had been careful about that.

"Try the beginning, my dear," Chokhmah prodded.

But it was Bonpo's eyes that made her sit up straighter in the plush armchair and take their curiosity seriously. He looked so fearful but at the same time it was clear he trusted her implicitly. She smiled at him in an attempt to reassure him and began, "Well, the truth is, nothing much really happened." At least as far as you all are concerned, she thought with not a little guilt. She'd been too focused on her attraction to the king to think of much else.

So she told them about the meal, the small talk, and then the final conversation in the parlor.

"In other words, we won't know anything at all until tomorrow night?" Gwrhyr stated in disgust.

"Well, at the very least, it prolongs our lives another day," Chokhmah offered.

"Always the optimist," Gwrhyr smiled at her.

"Until then, he told me I could explore the castle," Eluned added.

"You can explore the castle?" Jabberwock asked. "Not us?"

"Well, he didn't say you couldn't. As a matter of fact, he didn't say anything about what any of our restrictions might be. I intend to take advantage of it. Forgiveness being easier to receive than permission and all that. For example, I'd really love to go walk that labyrinth tomorrow. Anyone else up for it?"

"I tink I go kitchen and see what I can do dere," said Bonpo, hefting himself from the carpet.

"Actually, Captain Bleddyn has offered to show me where Arawn's men practice their weaponry," Gwrhyr said. "Perhaps I should take him up on that before I no longer have a chance."

"Really?" Eluned was amazed. "He already trusts you that much?"

"What can I say?" Gwrhyr smiled.

"I'm impressed," Eluned admitted. "Now what are the three treasures here again? The chariot, the chessboard and the halter? Shouldn't we all be keeping an eye out for them meanwhile?"

"Yes, definitely," replied Jabberwock. "The sooner we can relieve Arawn of his treasures and remove ourselves from his presence, the better."

"So are you interested in exploring tomorrow?" the Princess asked him.

"Yes, but I think I will do better on my own," Jabberwock said, "at least until the entire castle is aware of what I am." Eluned had to concede that he was right. "Chokhmah?"

"Of course, dear," she said. "It would be unseemly for you to explore alone."

"Den I tink it is time to say good night," said Bonpo, opening the door. "See you at bleakfast."

"Good night Bonpo," Eluned said, hugging her humongous friend. Bonpo hugged back, gently, then lumbered down the hall toward the soldiers' quarters.

"You never did tell us what you thought of King Arawn," Jabberwock reminded her.

She saw Gwrhyr's eyes light with interest and knew she had to be careful. "I'm not sure yet. He didn't look anything like I'd imagined, and he was as polite as he could be to me. I couldn't tell whether he liked or disliked me, or whether or not he believed a word I said. I got the feeling he was holding back, but in a good or bad way, I'm just not sure."

"So you'll meet him for dinner again tomorrow night?" Gwrhyr asked.

"That's what he said," Eluned agreed.

"Hmpff. Well, at least we don't have to worry about it again until then. I intend to make as much use out of tomorrow as possible," Gwrhyr said. "Good night, Princess. Chokhmah. Are you coming, Jabb?"

"Yes. Hold the door," he said. "We'll come by for you on the way to breakfast. Goodnight ladies."

Chokhmah and Eluned wished them a good night before closing and locking the door behind their retreating backs.

"Oh good," Eluned said, kicking off her shoes. "I can't wait to get in my nightgown and go to sleep. It was exhausting worrying about having to watch what I said. And, it has been a very long day. Hard to believe we weren't even at the castle this morning."

"Did I notice a certain sparkle in your eye when you were talking about King Arawn?" Chokhmah asked, helping Eluned loosen the ribbons that held the sleeves to her dress.

The Princess swallowed hard. Trust the gypsy not to miss a trick. "I have to admit that I thought thirty-three was going to look old, but there is something about him that is really striking."

"I have never seen him," she said. "What does he look like?"

"He has the longest hair I've ever seen on a man," Eluned said, breathlessly, removing the overdress. "It's long and straight and the color of copper. It looks so silky; I had to keep myself from touching it." She closed her eyes, remembering, before pulling the underdress over her head. Chokhmah handed her a nightgown so she could avoid getting chilled. "And his eyes, they bore right into you and they're the oddest color—they are . . . it's hard to describe, a reddish-bronze, maybe? I have to admit, he took my breath away."

"It sounds like you are quite enamored of him." Chokhmah attempted and failed to keep the worry from her voice.

"Perhaps, in a way. But," and she shivered, "I must confess that there was something about his mouth. It was nice enough, and there were times when it was definitely kissable, particularly when he was amused, but there was also a hardness there, or cruelty. I'm not sure. But it made me wary."

"Good for you!" she encouraged her. "You always keep

that in mind. He may remain always polite, perhaps even come to enjoy your company, but I am sure his reputation is based on fact."

"Meaning?"

"That while all the rumors may not be true, some of them most assuredly are. Be careful."

"I won't do anything to risk your lives, I promise."

"Thank you. Now go wash your face and brush your teeth like a good girl," Chokhmah laughed, patting her on the cheek.

6TH FEHARN

It was the sun streaming in through the window that awakened the Princess the following morning. Pulling her robe around her and hurrying to the window, she took stock of the coming day. Even without the fire, the room felt warmer than it had when they arrived.

It was going to be a great day to walk the labyrinth. It was something she had always enjoyed doing at Castle Mykerinos where they had labyrinths both indoors and outdoors because so much of the year was cold. They were her preferred way of meditating not to mention a way to remove herself from the hustle and bustle of castle life. Although, she decided, it was still chilly enough that she might wait until the day reached its ultimate warmth sometime after noon.

"Eluned," Chokhmah called, knocking politely on her door, "are you awake?"

"Come in!" Eluned acknowledged her. "I'm up."

"Breakfast is in half an hour. I let you sleep as late as possible."

"I can get ready in time. Oh!"

"What is it?"

"My clothes. Everything I had with me was on the floor by the bed and they're no longer there."

"I took those down to be washed while you were napping yesterday. They were returned while you were at dinner last night."

Eluned shook her head in displeasure. "I am such a princess," she moaned. "I could have taken them down myself."

"No, my dear, actually you could not have. You are a princess here remember? While it is perfectly acceptable to consider yourself an equal around the rest of us, you must treat us differently around King Arawn and his servants, soldiers, and anyone else who knows who you are."

"All right, I'll try. Omni forbid that I forget who and where I am at the moment."

"If it is easier, you could just always be the Princess Eluned."

"Are you serious?" Eluned was aghast. "After the hell Gwrhyr has put me through every time I've acted like one? I don't think so!" She wasn't sure if he'd get that peculiar smirking, supercilious look if she did so, or whether he'd just be disappointed, but either way, she wasn't willing to find out. "Regardless, thank you. I truly appreciate having clean clothes and not having to tromp around in a fancy dress all day."

"You are most welcome, my love."

She walked over to the armoire and pulled it open, "I can't believe I didn't even notice these were hanging here last night!"

"I do believe the stars were blinding you to all else."

"Stars?" Eluned regarded her blankly.

"In your eyes. The ones in the form of a certain king."

"Ah. Yes. Funny, I don't feel quite so smitten this morning."

"Interesting. Perhaps his eyes literally held a power over you."

"Like a mesmerist?"

"Something along those lines. Although I would say sorcery of some sort is more likely. Meanwhile, get dressed. The boys will be here soon."

"The boys," Eluned sniggered, reluctantly pulling her black wool skirt and white flannel blouse from the closet. She would much rather wear the leather pants and wool sweater. She absent-mindedly wondered what the laundry had thought about those particular garments.

THE PRINCESS HAD JUST PULLED HER HAIR BACK into a pony-tail and was pulling on her boots when there was a rap on the door.

"The boys are here," she called to Chokhmah, giggling.

"Well, they are all males," the Gypsy said, closing the door to her room, "and calling Jabberwock a 'man' does not fit somehow."

"Good point. I'll meditate on that while walking the labyrinth this afternoon—the perfect denomination for the trio."

"Excellent idea," Chokhmah replied, opening the door.

THIS MORNING, PERHAPS BECAUSE OF THE PRINCESS, they had been moved to another dining room. This room must have been used for the king's guests because it was larger and brighter, the windows looking out onto an inner courtyard. The furniture, china and silverware were of much better quality, as well. Tapestries covered the walls of stone, adding even more warmth to the room. A buffet table was overflowing with scrambled and hard-boiled eggs, bacon, kippers, ham, toast, broiled tomatoes, hashed brown potatoes, muffins and pastries as well as coffee, tea, cream and sugar.

"This feels much more friendly," Gwrhyr noted, pulling out a chair. "I thought we were stuck in the servants' dining room for the remainder of our time here."

As if that were her cue, a servant, who was really quite attractive, entered the room and asked if they had everything they needed. After assuring her they did, she backed out of the room.

"She was an improvement, as well," Gwrhyr noted.

"Why?" asked Eluned, sitting down next to him. "Did that sourpuss wait on you again last night?"

"Yes," Bonpo grumbled, pulling two seats together to hold his weight, "and not much food eider."

"What?" She suddenly felt bad about describing the exquisite meal she'd had.

"Sandwiches and salad," Chokhmah explained. "Plenty for me, but hardly filling for the," she paused.

"Boys?" Eluned filled in, helpfully, stifling a giggle by shoveling a forkful of eggs into her mouth.

"Boys?" Gwrhyr turned toward her in irritation. "You call us boys?"

"Only until I can think of something better," she explained. "Chokhmah and I are trying to come up with a group name for you three."

"What's wrong with 'men'?"

The Princess looked apologetically at Jabberwock, whose muzzle was in his plate. "I . . . hmmm, I'll think about it," she said, diplomatically.

Gwrhyr just looked at her, and shook his head. "Even guys would be better than boys."

"Fellows," Eluned exclaimed. "How about fellows? I think I like that."

"Fellows," Gwrhyr tried it out. "A friend or colleague. I could live with that."

"Fellows it is then," she agreed. "Now, I'll have to think about something else to meditate on while walking the labyrinth this afternoon. Although at this point, it might be more relaxing to think of nothing."

"Have you decided what you are going to do today?" Chokhmah asked the Bandersnatch.

"Well, in addition to my meeting with King Arawn, I . . ."

"You're meeting with King Arawn," Eluned interrupted.

"Let us just say that I have been summoned," Jabberwock informed her.

"When?" the Princess asked.

"This afternoon. Anyway . . ." he waited for the Princess to interrupt again.

"Anyway?" she asked.

"Anyway," he growled, "it is my intention to wander around the palace, itself, as unobtrusively as possible."

"I'll be spending the entire day with Captain Bleddyn in the practice yards," Gwrhyr interjected, "so I won't be here for lunch."

Eluned was disappointed, though she shouldn't have been. Hadn't she eaten dinner the previous evening without them? But she enjoyed the time she spent with her fellows . . . yet, she couldn't let him know that. "So," she turned toward Bonpo, "are you still going to the kitchen?"

"Yes. Cannot plomise I be 'ea fah runch."

"Jabb?" the Princess turned to him.

"As far as you know," he said drily, but his eyes sparkled with amusement.

"Very funny. Tell us what direction you intend to start working your way around the castle so that Chokhmah and I can head in the opposite direction."

"I think I shall go clockwise," he decided.

"Fine. Chokhmah, do you want to go back to the room first and then start upstairs?"

"Yes, that would be nice."

Eluned stood and looked around. "Do we leave our plates here?"

"Yes, Princess," Gwrhyr gave her a warning look, "we leave our plates here."

Eluned blushed and cursed herself, inwardly. She really had to be more careful.

AS THEY SET OUT FROM THE ROOM, counter-clockwise in order to avoid Jabberwock, Eluned wondered how much of the
castle would actually be open to them. Most of the doors they
passed were closed, and she was afraid to try opening them for
fear of startling a resident.

"This is ridiculous," she groused. "Maybe we should go
down a level. At least I know there are parlors and dining
rooms and such down there. I was so frightened last night that
I really didn't even pay attention to my surroundings."

Eluned and Chokhmah were now on the opposite side of
the castle having turned left at two towers already. The hallways were cold and drafty and she really just wanted to find
a heated room she could thaw in for a moment. Other than
the occasional suit of armor standing in a corner, and ancient
weapons or the heads of animals mounted on the walls, the
corridors were devoid of decoration.

The hallways were also awfully quiet. Perhaps there were
no other guests. It seemed highly unlikely. Surely some of the
officers had wives and children and lived in the castle. What
about his household staff—his seneschal, his chaplain (if he
had one), his butler or marshal? He wasn't married but surely
there were still chambermaids around? She knew he had a garrison of soldiers because she had seen some of them, and the
fellows were sharing quarters with them. Although, Eluned reflected, the military staff were probably up and out early each
day.

"You are being quiet," Chokhmah said, but Eluned noted
she spoke softly.

"It's so quiet here. Doesn't that seem odd? Aren't castles
usually noisy places? At least ours always is—both loud and
busy—everyone running around doing his or her job. Chambermaids laughing while they work at their needlework, people yelling to and at each other in the kitchen and the laundry,
and Papa's seneschal running around like a chicken with its
head cut off. Mother was always running to and fro overseeing

the work of her ladies-in-waiting and the chambermaids, as well as supervising the activities of the kitchen staff. She even kept an eye on all the spinners, weavers, and embroiderers. Speaking of which, we know the castle must be staffed that way because where else did my clothes come from?"

"You are right, my dear, something is not right. Do you think noise is forbidden within the castle walls?"

"Either that or, oh look, here's the staircase," Eluned pointed out, taking Chokhmah's arm and beginning to descend. "Either that or he has all his workers plying away outside the castle or in the dungeons."

"That is a scary thought. Perhaps it is a combination. No matter what, he seems to be a very private man."

They reached the bottom of the stairs and Eluned paused. "Let me think. Do we turn left or right?'

"Left if we want to continue in the direction we were already heading."

"Where do you suppose Jabberwock is?"

"Does it matter?"

"No, I guess not. It's just that I was hoping we'd see someone while on our walk."

Much to Eluned's surprise, the next door on the right was open. As a matter of fact, it didn't even have a door. "By Omni," she breathed in awe.

"I have never seen such a library," Chokhmah sighed.

"Paradise," Eluned agreed, entering. "I could spend my entire life in here, assuming there is something decent to read on one of these bookcases."

The two fireplaces on either side of the entranceway blazed away and Eluned collapsed into one of the armchairs that faced the fireplace to the right. "First priority: get warm. Then, I'll look at the books."

Chokhmah had already begun to peruse the nearest shelf. Once warm, Eluned stood up and turned to face the library. Where to start? At the back of the room, three long and narrow windows looked out on what was probably a lovely rose garden in the summer. At this time of year, all the bushes had been trimmed back and were patiently awaiting the final frost so they could send forth new shoots again. Would they be gone before the first buds opened? There was definitely a part of her that longed to wait out the last of the cold weather sitting comfortably in front of the library fireplace.

There were four floor-to-ceiling bookshelves at right angles to the far wall—two on each end wall and one on either side of the middle window. These latter two bookshelves, although they reached only halfway across the room, were two-sided. A round table, with six library chairs, filled the space in front of the middle window. A sofa and a coffee table sat in front of the window on the left; three armchairs and a coffee table offered comfortable reading to the right. Since Chokhmah was still at the bookshelf that covered the wall to the right, Eluned headed left.

The books on this shelf were apparently all nonfiction— books on philosophy and psychology, religion, sociology, anthropology and languages. Definitely some interesting books, but the Princess was looking for something lighter. She crossed over to the bookshelves in the center of the room. Fiction! So much fiction. How was she going to choose? There were classics and mysteries, romance, fantasy and science fiction . . .

"Let me guess," she called, but with a library voice, over to Chokhmah, "those are books on the sciences, arts, literature, history and geography?"

"Correct. Do not forget biography. And a wonderful selection of the Ancients—Eliot, Shelley, Browning, Herbert, and Lewis, Dumas, Brontë, too many to name."

"Ah, yes. So where are the reference books?"

Chokhmah pointed toward the wall on the other side of the fireplace, and Eluned nodded, and said, "It seems to be a very complete library."

"The King must have a librarian," Chokhmah noted, pulling a book from the shelf. "These shelves are extremely organized. I do not see one out of place. Do you?"

"No, the fiction seems to be arranged alphabetically."

Chokhmah glanced through the pages of her book for a moment before sliding it back onto the shelf, just slightly out of order.

"A test," she informed Eluned, who was watching. "So, the question is: would you like to pick out a book and read awhile or continue our exploration and return this afternoon to find a book."

"Let's come back this afternoon. I'd like to see what other rooms might be open."

Across the hall from the library, though she hadn't noticed previously, a door stood slightly ajar. Eluned pushed it open to discover a music room. "A harpsichord!" she squealed with delight.

"Ah yes, you did say you played," Chokhmah remembered, following her into the room.

Eluned rushed over to the harpsichord and was soon standing before it, fingers playing lightly over the keys.

"Are you not going to sit?"

"I prefer to play standing." Chokhmah watched, impressed, as the Princess, eyes closed, took a deep breath, and then opening them, began to play.

"I am speechless," Chokhmah said when Eluned finished the piece she was playing. "That was beautiful. What was that?"

"Thank you. That was from the First Movement of Bach's Italian Concerto."

"That is essentially a relic," Chokhmah observed.

"Good music never dies," the Princess smiled.

"Truer words were never spoken," a voice, from the direction of the door, said.

"Your Majesty!" Eluned exclaimed.

Chokhmah whirled around and curtsied, "Your Majesty."

Eluned was blushing furiously, "I had no idea anyone was around, that anyone could hear. I apologize if I disturbed you."

"There are worse ways to be disturbed," Arawn answered smoothly, stepping into the room. "Indeed, I was only passing on my way to a meeting, when the sound caught my attention. Very lovely. You are quite talented."

"Thank you, sir," she replied, her cheeks coloring again.

"Nonsense. Call me Arawn. We aren't that far different in age."

Eluned blushed in reply.

"I am having a dinner party tomorrow night, and I would like you to be there; as a matter of fact, you can entertain us with your Bach afterwards."

The Princess swallowed hard, "Of course, I would love to."

"As for tonight, urgent business will keep me away from the dinner I promised. A page should have delivered a note to your room?"

"Perhaps, but my lady and I have been in the library."

"Delightful, isn't it?" he said.

"It's heaven," Eluned agreed.

"Spend as much time there as you like," he offered.

"Thank you."

"Tomorrow night, then," Arawn said, moving back toward the door. He paused before leaving. "Wear the black dress."

Eluned blushed a final time. "Thank you for the dresses. They're beautiful."

"You are quite welcome."

Arawn left, and Eluned turned to Chokhmah in despair. "You knew," she whispered.

"I am sorry, my love," the Gypsy said, wrapping her arms around her in a hug. "His reputation precedes him."

"Tomorrow night," the Princess lamented, lowering herself onto the harpsichord's bench.

"Look on the bright side, my dear. This way you will go ahead and get it out of the way."

"That doesn't make it any easier."

"How about some tea? Why do you not go back into the library and sit by the fire? I will go to the kitchen and bring us back some tea."

"Actually, that sounds wonderful," Eluned stood up and moved toward the door. "We'd better find those damn treasures soon," she said under her breath.

"What my dear?"

"Nothing." She wandered into the library and decided to find a book before sitting down. She was afraid if she sat down, she wouldn't want to get up again. The problem was that she wasn't sure what she was in the mood to read. Definitely not romance. Murder mystery? Revenge? Suspense? Or an old favorite, perhaps? She tried to think of authors she liked to read and suddenly remembered Geillis Saille. She hurried to the S's, running her finger along the row of books. Saille wrote books that featured both murder and suspense, and, granted, a little romance, but they were the type of book Eluned had a hard time putting down, and that's what she needed right now.

Unfortunately, King Arawn didn't seem as keen on Mistress Saille as she was. There were only three novels by the prolific author and she'd read all of them, of course. But that didn't matter because the Princess could read some of her favorite books over and over again. She removed her most beloved of the three—*The Ghost of Loss*—and returned to the chair she had sat in previously. It had been very comfortable.

By the time Chokhmah returned with the tea (and some biscuits), Eluned was immersed in the book.

"Good, you have found something to read," she said, setting down the tray she carried on the coffee table.

"I've read it before," Eluned looked up. "But, I really like it and I don't mind reading it again. Mmmm . . . chocolate biscuits," she leaned forward and picked one up. "Perfect."

Chokhmah poured them some tea and walked over to glance at the shelf on which she had deliberately misplaced the book earlier. "Te bisterdon tumare anava," she suddenly exclaimed, cursing the king in her native tongue.

"What is it?" Eluned jumped up and ran over to the shelf.

"Look. This book. It is back in the correct order."

"I don't understand. We were gone from this room for no more than fifteen minutes, surely. How could someone come in, find one miss-shelved book, and fix it in that amount of time?"

"Exactly," Chokhmah agreed. "This is very scary."

"Is it magic?"

"Witchcraft, perhaps. Perchance I was correct about the sorcery earlier? It must have been the king."

"But I like this room."

"It is not the library, my dear, it is the man who owns it. Be very careful while you are here. We cannot be sure just how much he knows nor how he receives his information."

"Perhaps I chose the wrong place to run away to," Eluned said, practically whispering in case someone was listening.

"Do you mean we should have tried elsewhere first?"

"A neutral country at the very least."

"No," Chokhmah shook her head. "I believe, despite this, we were meant to come here. So, we must make the best of it and at least pretend we enjoy being here."

"What if someone hears you?"

"I don't think that is the kind of power the king has. He might be able to sense something is out of place, but he cannot hear through walls."

"Well, that's reassuring, at least."

"Finish your tea before it gets cold," the Gypsy directed. "I asked a page to let us know when lunch is ready."

The Princess settled back into her chair, opening her book and finding her place. Other than the occasional rattle of tea-cup against saucer and the nearly silent turning of pages, the only sound in the library for the next hour was the crackling of the fire.

Eluned was so deeply engrossed in her book that when the page knocked politely on the threshold of the door, she jumped. If her teacup had been in her hand, she would have spilled the entire contents all over herself and the armchair. Fortunately, it was long since emptied and resting neatly in its saucer.

"Your Highness," the page said, and bowed. It wasn't the same boy who had led her to the dining room and back to her bedroom the previous evening.

"Yes?" Her heart was pounding unreasonably fast.

"Lunch is served in the dining room," he was a very formal little lad, almost too serious for his age. And, Eluned thought, with his golden curls and cherubic cheeks, it didn't sit on him well at all.

"Thank you, kind sir," she curtsied to him and smiled her most winning smile.

"You are most welcome, my, I mean, your highness," he stuttered, cheeks flaming.

"Tell them we'll be right there, would you?"

"Y-y-y-yes, with pleasure." He bowed again and backed out of the room, and though he trod very formally back down the hall, there was a slight skip in his step.

"You would think," Eluned said, turning to Chokhmah, "that no one is ever kind to the child. He was so grim, and almost scared, at first."

"Is that so surprising?" Chokhmah asked.

"In this place? No, I suppose not." She looked at the book in her hand. "Curses," she scanned the library, "I need a book-mark and I don't see even the slightest slip of paper in here. Difficult to believe in a library."

"Do any of these tables have drawers?" Chokhmah asked. They began to search the coffee tables but not a single one of them had a drawer. After bending over to check the table in front of the sofa under the far left window, Eluned noticed something out of the corner of her eye as she was standing up. There was something peaking out beneath the sofa—a piece of paper. Was it the page of a book? She couldn't tell. She leaned down to get a closer look and slowly withdrew the vellum sheet from beneath the couch.

"What have you found?" Chokhmah asked.

"I'm not sure," Eluned frowned at the slip of paper. "I can't tell if it's a page from a really old book or an old letter or just notes."

"Do you mind if I look?" Eluned handed her the yellowed piece of parchment and Chokhmah studied it for a moment. "I just cannot tell. I will have to look at it more closely. Why do you not tuck it in your book and bring it with us?"

"Good idea. We need to get moving. I'd hate for them to think we're up to something or worse, being rude."

"True. I had better grab the tea tray as well, otherwise I may have to come back for it."

"I'll bet Jabberwock knows what this is," Eluned remarked as they hurried to the dining room.

"Why do you say that?"

"Because he told me recently that he has studied every kind of magic and spirituality that exists, and the writing or symbols or whatever they are on that sheet of paper definitely look mystical."

"I will grant you that," Chokhmah said, "but for some reason, the symbols look familiar to me. I just cannot remember where I have seen them before."

They had reached the dining room and much to Eluned's relief, Jabberwock was already there, clearly waiting impatiently for their arrival in order for the meal to be served.

"Where have you been?" he kvetched. "I have been waiting here for ten minutes already."

"I found something," Eluned whispered, sliding into the seat next to him.

"Found something?" It was clear he didn't know whether to be interested, or if this was just the Princess making another melodrama of the mundane.

"I found a piece of vellum under one of the couches in the library," she said, voice low.

"Heaven forbid," Jabberwock whispered back, glassy eyes rolling. "Tell me more."

Eluned bit her lip. Hard. "Notice me not saying what I'd like to say."

"You are showing great restraint, my dear. So, I take it that this is more than just a scrap of paper?" he looked to Chokhmah for confirmation.

"Yes," she said, "There are symbols, but I cannot identify them."

"May I see it?" But at that moment he was interrupted by one of the kitchen maids coming in to serve them.

A quick prayer to Omni later, they were enjoying their pasta and salad.

"The vellum?" Jabberwock asked.

"Oh, yes," the Princess pulled the page from her book and held it in front of Jabberwock's eyes, which reflected the yellowed page. He studied the odd symbols scrawled on the page before nodding his head in remembrance.

"You know what they are?" Eluned was breathless with anticipation.

"Indeed," he said. "Unfortunately, I am not sure if the paper is actually important."

"Why? What is it?"

"Well on the bright side, they are incredibly archaic symbols, which makes them interesting. They are Aegyptian, if I am not mistaken, but . . ."

"What does it say?"

"Princess," Jabberwock barked. "You must learn not to interrupt. It is extremely annoying."

Eluned took a deep breath. "I apologize."

The Bandersnatch gave her a warning look, but continued. "I was going to say that it doesn't actually say anything. They are alchemical symbols for different metals."

"Metals?" The Princess looked disappointed.

"Sorry. Clearly notes. It does mean whoever wrote this is studying alchemy."

"Whatever for?"

"Now that is a mystery," Jabberwock said.

"I'm not sure I understand alchemy," Eluned admitted.

"It is more than the transmuting of metals," Jabberwock said.

"Yes," Chokhmah agreed. "It is also a philosophy. Everyone thinks alchemy is about changing base metals into gold but most alchemists are actually looking for the elixir of longevity."

"And achieving ultimate wisdom," Jabberwock added.

"Well, that doesn't surprise me," the Princess said. "I don't know whether or not it was the king who lost that page of notes, but he strikes me as the type of man who would want to be young forever."

"I will not argue with that," Chokhmah said. "He definitely seemed . . ."

"Self absorbed?" Jabberwock said, but it was more rhetorical than a question. "He was definitely interested in my studies when I spoke to him earlier."

"You already talked to him?" Eluned asked. "I thought your meeting wasn't until this afternoon?"

"Yes, but I ran into him while I was wandering the halls and he asked to go ahead and meet," Jabberwock explained.

"Wait! We ran into him as well. Was he looking for us?" Eluned was not amused.

"He did say he had to leave on urgent business," Chokhmah said.

"Hmmmm," Jabberwock mused, "it is two days past so it cannot be that."

"By Omni, I had forgotten!" Chokhmah exclaimed. "It was recently the night of the vernal equinox," she informed the Princess.

"So?" Eluned asked, clearly frustrated by the turn of events. "How, by Omni, does that matter?"

"It is the first day of spring and some ancient religions have special ceremonies on that day," Jabberwock explained.

"I know what the vernal equinox is," the Princess was still annoyed. "So you're saying that King Arawn might be an adherent of one of these ancient religions and that these symbols are connected, as well? I don't understand."

"Highly likely," Jabberwock said, "as alchemy and old religions oft go hand in hand."

"Do I want to know what goes on at these ceremonies?" Eluned's voice echoed with trepidation.

"No!" both Chokmah and Jabberwock exclaimed simultaneously.

Eluned's eyes widened. "Really? That bad?"

Jabberwock conveniently found himself with a mouthful of pasta and vegetables in his mouth. Chokhmah was taking a long sip of her water.

"I see. Not to talk about." The Princess looked put out.

"Only because we do not actually know anything," Chokhmah assured her after swallowing.

"Yes, but you know the types of things that might go on," Eluned prodded.

"True," she said.

"But you're not going to tell me," Eluned's voice sank with the realization.

Chokhmah took a deep breath.

"Just tell her," Jabberwock said.

"Fine. You are not a little girl anymore. It is not uncommon for adherents of the old religions to practice fertility rites on the vernal equinox."

"Practiced," Eluned snorted. "That's one way of putting it.

I'm sure at this point, that those who celebrate are quite accomplished."

"I could not have said it better myself," Jabberwock remarked. "But it's not only fertility rites."

"Not human sacrifice, surely?" Eluned was aghast. "I thought those days were long gone."

"Nothing is ever gone if the interest still remains," Jabberwock said.

"It would have to be done very secretly, wouldn't it?"

"Oh yes, but that probably wouldn't be too difficult in one's own kingdom," he said.

"And, he is not alone in this," Chokhmah added, "as both the fertility rites and the sacrifice would need the involvement of a number of people."

"This is all conjecture," Eluned objected.

"It is true that that this scrap of vellum tells us next to nothing," Jabberwock agreed before hopping down from his seat.

"Wait, where are you going?" The Princess stood so abruptly that she nearly knocked her chair over. "You still haven't told me what metals these are. The symbols are difficult enough to understand, but the labeling doesn't help if I don't know what words like nub or asem mean."

"Do you have something to write with?" Jabberwock asked, clearly annoyed at the delay.

Chokhmah removed a short pencil from the pouch she carried at her waist.

"I hate to write on this vellum," Eluned pouted.

"Press lightly and you can erase it later," Chokhmah advised.

"Fine. So. Nub?"

"Gold," Jabberwock translated.

"Asem?"

"Electrum."

"What's electrum?" Eluned asked.

"An alloy of gold and silver," he replied tersely. "What's next?"

"Hat?"

"Silver."

"Xomt," she stumbled over the word. "Not sure how to say that."

"Close enough. It's copper."

"Men?" she giggled.

"Iron. Why is that so funny?" He looked annoyed.

"Nothing, just thinking of men as a type of metal amuses me. Teht?"

"Lead."

"And, finally, chesbet."

"That can be a blue stone, enamel or sapphire. Anything else?"

"That's it. See you at dinner?" The Princess asked as Jabberwock turned toward the door.

"Yes," the Bandersnatch affirmed. "Now, I'm off to explore. I want to take advantage of the fact that the king is not here."

"Oh, Jabb," Eluned said, after he'd taken a couple of steps.

"What is it?" He turned around.

"When Chokhmah and I were walking around the castle this morning, everything seemed abnormally quiet to us. Have you felt that as well?"

"Good point. It is both still and quiet here. Hmmmm."

Eluned watched him leave and then asked Chokhmah if she wanted to go back to their bedroom before checking out the labyrinth.

"Yes, that would be nice."

"Good. I want to leave this piece of paper there. Later, I can transcribe it into my journal, just in case. As a matter of fact, I think I will hide this paper in my journal until I do that. I don't want to risk losing it."

6ᵀᴴ FEHARN

Sitting on one of the benches in the gazebo located in the center of the labyrinth, Eluned turned her face toward the sun for the little warmth it provided. Granted, she had her wool cloak wrapped tightly about her, but the sun was working hard to spread as much heat through her body as possible. At least, that's how she imagined it. Chokhmah sat next to her, eyes closed, also enjoying this brief respite from the castle.

"I hadn't realized how claustrophobic the castle was making me feel," the Princess murmured. "Now that the days will be getting longer, I might be able to spend more time outside. That might help."

"It will if we must spend a significant amount of time here," Chokhmah agreed. "I do realize we saw only the library and music room, but surely the chessboard is not hidden. That seems like the type of thing the king would be proud to display."

"Maybe," Eluned paused, considering. "Unless, of course, he fears someone might steal it. It might be in his private chambers wherever those might be."

"I would imagine his rooms are in one of the towers," Chokhmah guessed.

"Why is that?"

"Because it would offer him several floors of space. The downstairs, from what we have seen at this point, seems to be for entertainment—the library, music room, the parlors . . ."

"And the kitchens and dining rooms," Eluned continued.

"And the laundry," Chokhmah added.

"Upstairs, though we heard nothing, are surely rooms for not just guests but residents," The Princess mused.

"And I would think the garrison occupies both floors on the north side," Chokhmah said.

"That makes sense. I wonder who rooms above the kitchens? Servants, maybe?"

"The kitchens would have to be the noisiest part of the castle," Chokhmah agreed, "so yes, in all likelihood they have rooms above the kitchen."

"I wonder what is in the towers? Maybe we should go back in and explore some more while the king is gone."

"Yes," Chokhmah said, standing, "we probably should not assume we have all the time in the world."

"Although it is awfully tempting to stay here until the sun no longer warms us," the Princess sighed.

"We are not here for recreation," Chokhmah admonished.

"I know, I know," the Princess groaned, slowly standing.

"I was reminding myself as much as you," Chokhmah sighed.

"Fair enough." Eluned descended the steps of the gazebo and re-entered the labyrinth. She had decided not to meditate on anything on her trip to the center, but she had found a certain peace while sitting in the gazebo. Perhaps the fact there was only one way in and one way out was reassuring. She couldn't be surprised by anyone sneaking up from behind.

There was only one entrance on the east side of the castle—directly across from the staircase that led up to the second floor. The huge doors were studded with iron and though standing open during the day, were securely closed come nightfall. Guards stood on either side of this portal and a door-keeper kept watch in the long narrow room inside. Similarly large doors, though closed at the moment, could be opened up onto the corridor inside the castle. The doorkeeper unlocked a smaller door on the right side of this postern gate that allowed them entrance into the castle proper, politely asking if they had enjoyed their time in the labyrinth.

They answered in the affirmative, and stood uncertainly in the hallway for a moment as the door was locked behind them.

"Which way should we go? We know the laundry is to the left. What's in the room next to it? That door and the one across the hall have always been shut when we walked by," Eluned asked.

"And apparently still are," Chokhmah noted.

"Well, then let's just finish the circle, so to speak, and we can either go back to the library from there or back to the room," the Princess decided.

Much to the disappointment of the Princess, the rest of the doors in the hallway were shut and she wasn't quite brave enough, yet, to try either opening them or knocking on them. At this rate, they would never find the treasures. On the other hand, they hadn't even been here two full days, and she told herself to stop panicking and keep her eyes open.

"Let's go back to the room," she said when they reached the staircase. "I just realized I left my book there, and if we have to go all the way back, I can just as easily read there as in the library. Besides, it's probably not that long until the fellows are done for the day. I imagine they'll drop by at some point."

"Indubitably. Our room is the logical gathering place while here," Chokhmah agreed.

"At least we'll all be eating together tonight," Eluned added, before lapsing into the quiet that seemed to permeate the very stones.

SHE WAS GLAD WHEN THEY FINALLY REACHED THEIR ROOM. It was warm, cozy even, and as she removed the heavy woolen cloak from around her shoulders and Chokhmah locked the door behind them, she felt as if a much heavier burden than the cloak had been lifted.

After she had replicated the alchemical symbols onto the pages of her journal, she looked for a place to hide the vellum. She hated that she felt like she had to conceal everything. At some point, she was going to run out of places in which to stash things. A slip of paper should be relatively easy to secret away, right? But either it had to be someplace no one would look, or alternately, in plain sight. There was a book of Scripture on the lower shelf of her bedside table. If she hid the vellum in pages containing the words of one of the minor prophets, surely no one would look there? Who would think that she might try to conceal something in a book that never moved from the bottom shelf?

Feeling much relieved, she picked up *The Ghost of Loss* from where she left it on the desk and settled in front of the fireplace to read until the fellows arrived.

AS EXPECTED, THE KNOCK CAME SHORTLY before they were expected for dinner. There was so much to say that instead they filled the short walk to the dining room with small talk instead.

They were served family style in the room in which they'd been served breakfast and lunch, and several minutes were spent passing round the roast chicken and potatoes and the sautéed chard. Simple fare but this time there was plenty of it.

No one seemed willing to bring up the events of their day except Bonpo. He regaled them with his day in the kitchens, which, he claimed, was mostly spent preparing for the fancy dinner that would be held by the king the next evening.

Eluned groaned. "It sounds wonderful, Bonpo, but I'm not sure if I will be able to eat a single bite."

"Why?" Gwrhyr wanted to know.

"The king has not only asked that she be present at the dinner, but she must also entertain them with her harpsichord music," Chokhmah informed him.

"It's worse than that," she wailed. "I have to wear that dress."

"Dress?" Gwrhyr frowned.

Eluned blushed and Chokhmah explained about how they had found the three beautiful dresses in the armoire upon their arrival.

"And why are you so upset about a dress?" he pressed.

"It's just so . . . revealing," she said, cringing as his eyes flashed and his fists clenched in anger.

"I should have known he'd be up to his old tricks," Gwrhyr growled.

"What tricks?" Eluned looked worried.

"Well, first of all, I have no doubt he wants to show you off and humiliate you in front of his friends."

The blood drained from Eluned's face and Chokhmah chastised him, "You do not know that at all. He was very nice to her today. The dress might not be exactly proper for a woman of her age and standing, but I have the distinct feeling that King Arawn has very little real knowledge of the women in his class."

"There is no doubt some truth to that," Jabberwock agreed. "I would imagine the king is more interested in what he wants than in what others might want. It probably never occurred to him he might be embarrassing the Princess."

"I'm sorry," Gwrhyr apologized to Eluned. "I just hate to see you being mistreated."

"I know you do," she said, placing her hand on his still-clenched fist, "and that's why I hadn't told you about the dresses yet. I knew it would upset you. When we're done with dinner, I'll show them to you and you can judge for yourself. So," she said turning toward Bonpo and changing the flow of the conversation, "I really do want to hear more about the fabulous creations in store for me tomorrow."

Bonpo nodded and began to tell them something about roasted peacocks and swans. Eluned pretended to be listening but her thoughts were elsewhere, specifically wondering where Arawn was now. Had he participated in those sexual rituals on the Equinox that Jabb and Chokhmah had alluded to? It was both provocative and terrifying at the same time. She both desired him and was repelled by him. It was all very confusing.

Eventually, they were ready to leave the table but not before Bonpo first went into the kitchen for a jug of wine and some mugs to take upstairs with them.

ONCE ENSCONCED IN THE WOMEN'S ROOMS, the pall lifted and the group began to relax. Mugs of wine in hand, they settled themselves in front of the fireplace and continued talking.

"And did you find out anything of value while spending the day with Captain Bleddyn?" Jabberwock asked Gwrhyr.

"Quite a bit, actually. For some reason Math really took a shine to me and let me in on some of the king's plans."

"Math?" Eluned asked.

"Captain Bleddyn."

"Wow, already on a first name basis, I see," she smiled and winked.

"Very funny. What's important is the fact that though Arawn's army is small now, they are in the planning stages of greatly enlarging it. They are working toward building training centers throughout the kingdom and recruiting soldiers from those areas."

"Interesting," Jabberwock mused. "I wonder if the others, particularly Hamartia, are working toward that as well?"

"I asked that very thing. Math seemed to think it was a strong possibility."

"Are they concentrating on anything unique, weapon-wise?" Jabberwock asked.

"Not as far as I could tell, mostly the ubiquitous archers with their longbows and crossbows, because they'll need to send more men out to do that training. Other than that, there were men practicing with the usual—polearms, battleaxes, maces, halberds, swords—that type of thing.

"It's amazing how inventive men can be when coming up with ways to inflict injury on each other," the Princess grimaced.

"Women can do just as much injury to others," Gwrhyr argued, "although they tend to deliver emotional rather than physical damage."

The Princess was silent a moment before conceding, "You have a point. And sometimes that type of abuse doesn't heal. But men can also inflict emotional damage. It's probably safe to say that humans excel at hurting each other in many different ways."

"Anyway," Gwrhyr continued, "the good news is that Math has said that if we end up being here a while, I am more than welcome to be trained as part of Arawn's army."

"That is significant," Jabberwock agreed. "Not only will that gain you more freedom but more trust."

"Exactly."

"What about you, Jabb? Did you find anything in your wanderings today?" Eluned asked.

"Absolutely nothing. You would almost think this castle is deserted. How about you two, other than the vellum?"

"What vellum?" Gwrhyr asked.

"Eluned found a sheet of vellum beneath a sofa in the library," Chokhmah explained. "It contained notes of alchemical symbols."

"I have it right here," Eluned stood. "I'll show it to you."

"Does it mean someting?" Bonpo asked after studying it for a moment.

"I can't imagine what," Jabberwock replied. "I wouldn't be surprised if King Arawn is interested in alchemy but these notes are conclusive of nothing."

"No doubt he is just dabbling," Chokhmah said, "but I believe your inclination that he is part of a cult today that worships at the equinoxes and solstices is more than likely correct. The rumors I have heard would suggest he practices pagan rituals regularly."

"Great," Eluned groaned. "Now I have to worry that he'll decide to use me for a virgin sacrifice or something."

"I could help solve that," Gwrhyr offered.

Eluned punched him hard in the arm. "You're hilarious. If I didn't know you were joking, I would be highly offended."

"What makes you think I was joking?" Gwrhyr attempted to ask with a straight face while rubbing his bicep.

"I see that sparkle in your eye," the Princess laughed. "You can't even keep a serious face! I hope you do better when lying to Arawn or Math."

"All right. All right. I surrender. Obviously I was harassing you. But, as far as Arawn is concerned, or with others that might just as easily take our lives as let us live, I can keep a very straight face. And, speaking of which, are you going to show us the dress you're so ashamed of wearing?"

"I will get it," Chokhmah stood. "It is quite stunning but . . . well, you will see." She removed the black velvet dress from the armoire and carried it over to the group by the fire. The Princess blushed again. Bonpo bit his lip and turned away and Gwrhyr stood, once again angry. Only Jabberwock seemed content to watch the reactions of his fellow travellers.

"That son of a," Gwrhyr clamped his mouth shut before he could say more. "What would cause anyone to believe this is appropriate apparel for a Princess?"

"I'm just not sure I can wear this," her voice was quiet. "My chest will feel so bare. I don't even have a necklace to wear that might draw eyes away from the neckline. I'm going to have to stand like this all night," she demonstrated by crossing her arms over her breasts. "Which is going to make it extremely difficult to eat."

"Or play the harpsichord," Chokhmah reminded her.

"I think I have the answer," Gwrhyr said. He walked over to the bed where he had tossed his leather jerkin and reached into a pocket on the inside. He returned to Eluned's side and extended his hand, palm open. "This might be just what you need."

Eluned picked up the collar of opals and emeralds inset in the filigreed gold. "Cuhvetena's necklace," she breathed. "I'd forgotten how beautiful it is."

"She gave it to me as we were passing through the door in the standing stone," he explained. "She said I might need it at some point."

"It is beautiful," Chokhmah said, "and if it was given to you by Cuhvetena, it must be enchanted as well."

"Enchanted how?" Eluned asked, but she was remembering the way Gwrhyr had gazed adoringly upon Cuhvetena, a willing slave to her every word. Perhaps it would be better at this point not to reveal that information. Being able to entrance Arawn, and perhaps, the other men she would meet at the dinner party, would definitely be to her advantage. But if Gwrhyr knew, he would be less likely to allow her to wear it.

"On the other hand, I cannot be sure." Chokhmah was saying. "It is also possible that the enchantment was broken once it was removed from her neck. You must let us know if you notice anything."

"Definitely," the Princess promised, wondering where to put the necklace for safekeeping. "Here, I'll return that to the closet," she reached for the dress. After hanging the gown, she slid the necklace into one of her wool socks. Surely no one would look there between now and the dinner party the following evening.

Gwrhyr had returned to his seat and when Eluned returned, she leaned over, planting a soft kiss on his cheek. "Thank you," she whispered in his ear. "I owe you one."

"You're welcome," he said, formally, taking her hand in his and kissing it, but his eyes spoke volumes and the Princess once again remembered that day more than two weeks earlier when she had felt his lips pressed against hers. She was still certain she hadn't liked it, but now realized that it no longer angered her, and that was an improvement.

"Well, I know what I'll be doing tomorrow," Eluned said, sliding into her armchair.

"Wat dat?" asked Bonpo.

"Practicing," she answered. "Followed by some more practicing. I figure I will need to feel comfortable with at least a couple of pieces, just in case. One may suffice, but I may be asked to play another."

"I wish I could hear you play," Gwrhyr said.

"Thank you. But I really do understand that bashing your fellow soldiers with maces and whatnots is so much more exciting."

"Don't make me take that necklace back," he laughed, finishing his wine and standing. "You reminded me. Early day tomorrow. Won't be there at breakfast, either. So, I will take my leave and perhaps find out tomorrow night what happened at the dinner party? If you can, try to remember as many of the guests as possible?"

"Yes," Jabberwock interjected. "It would be nice to know if it is just local dignitaries or if there is anyone there from outside the kingdom."

"I'll try," she promised. "Fear tends to shut down my brain."

"You do jus' fine, Plincess," Bonpo assured her.

"Thanks Bonpo," she said, ushering the fellows out the door. "Good night and see you tomorrow."

"Somehow I have the feeling that tomorrow night will never arrive and when it finally does, it will never end," she told Chokhmah as she began to get ready for bed.

"We will take it one step at a time, my dear. How about that?"

7ᵀᴴ FEHARN

Tomorrow night did arrive, and the Princess tried to still her quaking knees as Chokhmah fastened Cuhvetena's necklace about her neck.

"Take deep breaths," Chokhmah advised. "You look stunning. If there are any wives or girlfriends at this party, they are going to hate you. Perhaps we should try to dampen down your beauty although I am not sure how we might accomplish that."

The Princess did, indeed, look devastating. The black velvet glowed against her pale skin and the emeralds and opals in the collar were nearly as brilliant as her green eyes. She had insisted on wearing her raven hair down and her dark curls cascaded down her back and shoulders.

When the page knocked on the door, her stomach dropped to her knees and she clutched Chokhmah's arm, eyes pleading.

"Sweetheart, this is something you must do," she said, prying Eluned's fingers loose from her arm. "Remember that you are doing this for all of us. If you can get into the good graces of anyone there tonight, including King Arawn, it will bode so much better for our future."

Eluned took one final deep breath and straightened her

shoulders. "You're right, of course," she told Chokhmah, who was opening the door. "One for all and all for one and all that."

WHEN SHE REACHED THE DINING ROOM, she thanked the page. It was the little cherub from the previous day, and he seemed keen to please her in any way possible. She wondered, touching the necklace, whether it was the enchantment, although she thought the boy too young to be affected by it. She would later discover sorcery had nothing to do with it unless you count kindness as a sort of magic. He looked at her as if to say, "Are you ready?" Steeling herself, she nodded and he opened the door.

"Her majesty, the Princess Eluned of Zion," he announced. Thirteen heads turned in her direction and she could see immediately from the looks on their faces that the necklace still exuded some of its enchantment although perhaps not as strong as when it had adorned Cuhvetena's graceful neck. Most of the women looked either keenly jealous or downright disdainful. The men, on the other hand, except for a notable exception, appeared entranced.

Arawn crossed the room quickly to meet her. "You look ravishing," he said, quietly, but his eyes were burning embers and scoured her from head to toe. Taking her arm in his, he led her into the room and began introductions.

The Princess tried to focus carefully on each person she was meeting as Jabberwock had suggested. They would want to know who had attended. It was not surprising, she soon discovered, they were, all of them, members of the Awen Alliance.

"His majesty King Hamartia of Simoon," King Arawn said, introducing her to his most faithful ally. The King of Simoon looked to be in his early fifties. He was taller, though not significantly, than Arawn, and his dark hair was silvered at the temples. He was deeply tanned, and his hooded black eyes regarded her with obvious lust. The Princess would not have been dismayed if told the king was known for his myriad affairs, particularly with much younger women. She realized the jeweled collar was in part responsible for the attraction, but she was sure he would have been interested regardless. Eluned worked hard at keeping her face both polite and neutral as she curtsied before him. Unlike the thrill Arawn had given her when he had practically disrobed her with his eyes, she found Hamartia's "undressing" made her feel dirty.

She was glad to turn to the Queen of Simoon whose beautiful yet waspish face looked almost green with envy. 'Definitely a woman to avoid,' Eluned thought as she once again curtsied. Queen Foehn was also about fifty and nearly the same height as Arawn. Her hair, which was still black, was braided and coiled about her head. It made Eluned think of snakes. Wasps and snakes—there was a lot of poison packed into Foehn's too thin body with its angular hips and flat chest.

Relieved that particular introduction was over; she turned to meet Hamartia's chancellor, Matraqua. About fifty, as well, the man was short, stocky and heavily muscled. His flashing black eyes betrayed yet another philandering husband. White teeth gleamed through a thick black beard and mustache and Eluned wondered about Hamartia's lord high steward. Perhaps the king liked to have men like himself around. Didn't speak particularly well for Arawn, but she'd think about that later.

Matraqua's wife, the Lady Hilya, not only looked disinterested in Eluned, she seemed as if she might be a thousand miles away. She was probably about her husband's age but her dull and frizzy, mostly grey hair pulled tightly back from her face, faded brown eyes and dull skin made her look much older. Eluned decided she looked abused, perhaps not physically but emotionally, and almost as if she had had too many children and not enough time between each pregnancy to recover, and it had left her tired and careworn. She reminded her of one of her nannies. The woman had had a dozen children and looked constantly fatigued.

"His majesty King Hevel of Adamah," Arawn said of a

man about forty years of age. As Eluned curtsied before him, she noted that she was being introduced to the rare exception she had noted on entering the room. Of medium height with well-groomed chestnut hair, a neat mustache and goatee, Hevel was both slender and obviously fit. He was also dressed impeccably. Like the other men, his eyes seemed drawn to her cleavage. However, there was nothing but a distant curiosity in his dark blue eyes.

The Princess had a little experience with homosexuals because she had once befriended one of the castle's minstrels, and he, being pleased to have a uncritical confidant, shared everything with her—his hopes, fears, loves, losses. He had also introduced her to friends that were similarly inclined, and she realized immediately that Hevel must be like her minstrel friend because he was definitely unmoved by her presence. The necklace clearly enchanted those who would naturally be attracted to the one wearing it. Therefore, she was surprised when the woman standing next to Hevel was introduced as his fiancée. Apparently, he had felt it prudent to keep to tradition and marry a female.

It was with great consternation, then, as she was introduced to Yona, to feel the woman's obvious attraction to her. She was a good twenty years younger than her future husband, so only a year or two older than the Princess. She was quite beautiful, voluptuous even. She was maybe an inch or two taller than Eluned with long and wavy deep auburn hair and dark brown eyes fringed in long black lashes. Her mouth was as sensuous as her body, and the Princess was truly bewildered by the match. She couldn't think of anything more frustrating than being married to someone to whom you would never, could never, feel physical attraction.

Yona was still holding Eluned's hand, and the Princess suddenly experienced a moment of fear for her should anyone else note how enamored of the Princess she seemed to be.

"We should sit together at dinner," Eluned said. "It has been quite a while since I've had a female about my age to talk to."

"I would love that," she gushed, leaning forward to whisper, "I've been stuck with these old stick-in-the-muds for so long now, I'm going crazy." Eluned didn't think that was particularly kind to the young couple she noted waiting by the fireplace, but she nodded in understanding.

She was then introduced to King Hevel's chancellor—Chazak. He was older, too, probably about late forties to fifty, and no doubt one of the old fogeys Yona referred to. He had a full head of striking silver hair and an aquiline nose beneath eyes of cobalt blue that sparkled in obvious appreciation of Eluned's beauty. She had to wonder if she weren't wearing the necklace, if he would have been less obvious about the attraction, or perhaps, above it all.

Chazak's wife, the Lady Aviv, was clearly unimpressed. She greeted her politely but her thin mouth and stern brown eyes were definitely disapproving of Eluned's cleavage. She was shorter than the Princess with salt and pepper hair pulled back into a bun at the nape of her neck. She seemed to be about the same age as her husband. It wasn't so much that she was dumpy but rather that she seemed well settled into her middle age.

Arawn led her over to the fireplace where he introduced his lord high steward. Hywel couldn't have been more than thirty, Eluned thought. He was gorgeous, which explained why Hevel hadn't been able to keep his eyes from continually flicking in his direction. He was about as tall as Gwrhyr with broad shoulders and chest and notably well muscled. Thick blond hair the color of wheat poured down his back and eyes the color of sapphires bored into hers. She had a difficult time not responding to his interest.

Hywel's wife, on the other hand, was not amused. The Lady

Auron's pale blue eyes spoke volumes. "Leave my husband alone," they said. Eluned tried, unsuccessfully, she thought, to promise with her eyes that she had no intention of stealing her husband's affections. Auron, despite her name, had a frail, almost spectral beauty, definitely more white than gold. Her long hair was as fine as cornsilk and nearly as white. She was petite, barely over five feet tall, and Hywel struck Eluned as almost too alive for his mate.

Arawn's chancellor, Gethin, was also attractive, and the Princess wondered why the king preferred to be surrounded by beautiful people. In his mid forties, Gethin was about Arawn's height, fit and muscular with dark mahogany hair that gleamed in the firelight.

His wife, the Lady Celyn, was probably in her late thirties with carroty orange hair that curled tightly about her face. Her skin was pale and freckled and her dark green eyes betrayed her jealousy. Her full lips parted in greeting to reveal straight white teeth, and it was clear that Celyn worked hard on maintaining her appearance. Maybe that was why she was jealous, she thought. Celyn didn't come by her attractiveness easily, while at eighteen years of age, Eluned had yet to worry about her appearance. But who knew? When she was Celyn's age, she too, might have to put more effort into it.

She was now glad she had offered to sit next to Yona—it would keep her away from the overly attentive men and their resentful women. She was still glad Gwrhyr had offered her the necklace. At least she wouldn't have to work at impressing most of the men, and Hevel seemed happy to be relieved of entertaining Yona.

Actually, Arawn conveyed the impression that he approved as well. When they were called to dinner, he had rearranged the seating so that rather than sitting next to Hevel, Yona would sit next to Eluned.

Arawn and Hamartia took places at each end of the table and Eluned, who was placed to Arawn's right, wondered if the king didn't know Hevel better than she thought for he seated Hywel next to him. Eluned, sighed, quietly, as she placed her napkin on her lap. This was going better than she hoped. Now, she had only to make small talk with Yona and Arawn, or perhaps Hevel and Hywel across the table and she could avoid those from Simoon altogether. They truly gave her the creeps.

At one point during the meal, Yona was drawn into conversation with Gethin who sat to her right, and Arawn was talking quietly with Hevel. Eluned grabbed the chance to really look at the dining room, which she had neglected to do a couple of evenings before when she had been so distracted by Arawn. Her eyes were drawn to a large arras that covered the wall on the opposite side of the table. It was almost a triptych in that within the one tapestry it portrayed three completely different scenes.

It was quite striking. The first scene featured a young woman with long, shining hair the color of polished copper, not unlike Arawn's. She was seated amidst a sea of myriad flowers and a unicorn lay at her side, its head nestled in her lap. Eluned nearly gasped when she saw what the virgin was doing (for only a virgin can tame a unicorn, Eluned couldn't help but think). She was sliding a golden halter carefully over its pinkish muzzle. Eluned's eyes quickly slid to the next scene.

Her heart started beating more quickly. A tall and imposing woman holding the reigns for two unseen horses in one hand and a spear in the other stared menacingly out of the tapestry. She had snakes for hair—vipers that twisted and curled and hissed about her face. But it was what she was standing in that drew Eluned's attention. A chariot! The chariot, no doubt. It was quite simple with what looked like iron-rimmed wheels and constructed from wood and wickerwork. It was a conveyance built for warfare and the warrior looked ready to kill. The Princess was glad it was only a tapestry.

That left only the chessboard. Eluned's eyes flicked to the final scene. On a small marble table sat a chessboard of silver and gold. She wasn't sure how but somehow the creator of the tapestry had managed to convey that the pieces were moving themselves. On each side of the table, a king leaned forward watching the progression of the game intently—one with robes of red velvet and ermine and a gilded crown studded with jewels resting upon the golden hair of his head; the other wore a cloak of black silk embroidered with silvery moons, stars and other symbols. Upon hair black as obsidian sat an intricately filigreed crown of silver.

"You've noticed my treasure," Arawn interrupted her absorption.

"Excuse me?"

"The arras on the wall. It is quite a treasure, is it not?"

"I don't think I have ever seen one so detailed. It's breathtaking."

"And, of course, it depicts the three treasures of my kingdom."

Eluned looked at him, confused. At least, she prayed she looked confused. "Treasures?"

"You're aware of the Thirteen Treasures of the Thirteen Kingdoms, of course?"

Eluned blushed because she would have to lie once again, and was thankful for once for the uncontrollable reddening of her cheeks. "No, I'm not sure I've heard of them. What are they?"

Arawn raised his eyebrows in surprise. "I guess they are so much a part of the history of this kingdom that I just assumed everyone, particularly a princess, would know about them."

Eluned blushed again. This time it was because she hadn't known about them before she'd left her father's kingdom. "I feel I am sorely missing a part of my education."

"Not to fear, my dear. We have plenty of time. It is a long story, and I will regale you with it on another evening."

The Princess gave him her most winning smile and gently caressed his hand. "It will be a pleasure."

"The pleasure will be all mine," he assured her.

Somehow she had no doubt that that would be true. She hoped she had convinced him about her ignorance of the treasures. The last thing they needed was for him to be suspicious.

THE MEAL WAS EVERYTHING BONPO HAD PROMISED it would be, but by the time they got up from the table and headed toward the music room for after dinner drinks and entertainment, Eluned had lost track of what she'd eaten. Fortunately, she'd had enough wine to remove any inhibitions about playing and was looking forward to stunning the mostly appreciative crowd with her rendition of the First, and perhaps, Second, Movements of Bach's Italian concerto.

She was glad she stood to play because it prevented anyone from joining her on a bench. She played beautifully and after she had finished the First Movement, Hywel joined her at the harpsichord.

"Are you familiar with Bársony's Variation Number Thirteen?" he asked, referring to a composer more contemporary to their time.

"Yes, of course," she replied.

"Why don't you play the bottom keyboard, and I shall play the top," he said, managing to make it sound sexual. Then, much to her chagrin, he stood behind her, reaching around her on either side to place his hands on the keys. She felt caged in, but decided to act as if it were the most natural thing in the world to play this way. She focused on the keys and not on the way his body pressed against her back or the warmth of his breath against the top of her head. Auron was going to kill her or him, one. And she wouldn't blame her a bit. She was glad when the piece finally ended and Hywel was forced to step away from her. She could feel her cheeks flaming, which embarrassed her even more.

"Shall we withdraw to the parlor?" Arawn asked, rescuing her from the awkward moment. Sliding her arm through his, they led the way back down the hallway to the parlor they'd spent time in the night she had dined with him.

Arawn handed her a snifter of brandy from the tray already set up on the coffee table before leading her to a small sofa in front of the fireplace. The others picked up their drinks and scattered around the rest of the room. Yona pulled up a chair to sit to Eluned's left. It was apparent that Hywel wanted to join them as well, but Auron, with a warning glance, led him off to a couple of armchairs that were off by themselves in the back of the room.

Eluned's heart sank as Hevel sat in the armchair next to Yona and the King and Queen of Simoon took the other two armchairs in front of the fireplace. Not only were they all royalty (or soon to be), but also Eluned got the distinct impression that she and Arawn were being thought of as a couple, despite the fact she was betrothed to King Uriel. After all, that would hardly be an impediment to his marrying her should they both wish to do so. She just hoped he wasn't in any hurry to seal her fate in that particular way. He was quite attractive, yes, but she could never live with a man who would be happy to see her father on the opposite side of a battlefield.

She spent the next hour or so fending off probing questions about what was going on in her father's kingdom. Fortunately, with her age, she was able to play dumb to some degree and the excuse, "I was so busy planning my escape from Zion that I wasn't paying attention to what was going on," was getting well worn by the time Arawn's guests began retiring for the night.

"Why don't I spend the night with you?" Yona asked Eluned as Hevel stood to take his leave. "I'm just here with my ladies-in-waiting, and I would love to get to know you better, you know, just have some girl time for a change? We could have a slumber party."

"I think that would be lovely," Eluned said, graciously, but wondering. A slumber party? Really? She'd never experienced a slumber party. It would certainly be a good way to find out what everyone had been up to, and having a friend on the inside, so to speak, was never a bad idea. Besides, she wanted to ask her about her espousal to King Hevel.

Hevel raised an eyebrow and smirked, but said he had no problem with it. "We return to Arberth tomorrow, though," he reminded her.

"Tomorrow!" Yona wailed. "Can't we stay here a few more days? We only just arrived."

"Arberth?" Eluned asked.

"My winter palace, Castle Emrys, is there." Arawn said. "It's on the coast. Most of my staff winter there every year."

"Oh," Eluned said, understanding dawning. "That explains why it has been so quiet around here."

"Ha!" the king laughed, "I hadn't thought it might seem unusually quiet to you. What must you have thought?"

"I admit I did wonder," she laughed, "but I was sure there was an explanation and so there is." But, she felt, that still didn't quite explain it. One would think the castle would be just as noisy, even noisier, perhaps, when the king was gone. As the saying goes . . . when the cat's away . . . She shivered.

"Cold?" Arawn asked, concerned.

"No, a rabbit ran over my grave."

"A rabbit ran over my grave," Hamartia chortled. "I have never heard that expression.

"Really?" Eluned asked, "What do you say when one shivers for apparently no reason?"

"A ghul has breathed on my neck."

Eluned shivered again. "Yes, I can see that, or feel it, rather."

"So," Yona interrupted. "Can I stay here at least a few more days? Please?"

"Yes, yes, my dear," Hevel acquiesced. "I see no harm in it, do you?" he deferred to Arawn.

"No, absolutely not. I will be busy most days, and Eluned will need entertainment."

"Thank you," Yona squeezed Hevel's arm. "I truly appreciate it, my love."

"As a matter of fact," Arawn added, "if you would like to return to Arberth, I would be more than happy to escort Yona when I travel there next Deethyai. Perhaps Eluned would like to come along and spend some time there as well before we return to Castle Pwyll for the summer?"

"I don't know what to say," the Princess stuttered. "It sounds wonderful. Is it warm there?"

"Warmer than here," Arawn said, "but it is a nearly four-day journey south. King Hamartia and Queen Foehn and their retinue will be returning to Simoon, of course. But, the others will spend a few more months there."

Chokhmah, no doubt, would be allowed to accompany her, but she didn't think the others would be invited.

"We might ask your Jabberwock to come along as well. He might be entertaining," Arawn mused.

"Jabberwock?" Hevel asked.

"You've heard of the Janawar?" Arawn asked.

"Yes. I thought they had all been exterminated. Wait, this couldn't be the creature that ran away with Queen Fuchsia of Zion?"

"The very one."

Hevel began to laugh although it sounded quite mirthless. Hamartia and Foehn began to chuckle as well.

"What's so funny?" Yona asked. Eluned's cheeks were blazing.

"I am amazed that Seraphim allowed him any contact with his daughter," Hamartia said.

"Or that he even allowed him to return to Zion," Hevel added.

Now that they said it, Eluned wondered as well. Why had

her father allowed her to spend hours nearly every day for the past eleven years with the Janawar that had helped disgrace his family's name?

"It doesn't make sense, does it?" Arawn queried the Princess.

She shook her head in wonder. No. It didn't.

"Perhaps your father is too kind hearted for his own good," Hamartia said, managing to make it sound both deprecating and condemnatory.

"I'm sure you do not have to tell her that," Arawn said, sliding an arm around the Eluned's waist and drawing her closer. "After all, she is the one who ran away. Correct, my dear?" He pinched her cheek, albeit gently, like she was a young child.

Eluned blushed again. What could she say? It was "the story" after all. She felt the tears prick her eyes.

Arawn's lips brushed her cheek. "It was that miserable?"

Eluned nodded, allowing the misunderstanding, and a tear escaped the barrier of her lid and slid down her cheek. Arawn kissed it away and the Princess did her best not to shudder.

"I still don't understand," Yona grumbled.

"I'll explain later," Eluned promised her.

"Well, I say most definitely invite the Janawar." Hevel agreed. "What did you say he calls himself? Jabberwock?"

Eluned decided she'd let the Bandersnatch explain that one himself.

"She arrived with a most unusual entourage," Arawn continued, enjoying himself. "In addition to the Janawar, there is also a giant and a gypsy as well as a young man who appears to serve multiple purposes."

"A giant?" Foehn asked. "From Dziron, I presume?"

"Yes, Madam, he is my cook," Eluned explained.

"I understand he has made himself quite useful in my kitchens." Arawn added.

"He helped with tonight's meal, I believe," the Princess said. "I hope you were pleased. He would love to be useful to you."

Everyone agreed the meal had been wonderful.

"And the gypsy?" Hamartia asked. Trust him to be interested in the females in the group.

"Chokhmah is my maidservant but she is also a healer, which I felt would come in useful."

"Does she tell fortunes?" Yona asked, eyes lighting up.

"I believe tarot cards are her specialty," Eluned said.

"Oooh. Do you think she'd do a reading for me?"

"She'll do whatever I ask her to do," Eluned said, grimacing inwardly at the presumption.

"And the young man?" Hevel asked.

"Gwrhyr speaks many languages and there seems to be very little he can't do," Eluned tried to remember the annoyance that often caused and emphasized that in her tone. "But, I understand he is keen to join your army."

"Indeed? That must be what Captain Bleddyn wants to speak to me about. Well, one can never have too many soldiers, right Hamartia?"

"Agreed. Well, your Highness," he said, taking Eluned's hand and pressing his lips to it; they were cold and wet and very unpleasant, "it was a pleasure meeting you and I, personally, am glad you chose to run to Annewven rather than Tarshish or Naphtali. Although, I would have been happy to welcome you to Simoon."

I'll bet you would, Eluned thought and nearly gagged.

Queen Foehn bowed to her politely, "Princess. I am sure we will meet again."

"It was an honor meeting you," the Princess returned the bow, praying with all her might that they might never cross paths again. Thank Omni they were returning to Simoon on the morrow.

"Your Highness," Hevel bowed. "I look forward to seeing you in Arberth."

"Thank you, Your Majesty," she curtsied. Hevel didn't bother her nearly as much as the King and Queen of Simoon.

Yona kissed Hevel's cheek. "I'll see you in a week, darling."

"Enjoy your time with the Princess," he said, kindly.

"Thank you so much. I really am looking forward to it."

Before the young women said their farewells to Arawn, he asked Yona to inform her women to return with the party travelling to Arberth on the morrow.

"If it is to be just the five of us," he explained, "we can take the phaeton and arrive the day after the main party."

"Hevel and the others will travel there by the phaeton tomorrow," Yona explained. And then a servant will bring it back."

"I don't understand," Eluned said.

"Oh," Yona exclaimed, "he has this magic coach that can take you wherever you want to go in an instant."

Eluned's mouth dropped open in faux astonishment but her mind was racing. That was the answer. If they could steal Arawn's phaeton, obviously constructed from the chariot of Morgan the Wealthy, they could be in Favonia immediately. There were only five of them. Bonpo might be a problem, though. She'd have to see the carriage first but it looked as if she'd get to experience it first hand.

Before heading off, arm and arm, toward the staircase, Eluned reminded Yona that they needed to stop by her room first.

"Ah, yes," Yona agreed. "I will need to gather my things before my ladies leave in the morning."

ELUNED BREATHED A SIGH OF RELIEF when they reached her room and only Chokhmah was present. It would have been hard to explain why Bonpo and Gwrhyr were there. She introduced Yona to the gypsy and Chokhmah promised her a tarot reading the next day, warning her, as she had Eluned, to meditate on the question she wanted answered. While Yona was getting ready for bed, Eluned asked Chokhmah if she'd heard from the fellows. But Bonpo was still in the kitchens, Gwrhyr with the soldiers, and Jabberwock had retired early. Feeling a bit lighter for the moment, Eluned took her turn performing her nightly ablutions before the girls settled down in front of the fire to chat a bit more.

"I've been dying to ask you," Eluned said without preamble, "why on earth you're engaged to Hevel. I can't think of a more miserable match."

"You're right,"" Yona replied. "It should have been. My father arranged the betrothal because he thought it would take care of my little problem."

"Problem?"

"The fact I prefer women to men. He was greatly embarrassed by it. But, it turned out that Hevel thought it an excellent solution because we wouldn't have to pretend to be who we aren't as long as we are discreet about it."

"Ah," Eluned said, understanding. "A marriage in name only, so to speak."

"Granted, I would much rather fall in love and be married to whoever she might be, but I wasn't really offered a choice in the matter. Fortunately, Hevel and I get along quite well and he gives me a fair amount of freedom when I am with him. At home, my parents practically keep me prisoner for fear I might shame them in some way."

"That's good to know," Eluned said, before switching the subject to Arberth and Castle Emrys and what they might do while there.

8ᵀᴴ FEHARN

The gentle warmth of the sun against her eyelids plucked her from a dream in which a gorgeous young man was embracing her from behind, his face buried in her neck, breath hot against her throat.

As the fogginess of sleep dissipated, she realized that reality had intruded upon her dream and that it was Yona's arm draped over her waist. Her face was buried in the Princess's hair and Eluned could feel her warm, moist exhalations against her neck. It wasn't unpleasant, and she hated to risk waking her new friend, but she really needed to get out of bed. Carefully lifting Yona's arm, she slowly rolled away from her and off the bed.

While in the bathroom, she could hear Chokhmah puttering, albeit quietly, about her room and she tapped on her door before opening it.

"Good morning, my dear, did you sleep well?"

"I must have. Surely it's close to noon?"

"Nearly."

"I'm starving. I was so nervous last night I barely ate."

"Then, perhaps, you should awaken your friend. By the time the two of you get ready, lunch will be served."

"True. I'll wake her up." But Yona was already sitting up in the bed, stretching, when Eluned returned.

"It looks to be a beautiful day," she said, nodding at the window through which the deep azure of the sky could be seen.

"I have an idea," Eluned said, walking over to the window and studying the labyrinth below, "Why don't we pack a picnic and have our lunch in the labyrinth gazebo? Seems like a perfect day for it."

"What fun!" Yona exclaimed, joining her at the window. "I haven't been down there yet."

It didn't take long for them to get dressed and head down to the dining room where Chokhmah was waiting for them, basket in hand.

They took turns carrying the basket as they twisted and turned their way to the center of the labyrinth. It was heavy and Eluned was dying to know what was in it. She was sure she could smell chicken and freshly baked bread . . .

. . . in addition, she found a cluster of grapes, a small wheel of cheese and a bottle of fruity white wine tasting of crisp pears and apples.

Eluned was so busy eating at first that she paid little attention to her surroundings, but as her hunger was sated, she began to take more note of the gazebo. The previous time she'd been here, both Arawn and the castle had consumed her thoughts. This time, her eyes were drawn to the floor, which was composed of wood in an intricate parquetry pattern. The motif was beautiful but it was the very center of the floor that incited her heart to jump painfully against her ribs. The design was a heptagon and in each of its seven slices was one of the alchemical figures she had found on the scrap of parchment in the library. Each symbol apparently inlaid into the wood in its own metal. Whatever did it mean?

She wanted to talk to Chokhmah about it but wasn't sure

how much she could trust Yona. She would just have to act as if it were a pretty design, nothing more.

"What an unusual design," she said, standing up and walking to the center of the gazebo. She crouched and traced the alchemical characters with the tip of her finger. Chokhmah and Yona joined her. "Do you know what they mean?" she asked them.

"I have no idea," Chokhmah said.

"Me either," Yona added. "How truly bizarre."

"Perhaps it meant something only to the person who designed it," Chokhmah suggested.

A narrow band of bronze separated the heptagon from the rest of the floor almost as if it were a very large medallion. Eluned was sure there was a purpose for it being there but she wasn't sure she'd have time to discover what that might be until she returned from Arberth.

Chokhmah stood and returned to the bench. "Do you two have any plans for the rest of this afternoon?" she asked as she stowed the remains of their lunch in the basket.

Yona and Eluned looked at each other blankly. "What I'd like is a nap," Eluned laughed, rubbing her full belly, "but I probably need to walk. Have you explored the town? Do you think we'd be allowed to do that?"

"No, I haven't," Yona said, "but I imagine it's warm enough for the market to be open. That might be fun."

"Agreed. Who knows what we might see. Or find, for that matter."

"It is Deethseel," Chokhmah warned. "The market may not be open."

"Oh, King Arawn doesn't care about that," Yona said, "He doesn't worship Omni. But for courtesy's sake, it cannot open until the noon bells ring. At least, that's true in Arberth."

"What time is it?" Eluned glanced at the sky. "It must be past noon."

"I would say it is closer to one o'clock," Chokhmah guessed. "The bells were ringing noon as we were walking to the gazebo."

"Ah, yes," Eluned remembered. "Then let's return the basket to the kitchen and walk down to the town."

THE MARKET WAS CROWDED, noisy and raucous as the merchants cried their wares and townsfolk haggled over the various goods, but as the first truly warm day of the year, you could hear the joy in their voices.

Salted fish from the coast, chicken, fresh and salt meats, garlic, honey, onions, rhubarb, cabbages, parsnips, eggs, leeks, lettuces and other greens were among the winter's bounty. In addition, there were fabrics of cotton, silk, wool, flax alongside stalls selling household items and livestock. If they hadn't just eaten, they could have had purchased pasties filled with fruit, chopped ham, chicken or eel, and seasoned with pepper, soft cheese, or egg. Eluned would have bought one to take back to the castle for dinner had not she and Yona been invited to dine with Arawn that evening. Doubtless whatever they would dine on that evening would be far superior to a pasty, but she craved one anyhow.

While there really wasn't anything she needed, Eluned found a stunning pair of earrings at a jeweler's stall. The chandelier-style earrings were decorated with multi-colored gemstones—amethyst, turquoise, coral—all inset within intricately wrought silver.

Yona insisted on buying them for her and Eluned was willing to accept the gift on the condition they return to the booksellers where Yona had debated the purchase of a book of poetry by the renowned poet Schlomo, and allow Eluned to purchase it for her.

"Do you see something you want?" she asked Chokhmah.

"I have yet to see anything without which I cannot live,"

she said as they moved on. But, as they passed by the stall of the herbalist, the gypsy halted so suddenly Eluned ran into her.

"Actually," she said, browsing the herbs, "I could really use some of these." She lifted a bundle of belladonna and sniffed it.

"Gather what you need," Eluned said.

Groundsel, St. John's Wort, chamomile, poppy seeds and valerian were added to her parcel along with the belladonna.

"Thank you, my lady," she said with a wink.

"You're quite welcome. You take very good care of me," Eluned squeezed Chokhmah's free hand. Shortly thereafter, the bells chimed the hour of four and the women decided it was time to return to the castle to prepare for the evening.

"THOSE ARE VERY INTERESTING EARRINGS," Arawn remarked as he poured wine into the women's goblets. "I've got the strangest feeling that I've seen them before."

"Well, I know they don't actually match my gown (she was attired in the cream silk) but Yona bought them for me today and I was dying to wear them."

Arawn studied them a moment longer and was just shaking his head as if he just couldn't remember when his expression froze. "No, that can't be right."

"What is it?"

"I thought I remembered. But no. Impossible. Where did you get them?" His eyes flashed with barely controlled rage.

"It was a jeweler's stall in the market, not far from the Cathedral."

"Hmmm, well perhaps they're just reminiscent of the pair I'm remembering," he tried to recover.

"Were they yours?" Yona asked. "I mean, were they a pair you gave to someone?"

"No. Not mine. Let's just say they belonged to a lady friend. So," he changed the subject, "did you enjoy your trip to the market?"

"It was very entertaining. So much to take in. I can't imagine anything that there was anything that wasn't available for sale," Eluned enthused, "Right, Yona?"

"It's true. We had a wonderful time."

"It was all I could do, though, not to bring back one of those pasties," Eluned continued, "even though I knew the food here is far superior," she glanced down as a bowl of soup was set before her—it appeared to be egg and broth ladled over spinach chiffonade—and knew it would taste exquisite.

"You should have the kitchen prepare you pasties for lunch tomorrow," he said more to the server than Eluned. "Any preference?"

"I haven't had eel in a long time," she informed the server, who nodded and returned to the kitchens with the message.

"I want to know more about the arras," Eluned said, lifting a spoonful of soup to her mouth. "What is the treasure in the first panel? The necklace?"

"Necklace?" Arawn glanced over at the tapestry. "No. No. It is a piece of jewelry that has been handed down in the family, but it is the halter that is the treasure."

"A halter?"

"The Halter of Clydno Eiddyn," Yona said. "They say if it is attached to the foot of your bed, whatever horse you wish for will fill it."

"Unfortunately," Arawn scowled, "my great-great-grandmother lost it in the very way you see portrayed."

"What?" Eluned exclaimed. This was bad news.

"Yes, it was more than a century ago," he stared gloomily at the tapestry for a moment. "According to the story that has been told through the generations, when my second great-grandmother was a young woman, perhaps about sixteen years old, she decided to discover if there was any truth to the rumor that a unicorn made its home in the Forest of Avalach, not far from the family castle at Arberth." He sighed and sipped his soup for a moment, lost in thought. Yona and Eluned were wise enough to remain silent.

"At any rate," he said, shaking his head to clear his thoughts, "she, the Princess Morrighan, not only found the unicorn but she managed to tame it. Apparently, it was her wish to put a halter on the creature and lead it back to the castle. Why she chose to use the treasure, we'll never know. Perhaps she thought she needed something magical to capture such an otherworldly beast or maybe she thought her unicorn deserved something both beautiful and valuable. Regardless, she slid the halter over the animal's muzzle and it reacted violently. It gored her in the left shoulder with its horn and fled, never to be seen again."

"Obviously she survived," Eluned said, "but did it do any damage?"

"She never used her left arm again and she refused to talk about it other than what I've told you," he said.

"By Omni, what a story," Yona said. "She must have felt awful for having lost one of Annewven's treasures."

"Her father never forgave her, but she was, unfortunately, his only remaining child. Two sons died in infancy, and another daughter was also sickly and died when she was eleven. He was left with no choice but to pass on the monarchy to Morrighan and her husband, Arawn."

"Your namesake?" Eluned asked.

"And my great-grandfather's, and my grandfather's and so on."

"No lack of healthy sons since," Yona laughed.

"No indeed," Arawn agreed. "The queen did redeem herself in that aspect, at least."

The server entered again and removed the soup bowls while another servant replaced them with plates containing beautifully arranged salmon with potato fans and asparagus and watercress timbales.

As she tasted her timbale (which was, no surprise, excellent), Eluned reflected on the story. Was the halter gone forever? Would they be able to bring peace without it? How long did unicorns live? Gwrhyr and Jabberwock were not going to be happy to hear this. "Well, I know the chariot is safe," she said, studying the middle panel, "or, at least I assume the chariot and the phaeton are one and the same."

"You assume correctly," Arawn confirmed. "The family has always chosen to either use the treasures or keep them where an eye can be kept upon them rather than hide them away and risk them disappearing through rot or theft or what have you."

"That makes sense," Yona said. "After all, it was one of the family that lost the halter so at least you know what happened to it."

"So who is the woman in the chariot?" Eluned asked.

"The artist's interpretation of the warrior queen to whom the chariot first belonged," Arawn replied.

"Intimidating," Eluned remarked.

"But I thought Morgan the Wealthy was male," Yona said.

"No, you assumed. The story in our family is that Morgan was a she and as the treasures originated in Annewven . . ."

"Then you would know," Yona acknowledged.

"With all due respect," Eluned spoke, "it would seem, in that case, that Annewven was once matriarchal or, at least, that men and women were equal. When did that change?"

"Centuries before my time would be my guess although I accede your point. Perhaps the pendulum will eventually swing back that way."

"You never know," she agreed, leaning back to allow the server to take her plate.

They finished the meal with almond cheesecake while Arawn explained the final panel of the arras, which portrayed the Chessboard of Gwenddolau.

"I can understand that the pieces will continue to play once set up," Eluned said, "but to what purpose? The only thing

I can think of is to help determine the outcome of something without using violence."

"Exactly," Arawn said. "It was supposed to be used to avert wars, but monarchs rarely like to be told by magic that what they want belongs rightfully to the other."

"In other words, they prefer might to right," Eluned frowned.

"It would appear so," Arawn agreed.

"Will I get a chance to see it?" Eluned asked.

"Of course you shall. Perchance one day we shall even 'play' a game."

"Do you have to physically make the first move?" the Princess asked.

"The first three, actually."

"Then how one begins the game is quite important," Yona noted.

Arawn laughed. "Always, my dear, always. Shall we retire to the parlor?"

"Didn't you find it odd?" Yona asked later when they were ensconced in Eluned's room.

"What?"

"Just how strange the king acted when he saw your earrings," Yona said.

"That was bizarre wasn't it?"

"I think he was lying," Yona continued. "I think he gave them as a gift to some woman, probably one of his paramours, and she sold them after he discarded her."

"Discarded? That sounds like she was rubbish," Eluned said in dismay.

"Well, that's what they say."

"What who say?" Eluned asked.

"The rumor is that Arawn uses a woman until he's had enough of her and then moves on to the next," Yona explained.

"Discarding her like trash," Eluned said, comprehending.

"Without a stipend or any other support even if she sires one of his brats."

"Brats?" The Princess was aghast.

"Oh, look closely next time we're in town. You're sure to see a little Arawn or two running around."

"That's horrifying!"

"Well, he would never treat you that way; you're royalty. I imagine he intends to make you his queen at some point," Yona attempted to console her, "so until then he'll be on his best behavior."

"That's hardly reassuring."

"Don't worry too much," Yona said, hugging her a little more suggestively than Eluned liked, "I'll always be there for you."

"Thank you," Eluned replied returning the hug a little less enthusiastically. She wasn't sure that news was completely comforting either. On the other hand, to have a friend on the enemy side, so to speak, could be to her advantage, and she certainly didn't want to cause Yona to be her adversary. She was going to have to make a concerted effort to convince the beautiful young woman that she was truly interested in being her friend. Not too difficult a task, really, she thought, as she already liked her quite a lot. She hugged her a bit tighter. "Thank you," she whispered. "I really need a friend."

THE FOLLOWING MORNING ELUNED BOWED OUT OF, as gracefully as possible, going with Yona to get a pedi- and manicure. "Hevel insists," Yona explained. "As does my mother. They don't want me to embarrass them."

Eluned's mother had lost that battle years ago when she was a young teenager. The simple problem was that the Princess used her hands too much. At the rate she cracked and chipped her fingernail polish, she would need a daily manicure. She could almost swear that all she had to do was look at her nails and the polish would flake off. There was a simple solution to her problem—she kept her nails short, very short, and buffed them (for her mother's sake) nightly. Although she had been somewhat derelict in that department since she began her journey. She promised herself she would buff them that evening before dinner with the king. Meanwhile, she was desperate to get to the gazebo and back before Yona was finished. Chokhmah was waiting for the word that all was clear.

As soon as Yona left the room, Eluned retrieved the scrap of vellum from the book of Scripture and called to Chokhmah. They hurried down the stairs and outside and it wasn't long before they stood, breathing heavily from nearly running the entire way, on the parquet floor of the gazebo.

Kneeling on the floor, they studied the design more intently. The heptagon was about two-and-a-half feet in diameter. Suddenly Eluned gasped. "Look at this! I didn't notice it yesterday."

"What?"

"See how each of the symbols involves three circles as part of the design?"

"Yes," Chokhmah affirmed.

"Look at the third circle of each."

"They are not quite the same as the other two circles," the gypsy was nodding her head.

"Each one is outlined by another metal. What is that? Titanium, perhaps?"

"It could be."

"But why? Eluned wondered.

"I might be wrong," Chokhmah mused, "but it looks as if each of those circles are perhaps buttons that can be depressed. See how they have managed to set each of the third circles in the same position near the center of the heptagon?"

"Yes? But why on earth?"

"I cannot imagine," Chokhmah said, pressing the tip of

her finger against one of the circles. "No, they are too inset into the floor. We need a tool of some sort and I didn't bring my bag." She looked around the gazebo but it was clean.

"What about a twig? I'll go look at the roses." Eluned returned shortly with a small piece of deadwood from one of the bushes and pushed the end of it against the third circle of the xomt design. It did, indeed, depress, but nothing happened.

"Perhaps we need to press all of them," Chokhmah suggested. Eluned pressed each of the seven buttons. Still nothing happened. "Let me see the scrap of vellum."

Eluned handed it to her, leaning forward to study it with her. "The order of the metals on the parchment is different than the order on the floor. Look. Start with nub."

"Nub, men," Chokhmah read in a clockwise direction, "hat, chesbet, asem, xomt, teht."

"Now read them from the vellum."

"Nub." The Princess depressed the nub button. "Asem, hat, xomt, men, teht, chesbet." As she read them, Eluned continued to depress the buttons, and as she pressed the last, there was a slight whooshing noise and a rush of cool air as the heptagon slowly rose upward on two metal tubes, revealing a descending tunnel beneath.

"It was a code," Eluned whispered. "What do you suppose is down there?"

"It looks like a ladder," Chokhmah said, "but I cannot see more than a few feet down."

"And we're going to need time to find out."

"And light."

"Neither of which we have right now. We're going to have to wait until we return from Arberth to explore it."

"At least we will not have to work around Yona," Chokhmah said.

"That's true. Hopefully, we'll have a bit more freedom. I wonder how we get it to close?"

For the next five minutes the women tried everything they could think of from pushing on the heptagon, which had risen a good three feet into the air, to looking for another button within the rim of the of ladder tunnel.

"Perhaps the button is at the bottom of the ladder," Chokhmah mused aloud.

"I can't figure out how these tubes work," Eluned groused, "and we can't risk leaving it open. Arawn knows we spend time out here and so do his guards."

They stared at the open hole, which now seemed somehow malevolent. What were they going to do? Eluned started taking deep breaths.

"What are you doing?" Chokhmah asked.

"I'm trying not to panic. Have you thought of anything?"

"No," Chokhmah moaned. "There must be a way to close it, though. I can see closing it from below when one enters here, but surely it is an exit as well."

"Do you think there is another code we didn't find?"

"That seems too complicated, but let us try the code backwards."

That didn't work either. Eluned stood and started pacing. "What are we missing?"

Chokhmah retreated to the bench and stared at the gaping hole in growing frustration. And then, seemingly of its own accord, the heptagon slowly descended into place.

"That was freaky," Eluned said, stopping mid-stride.

"It must be on a timer. It feels like much time has passed but it has probably been no more than ten or fifteen minutes."

"True, but I guarantee you that's probably a fail safe. There must be some way to close it immediately."

"I agree. We must think about it while we are in Arberth. I imagine, though, that if it is another code, we will probably never find it."

AFTER A LUNCH OF THE PASTIES Eluned had craved, the women hurried to the market in search of the jeweler who sold the earrings to Yona.

"Something's just not right," Yona said, trying to explain her reason for wanting to go back. "There was something he wasn't telling us."

Eluned found herself not only quite pleased with Yona's quest, but also trusting the young woman a bit more. Perhaps she needed to return that trust in some small measure. Chokhmah left them to purchase a few more herbs, agreeing to meet them at the church when she had finished.

Fortunately, the jeweler's stall was in the same place, and soon Yona was questioning him about the earrings. "Did you make these?" she asked, displaying them in the palm of her hand.

"I doesn't make ther jewry," he explained, "I buys it off them that does."

"So, who sold you these?" Yona asked.

The vendor stared at the earrings for a moment trying to recollect how they'd come into his possession. His eyes widened slightly as he remembered. "It were a man I'd never seen before nor has seen since. He said, he uh, found'em."

"Found them?" Eluned prompted. "Did he explain where?"

"I didn't ask as he were willin' to accept less than they was worf fer payment. I jus' has ter clean'em up a wee bit."

"I don't understand." Eluned's brow was creased in perplexity.

"To be perfeckly honest yer highness, he give me ther impression he stole'em off'n a corpse." He colored. "I unnerstan if you wants to return'em."

"A corpse!" Yona paled, realizing the implication.

"No, no," Eluned assured the vendor. "We'll keep them. But why did you have to clean them?"

The man flushed again. "I can't be certain, but ther' seemed ter be a spot o'blood on'em."

Yona moaned and swayed. "Do you have a seat?" Eluned asked.

The vendor handed her a small stool and Eluned pushed Yona down onto it. "Breathe deeply and slowly," she advised.

Yona was shaking her head and muttering, "I just can't believe it."

"It ain't that uncommon ter sell dead folks jewry," the man said in his defense.

"It's not that," the Princess reassured him. "She's just faint of heart. She'll get over it. Won't you?" Eluned kicked her shin, gently.

Yona took a deep breath and stood. "The Princess is right," Yona said, trying to recover before the vendor started asking them questions. "It just caught me off guard, that's all. I'll be fine. Thanks so much for your help." She reached into her pouch and pulled out a coin, pressing it into the man's hand. "Thank you again."

"Yer mos' welcome, me ladies."

In the quiet darkness of the church, Eluned and Yona seated themselves in a back pew and waited for Chokhmah's arrival. Eluned was trying to understand the implications of what they'd been told. If the woman who had worn the earrings had died violently enough that blood splattered on them, and if Arawn recognized the earrings, what did that mean? Of course, they could easily be unrelated incidents but somehow she didn't think so, and the only reason she didn't is because of the way Arawn had reacted to the earrings. The anger. The backpedaling. He had even admitted they belonged to a lady friend.

"What are we going to do?" Yona whispered.

"Absolutely nothing, as far as the king is concerned,"

Eluned replied, "because we don't know anything for sure. But, we should definitely keep our eyes and ears open."

The creak of the door as Chokhmah entered the church interrupted them. They jumped up and were practically out the door before she'd even finished shutting it.

"What is going on?" she asked, following them back into the street.

"We really can't talk here," Eluned looked around, nervously, as if the king had spies lurking on the street corners.

"Why don't we go back to the pavilion in the labyrinth," Yona suggested. "At least there no one can sneak up on us."

"Good idea. Can we go straight there or do you need to go back to our room first?" Eluned asked Chokhmah.

"We can go there straight away assuming I do not die of curiosity first."

Eluned laughed. "Don't worry. We're probably making carracks out of coracles."

But Chokhmah's forehead creased with worry as the girls told her what they had discovered from the jewelry merchant. Without thinking, her hand flashed the sign to ward off evil.

The women were once again sitting in the pavilion in the center of the labyrinth. It had taken them a good five minutes to regain their breath after hurrying uphill toward the castle before they could relate the story to Chokhmah. Eluned found herself glancing continually at the design in the floor certain the hidden door would suddenly spring open to reveal the King or one of his spies. Despite that particular fear, she was still dying to explore the tunnel and discover its true purpose. Unfortunately, she didn't yet trust Yona quite enough to let her in on its existence.

And now they had the mysterious earrings to deal with as well. And just two more days before they left for Arberth! Not to mention the fact that they still had to figure out how they were going to acquire the chessboard and chariot and somehow find the missing halter. The Princess inhaled deeply, trying to control her rising panic.

"I think that perhaps this is something we must bring to the attention of the fellows," Chokhmah advised.

"The fellows?" Yona asked.

"Jabberwock, Gwrhyr and Bonpo," Eluned explained.

"Oh yes, I remember them being mentioned at the dinner party. Why them?"

"Because I've counted on their wisdom more than once on the journey to Castle Pwyll," Eluned explained.

"And perchance they will not find this as disturbing as we do," added Chokhmah, standing. "I think I shall see if I can send them a message to meet us tonight."

"Good idea," Eluned said, standing as well. "In which case, I could use a nap before dinner and another late night."

"Me too," Yona yawned, stretching out her hand toward Eluned. Understanding immediately, the Princess grasped it and pulled the young woman to her feet. "I suddenly feel like the weight of the world has descended upon my shoulders," Yona sighed, sliding her arm around Eluned's waist and resting her cheek against the top of her head. "Our room seems miles away."

"It certainly does," Eluned yawned. "I feel as if I could curl up right here under the rose bushes and sleep forever."

"Now that sounds like the beginning or end of a fairy tale," Chokhmah chuckled, stifling a yawn herself.

Eluned's giggle was interrupted by another jaw-cracking yawn. "I think the roses would have to be blooming in a fairy tale. Then, at least, we might be able to claim that their scent was to blame or that they were poppies in disguise."

"Don't say that!" Yona admonished, laughing, tickling Eluned's ribs. "I don't want it to snow. Let's just hurry and get to our room."

Eluned tittered in surprise. It seemed some of the old fairy tales were universal. She then picked up her pace. "Last one there doesn't get to sleep as long," she teased.

CHOKHMAH PARTED WAYS WITH THEM at the staircase. Once they reached the room, they discovered an envelope, one of the King's ornate and wax-sealed vellum envelopes, on the floor of the room, where it had obviously been pushed under the door. Eluned retrieved it from the floor and broke the seal.

"What does it say?" Yona asked, peering over her shoulder.

"I regret to inform you," she replied, attempting to make her voice sound as affected as Arawn's, "that I will not be able to share dinner with you tonight. Please accept my apologies and I look forward to seeing you tomorrow. Your servant, Arawn."

"Your servant," Yona snickered. "Nice touch. If he knew what we know, he'd be groveling at our feet."

"And praise be to Omni that we don't have to hide it from him tonight."

"True!" Yona gasped, clutching her chest as if to still her heart. "I hadn't even thought of that. What sweet relief. What do you say? A snifter of brandy to calm our nerves before a well-deserved nap?"

"Perfect, but I want to put on my nightgown, first. This room is too warm for these clothes."

CHOKHMAH WOKE THEM an hour before dinner. "I have arranged for us to be served dinner in our room," she explained, "although I should warn you, it will not be anything fancy. The fellows should be joining us about nine o'clock."

"Wonderful," Eluned said, stretching. "In that case, can I just throw on the pants and the sweater? I don't feel like dressing."

"Certainly," she replied, going to the armoire to retrieve the garments.

"Do you always ask Chokhmah what to wear?" Yona teased her.

"Only when I'm worried about breaching etiquette. If I had my choice I'd wear men's clothes all the time. They are so much more comfortable."

"I'm jealous," Yona said. "I've never worn men's clothes. I have a friend who does, but I just never have. "

"You should try it some time," Eluned enthused. "Something tells me Hevel won't have a problem with it."

Yona laughed. "He would probably find it very intriguing."

PRECISELY AT SEVEN O'CLOCK, a servant knocked on their door, and she and a couple of pages preceded to carry in trays containing cold chicken, bread and cheese, dried figs, apples and hard boiled eggs along with a pitcher of mulled wine.

"Thank you," the Princess said, escorting them from the room and discreetly pressing a coin into each of their hands. She wasn't sure if Arawn would approve, but they had gone out of their way. "We'll leave the trays outside the door when we're finished."

"SO, WHAT ARE WE GOING TO DO for the next hour or so?" Yona asked after Chokhmah had placed the remains of their meal in the hallway.

"Good question," Eluned stated. "I don't feel like reading. We could play cards. I'm sure we could send for some."

"Do you know tarok? We can play it using my tarot cards," Chokhmah offered.

"Tarot cards," Yona sat up straighter. "You promised to give me a reading."

"True, but an hour is not enough time. It is very personal. Perhaps first thing in the morning? Right after breakfast?"

Yona looked disappointed but agreed. "So what is this tarok?"

"I'll show you. Let me get my cards." Chokhmah left the room and soon returned with her cards.

The next hour flew by quickly as the girls learned the game and began to play. Luck was with Yona that evening and she was well ahead in points, taking trick after trick, when there was a rap at the door.

"They're here," Eluned jumped up and rushed to the door. Her heart was beating wildly although she wasn't self-aware enough to realize that it was the prospect of seeing Gwrhyr again that had set her pulse racing. She swung open the door, grinning widely.

"I feel like I haven't seen you all in ages," she practically squealed, standing aside so they could enter the room.

Gwrhyr arched an eyebrow but didn't comment as he noticed there was an additional person in the room.

"Your beard," Eluned exclaimed, as he passed her. It had been closely cropped and she could more clearly see his cleft chin and the dimples at either side of his mouth. His hair was pulled back in a low ponytail, as well.

"The king insists that we either shave completely or keep our beards trimmed and our hair must be cut short or pulled back," he explained.

She nodded. "It's actually quite attractive. I like it."

Gwrhyr's cheeks colored, slightly, but Eluned was already introducing them to Yona. "Gwrhyr, Jabberwock, Bonpo," Eluned said, "this is Yona. She is betrothed to King Hevel of Adamah. She's staying with me until we leave for Arberth on Deethyai."

"My lady," Gwrhyr said, brushing his lips against the back of her hand.

"It's a pleasure to make your acquaintance," Jabberwock said. "I'm sure we'll be spending more time together in the coming weeks."

"Nice meet you," Bonpo bowed.

"You're so big," Yona breathed. "I've heard about the Dzutch, but never met one. I understand they rarely leave Dziron."

"Vely true. I mus' reave. Banish."

"Ah," Yona nodded. "I'm very sorry."

"Tank you."

AFTER THE GROUP HAD SITUATED ITSELF—Jabberwock curled up in front of the fire, Bonpo filling the corner between the window and fireplace, Chokhmah in Eluned's desk chair between the two armchairs, Gwrhyr took one of the armchairs and Yona snuggled into the other with Eluned. The Princess caught the flash of amusement in Gwrhyr's eyes before he settled back into his "neutral" face.

Why was he always amused by her possible discomfort? Just to annoy him, she clasped Yona's left arm and pulled her closer. She must have seen something in Gwrhyr's eyes as well, because she twined her fingers through those of the Princess and whispered something into her ear.

She only whispered, "Someone's jealous," but did a good job of making it look like she was saying something a lot more provocative.

"Indeed," Eluned whispered back and lightly nuzzled Yona's ear for good measure.

Jabberwock and Chokhmah watched the interplay with thinly disguised amusement as they both knew the Princess and her friend were putting on a show for Gwrhyr's benefit.

Before he could lose his temper, though, Chokhmah cleared her throat and said, "You are, no doubt, wondering why we have asked you here."

"We are indeed," Gwrhyr's voice was gruff.

"Why do you not tell him, Princess?" Chokhmah suggested.

"Gladly. Yesterday, after lunch, we decided to go explore the village . . ." She carefully explained everything from buying the earrings to the King's reaction to questioning the jeweler that afternoon. At one point, early in the story, Chokhmah left and returned with a few more mugs and another pitcher of wine.

Afterwards, Gwrhyr stared into the depths of his mug as if it were a scrying bowl, Jabberwock's eyes reflected the myriad colors of the dancing flames and Bonpo could have been asleep, but it was the latter that spoke first.

"I be vely caleful if I were you."

"Why? What do you suspect?" Eluned wanted to know.

"I may be mistaken but might be litual kirring."

"Like human sacrifice?" Eluned asked, swallowing hard.

"Just knowing what we know about King Arawn," Gwrhyr said, taking a long sip from his mug, "it wouldn't surprise me at all."

"That being said," the Bandersnatch added, "there is no way he'd risk harming either you or Yona. He needs his allies and he needs you, Princess."

"So like Yona said last night? She was probably one of his concubines?"

"That's a nice way of putting it," Gwrhyr laughed.

"A whore then? Is that what you mean?" Eluned demanded.

"Nothing that crass," Gwrhyr said. "He did give her earrings after all. Concubine implies that he took care of her."

"I hadn't realized there were so many degrees of bad women although I guess calling them bad is kind of judgmental," the Princess mused.

"She was probably more of a doxy or courtesan," Jabb said. "Promiscuous but monogamous to the king while he used her. And you cannot necessarily blame her . . ."

"Really!" Yona interjected. "As I told you last night, Eluned, the King kind of has that reputation. He takes who he wants unless it would mess things up for him."

"Wow. You learn something new every day," Eluned said.

"Regardless," Jabberwock sighed. "We must be very careful."

"Bonpo and I will nose around a bit while you're gone," Gwrhyr said. "Between the house staff and the army, someone's bound to have heard some rumor."

"Will we see you again before we leave?" Eluned asked as the fellows stood to take their leave.

"I doubt it," Gwrhyr said. "The army is heading out for maneuvers tomorrow for a week."

"Oh." Eluned wasn't sure why she felt so disappointed, but didn't rebel when Gwrhyr hugged her.

"Be careful," he said, hazel eyes boring into hers. "I'll see you when you return." And then he was striding down the hallway toward the soldiers' quarters.

Bonpo said his goodbyes, and ambled down the hall toward the kitchens. Eluned looked at Jabberwock questioningly.

"He's staying with the kitchen staff now," he confirmed.

"So are you alone?"

"I don't mind. I've spent most of my life alone."

"You're always welcome here," she offered.

"Thank you. I will take that under consideration." And he trotted down the hall toward the empty barracks room.

10ᵀᴴ Fᴇʜᴀʀɴ

A cymbal crash of thunder jolted the Princess out of a disturbing dream in which monster-masked men were strapping her to the altar stone atop the hillock in Ruisidho. She sat up, heart racing, causing Yona to stir in her sleep beside her.

Sliding out of bed, she padded on bare feet to the window. Another flash of lightning, followed a few seconds later by a ferocious boom, sent Eluned scurrying back to bed. Definitely a day to sleep in.

It was still raining when she reawakened, and she and Yona were forced to remain inside that day. After breakfast, while Yona was getting her much-anticipated tarot reading, Eluned returned to the library where she spent the next few hours finally finishing The Ghost of Loss, but not until after she'd researched unicorns. Just in case.

Eluned joined Chokhmah and Yona for a lunch of deliciously warming chicken and rice soup in the dining room before they all returned to the library. The women spent the remainder of the afternoon snuggled into the armchairs in front of the fireplace where they played cards and a few of the various board games they'd found on the lower shelf of a bookcase.

About five o'clock, they returned to their rooms to prepare for dinner.

But, even dinner with the King was a non-event. Despite the fact that the food, as always, was fabulous, Arawn seemed distant. And, sometime between dinner and dessert, he stood abruptly and excused himself, professing that he was ill, and left the room before either woman could offer their commiseration.

Yona and Eluned glanced at each other and remained silent until they were sure he was gone.

"What was that all about?" Yona whispered.

"I don't know. He didn't look sick," Eluned whispered back.

A servant entered at that moment carrying a tray with a chocolate éclair for each of them, stopping short upon seeing the King's empty seat.

"He wasn't feeling well," Eluned explained. "I'm sure he won't be back."

The servant bowed and served them. "Will you be retiring to the parlor then?"

"No, I don't think so," Yona replied. "Just bring our brandy here."

"Yes, m'lady." He bowed again and slipped out of the room, returning about five minutes later with two snifters of brandy. "Will that be all, yer Highness?" He asked the Princess.

"Yes. Thank you." She paused as he left once again. "Why don't we take these back to the room," she said, pushing away from the table.

"Excellent idea. For some reason it feels really sinister down here now." They remained silent until they reached the room, but no matter which way they turned it, they could make no sense of Arawn's behavior. They both agreed he certainly hadn't seemed ill. Preoccupied, yes. Sick, no.

"How very peculiar," Chokhmah commented. "Perhaps he is still worried about the earrings."

"Well, I know one thing for sure," Eluned said. "I don't intend to wear them in his presence again. Perhaps I should leave them here when we leave for Arberth. Out of sight, out of mind, right?"

"Hopefully," Yona said, collapsing into an armchair. "I'm sure things will be better once we're back on the coast. At least Hevel and the others will be there to entertain us."

"And Hywel," Eluned groaned. "You'll have to protect me from his wife."

"Gladly!" Yona laughed. "I don't particularly like the Lady Auron either. Believe it or not, she's even jealous of me."

"So she's an idiot as well?"

"You said it, darling."

DEETHMERKER DAWNED CLEAR AND BRIGHT. "It looks as if the rain scrubbed everything clean," the Princess remarked looking out the window. "It has now been exactly a month since I left home and now it's our last day here for awhile," she said, almost wistfully. "What shall we do today?"

"How about a picnic?" Yona suggested. "Perhaps they can prepare a coach for us, and we can go down to the river. It's a perfect day to be outdoors."

"Or we can take the horses," Eluned suggested. "I haven't seen Honeysuckle since we got here. I hope she doesn't feel abandoned."

"Or Halelu," Chokhmah chimed in. "He comes from a long line of Roma stock. I do not wish to lose him."

"So, let's get word to the stables and the kitchens then," Yona said, pulling the bell chord that would summon a page.

THE WOMEN RETURNED TO THE CASTLE AT DUSK, pleasantly worn out from the day, which included a hike up to some rocks that offered an outstanding view of the Duir River valley. They spent a couple of hours watching as the river curled like a ribbon through pastures where fluffy white clouds of sheep nibbled at the new spring grass. Even the shepherds seemed keenly aware that it was an exceptional spring day and frolicked with their dogs while their complacent sheep ignored them.

It was one of those days where everyone seems to be in a good mood, wishing each other blessings and a good day as they went about their business. It was one of those days when you forget that you actually live under the thumb of a despotic and evil king whose only wish seemed to be to make war on those kingdoms that did not give him the honor he felt was his due.

"Isn't it nice to have days like this in which we can actually forget our real problems?" The Princess commented as they made their way back down to the river.

"Amen," Chokhmah and Yona agreed simultaneously.

If the Princess thought she could get away with not going to Arberth, she would stay in Prythew, but she knew that wasn't actually an option.

A PERFECT END TO THEIR NEARLY PERFECT DAY would have been for Arawn to bow out of dinner again. But that was not to be. Tonight, he seemed eager to discuss their departure on the morrow, and some of the things they might be doing once they arrived in Arberth.

It seemed even the King could be influenced by the splendor of the day and both Eluned and Yona were pleased to sit back and let him ramble on about his plans.

They were to leave shortly after breakfast, so the girls excused themselves after dessert so they could pack and be ready to leave on time.

"And get a good night's sleep," Yona added. "I realize we'll be there instantly, but I haven't ridden in the phaeton enough to get used to that disorienting feeling."

"Disorienting feeling?" Eluned asked.

"It has been quite a while since I have experienced that," Arawn said, leaning toward the Princess, who was unexpectedly distracted by the king's coppery hair, which had rippled forward over his shoulders as he leant toward her. Sometimes she forgot how long and shiny it was. She had a sudden urge to run her fingers through it to see if it was as silky as it looked. She looked down in horror as her hand, seemingly of its own accord, began to move toward Arawn. Before she could snatch it back, Arawn had clasped it in his own cold hand and brought it to his cheek. The look of lust in his bronze eyes nearly made her gag, and she bowed her head and blushed instead.

"Don't be shy," he said, kissing each one of her fingers. She could feel the tip of his tongue on each, as well, and her gorge rose again. Omni have mercy, she thought, how am I going to make it through this trip? She flushed again and made herself squeeze his hand. It appeared as if she'd have to keep Yona as close as possible when they arrived at Castle Emrys.

"It's hard to explain," Yona said, coming to her rescue by pulling her out of the chair. "I always have to lie down for awhile afterwards until the world stops spinning, so to speak."

"You'll be fine by dinner time," Arawn assured her. He looked perturbed at being interrupted by Yona, but there were obviously some advantages to being betrothed to both a king and an ally of Arawn's.

Murmuring their good nights, they retreated from the dining room.

YONA HADN'T BEEN JOKING about the disorientation. After they all had been ordered to think "Castle Emrys," it was as if a streaming darkness had descended on them and in no time they had arrived. But what was 'no time'? She couldn't even define that, really. It was just a sense. When they arrived on the lawn at Arberth, Eluned, feeling an extreme dizziness, was forced to keep her eyes shut until she was led to her room.

There, Chokhmah, who was a bit green at the gills herself, administered a sleeping potion to both of them, and they crawled into bed to sleep it off.

THE PRINCESS AWAKENED to the suffused light of late afternoon. She felt significantly better and propping herself against her pillows, she took stock of the room. Not surprisingly, it was as stunning, if not more so, as her room back at Castle Pwyll. The bed in which she reclined, and the entire room for that matter, was decorated in tones of sapphire blue and pearly white with a few accents of emerald green, lemon yellow and bougainvillea pink.

To the left of her bed, against the wall, stood an austere yet elegant armoire painted white and decorated with an uncomplicated wave-like pattern in blue. There were three windows on the wall opposite the bed—one, tall and arched in the center, two long and narrow on either side of it. Sheer curtains helped dim the room.

A small table flanked by two delicate armchairs had been placed in front of the center window. A small writing desk sat in front of the narrow window to the left. To the right, in the far corner of the room, Chokhmah still slept upon a cot that apparently had been placed there just for her use. I will be so happy when this part of the game has ended, Eluned thought. Poor Chokhmah had left her beautiful vardo only to be treated like a servant. The Princess would do anything to trade places with her.

To the right of Chokhmah's cot, a fireplace with an ornately carved mantle of white marble occupied most of the wall. A sofa and coffee table had been placed in front of it. Beside the mantle, and apparently leading to a bathroom, was a closed door. On the wall, to her right, beside her bedside table, was a bookcase.

Eluned quietly slipped out of bed and padded around the

table and armchairs to the center window behind them. The view caused her to gasp in awe. The room was located high above the ocean. It looked as if the castle must rise out of the sea from where she was standing. There was a small balcony just outside the window and she opened the window and stepped onto it. Holding on tightly to the railing, she peered over and saw that there was another floor with a larger balcony beneath her and that there was actually some pavement in front of the castle before the rocky shore dropped away to the pounding waves beneath it.

To her right, the western sky was painted in hues of orange and yellow and even purple. The sea glowed azure and turquoise and gold in the lambent light of approaching dusk. It was absolutely breathtaking. If it weren't for Arawn, she could be very happy.

The sharp intake of breath behind her alerted her to Chokhmah's presence. "Isn't it incredible?" she asked, turning to greet her. The gypsy stepped through the window to join her on the balcony.

"Words escape me."

They enjoyed the sunset for another ten minutes before a knock on the bedroom door made them jump.

"Reality intrudes yet again," Eluned groused, returning to the room.

A servant, bearing a small decanter of cordial on a silver tray, waited patiently to be acknowledged. Thanking her, Chokhmah took the tray. Beside the decanter lay the ubiquitous vellum note bearing the king's red wax seal.

Rolling her eyes, the Princess opened it. "Damn!"

"What is it?"

"He's getting more and more familiar. Look." Chokhmah read over her shoulder:

"I thought perhaps you could use a little pick me up to aid in your recovery, my dear," the note read in the Arawn's precise script. "I look forward to seeing you tonight at dinner. A page will arrive to lead you to the dining room at 8 o'clock."

"Well, I'll be cursed if I'm wearing that black dress," Eluned groused.

"The blue one again?"

Eluned sighed. "I may need more than one glass of that cordial. Or maybe I should just drink straight from the bottle."

THE PRINCESS WASN'T SURE who she dreaded seeing more—the king or Hywel and his jealous wife, Auron. But she was completely unprepared for what actually greeted her—a romantic tête-à-tête with Arawn.

"I didn't want to overwhelm you on your first night at Castle Emrys," he explained.

It was all she could do not to guffaw in his face. If only she had feigned illness and asked for broth to be sent to her room. But it was too late to be anything but gracious. What was it they said in her great grandmother's books? The show must go on? So, she said, "Thank you, I appreciate that."

He helped seat her before joining her across the small candlelit table.

"I asked them to prepare something light as I wasn't sure how you'd be feeling."

His continuing attentiveness was starting to irritate her. Why couldn't he revert to the louche she knew he actually was—the one who used women and, on occasion, if the earrings were the proof, killed them sacrificially? But, she said, just as politely, "That was kind of you. I am still feeling somewhat lightheaded."

"I've been traveling in the phaeton since I was a boy, but I was horribly ill the first time. It does get progressively better, I assure you."

"That's good to know."

"Wine? This is from my southern vineyards, and it has a most refreshing bite to it."

"Please." She sipped it, tentatively. True to his word it was quite good with a pleasant aftertaste. "Nice. What is that flavor? I feel as if I am tasting a forest."

"There is a tinge of pine, is there not?"

"That's it. I like it."

"I'm pleased," he said and seemed to mean it. "People either seem to enjoy it or they cannot abide it all."

A servant entered and placed bowls of a steaming lemony rice soup before them followed by chicken with rosemary and green beans. Despite her trepidation, Arawn remained convivial through the remainder of the meal. It was as if he was a different man in Arberth and she had to wonder why.

"Perhaps you would like to go riding tomorrow? The forest behind the castle is lovely and has numerous trails."

"Avalach?"

"Yes! You remembered."

"Of course I remembered," she laughed. "Princesses are required to remember forests that are home to unicorns."

"I am sure that unicorn is long gone," he smiled.

"Perhaps, but it's the mystique that makes it so special."

He kissed her cheek, and this time she managed not to cringe. "Ten o'clock then?"

"I look forward to it." And the truth was, she actually did, because it would give her a chance to explore the forest and look for signs of the unicorn.

"You look as if you had a pleasant time," Chokhmah remarked, eyebrows arched in surprise, when Eluned returned to the room.

"It was certainly a lot less painful than previous meals with the King," she replied. "He has me actually looking forward to going out riding with him tomorrow. But, that may be in part because we'll be riding in Avalach."

"May wonders never cease," Chokhmah laughed. "Why the change in attitude?"

"I guess I just decided that if we were going to have to spend Omni-knows-how-long in Arawn's kingdom, I might as well enjoy myself. It's Mid-Faharn. How long will it be before we even return to Prythew?"

"I believe I heard that the King prefers to be back at Castle Pwyll before the summer solstice."

The Princess looked horrified. "Nearly three months! I haven't even been gone from home that long!"

Chokhmah chuckled. "Try not to fret too much, my dear. We have nearly three years before we need to return you to Castle Mykerinos. Three months will end up feeling like a week in that amount of time."

"True," Eluned sighed. "I really shouldn't be panicking yet. After all, we already have access to three of the thirteen treasures, and know for sure where there are two others. But the harness is on the unicorn, which according to Arawn, has disappeared."

"That is troubling," Chokhmah admitted.

"Fortunately, if we're going to be here for three months, I'll have plenty of time to search Avalach for signs of the unicorn."

"Yes, and if you remain in the good graces of the King, you might later have an easier time acquiring both the chariot and the chessboard."

Eluned sighed again. "I know, I know. What is it they say, 'You can content more kittens with cream than crumbs'?"

"Exactly."

BY THE TIME MORNING ARRIVED, Eluned was beginning to dread having agreed to spend the day with Arawn.

"You are going to have to stop drinking wine," Chokhmah teased her, "it seems to make you too malleable."

"I didn't even drink that much last night," she complained. "It's just that he was being so nice."

"Well, I imagine that will not change today. We know that

if he does not wish to be in your presence, he has no compunction about cancelling a meeting."

"True, but I wish I could wear my pants. They're so much easier to ride in."

"Do it. If he does not like it, you may explain to him that you have no proper riding clothes."

Eluned chuckled. "I like the way you think."

So, DRESSED IN LEATHER PANTS and a white cotton blouse, the Princess presented herself to the king at the appointed time.

Arawn arched an eyebrow. "No riding clothes, I take it?"

"Nothing appropriate. I picked these up in Mjijangwa and I have to admit, they make riding much easier."

"No doubt, and they are quite attractive on you," he said, eyes lingering on her hips.

Eluned gritted her teeth. She always felt dirty when Arawn made obvious his attraction to her. It annoyed her when Gwrhyr did the same, but she didn't feel like she needed to take a bath afterwards.

BUT, THE PRINCESS ACTUALLY ENJOYED her outing with the king. The first couple of hours were spent touring Arawn's vineyards and the well-manicured grounds around Castle Emrys. About noon, they handed off their horses to a groom and walked down to the beach. There, beneath a canopy, they lunched on seafood salad, fruit and cheese and more of his private label wine.

Following a surfside stroll, they returned to their horses and explored the forest of Avalach for an hour. It had been extremely peaceful under the whispering branches of the tall pines, the horses' hooves nearly silent on the pine needles, but Eluned caught nary a glimpse of the unicorn.

Eluned wasn't too surprised, really. It was highly unlikely that she would see the unicorn when accompanied by the

King, or anyone else, for that matter. She would have to arrange to search the forest alone at some point.

The Princess returned to her room mid-afternoon to take a brief nap before the dinner party that evening. Once again she would be reunited, so to speak, with Yona and Hevel, Chazak and Aviv, Hywel and Auron, and Gethin and Celyn. And Jabberwock? She hoped so. At least Yona would be present and, no doubt, highly protective. That would be a relief.

She toyed with the idea of wearing Cuhvetena's necklace along with the black dress before Arawn ordered her to do so again, but decided that not only did she not want to vex the women neither did she wish to titillate the men.

She decided to go with the cream and periwinkle dress, which struck her as the second most demure of the three, a compromise dress. With that decided, she crossed to the windows to pull the curtains closed and for the first time, wondered what had become of Chokhmah.

"I'm not my gypsy's keeper," she reminded herself, and if it came to it, she was perfectly capable of dressing herself for dinner. Maybe. She was too tired to worry about that now and crawling into bed, soon drifted off to sleep.

THE SCENT OF ROSEMARY ROUSED HER from her dreams and Eluned awoke to find Chokhmah setting a tray of tea and biscuits on the table in front of the windows.

"Good afternoon," the Princess yawned as Chokhmah drew open the curtains.

"Did you have a pleasant morning?" she asked as Eluned slid out of bed and padded over to the table.

"It was better than I feared," she said picking up a chocolate biscuit. "I did get to see a lot."

"No sign of the unicorn?"

"No, not that I'm surprised. I'm looking forward to exploring on my own a bit. I have a feeling I will have to be alone to see a unicorn."

"It is true that tradition says that only a virgin can entrap a unicorn."

"I don't like the word entrap, but I wrote in my journal this quote from one of the Ancients, Leonardo da Vinci," she pulled her diary from the desk drawer, and read: "The unicorn, through its intemperance and not knowing how to control itself, for the love it bears to fair maidens forgets its ferocity and wildness; and laying aside all fear it will go up to a seated damsel and go to sleep in her lap, and thus the hunters take it."

"Interesting. Where did you find that?"

"It was in a book about unicorns in Arawn's library in Castle Pwyll."

"That is a lovely drawing of a unicorn," Chokhmah said, looking over her shoulder.

"Thank you. I was trying to get down the basics of what they are said to look like."

"The cloven hooves? The billy goat beard?"

"Exactly. Not that I imagine I will be confused if I ever see one."

"That seems very unlikely. Do you know the name of the unicorn that Morrighan put the halter on?"

"You know, I forgot to ask. I'll ask Arawn tonight."

ABOUT 6 O'CLOCK THERE WAS A KNOCK on the door. Chokhmah opened it to find Yona with wine bottle in hand.

"Yona," Eluned found herself smiling, "Welcome! Come on in."

"I come bearing gifts," she said. "I figured we could use a little help before facing the hordes tonight."

The Princess laughed, "I'm not sure less than a dozen can be considered a horde, but I know exactly what you mean."

"I know they are my allies, but they make my skin crawl."

"It's too bad I can't introduce you to Queen Njima," Eluned teased.

"Of Naphtali? Why?"

"I assumed you would know about her. Not only are they a neutral kingdom but also the Queen is single. She hasn't found the right partner yet."

"Partner?" Yona looked interested. "You mean she is going to defy tradition and marry a woman?"

"That's what I heard. I had a minstrel friend who told me all about it. It was quite a scandal a decade ago when her parents tried to force her to marry her betrothed. She refused."

"Who was her betrothed?" Yona asked.

"Aahil, the son of King Dodi and Queen Chahindra of Tarshish."

"Oh my, they must have been furious!"

"That's an understatement. Instead, despite the fact they still claim to be neutral, they allied themselves to Dziron by betrothing him to Xiang, the six-year-old daughter of King Zhang and Queen Ling."

"Is she heir to the throne? I really need to learn all this, especially if I am to be Queen of Adamah."

"No. They had three sons before her—Qiang, Chao and Huang. And Aahil is not first in line for the throne of Tarshish, which is another reason breaking the betrothal was so inflammatory. But Xiang is only now sixteen. It will be two more years before they marry."

"He must be significantly older than her by now."

"He's twenty-eight."

"Twenty-two years; nearly as much a difference as between Hevel and myself. But, at least I don't have to touch him. Well," she paused, "other than how ever many times it will take to get pregnant and bear the expected heir. Not looking forward to that."

Eluned grimaced in sympathy. "Anyway, that makes Njima only about eight years older than you."

Yona smiled. "Hmmm . . . wonder what she looks like."

"I don't know, actually, but I bet Gwrhyr does. He seems to know everything about everyone."

"Too bad he's not here."

"Maybe Jabberwock knows."

Yona upended her glass and swallowed the rest of her wine and sighed, "It's just wishful thinking. I'm betrothed to Hevel." And she sighed again.

"This calls for another glass of wine," Eluned said.

"Anesthetize me, my dear." Yona held out her glass.

THEY WERE BOTH A LITTLE GIGGLY by the time they arrived, but it also made them oblivious to the cool stares they received from Aviv, Auron and Celyn. While Hevel only smirked, the other men, excluding Arawn, maintained their distance. That was fine as far as Eluned was concerned. She wanted to ask Arawn about the unicorn.

When they had a moment alone, Eluned asked if the king was aware of the name of the unicorn. "We keep talking about the unicorn, but it's my understanding that all unicorns have names," she initiated the conversation.

"That's true." Arawn said. "At least, it is true that my great-great-grandmother called the unicorn she tamed by a name. I am not sure whether or not it was of her own devising, but I seem to remember it was something quite simple," Arawn closed his eyes in thought for a moment. "What was it?" he murmured to himself. "Styx? No, that's not right. Nyx. Yes, that's what I was told. Nyx."

"Nyx," Eluned repeated. "Interesting. I like it. Maybe I'll be lucky enough to meet her someday."

"Sooner rather than later," Arawn said with a rather lascivious expression on his face.

The Princess blushed, and inwardly gagged, and was extremely thankful when Yona appeared at her side with a glass of champagne.

"Just can't resist the bubbly stuff," she laughed before noticing the look on Eluned's face. "Are you feeling quite well, my dear? You look a bit flushed."

"Just too much sun today," Eluned said, trying to recover quickly.

"You should probably go ahead and take a couple of tablets," Yona replied. "They could help quell any possible side effects. Right, Arawn?"

"Absolutely," he agreed, completely oblivious.

"Come with me," Yona said, putting her arm around Eluned's waist and leading her away from Arawn. "We'll get those before they serve dinner. We'll be right back," she smiled at the king over her shoulder.

"See you soon."

"WHAT HAPPENED?" YONA ASKED once they were in the powder room.

"It's me, really. I am just continually shocked when Arawn makes some allusion to the fact he wants to bed me. Does he forget that I am a Princess?"

"Apparently. As I said, he is used to a completely different class of woman."

The Princess shuddered. "I expect behavior like that from Gwrhyr," she stopped suddenly, remembering the kiss, and flushed, because it really had been different somehow. "But a king!"

"Clearly if he has his way, you will be married before summer's end."

Eluned felt the strength drain from her legs and she collapsed into one of the room's two armchairs.

"I don't blame you," Yona sympathized. "Sometimes I really wish I was poor. At least then I would have some chance of living my own life."

Eluned's mind was racing. She wasn't about to marry her father's enemy nor was she about to give up the three years of "freedom" she'd been given. Marrying Arawn was just as bad, nay worse, than marrying Uriel. At least she had nearly three more years before she had to marry him. Look how much she'd experienced in just one month! How could she give up thirty-five, or even thirty-two assuming they married in Teeneh, more months? Impossible. She needed to talk to Chokhmah and Jabberwock, and for once she actually regretted not having Gwrhyr around to counsel her. Know-it-all or not, he was really quite knowledgeable. At any rate, it was clear they were going to have to figure out a way to gather the three treasures in Annewven and get out of the country before the king insisted on a wedding.

"Take these," Yona handed her the tablets, "and take a big sip of champagne. Don't fret. We'll figure out something."

Eluned squeezed her hand. "Thank you, Yona. I'm not sure what I would have done without you." And she meant it. Because of her position in society, Yona was the only one of her companions that had access to the same places she did. It was becoming more and more clear to the Princess that Yona might be of more use as an ally than as a potential enemy. But, how to go about it? She would have to discuss it with Chokhmah.

Meanwhile, it was time to get back to the dinner. Taking a deep breath, she stood. "All right, I think I can handle this now. I need to learn not to react to him."

"Yes, you do," Yona replied, opening the door.

THEY RETURNED TO THE DINING ROOM just in time to be seated for dinner. Eluned was once again between Arawn and Yona with Chazak and Auron seated across from them. With Hevel at the opposite head of the table and Gethin and Celyn to his right, and Aviv and Hywel to his left, the party was complete. No sign of Jabberwock, the Princess noted, but maybe Arawn thought it was too early to subject his friends to the Janawar. She hoped, belatedly, that he had made the transition to Arberth in good health. Why hadn't she checked on him yet? Curse her selfishness! When would she learn? That would be the first thing she would do in the morning, she promised herself.

Her thoughts were interrupted by a question from Chazak, and before she knew it, the meal had passed in polite conversation with those around her. By the end of the meal, when it became clear that the Princess did not have designs on their husbands, the tension in the room lifted, and Eluned returned to her room having promised to meet Yona, Auron and Celyn for a morning trip to the beach.

Of the four women, only Yona's skin was dark enough to spend an extended amount of time out in the sun. Eluned's cheeks were already pink from the horse ride and the brief stroll she had taken with Arawn earlier in the day, but at least the pain tablets had soothed some of the heat-related symptoms.

"I am sure we can find you a parasol to protect your beautiful skin," Chokhmah assured her. "Now tell me all about the dinner. I feel so out of touch."

Eluned was exhausted. It had been quite a long day, after all, but she took pity on her friend who was once again holed up in their room alone. Surely not what she had bargained for when undertaking the journey.

"This changes things," Chokhmah agreed when Eluned's story was finished. "I cannot risk letting any of our enemies know that I am the niece of the queen of Favonia. As your handmaid they will overlook most of what I say or do. But you are right in saying that it might help us if we can get Yona to be a part of our little group. I just worry that if she were to publicly renounce her engagement to Hevel, and befriend you at the same time, it might cause us trouble in Dziron, Kamartha, Simoon and Adamah."

The Princess stamped her foot in frustration. "Why oh why do most of the treasures have to be in the kingdoms of our enemies? Other than the Mantle of Arthur, my ring and the sword, we have only one in a neutral territory."

"Two."

Eluned felt the color drain from her face. How had she forgotten? One of the treasures, the knife, was rumored to have disappeared in the lost Kingdom of Pelf. How were they to face the Aberrations of the Devastation? This was all beginning to seem so hopeless. "We'll never find all the treasures," she felt her eyes filling with tears. "The halter is lost on a unicorn that hasn't been spotted in a century or so, the knife is somewhere in the Devastation of Pelf and nearly all the treasures are in the hands of our enemies!"

"It does, indeed, seem hopeless," Chokhmah sighed. "I still think that Yona will be most helpful to us as the fiancée of Hevel. At the very least, she will still be able to travel freely in Adamah and Simoon. Kamartha and Dziron may be our enemies but they are so far distant from Simoon, Adamah and Annewven that I think they will be less of a problem. It is true that once we steal the treasures from Arawn, whether or not we find the halter, and assuming we can escape from his kingdom, that we will become his sworn enemies. I have no doubt he will hasten his preparations for war if that happens."

"We need to talk to Jabberwock. Have you seen him today?"

"I think he was doing a little nosing around on his own."

"Ah yes, Gwrhyr's ghost. The next best thing to invisibility."

"Exactly. I imagine he hears a lot more than we ever shall."

"If only Gwrhyr and Bonpo were here. We could figure all this out together."

"We will just have to make the decisions on our own. Until we can get together with Jabberwock, we will continue with our current ruse, correct?"

"It's working so far."

14ᵀᴴ Fᴇʜᴀʀɴ

Eluned decided to do a little nosing around of her own the following morning. And, after the women had settled into their beach chairs with only Yona hoisting her skirt high so that her long legs could bronze under the gentle rays of the sun on this early Spring day, the Princess began to somewhat carelessly press the affianced woman about her upcoming wedding.

"I'm sure Celyn and Auron know all about it, Yona, but I haven't heard about your upcoming wedding. I don't even know when it is! I apologize for never having asked."

Yona gave her a strange look. She knew that Eluned didn't give a pauper's pickle about her wedding. What was she playing at? She decided to go along. One way or the other, she'd find out. "It won't be until I am twenty-one, which means I agreed that on my twenty-first birthday I would set a firm date for the wedding."

"And when is your birthday?" Eluned asked.

"The fifth of Hetel."

"Seven more months of freedom."

"I am tempted to see how long I can prolong the actual ceremony, though," Yona admitted.

"Whatever for?" Auron looked surprised. "I'd be anxious to get married as soon as possible."

Yona and Eluned looked at her blankly. "Why?" they asked simultaneously.

"Queen Yona?" Auron said in a tone that clearly implied she was speaking to madwomen.

"What's so great about being queen?" Eluned asked while contemplating the marriage that would make her queen of Aden.

"What isn't?" Celyn exclaimed. "Clothes, jewels . . ."

"A servant for your every need, and the power to command them," Auron added.

"Your every wish fulfilled," Celyn drifted off, dreamily.

"I hate to disappoint you, but you know the old adage: With great power comes great responsibility? It became an adage for a reason. A queen has a responsibility to her people and her household. It's a never-ending job. My mother is always busy with her duties as queen. There is very little room for selfishness. That's why I am enjoying my last few years as a princess."

"Not if the king has his way," Auron snorted.

"Oh yes!" Celyn laughed. "Gethin says he'd marry you tomorrow if he felt he could get away with it."

"Get away with it?" Eluned's throat felt as dry as the sand on the beach. As a matter of fact, it felt as if she were trying to swallow a mouthful of it.

"Political repercussions," Auron explained.

"Oh. In other words," Eluned suddenly understood, "I would have to convince my parents it is what I wanted."

"Exactly," Celyn agreed.

"Difficult," Eluned lied, "but not impossible to surmount although it may take a little while. That is, the longer I have a chance to 'get to know' the king, the more likely they will believe me."

Celyn and Auron nodded, pleased.

"That sounds like a good plan," Yona said.

"So is that why you aren't ready to marry King Hevel?" Auron asked. "Enjoying your freedom?"

"Not as much as I'd like to," Yona joked, but they were oblivious to what she really meant though Eluned understood, and giggled. "Where's my champagne?" Yona laughed.

"Champagne and strawberries!" Celyn agreed.

Eluned nodded to the servant that was hovering nearby and held up four fingers. "Thank you," she called after him as he hurried to do her bidding.

"You're thanking a servant?" Auron was scandalized.

"That, my dear, is one of the first lessons my mother taught me. 'Always treat your servants as humans, Eluned', she'd say, 'and you will win their undying devotion.'"

"But they're still servants?" Auron pressed her.

"Well, of course," Eluned agreed, but she felt extremely guilty about saying it aloud. Damn charade. She felt a sudden and intense longing for those few days when she had traveled alone with Gwrhyr, Bonpo and Jabb. She closed her eyes against the sun, and immediately felt something land on her legs. She nearly shrieked but caught herself as she recognized Jabberwock's small form settling in her lap.

"By Omni, where'd that ugly cur come from?" Auron grimaced. "Shoo him away."

"But he looks so friendly," Eluned said, arching an eyebrow at the Bandersnatch, trying to determine if he was still playing at Diptera or trying to make fools of Auron and Celyn. She stroked his domed forehead and he licked her hand. Still the fly then. "Isn't he adorable?" she turned toward Yona.

"Yes he is," she cooed, scratching the coarse fur on his neck. "I think we should adopt him while we're here."

"Maybe I'll even take him back to Prythew," Eluned considered. She was enjoying this. "I've always wanted a little dog for my own." She felt Jabb's claws dig into her legs and had to stifle a giggle. It was warning enough.

The servant soon arrived with their refreshments, and the women spent the next couple of hours in idle chatter despite Eluned's occasional attempts at leading them toward more interesting topics.

The Princess was greatly relieved when it was time to retire to their rooms to ready themselves for the luncheon and Jabberwock made a point of tagging along behind her.

"Don't feed him," Auron warned her. "You'll never be able to get rid of him."

Eluned laughed and turned around before rolling her eyes and mumbling something that Jabberwock felt sure he was glad not to hear.

As soon as they were tucked away in her room, she collapsed on the bed and moaned, "By Omni, I'm not sure I can keep up this masquerade for three more months. It's killing me."

"You would feel quite at home on The Masala, my dear," Jabberwock chortled. "You excel at theatrics."

Eluned sat up. "Where have you been? I feel like I never see you any more."

"Just listening," he replied. "Mostly to nonsense, but occasionally something interesting will crop up."

"Such as?"

"You, my dear. There is plenty of chatter about the King's intentions towards you."

"Yes," she groaned. "I've been hearing that, as well. Jabb, I can't marry Arawn! I'd rather be drawn and quartered. And now I am stuck here with him until we return to Prythew in Eahth."

"Which means that shortly thereafter, we must recover what treasures we can and leave this kingdom," Chokhmah chimed in.

"Well at least we know where two of them are," Eluned said, "but I am not sure I'll be able to find Nyx. No one has seen her since Morrighan put the halter on her."

"At this point we have no choice but to do the best we can," Jabberwock maintained.

"Well, we do have a possible ally," Eluned ventured.

"Yona." It was a statement.

"By Omni, I'd forgotten you could do that. What do you think?"

"She will need to be working on retrieving the hamper from Adamah while we're repossessing the treasures in Annewven," Jabberwock said.

"How will we get the whetstone in Simoon?" Chokhmah asked.

"That may take a bit of magic. Let me work on that. I have the feeling that the more treasures we have in our possession, the easier it will be to find the others."

"I don't understand," the Princess said.

"Almost like a burgeoning of power," Chokhmah's eyes shone in understanding. "The treasures were meant to be together in one kingdom."

"So they will feel themselves coming together again," Eluned said. "Is that what you're saying?"

"Do not misunderstand me," Jabberwock cautioned. "I do not think it will be an easy task. But, once we have more than half the treasures, the quest will be in our favor."

"I have one major worry, though," Eluned admitted.

"Bonpo." Jabberwock stated.

"Stop reading my mind!" the Princess scolded him. "I think that Gwrhyr, Chokhmah, you and myself can all fit comfortably enough in the chariot and end up in Favonia, say. But, how will Bonpo get there?"

"We need to get him to Arberth now," Chokhmah said. "It will be easier to arrange to get him to Favonia from here. We have nearly three months to figure out a way for him to cross the sea."

Eluned chuckled and they stared at her, aghast. "I'm sorry," she apologized. "I was just imagining the abominable snowman in the tropics."

Jabberwock snorted. "Amusing, but I am sure he would much rather deal with the heat than death."

"Then how do we get him here?"

"I'll leave that up to you my dear," the Bandersnatch replied. "After all, you hold the key to the king's heart, so to speak."

"And I guess recruiting Yona is my job as well?" she asked.

"That goes without saying."

"Hmmm. You don't happen to know anything about Queen Njima?" Eluned asked him.

"Queen Njima? Oh," he said, receiving the image from her mind. "I happen to think quite highly of Njima. You have to admire someone who is willing to defy tradition the way she has. She is quite lovely. I am sure we can find a way to introduce her to Yona eventually. After all, Naphtali is home to the crock and dish so we will end up there at some point."

"And by that time," Chokhmah added, "Yona's reputation will have preceded her."

"You mean by then she will have broken her engagement with Hevel?" Eluned asked.

"Yes," Chokhmah answered, "and perhaps she will need to avouch the reason she has done so. It will not harm her, necessarily, but could cast a shadow on Hevel's reputation."

"Or maybe give him the courage to defy tradition himself." Eluned said. "Wouldn't that be nice?"

"Yes, it would," Jabberwock agreed.

"Have you heard anything else besides talk of me?"

"There are the constant rumors about why the King must always return to Prythew before the summer solstice," Jabberwock noted.

"I'm hesitant to ask," Eluned said.

"Sacrifice." Chokhmah stated.

"I am afraid so. It is said that the king's religion requires a human sacrifice during the celebration of the longest day of the year."

"As well as the vernal equinox?" Eluned asked, remembering their discussion at Castle Pwyll when she'd found the scrap of vellum.

"And, no doubt, the autumnal equinox and winter solstice, as well," Jabberwock added.

"Four times a year! That's horrible!" Eluned's face drained of color. That was four murders a year. Did his subjects not realize that people were constantly disappearing or were they too afraid to do anything about it?

"And once at the vernal equinox was forgivable?" Jabberwock was saying.

"No! No!" Eluned was vehement. "I just somehow continually manage to repress that memory. It's as if my mind refuses to admit the evil of it all because I am forced to deal with that monster on a nearly daily basis." She had yet to wear the earrings from the market again. Eluned would have thrown them away but she considered them the poor unknown woman's last testament to having lived. If they were gone, she might be forgotten. "In that case, we need to be escaping with what treasures we can manage to get our hands on while he's preoccupied with the solstice."

"I could not agree with you more," Chokhmah said.

It was during lunch that Eluned found the inspiration she needed to get Bonpo to Castle Emrys. They were enjoying an array of local favorites, including grilled octopus in vinegar, oil and oregano along with fresh green beans stewed with potatoes, zucchini and tomato sauce, and plenty of Arawn's wine when the Princess noted to the King that Bonpo would be thrilled by Arberth's cuisine.

"And why is that?" Gethin asked.

"His passion is cooking," Eluned explained and then went on to rhapsodize about some of the food he had prepared on the journey to Annewven, from the stuffed dumpling soup and apple turnovers at his inn to the wonderful fish in fig leaves he had prepared their final night in Sheba.

"Then he shouldn't be wasting his talents at Castle Pwyll for the next few months," Arawn declared. "Why don't I send a pigeon to my castellan asking him to send Bonpo down here. He could be here within a week."

"Really?" Eluned placed her left hand on Arawn's right forearm and squeezed, gently, "You would do that?" She did her best to look at him all starry-eyed, as if she couldn't imagine another pair of eyes she would prefer to drown in, and, not surprisingly, he fell for it. She felt Yona kick her shin under the table and tried not to react to it.

"I would be more than happy to do that for you, my dear," he said, placing his left hand atop hers where it still lay on his arm.

Now came the tricky part—politely breaking contact with his mesmerizing eyes. She graced him with a brilliant smile, squeezed his arm again, then turning to Yona said, "What did you say?"

"I," Yona faltered, and squeezed her eyes shut pretending to remember. "Oh yes, I was wondering whether you'd like to attend the service at Saint Yorgos with me tomorrow? It is only a week away from Pascha."

Arawn had removed his hand from over hers, and she slowly slid her own hand back into her lap. "I'd love to," she enthused. "I haven't been to worship in more than a month."

"Would anyone else care to go?" Yona asked, looking around the table. Hywel looked like he really wanted to tag along with them, but dropped his eyes when Auron elbowed him in the ribs. Everyone else demurred politely.

Hmmm, Eluned thought, as she allowed the king to refill her wineglass, apparently Yona had yet to be initiated into whatever pagan religion they practiced. Perhaps that wouldn't happen until she was married to Hevel. Clearly the others no longer even pretended to be faithful to Omni, which she found surprising. No wonder the king's religion was the subject of much rumor.

"I have business to attend to tomorrow," Arawn explained as the dishes were being cleared, "but I would be honored to attend the Pascha service with you next Deethseel."

"Wonderful," she beamed at him. "I would truly enjoy that."

"It is, perhaps, our biggest feast day of the year, next to the Feast of Saint Yorgos, which occurs later in the month. We are lucky to be part of both while here."

"And, of course, he has his official part to play in both," Celyn added almost coquettishly, finger twirling one of her carroty curls.

Who was she flirting with, Eluned wondered. The King? Just to spite her, the Princess leaned closer to Arawn until her upper arm was in contact with his. "I have no doubt your people are thrilled to have you take part in their celebrations. I am sure they adore you."

"I like to think so," he said, but under the table his hand was squeezing her knee and Eluned had to bite her tongue, hard, to keep from protesting. When he began caressing his way up her thigh, she nearly fainted. What was she going to do to distract him this time? Damn him. Give him a pence and he took a pound. Unbelievable.

But, once again, Yona came to the rescue. "And what shall we do the rest of the afternoon, your majesty?" she leaned across Eluned to ask the king. "Are there plans?"

"I have business to attend to at the vineyard. Feel free to entertain yourselves." He stood. Taking Eluned's left hand, he kissed it, courteously, and said, "I will see you at dinner tonight, milady."

The Princess smiled, graciously, and bowed her head, "As you wish, sir."

"So," Yona grabbed her hand and pulled her up. "Have you seen the music room? They have a harpsichord."

"What about a library?" she asked as Yona led her away from the table leaving the others with mouths somewhat agape at the abrupt ending to the meal.

"I DON'T WANT TO DO THAT AGAIN," ELUNED SAID once they were ensconced in the music room with the tinkling of the instrument covering the sound of their already muted voices.

"It is a dilemma," Yona acknowledged. "If you don't touch him, he'll think he disgusts you, but when you do touch him, he can't keep his hands off you."

"I know," she moaned. "There's got to be a happy medium, I'm just not sure what it is. I'm just not practiced in the art of courting. I've never been courted or wooed because I've been betrothed since I was a child." She really wanted to open up and be completely honest with Yona, but she couldn't risk being heard nor could she risk a bad reaction on her friend's part. She was pretty sure that Yona liked her as a friend, as well. But what if it were entirely sexual? Everything she had said so far caused her to believe that Yona was engaged to Hevel for political reasons only, and that she valued her relationship with the Princess because it offered her a chance to be herself. Tomorrow, she decided. Tomorrow on the way home from the service, she would talk to her.

"At this point, I can only advise you to pull back just a bit if you feel he's overstepped bounds." Yona said. "Maybe if he thinks he's pushing you too hard, he'll realize the error of his ways, so to speak."

"I hope so. I will try," she sighed before brightening as she remembered, "So where's the library?"

As they were walking to Saint Yorgos the following morning, Yona seemed lost in thought.

"Is everything all right?" Eluned asked.

"Do you remember when I had my tarot reading?"

"Of course. It was the morning it rained, just a few days ago. Why?"

"Chokhmah didn't say anything?"

"No, of course not! She wouldn't have unless you asked her to do so. Did you?"

"No, but neither did I say she couldn't. It didn't occur to me either way."

"Is there a reason you ask?" Eluned said.

They were walking along the beachside promenade, within sight of Saint Yorgos and its beautiful gilded dome, when Yona took Eluned's right hand and led her over to a bench. "We have time," she said. "Let's sit for a second." She then took Eluned's other hand, took a deep breath, and said, "I'm not really sure how to say this. I don't want you to get the wrong idea, you see."

"Yona, you're scaring me."

She laughed, nervously. "It's nothing bad, I promise. It's just that having spent time with you, and with Chokhmah, and even with your fellows, my eyes have been opened to a way of life I could never have imagined for someone of my rank."

"Rank? What do you mean? Are you serious?"

"Very. I've never felt so free to be myself except when I was at the docks and, if my father had known who I was spending time with, he'd would've locked me in my room." She paused. "Actually, maybe he did. I'm sure that's why he set up the engagement to Hevel. But, the important thing is that I've spent my entire life hiding who I really am, and pretending to be the person my parents asked me to be. It was actually quite a blessing when Hevel and I discovered that we could be ourselves with each other even if we had to hide that particular aspect of our lives."

"Yet?" the Princess prompted her.

"And yet, why should I settle for that? I'm not royalty. I'm just the daughter of one of Hevel's minor lords. I don't need to bend to my parents' wishes for me. Why can't I be happy in life?"

"I know exactly what you mean."

"Maybe something will happen in the next three years to change that. You don't want to marry Uriel or Arawn. I understand that. You want to spend your life with whom you choose. So do I."

"And what does this have to do with your tarot reading?" Eluned wanted to know.

"I asked in what ways I might change things to live the life I want to lead," Yona explained. Eluned felt unexpectedly silly for the question she had asked. But that was nearly a month ago. Life was different now. And yet, she still wanted to fall in love.

"And?" Eluned prompted again.

"It just clarified for me that I don't want to be married to Hevel; that I truly dislike where I am from. I hadn't realized that there are people out there who don't live in fear, who actually want what's best for all. It has been amazingly enlightening spending time with you."

"Thank you," Eluned said, squeezing Yona's hands for emphasis. "You might be surprised to learn that until I left Zion, my only real friend was Jabberwock. Now, I can't imagine a life without Bonpo, Gwrhyr, Chokhmah and, most especially, you. I've never known what it meant to have a female friend."

The bell began to ring for worship and the women jumped up and hurried to the church, scurrying in behind the procession and before the doors closed, feet crunching on the palms that had been dropped on the floor of the narthex.

"WELL, THERE'S ANOTHER BIG DIFFERENCE," Eluned said. They had returned to their seaside bench, prior to returning to Castle Emrys, in order to give themselves a few more minutes of solitude.

"What's that?" Yona asked, eyes closed, face turned to the breeze.

"We're the only two that were at the table yesterday who seem to go to worship because we enjoy it."

"To be perfectly honest, I think Arawn and his friends are into something freaky. They haven't said anything but neither have they allowed me to be a part of whatever they are doing."

They heard footsteps behind them and both women, turned, guiltily, to see if they had been heard.

"Oh, Chokhmah," Eluned smiled her relief. "Thank Omni it's you! Are you coming from Saint Yorgos?"

"Yes, I stayed to talk to the priest, Father Addogar. May I join you?" she asked.

"Certainly," Yona said, making room. "I was telling Eluned about my tarot reading."

"Yes?"

"And I was about to ask her if she wanted to join our 'secret circle,'" Eluned said.

"Secret circle?"

"I meant that kind of tongue-in-cheek."

"I don't understand," Yona looked confused.

"I guess I need to ask you, first, if you meant what you said about not wanting to be a part of the Awen Alliance?"

"I hadn't thought of it that way," she admitted, "but, in my heart-of-hearts, the answer is that I want no part of them. They scare me. Why do you think I was so eager to stay with you at Castle Pwyll?"

"Then we can trust you completely? You can promise to play your part?"

"Play my part? What does that mean? What does it mean for my future?"

"Should you not start at the beginning, Princess?" Chokhmah advised.

Eluned hesitated, and Yona once again took her hands. "Trust me, Eluned. Please? I promise, no matter what, my lips will remain forever sealed, if necessary."

The Princess took a deep breath, and began the story . . .

"WOW," YONA BREATHED, AND STOOD UP, beginning to pace back and forth in front of the bench. "And what would be my part?"

"Do you know where the hamper is kept in Adamah?"

"I do," she said. "It is on display in Castle Lavieven in Stonehelm. It is very well guarded, or at least it appears to be whenever I've been there."

"But surely he doesn't have a guard on it twenty-four hours a day," Eluned said.

"I doubt it," Yona agreed. "There's a reason we spend so much time in Annewven each winter."

"Why is that?" Chokhmah asked.

"Because Hevel is incredibly miserly except where it concerns himself," Yona explained. "I've only been to Lavieven for formal occasions—our engagement, once or twice after that. He even has a nice little palace in Seagirt, but he'd rather let Arawn pay for his holidays."

"And when you return to Adamah in Eahth, where will he go?" Eluned wanted to know.

"Oh, definitely back to Stonehelm," Yona said.

"And you?" Eluned stood.

"I suppose I'll stay with my parents. At their home in Seagirt," Yona replied then realization dawned. "Ah, but you're wondering if I can return to Lavieven with Hevel and steal the hamper, aren't you?"

"Yes." It was more of an exhalation. "And then meet us in Favonia."

"Hmmm . . . I suppose in the next few months I can come up with a plan to do that," Yona reflected. "Returning to Seagirt might be a bit more difficult."

"What's in Seagirt?" Eluned asked.

"The harbor. And, more importantly, the people I grew up with there and a way to Favonia," she replied.

"Why? What does your father do, Yona?" Chokhmah asked.

"He is the commander of Hevel's fleet, small though it is. But, what he doesn't know is that in addition to the sailors and others who work under my father, I also got to know the smugglers and pirates. I spent a lot of time hanging out at the docks. It was so much more interesting than needlepoint."

"Ah," Chokhmah smiled. "In other words, you know someone who can get you to Favonia."

"Some ones, fortunately. Libni, definitely. Merari and Azariah would also help. Perhaps others. It will depend on who's in port at the time. But, I have no doubt they'd lend me aid. The King isn't exactly loved by his people."

"Kind of like Arawn, huh?" Eluned noted. "Now that I think of it, though, I am not really sure how the people of Zion feel about my father."

"Do not worry, dear," Chokhmah reassured her. "I have heard nothing but good about King Seraphim."

"That's good to know," the Princess said. "And speaking of harbors, maybe we should start frequenting this one. Bonpo is going to need a way to get to Favonia, himself."

"Good point," Yona said. "I would not be surprised if we ran into some of the same people I know in Adamah. Smugglers and pirates aren't choosy when it comes to ports and potential clientele."

"At the moment," Chokhmah said, "we should be returning to the castle. We do not want the kings to be sending out a search party."

"True," Eluned agreed. "We don't want Arawn suspecting we're plotting something behind his back. He strikes me as a little bit paranoid."

"That's an understatement," said Yona.

"We must discuss this with Jabberwock, as well." Chokhmah stood. "He needs to be aware of all of this."

22ND FEHARN

The following week seemed to drag along at an interminable pace for the Princess. She realized that she needed to get accustomed to the daily, or rather what would become weekly, pattern at some point: The horsebacks rides in various combinations—Eluned and the King; Eluned, Arawn, Hevel and Yona; Eluned, Yona and Chokhmah; and so on and so forth.

There were the morning or afternoon rambles on the beach, hours spent in the library or music room, long lunches and even longer dinners. Eluned had only run into Jabberwock once during the week. He had quickly informed her that he was busy ingratiating himself to Arawn, but that he would be sure to catch up with them in the week following Pascha.

The only highlight of the week, as far as Eluned was concerned, were the fittings for the native costumes they would wear that weekend to the Paschal service and festival that followed it.

She was tickled by the outfit, which consisted of a short undershirt (hers was lavender, Yona's a deep ruby red), which was mostly covered by a long brocade dress with broad sleeves (she loved the shimmery sea green of her brocade and Yona looked striking in the brushed gold of hers. Over this they wore the long velvet black vest trimmed with golden embroidery that was characteristic of the region. A headscarf, which matched their undershirts in color but decorated with gold trim along the edge, completed the outfits.

That may have been the highlight, but Eluned was going to miss the daily pattern she, Yona and Chokhmah had developed of attending the early morning Sacrament at Saint Yorgos; something they could get away with doing because it was the Holy Week. The sunrise walk gave them time to be together, alone. It also gave them a chance, following the service, to hurry down to the wharves to see if they could spy Libni, Merari, Azariah or any other of Yona's childhood friends. Unfortunately, as of the Deethsadoorn morning prior to Pascha, they had yet to see anyone. By Deethyeen, they would have to devise another reason for the threesome to enjoy their seaside walks. Although at this point, running into one of Yona's friends was apparently moot as Bonpo had yet to arrive at Castle Emrys. Eluned steeled herself to ask Arawn about the giant again after he was well lubricated from the Pascha festivities. She hoped he'd be a bit more tractable then.

THE PRINCESS AWAKENED DEETHSEEL MORNING to the castle almost literally buzzing with excitement. Arawn hadn't been overstating the fact it was one of the biggest festivals of the year. After she had donned her new costume, along with Cuhvetena's necklace (because it complemented it so nicely), she and Chokhmah hurried downstairs. Eluned was surprised to see smiles on the faces of even the most dour of servants. Was it the only time they were allowed to be happy?

As she entered the dining room, Eluned was caught off guard by the men's clothing. Most of the men seemed to carry off their costumes with varying degrees of success—Hywel looking the most masculine and Arawn looked downright silly. Even Hevel looked more masculine that the King of Annewven. All the men were dressed in waistcoats of various colors that were embroidered on the front and back. Underneath this they wore a white skirt-like garment with hundreds of pleats; a full-sleeved shirt, also white; a waistband that matched their vests; garters that draped from the knees, and tight, white trousers. Their shoes featured a large pompom on the front. While Hywel, Gethin and Chazak wore a short, cylindrical hat, which also matched their vests, both Arawn and Hevel wore their crowns.

Eluned decided it was the combination of the crown and the tight pants that made Arawn look ridiculous. The crown, in and of itself, was lovely—red gold featuring an intricately fashioned dragon studded with deep crimson rubies. It even looked nice against his coppery hair. But, it was his long and flowing hair combined with the puffy skirt and skintight pants that made his scrawny legs stand out even more. From behind, he looked like a teenage girl in her gangly, gawky phase. Hywel had wisely pulled his hair back into a long braid. And, King Hevel's crown was a simple silver ringlet adorned with gold leaves.

The Princess found herself blushing in embarrassment for him and tried to avoid looking directly into his eyes. She also found herself wondering what Gwrhyr would look like in the costume and that made her flush as well. Eluned decided she really needed to distract herself, but there was no food available on the sideboard.

Yona saw her looking quizzically at the empty buffet, and quietly informed her that it was traditional to fast until after the service, but they could allow themselves one cup of black coffee before heading into Arberth.

"I guess that makes sense," she murmured. "In Zion, we eat only a hard-boiled egg and a piece of toast before the service."

Booming laughter from behind the door that led into the dining room caused the Princess to slosh her coffee in surprise. She had to force herself not to jump up and fling open the door. "Bonpo?" she asked, trying to keep her voice steady.

"Yes," the king replied, "I understand that he arrived late last night."

"What a wonderful Pascha gift," Eluned smiled at him before quickly taking another sip of her coffee in case he could see in her eyes how foolish she felt he looked. Inside, though, her heart was beating like a hummingbird's. Praise Omni, she thought. She had been worried that he might never actually make it to Arberth, which would assure his doom. If they couldn't get him out of here, first, he would surely die once they managed to steal the treasures and flee to Favonia. Now it was even more important they find one of Yona's friends.

The entire group soon left, en masse, for Saint Yorgos. The men formally escorted the women as if it were a tradition and not your ordinary Deethseel outing. The servants, including Chokhmah (although the newly arrived Bonpo stayed behind with some of the other kitchen staff to make sure the side dishes, among other things, would be ready and at the town square when the service ended), maintained a steady, if subservient, distance behind the king and his party.

Not surprisingly, there was special seating in the very front of the church for the king and his guests and they processed up the aisle with more pomp than Eluned was comfortable with. Fortunately, once seated they were less of a distraction although she had no doubt that she was the subject of much of the whispering. Thank Omni she'd left her crowns in Zion. But, she thought with surprise as the King got up to say the blessing that would begin the service, it seemed odd that Arawn hadn't had one made for her. Surely, it was in his best interests to boast to his people that the woman on his arm was a princess? How very odd.

Once the service had ended, the King and his party joined the recessional out of the church where they were led to a large tent that held a formally set table. They were seated, and soon a never-ending procession of food was placed before them.

As they waited for the lamb to finish roasting on the spits outside the tent (and Eluned had noticed there were a number of tents set up in the vicinity of Saint Yorgos, all accompanied by lambs on spits over roasting fires), they were served small triangles of cheese pie, olives, sliced cheese, stuffed grape leaves, and fresh vegetables and flat breads to dip in either a spicy cheese sauce or cucumber-yogurt spread. In addition to water, there was a highly alcoholic drink, which, Arawn informed her, was made from the must-residue of his winepresses. That, of course, meant she had to try it, and then she had to praise him lavishly despite the fact it brought tears to her eyes.

But, the Princess was most interested in the red eggs that filled several baskets along the table. This was the tradition she was comfortable with. She always ate her red egg first before tasting anything else. The deep red of the shell signified death and rebirth and she was superstitious enough to believe that if she didn't eat the egg, first, then bad luck would plague her in the coming year. As a matter of fact, she probably ought to eat two, just in case.

"Superstitious, my love?" Arawn asked, picking up an egg, himself. The remainder of the table followed suit and Eluned blushed. She hadn't meant to start anything. As per usual, Yona rescued her.

"I always eat a red egg first," she claimed. "Why risk bad luck when it's so easy to avoid, right?"

"Absolutely!" The Princess exclaimed with enthusiasm. "And nothing has gone wrong, yet. Why jinx it?" And she forced herself to look adoringly at the King. He kissed her cheek and she tried not to shudder. His lips felt like the brush of a spider's legs against her soft skin.

Once Eluned had finished her eggs (two for double luck!), she wisely decided to only nibble on what was placed before her, realizing that there was, no doubt, much more to come. She knew Bonpo was involved in the preparations but she had yet to see him.

The main meal soon followed with lemon-egg soup, slices of spit-roasted lamb, grilled chicken and roasted potatoes with lemon, oranges and oregano, spinach pie with cheese, lettuce with dill and spring onions along with hot and crusty bread. And, if that wasn't enough, desserts soon arrived, as well: sweet bread with yogurt, custard-filled pastries, butter cookies and fruit and plenty of the King's wine, liquor and liqueurs. And, most fortunately, as far as Eluned was concerned, there was strong black coffee.

When the meal was drawing to a close and most of the party was groaning over their full bellies, the exodus began. First to excuse himself was King Hevel. He looked at Yona, inquiringly, and she, in turn, pivoted toward Eluned, who sat to her right.

"Are you heading back?" she asked Eluned.

"I really wanted to stay and see the market. Isn't it supposed to be the biggest day of the year in terms of the number of stalls?"

"Except for the Feast of Saint Yorgos and May Day," Yona replied.

"May Day?"

"It's the 17th of Saitheh. In the distant past, it was a pagan holiday that occurred on the first of a month called 'May.'"

"Interesting." Why was she not surprised that the king publicly celebrated a pagan holiday. The Princess turned to Arawn, prepared to plead.

"Of course you may stay," he said. "I am sure we can find your gypsy to accompany you."

"Oh, that would be wonderful, thank you."

The King signaled a servant and sent him in search of Chokhmah. Then he stood. "I, on the other hand, have some things to attend to." The Princess had just pushed back her chair and was beginning to stand when Arawn pulled her into his arms and pressed his lips against hers. "I will see you later, my love."

Eluned was too shocked to stutter little more than her goodbyes. She caught a flash of jealousy in the Lady Celyn's dark green eyes as she took Gethin's arm to begin the journey home. "I'm truly ready for a nap," she said with a meaningful look at Arawn. No one else seemed to be paying attention, but Eluned could have sworn she saw an answering spark in the king's eyes. Shocked again, she turned toward Yona who had clearly missed it.

"What?" Yona whispered.

Eluned said nothing but took Yona's arm. "Look, here comes Chokhmah."

"Anyone else care to join us?" Yona asked. Auron looked paler than normal except for two bright spots of color high on her cheeks. Too much food and alcohol, Eluned thought, and it was clear Hywel wanted to get her back to the palace as soon as possible. Apparently, Arawn's business included Gethin and Hywel, as he said he would meet them in his parlor in an hour before striding off alone. Chazak and Aviv, who were the eldest of the party, were clearly looking forward to a nap. So, once again, Yona and Eluned were left to their own devices. It seemed too good to be true.

As soon as they were out of sight, Eluned spoke. "I think Celyn is having an affair with Arawn."

"What?" Yona gasped. "Why do you think that?"

"Just little things. She seems jealous of me. And, more importantly, I've seen some of the looks that have passed between them. I just can't bring myself to believe it is innocent flirting. And, he said, he had to get back to the castle on business but clearly gave himself enough time to see Celyn first."

"Interesting," Chokhmah said. "He most certainly has that reputation, and I cannot imagine that Gethin would risk opposing anything the king wants, even if it is his wife."

"Really," Yona agreed. "We all know what happens to those who anger the king."

"No," Eluned said. "We don't all know. What happens?"

Yona slowly drew her finger across her throat, and Eluned blanched significantly.

"Omni have mercy," the Princess muttered. "What have we gotten ourselves into? We're going to be lucky to get out of here alive, aren't we? I am just so glad that Bonpo is here now. At least he will now have a chance of escaping this kingdom."

"If one of my friends would just show up here," Yona lamented.

"Do not worry," Chokhmah assured her. "We have plenty of time yet. We will not be returning to Prythew until late Eahth. Surely someone will show up in that time. We have only to be sure that at least one of us checks every day. Today, why not let us enjoy the festivities?"

The women spent the remainder of the afternoon browsing the stalls and stopping occasionally to listen to a minstrel or watch a puppet show or skit.

Toward sunset, they worked their way toward the quays to see if, perchance, any of Yona's friends happened to be docked there. As they reached the last of the market booths, Eluned stopped so suddenly that Yona, who was right behind her, ran into her.

"Ouch!" she exclaimed. "Why did you stop?"

"Isn't that him?"

"Who?"

"The guy in that stall. Isn't he the one you bought the earrings from?"

Yona walked a few steps closer. "Why, yes. I think it is. I assumed he was local to Prythew. He must be a journeyman."

"I wonder if he has any more dead women's earrings?" Eluned said without humor.

"Not funny, Eluned," Yona groaned.

"Hmmm," she mused aloud.

"I see that glint in your eye," Chokhmah said. "What is it that you are thinking?"

"I was just thinking that I might like to see what jewelry he has to offer, after all."

Chokhmah shivered, then frowned. "I am getting the feeling this is a very bad idea."

"It's only jewelry," the Princess laughed as she began walking purposefully toward the booth. "What harm can come from looking at it?"

Yona and Chokhmah exchanged a troubled glance before following her.

"Yer highness," the vendor blurted and did a half bow as Eluned walked up to his booth.

"I was so pleased to see you here," Eluned lied. "I just had to come over and see what kind of jewelry you have with you."

He looked at her, confused.

"This jewelry is for sale, correct?"

"Aberlutely, yer higness. It's jest that yer friend seemed ser upset ther last time I sees yer."

"Oh, she's fine now. Aren't you, Yona?"

"Uh, y-e-s." It was clear she was wondering what the Princess was up to. Even the vendor continued to look a bit skeptical as Eluned considered what he had displayed on the table.

"Is ther anerthin' partikler yer lookin' fer?" He asked.

"Are these the only bracelets you have?" There were mostly cheap wooden bangles and glass beaded circlets scattered amongst the necklaces and earrings.

He colored a bit. "I'm sorry, yer highness, I was fergettin' who yer is. I keep ther nicer jewry in here," he said, bringing a box up from behind the display table.

Nicer being in the eye of the beholder, Eluned thought when he opened the box. She wasn't exactly sure what she was looking for but she knew it had to be distinctive, just as striking as the earrings had been. She guessed she could ask outright if he had bought anything other than the earrings off the mystery man, but she suspected that would make him clam up.

It was clear he regretted the day he sold them the earrings. So, she picked up each piece in the box and considered it seriously, or at least pretended to do so.

The bracelet was at the very bottom of the box. It probably wasn't even connected to the earrings as it was a lovely torque in a slender braid of red, yellow and white gold and the earrings were silver. She slid the torque over her hand, admiring the way it wound up her slender forearm. The gold had been fashioned to look somewhat like a dragon. Or was it supposed to be a wyvern, the Princess wondered. It was difficult to determine as it had neither wings nor legs. One end featured a dragon's head with rubies for eyes (not unlike the king's crown, she thought); the other tapered into a tail that ended in a spade of carved amber. And there was something in the amber. She looked at it more closely but she couldn't quite make it out. A bubble? A small fragment of rock? She couldn't tell, but she liked the way it seemed to sparkle. Perhaps it was a diamond chip.

Regardless, it was clearly unique and she had already fallen in love with it. "This is it!" she exclaimed, holding her arm up so Yona and Chokhmah could admire it.

"This is what?" Yona asked, worried.

"Exactly the type of bracelet I was looking for," she enthused. "Isn't it lovely?"

"It is, indeed," Chokhmah said though she was eyeing the trader with suspicion.

"Well, I intend to get it." She didn't have to haggle for long. The sun was beginning to set and the vendor, at this point, just wanted to shut down his booth and find a pub. Besides, Eluned's offer was more than generous.

"Do we still have time to make it to the wharves?" Eluned asked as they walked away from the stall.

"We can make them a part of our return trip," Chokhmah

said. "And on the way you can explain to us what that," she pointed over her shoulder, "was all about."

"I was hoping I would find a bracelet, or even a necklace, for that matter, that seemed like it matched or coordinated with my earrings. Unfortunately, as you saw, there wasn't even anything remotely similar."

"So why were you so excited about the dragon torque?" Yona asked.

"Are you joshing me?" Eluned looked at her in amazement. She held up her arm again, admiring the way the rosy light of the setting sun shimmered off the gold. "Don't you think it's beautiful?"

"Oh." Yona said, understanding dawning. "It has nothing to do with anything else. You just liked it."

"Yes, silly," She said, taking Yona's hand in hers. "Not everything's a mystery."

"Sorry," Yona said, squeezing her hand and sighing. "I guess I allowed my imagination to go into overdrive. I had visions of severed heads and blood-stained jewelry."

The Princess stopped and hugged her friend. "We're in this together, and we're going to do everything possible to make sure we all arrive in Favonia safely."

"With the treasures," Chokhmah added.

"Well, there's always a catch, isn't there?" Eluned chuckled, starting to walk again.

"At least you're in high spirits about it," Yona smiled.

"I did eat two eggs for luck!"

ALAS, THE QUAYS SHOWED NOT A SIGN OF LIBNI, Azariah, Merari nor any of their vessels.

"Maybe the luck part starts tomorrow," Eluned suggested.

"I sure hope so," Yona said. "I'll be glad to get back to the castle. I'm exhausted. My feet are throbbing too."

"I agree," Eluned yawned. "I just want to sit down and have a glass of wine and relax."

"Is that . . ." Chokhmah began.

"Leened!" Bonpo's booming voice split the darkness.

"Bonpo!" Eluned laughed, picking up her pace. "Were you sent to make sure we are still among the living?"

"King get worry," he explained.

"King wants me on a shorter leash," Eluned said under her breath.

"Amen." Yona whispered.

ELUNED FELT LIKE A CHILD AGAIN, and that infuriated her. She had been summoned by the King, and was sent immediately to the parlor he used as a throne room at Castle Emrys. She found him sitting on the overly ornate chair he used as a throne both white-knuckled, and with his lips pressed so firmly together that his mouth looked like a scar. Clearly he was very angry.

She bit her lip to keep it from trembling and stared at the floor, trying hard not to cry as he lectured her about how inconsiderate she had been and 'what if' this and 'what if' that.

She truly did not understand why he was making such a big deal about the fact they'd arrived back at the castle shortly after dark. She couldn't believe he was actually worried about her. He was too self-centered for that. She could only assume that he was distraught about how her behavior might reflect on him.

"By the sacred three," he hissed, "what were you thinking?"

"Apparently, I wasn't thinking," she said, though her head was reeling. Sacred three? What is the sacred three? He must have been really angry to let that slip.

She decided the best way forward was to apologize. Profusely. "I am so sorry, my lord. We were on our way back, and I made Yona and Chokhmah stop at a jewelry booth with me so I could see what he had."

"There are dozens of jewelry booths at the Pascha market. Why this one?"

Eluned felt her cheeks burning. "It was the same vendor as the one in Prythew that Yona bought my earrings from. I just wondered if he had anything else that was as unique as the earrings. Plus, all the other stalls had only tawdry looking jewelry."

"And did he?" He asked coldly, eyes narrowed.

The Princess pulled back her sleeve and held up her arm to display her torque. Arawn's face paled considerably but he didn't say anything, just stepped closer to Eluned, grasping her wrist to take a closer look. She grimaced in pain, but held her tongue.

"Exquisite. You certainly have a knack for finding incomparable baubles."

I am a Princess, Eluned thought, but said, "Thank you," although she was pretty sure it hadn't been a compliment.

"Promise me," he said, pulling down her sleeve and letting go of her wrist, "that you will not be abroad after dark here in Arberth unless accompanied by me, King Hevel, Hywel or Gethin or, alternately, one of my soldiers."

"I promise," she whispered, tears brimming in her eyes again. She angrily blinked them away. She refused to let him see her cry. He "dismissed" her by leaving her standing alone in the parlor. She counted slowly to thirty to make sure he was gone before returning to her room. By the time she got there, she was fuming.

"Who does he think he is? My father?" she raged to Chokhmah. "If I had wanted to be treated like a child I would have stayed in Zion. Unbelievable. I'm not sure I can stand him for two more months. I might kill him first, if not myself."

There was a sharp rap on the door and Eluned's eyes widened. Had someone outside heard her griping? She opened it to find Yona.

"I just couldn't wait until tomorrow to find out what happened," she explained.

"Did Hevel reprimand you?"

"No, of course not! He seemed to find it rather amusing that Arawn was so angry with you. It wasn't that late in the evening, after all."

"Then what was he worried about? I know it wasn't me."

"I'm at a loss to explain it," Yona said. "I think we could use a glass of wine."

"I agree," Eluned said, and walked over to the couch in front of the fireplace. A decanter of wine and several glasses waited on a tray on the coffee table. The Princess collapsed onto the center of the sofa, sighing. Yona joined her as Chokhmah poured them each a glass. Then she settled on the other side of Eluned.

They sat in silence for a while, sipping the deep red wine, and staring into the flames of the small fire that burned brightly in the fireplace.

"Well," Eluned finally said. "There were a couple of weird things he said and did."

"What would that be?" Chokhmah asked as she refilled their glasses.

"Well, first he swore by the sacred three. What's the sacred three?" she looked at Chokhmah, who always seemed to know nearly as much as Gwrhyr.

The blood drained from the gypsy's face. "Oh dear," she murmured, unconsciously making the sign to ward off the evil eye. "I guess that is our confirmation."

"I don't understand."

"Three ancient gods. They are connected by their demand for human sacrifice—by burning, drowning and flaying. I think over time just one sacrifice per the three became sufficient, but I really do not know any more than that. I thought people had long since stopped worshipping them. But, I guess that I am not really surprised. I had heard rumors that the Crimson King performed human sacrifices . . ."

"And then his reaction to the earrings I bought Eluned," Yona interrupted.

"And that's the other thing," Eluned chimed in. "The way he reacted when he saw my bracelet. He kind of went pale, and hurt my wrist looking at it more closely."

"He did not say anything?" Chokhmah asked.

"No. Actually he acted like it was an interesting piece of costume jewelry. But I know the gems and gold are real. It was almost as if he was trying to be casual about it in his freaky Arawn sort of way."

"We may never know the connection," Chokhmah said, "but that might be the last piece of jewelry you want to buy while we are in Annewven."

"I couldn't agree with you more," Eluned said. "Also, I think I want to continue our habit of going to the early mass at Saint Yorgos. It may be our only chance to keep an eye on the quays. I doubt that King Arawn will prevent us from going. It would only make him look bad."

"True." Yona said, "and I know that Hevel won't mind if I go. It's always an advantage to the king to have a pious wife."

"Especially when you're involved in worshipping pagan gods and offering humans in sacrifice," Eluned grimaced.

23RD FEHARN

After a few hours of exhausted sleep, Eluned found herself suddenly wide-awake, heart racing and butterflies dancing in her belly. She wasn't sure what had caused the anxiety attack. So many things had happened the previous day—the tension of attending the Pascha service with Arawn and his cronies along with the rich food at the Paschal feast, the stress of the charade with the jewelry vendor, or the anger she felt at the way she had been treated by Arawn.

Perhaps all three, she thought as she tried to calm herself in various ways. But slow and deep breaths, prayers, and even allowing her overactive imagination to take rein and gallop about at will did not help. She was still tossing and turning, trying to get comfortable and fall back asleep when Chokhmah began to stir. Already a pearly gray light could be seen at the windows.

"Morning already!" she groused as Chokhmah pulled the curtains back.

"Did you not sleep well?"

"I barely slept. I couldn't turn my brain off, and my heart kept racing and I was nauseated."

"You should have awakened me."

"I couldn't do that! You were sleeping so soundly."

"But Eluned that is exactly what I am here for."

"Only publicly."

"I meant that as your friend, I am here to help you."

"Oh," the Princess felt chastened. "I'm never sure when I am crossing the line."

"Rest assured that I am more than happy to make you aware when you are doing so. Would you prefer to miss the service this morning?"

"No," Eluned said, swinging her feet over the side of the bed. "We need to go ahead and set the precedent. I can take a nap later today if I need to do so. I could definitely use a cup of coffee though!"

Chokhmah opened the window and stepped out onto the balcony. "Goodness!" she exclaimed.

"What is it?" Eluned asked, joining her. "Oh my! I can't even see the ground. Or the ocean, for that matter. Where did the fog come from?"

"It does seem unlikely after the beautiful day we had yesterday. It is just the vagaries of spring, I suppose. You might want to bring your cloak along. It may take a while for the sun to burn the fog away."

"It's spooky, isn't it?" Eluned's voice registered barely above a whisper as they began walking along the promenade. "I can barely see but a foot or two ahead."

"What is it about fog that makes you want to speak quietly?" Yona asked, talking softly, herself.

"It is almost as if sounds are amplified," Chokhmah also spoke in low tones. "Listen. I hear voices ahead. Something is happening." They stopped in order to hear more clearly. It was true. They could hear muffled voices, but they seemed to be excited or distraught. It was hard to tell, though, as the fog seemed to cloak all their senses not just their sight.

They continued ahead, slowly, straining their eyes to put bodies to the voices but the mist was just too thick. Suddenly, the voices grew louder and they stumbled upon a group of fisherman working to pull something out of the water that lapped against the sea wall.

"What is it?" Chokhmah asked one of the men.

He turned a grim and weathered face toward her. "You might want'a stand back, Missus," he warned her. "They be pullin' up a body."

"A body?" The Princess echoed him. She wasn't sure she was ready to see a drowned body.

"We should go on," said Yona.

"No," Eluned gritted her teeth. "We should stay. Someone may need to be told and it would be better if we were the ones to bring the news." It would help the King if his "betrothed" took an interest in his people. Not that she relished the idea of informing some poor woman or man that their spouse or parent was dead.

"Arright, pull!" someone out of sight below the wall shouted. Several of the men gathered along the wall were grasping a rope that ran over the edge of the sea wall and then downward and out of sight. Standing one behind the other, they braced themselves before beginning to strain against the rope. It didn't take them long to pull the body over the wall and lay it out on the pavement of the promenade. There were a number of gasps and several flashing hands attempting to ward off evil.

"What's wrong?" Eluned asked, stepping forward to look down at the drowned man. His skin was so white that his lips looked almost blue. A jagged red wound gaped across his neck. Eluned heard Yona stifle a cry before she ran to the wall and lost her coffee to the ocean.

She turned to look at Chokhmah, surprised at the depth of the anger she felt. The older woman's eyes reflected her dismay.

"Does any un recornize 'im?" someone was asking.

"Yes," the Princess began, but nothing came out but a whisper. She cleared her throat and tried again. "Yes. I do. It's the journeyman. He had a jewelry stall at the fair yesterday."

"She's right," said one of the fishermen. "I saw 'im down ter ther Ship and Castle. Kept ter 'imself, he did, and lef' quiet-like. Mayhaps that's ther reason I noticed 'im."

"In other words," Chokhmah said, "he was not causing any trouble."

"'Zac'ly," the fisherman agreed. "Some un muster robbed 'im."

"I don't know where he's from," Eluned sighed. "I saw him in Prythew, as well, but that doesn't mean anything."

"Might as well let ther sea take 'im then," said another of the men who helped pull him up. "Canna leave 'im here."

"There's no one to bury him?" Eluned asked.

"It'll cost," a third man said.

Eluned pulled some silver from the pocket of her cloak. "Will that see that it gets done?"

The third man assented, quickly pocketing the coins.

"Thank you," she said, despite the fact she had a strong feeling the burial would still be at sea.

SHE AND CHOKHMAH WALKED over to the bench where Yona sat pale faced and shivering.

"Are you all right, my dear?" Chokhmah asked.

Yona nodded and stood. "I'm sorry. It's not that I haven't seen my share of drowned bodies. It was a part of growing up on the docks. It's just that we were talking to him yesterday, and now he's violently dead, and I can't help but think that the King had something to do with it."

She had said it quietly but Eluned glanced around, nervously. The fog was still thick and she could barely see the body on the ground much less any eavesdroppers. She also realized the men who had pulled the body from the water were shifting from foot to foot, obviously waiting for them to leave before disposing of the body. She put her finger to her lips warning Yona to be silent and said, a bit too loudly, "We're going to be late for the service. We should hurry."

SOON THEY WERE SAFELY ENSCONCED in the chapel where the morning service was held. They were forced by the quiet of the church to keep silent. Once the service started, it wasn't clear to the priest just how present the women were during the liturgy, as they all appeared deeply absorbed in their own thoughts rather than in the service. Only Chokhmah gave some semblance of taking part, murmuring the responses and standing and kneeling as required.

After the service, as they filed out of the chapel, the priest stopped the women and asked, "Is there something wrong?"

"It is nothing important, Father Addogar," Chokhmah replied.

"We were just surprised by the sight of a drowned man being pulled out of the sea on our way here," Eluned chimed in. "It was very disturbing."

"Omni have mercy!" he exclaimed. "Was it someone you knew?"

"No, just one of the vendors at the fair yesterday but it was shocking nonetheless," Chokhmah explained.

"How tragic," he agreed.

"He probably over indulged," Eluned said, quickly. "The last place he was seen was at the Ship and Castle."

The priest nodded in understanding. "Sad, indeed. May Omni have mercy on his soul, and may he rest in peace."

"Amen," the three women agreed. They seemed to be in unspoken agreement that the man's murder should not be mentioned, or, at the very least, they should act as if they had not recognized that it was the vendor who had sold them the jewelry on the off chance Father Addogar said something to the King to alert him to that fact.

OUTSIDE, THE FOG HAD DISSIPATED SOMEWHAT but it was now clear that the sky was overcast. A brisk wind had cleared most of the mist close to the ground, but it also forced the women to pull their cloaks more tightly around them.

"We still need to go down to the wharves," Eluned said, once they moved away from the church. "Although I'd prefer to return to the castle and hide in my room.

"I'm not sure I can face Arawn again," Yona muttered.

"He's certainly living up to his nickname," Eluned agreed.

All was quiet down at the docks as well. A few people could be seen here and there, but apparently most of the population was still sleeping off the effects of the previous day's celebrations. Several diehards could be seen out on the horizon fishing in the deeper waters of the bay, but the gusting wind, light fog and generally gloomy weather seemed to be keeping most people indoors.

"Unless, of course," the Princess noted, "they've heard about the death of the journeyman, in which case they're probably avoiding the king's men."

"Not beyond the realm of possibility," Chokhmah agreed. "Let us return to the castle. I think we can easily plead exhaustion and hide ourselves in the room the rest of the day. I agree that we need some time to compose ourselves before facing the Crimson King again."

THEIR PLAN WAS EASIER TO PULL OFF than they hoped. When they returned from the morning Mass, most of the castle was still silent. They could hear noise coming from the kitchens, and Chokhmah stopped in for a tray of bread and cheese along with some hot tea to break their fast.

They managed to avoid being seen on their way up to the room, and breathed a collective sigh of relief as they removed their cloaks before settling in front of the fireplace. Chokhmah stoked up the fire as Yona poured the tea.

"It's at times like this," Eluned said, "that I almost long to be back in the Mountains of Misericord."

"Why is that?" Yona asked.

"I was miserably cold most of the time," she explained, "but I had yet to learn of the treasures, and I was still unaware that the plan was to come to Annewven. Everything was so simple—food, water and shelter. I miss Hayduke. And Bonpo's laughter. I miss sitting around the campfire and talking with Bonpo and Jabb. I even miss arguing with Gwrhyr. Now, he's back in Prythew or wherever they're training, and here we can't even talk to Bonpo or Jabberwock very often. The next two months are never going to end." Then she stopped abruptly, realizing how that sounded. "But, of course, those days would have been even more perfect if you two had been there as well. I wasn't trying to say that I don't like being here with you."

"Don't worry," Yona said. "I understand completely. I was about to go insane having to spend all that time with King Arawn and his cronies. So, while I can't appreciate what it was like before I arrived on the scene, I am so very glad that I did meet you and that you did come to Annewven. You've changed my life in a good way and for that I will always be thankful."

"Yes," added Chokhmah, "I do not regret in the least having joined you and your fellows on this journey. I cannot yet see what lies ahead of us, but I rest assured that we are doing the right thing."

AS EVENING APPROACHED, a scratching at the door startled them. Eluned's eyes widened in fear and her heart began to beat faster until she realized the reason for the rasping sound. "It's Jabberwock," she said, breathing a sigh of relief and rising to open the door. "He can't knock."

The Princess let him into the room saying, "I'm so glad you're here. We've been dying to talk to you."

"You look fine to me," he observed as he pattered over to the fireplace.

"I am fine. Why?"

"I heard a rumor that all of you were feeling under the weather," he said as he sat down on the hearth, back to the flames. "Ah, that feels wonderful. The king keeps his parlor downright chilly."

"It was the only thing we could come up with that would seem like a viable excuse in order to avoid the king," Eluned admitted.

"Indeed?"

Then, haltingly at first, the women filled him in on what had been happening the past couple of days.

JABBERWOCK TURNED TO FACE THE FLAMES and stared into the fire for a long while after they were finished. Eluned could see the orange and yellow of the flames reflected in his eyes. "This recess in Arberth is frustratingly long considering we wanted to get in and out of Annewven as quickly as possible," he began. "It has certainly given us more than enough time to find out just how dangerous Arawn can be. You're really going to have to lay low the next two months and do as much as you can to truckle the King."

"Truckle?" Eluned interrupted.

"Bootlick, brownnose, butter up," he explained.

"Grovel," Chokhmah added, smiling.

"Kowtow, toady," Yona giggled.

"Are you saying you want me to fawn over him?" Eluned was laughing but she wasn't sure it was funny.

"All right, all right," the Bandersnatch snorted in annoyance. "You get the idea. He needs to have complete trust in you or we'll never make it out of Annewven alive."

They agreed, but only because they feared Arawn and trusted Jabberwock's wisdom.

"At least Bonpo and Yona won't have to go back to Castle Pwyll," Eluned muttered.

THE TIME TRICKLED BY, Feharn passing into Saitheh: Three weeks of morning walks to Saint Yorgos followed by a surreptitious pass through the wharves; never once happening upon any of Yona's friends. Eluned tried not to panic. Occasionally, Father Addogar was invited to Deethseel lunch or dinner, offering them a brief respite from the never-ending meals with Arawn, Hevel and the others.

There were plenty of days spent on horse back although Eluned never found a chance to go riding alone in Avalach and therefore, never had a chance to look for Nyx. It was clear Arawn never meant for her to be left alone, and she and Yona and Chokhmah were only un-chaperoned when they attended the early service each day. This was clearly a blessing in disguise as it gave them a chance to look for Yona's friends. Of course, that never took them much time. They would have to come up with an excuse for the extra time spent on arranging Bonpo's passage once they did find someone.

There were mornings or evenings on the beach and days trapped indoors by frequent showers. The library at Castle Emrys was sadly inferior to the one at Castle Pwyll and the Princess quickly ran out of things to read. Instead, she became quite practiced at the harpsichord and took up drawing and painting again as well.

And still the days seemed to drag on. The only bright spot was Bonpo's happiness in the kitchens where he quickly excelled at reproducing the local dishes.

The Princess also became proficient at keeping Arawn at arm's length although he had yet to propose marriage. A fact that left her simultaneously unnerved and relieved. She was glad to be left alone, and by the end of the month, the King had apparently grown tired of Celyn and had begun flirting with the pale and flaxen-haired Auron. She doubted he could even be faithful to a wife.

Eluned and Yona spent as little time with Celyn and Auron as they could possibly manage. Hevel's chancellor, Chazak, and the Lady Aviv had returned to Adamah shortly after Pascha when they received news that Chazak's father was ailing and not expected to live much longer. Hevel seemed content to spend most days in the company of Arawn, Hywel and Gethin. The only time he required Yona at his side was on the Feast Day of Saint Yorgos when the remainder of the party processed into the church once again.

Fortunately, as far as Eluned was concerned, only the hardiest of souls stayed to celebrate the holy day in the driving rain. Yona declared that nearly half the usual number of booths were scattered along the road leading to the harbor. The holiday was truly a miserable day and Eluned was glad to be curled up on the sofa in her room playing tarok with Chokhmah and Yona. Only two weeks had passed since they'd seen the journeyman, throat slashed, lying on the promenade. And at that point, if she never attended a fair again, it wouldn't be too soon.

The sixteenth day of Saitheh was a week later and by then, the temperatures were more consistently warmer and the storms much less frequent. Arberth was abuzz with preparations for the May Day festival that would take place the following day. A May Pole had been set up in the square in front of Saint Yorgos and the children had been practicing the dance they were to perform around it for nearly a week.

As they were making their daily pilgrimage from the church to the docks that morning, booths were already being erected along the streets and the square. Carts and barrows overflowed with the flowers that would be strung to decorate everything from those stalls to the statue of the first King Arawn that stood in the center of the square.

The Princess inhaled the aroma of the cakes and pies, hams and roasts, and the myriad other delicacies being prepared for the big day. Her stomach rumbled in response. She'd had nothing but a cup of coffee before the service, and now she couldn't help but wonder what Bonpo was preparing for their lunch. It would probably be something easily thrown together as the servants in the kitchens were working furiously to prepare the food for the last big festival before the King left for Prythew.

Even so, Eluned couldn't help but feel the excitement in the air and she felt a glimmer of hope ignite in her heart. They were scheduled to return to Prythew and Castle Pwyll on the twenty-seventh of Eahth. Just a month and eleven days left before they could begin to plan in earnest the stealing of the treasures and their escape from Annewven. Surely, now that the seas were calmer again, one of Yona's friends would turn up at the quays and they could plan Bonpo's departure to Favonia.

DESPITE THE FACT EVERYONE ELSE SEEMED to be in a fever about the May Day festival and were somewhat aghast that they chose to do so, Eluned, Yona and Chokhmah made their daily trek to the morning service at Saint Yorgos. They were too entrenched in the pattern not to go and even though they would probably have a chance to visit the quays later in the day, it seemed ill luck not to keep to the paradigm they had set.

So, following the service, they hurried once again to the docks, and, after more than a month of searching, Eluned and Chokhmah were completely unprepared for the near shriek Yona suddenly emitted.

"By Omni," Eluned gasped. "What is it? My heart nearly stopped."

"I'm so sorry," Yona apologized, eyes filling with tears. "I hadn't realized I'd essentially given up hope of ever seeing any of my friends again."

"What! One of your friends is here?" Eluned sounded a bit teary herself.

Yona pointed to one of the vessels tied up at the nearest

dock. "That's Libni's sloop," she said. "In its non-pirate mode, of course." The smallish ship had one mast rigged fore and aft, carrying a mainsail, gaff-topsail, jib and fore staysail. "Pirates, and smugglers for that matter, prefer small ships like that," she explained, "Because they can easily be altered for various sail combinations. Makes it easier to escape, you see?"

"Makes sense to me," Eluned replied.

"See," Yona pointed again, "she's flying the flag of Adamah."

Eluned could see the lion rampant, gold on silver, fluttering in the light breeze. "As opposed to?"

"Her pirate flag," Yona stated as if Eluned should have known. "The name is a dead giveaway," she continued, "though I'd recognize that sloop without it."

"*Queen of the May*," Eluned read the flowing letters on the bow. "That's an odd name for a pirate ship, but it strikes me as quite propitious today."

Yona laughed. "True. But that's Libni. She probably knows I am here and planned on being in Arberth on May Day. Let's go see if she's aboard."

Queen of the May was probably between forty and fifty feet long, Eluned calculated. When they got closer, she counted more than a dozen cannons, assuming there was a matching set on the port side. She only hoped that Libni would be willing to return and take Bonpo to safety at least a week before they traveled back to Prythew. She feared he might be required to return to Prythew earlier than Eluned and Chokhmah because he couldn't use the phaeton and it took days to travel by foot. It might keep Arawn from suspecting the Princess if he disappeared first but she stayed on. At least, she hoped so.

"Mahschlomchem!" Yona called out as they stepped onto the dock. Eluned didn't know what she was saying but it sounded like some form of greeting.

"Yona?" They heard a voice call back. A few seconds later,

a tall woman was barreling down the gangplank and enfolding Yona in her muscular arms. "Yona, schlomitov, now that you are here." She kissed her, heartily, on both cheeks and on the lips before stepping back to look at her, although her hands remained firmly on Yona's shoulders.

The whole exchange had happened so quickly that Eluned hadn't had a chance to look at the female pirate other than to note she was tall and muscular. And while it was true that she was a large woman, she was also quite striking with dark, almost black almond-shaped eyes, long blue-black hair pulled into numerous plaits, which in turn were filled with charms, feathers and beads that were braided, tied or even just lodged in her hair. She had full lips and her nose had apparently been broken more than once, and a ragged scar ran along her left cheekbone. Libni looked to be at least ten years older than Yona.

The pirate was wearing men's leather trousers and jerkin over a red cotton sweater, and Eluned was reminded that she and Yona had wanted to invest in some male clothing for themselves. Well, an outfit for Yona; the Princess just wanted a lighter sweater and a shirt to wear with the trousers she already owned. They would have to make sure to take care of that today as they would probably be given a bit of freedom for the last time.

Libni invited them on board and led them to the galley where she poured them each a shot of a clear liquid. The Princess looked around the compact but comfy room. It was rough but clean and mostly filled with a large wooden table that looked to seat maybe a dozen people at a time. Eluned imagined the crew must eat in shifts.

"L'Chayim!" Libni raised her glass in a toast once she had finished pouring.

"L'Chayim!" Yona returned and downed her glass. Eluned and Chokhmah followed suit and it was all the Princess could do to keep from choking as the fiery liquid burned its way down her throat.

"I'm afraid we can't stay long, right now," Yona apologized to Libni. "Arawn watches Eluned like a hawk, and will soon be wondering why she isn't back from Mass. But, I imagine Hevel will allow me some time to visit later and we have a huge favor to ask of you."

Libni arched her eyebrows. "Then definitely you must come back and tell me more of this favor."

"Thank you," Yona said, hugging her. "I'll be back once the festivities end following the maypole celebration."

"I look forward to it, my treasure," Libni said, kissing her again, this time a bit more passionately.

"Friend, huh?" Eluned asked once they reached the promenade.

Yona smiled, almost wistfully, "Maybe a little more than a friend," was all she would admit.

"That's probably a blessing," Eluned said. "I imagine it will make her more willing to help us out."

"Possibly." Yona seemed doubtful.

"Have you asked anything of her before?" Eluned wanted to know.

"No," she shook her head. "Well, kind of. We've always been close, sometimes closer than others, but," she sighed. "When I was sixteen, I wanted to join her crew and sail off with her. I didn't care what my family thought. But, she dissuaded me. Said it would make life even more dangerous for her because my father was sure to come after me. She took off shortly after that and I didn't see her for another couple of years. By then, I was betrothed to Hevel, which, of course, made it impossible to remain with her."

"I'm sorry."

"She was correct, of course," Chokhmah murmured.

"Yes," Yona sighed again. "But it broke my heart."

"Well, you seem to be on good terms now," Eluned said.

"True. We remain good friends. Better to have a little than nothing at all."

Eluned experienced a flash of jealousy. She'd never even been in love much less had her heart broken. Now she was stuck in Annewven; might not even make it out alive. What if she never had a chance to experience love and passion? Part of her wanted to burst into tears of self-pity, but she would wait until she was alone for that. She most certainly wasn't going to arrive at Castle Emrys with swollen and red eyes. They were surely already going to have to explain to Arawn why they were nearly half an hour later than usual.

ONCE AGAIN, YONA RESCUED HER. They had barely reached the parlor where everyone was gathered to begin the procession to the square before Yona began apologizing.

"I am so sorry we are late. We ran into a friend of mine from Seagirt," she explained, "and it took a few minutes for me to explain that we had to rush back to the castle but that I would see her later in the day."

"A friend from Seagirt, you say?" Hevel said. "Who was it?"

"It was Libni."

"I'm not familiar with him."

"Her." Yona said. Had he not been paying attention? It both annoyed and relieved her as it might mean she could get away with a lot more.

The King raised his eyebrows at that. "Libni is a man's name."

"Her parents wanted a boy."

"And what is Libni doing here?"

"She's a trader," Yona lied.

"She has a lovely sloop," Eluned said, then stifled a giggle because somehow that sounded completely inappropriate.

Yona looked at her oddly, but explained. "Yes, her vessel is *Queen of the May*. She decided to make port in Arberth for May Day because she knows I spend my springs here."

"Then you were lucky to run into her already," Arawn said, losing interest. "Are we ready to process to the square?"

THANK OMNI THIS IS THE LAST OF THE PROCESSIONS, Eluned thought, as she took Arawn's proffered arm. At least he didn't have to wear that ridiculous outfit this time. They'd had to wear their traditional costumes on Saint Yorgos' Day, and Arawn had once again looked like an idiot as far as she was concerned.

Today, she was wearing the green skirt and blouse that Chokhmah had given her. They seemed appropriate, somehow, for May Day. She glanced at Arawn realizing she had never really paid attention to what he wore. At first, it was because his eyes were so mesmerizing she'd had a difficult time not staring into them; later, it was because she avoided looking at him at all.

He was wearing black leather pants that were indecorously tight. She was pretty sure she didn't want to see that much of him. He was also wearing an overly puffy white silk shirt that might have looked masculine on Hywel or Gwrhyr but managed, once again, to make him look like a girl. In addition, he wore a black silk robe not unlike the one in his tapestry back at Castle Pwyll. She hadn't noticed him wearing it prior to this time. It was quite striking covered as it was in silvery moons and stars and symbols that were unfamiliar to her. It was almost as if he was trying to look like a dashing young mage or something. His crown was silvery as well (titanium, maybe?) set with sapphires and emeralds. Beautiful crown, she thought, but it looked odd against his copper hair.

They soon reached the square where they were led to a dais from which they were to view the celebration. The King stood up and gave a short welcome speech and the festivities began.

The children were absolutely enchanting as they wove the ribbons around the pole in an intricate dance, but Eluned couldn't wait for it to be over so that she and Yona could "escape" back to Queen of the May. But that was not to be. After the children had decorated the May pole, a beautiful young woman, hair shining like gold and adorned with flowers, got up to sing a hauntingly beautiful song about summer and love and loss. This was followed by the ceremony crowning her as the May Queen.

The King stood, and much to Eluned's surprise, took the May Queen's hand and led her in a formal dance that was uniquely choreographed and, according to Hevel, performed every year by the King and the current May Queen. Once the King was re-seated, a group of dancers stepped forward and performed yet another ceremonial but definitely cruder gambol clearly symbolizing fertility rites. Eluned found herself blushing yet again.

She glanced at Yona to see whether she was enjoying the interminable festivities, but she had obviously known what to expect and seemed oblivious of anything but what was going on in front of her. Or was she daydreaming about Libni? Eluned wished she had someone real to fantasize about. The imaginary lover she'd left Zion with no longer enticed her the way he once had. She wanted to picture herself on the beach with someone she actually knew, she thought, grinding her teeth to prevent herself from yawning.

The dancing and singing finally ended, but then they were led to a tent where they were seated at a beautifully set table, and once again treated to course upon course, and dish upon dish of the May Day feast. The Princess was finding it difficult not to scream in frustration. She'd lost her appetite and just wanted to meet with Libni so she could finally rest assured that Bonpo would escape. Yet, the King was at her side and she had to, at the very least, nibble at what was set in front of her.

When the meal had finally ended and what would happen next was being discussed, Eluned prayed that Auron would distract the king much the same way Celyn had done at the Paschal meal. Instead, he turned to her and said, "Shall I escort you around the fair? Perhaps you would like another piece of jewelry? A ring, perhaps?"

It took every thing Eluned had within her not to cry. She had no choice. He was not going to let her roam around the vendors' stalls on her own ever again. So, wailing inwardly, she pulled herself together (at least, she hoped so) and consented. "But I'd rather look for a light sweater and blouse," she heard herself saying.

"We can get one of the women at the castle to knit you a sweater and sew you a blouse," he said. "Perhaps we will find your favorite jewelry vendor. No doubt he is here yet again."

The nerve, Eluned thought, glancing at Yona. She had overheard the King and looked stricken as well. No doubt he is in his watery grave, Eluned clenched her hands in anger. She might have to replace her unsatisfactory visions of love with inventions of different ways to kill Arawn. "Let me give my apologies to Yona," she said. "I was supposed to go with her to meet Libni."

"By all means."

She quickly scooted around Arawn and Hevel, who had oh so conveniently prevented them from conspiring during the meal, and apologized, gripping her hands, urgently.

Yona hugged her and said, "Don't worry, I am sure Libni will understand." She then whispered in her ear. "I know what to do. Trust me."

She would have to trust her. She would also have to keep herself from being too jealous. Yona had now been granted time alone with Libni. She was practically glowing.

"I'm ready," she said, trying not to grimace as she took the King's arm.

17ᵀᴴ Saitheh

Eluned was in an agony of suspense for the remainder of the day. She could barely pretend interest in the booths, and the thought of even looking at jewelry horrified her. The Princess just wanted to get back to the castle, crawl into her bed, and hide until Yona returned. Finally, finally, finally, after Arawn had insisted they look at every single stall (he was punishing her, she was sure of it), he asked her if she was ready to return to the castle.

It was all she could do not to weep with joy. But, she continued to play the part (she hoped that Queen Fuchsia would have been proud of her acting skills), and began to feign a headache so that she could retreat to her room once they returned.

There she discovered Chokhmah waiting patiently to hear what had happened with Libni.

The Princess threw herself onto the couch and finally vented all her many frustrations with the day.

Chokhmah commiserated. "I am so sorry that your day was so unsatisfactory for you. Perhaps, you must learn to be a little more patient. We still have ample time to get things arranged here. An entire month, in fact."

"Another month!" Eluned lamented, jumping up from the couch and pacing the room. "I'm not sure I can make it another day much less another month."

"Another month and eleven days," Chokhmah pointed out. "Or, thirty-seven days if you do not count today and the day we return."

"Omni have mercy!"

"Amen!"

"Well, it helps to know that I am not the only one counting down the days," Eluned sighed. "I wonder when Yona will be back?"

"I suspect we will not see her until tomorrow."

"Tomorrow!" The Princess wailed. "Why?"

"You know as well as I do. She has been granted some time with a good friend . . ."

"And lover." It was more of an accusation than a statement of fact.

"Correct," Chokhmah said trying not to smile. "I imagine she will return to the castle as late as possible, if not first thing in the morning."

"Omni have mercy," Eluned groaned. "I need some wine."

"And you should eat a little something. There is no point in making yourself ill from dissatisfaction. I shall return shortly," and Chokhmah left the room leaving Eluned staring bleakly out the window.

As Chokhmah had surmised, they didn't see Yona again until the next morning at Saint Yorgos. She slipped into the pew and sat next to Eluned a few minutes after the service began. The Princess looked at her in reproach before turning away and ignoring her for the remainder of the Mass. She had apparently come straight from Queen of the May as she was still wearing the dress she had worn the previous day.

Yona apologized profusely after the service, and Eluned did her best to remain staunchly unforgiving, but relented by the time they reached the promenade. In truth, not only could she not stay mad at Yona, but also she actually understood her taking as much time with Libni as possible. She would have done the same in a similar situation.

They hugged and Eluned tried to explain how agonizing the previous day had been for her. "Please give me some good news," she finished. "Please tell me that Libni will return and take Bonpo to Favonia."

"Yes, she is more than willing to do that for us. She says she will sail into port after midnight on the nineteenth of Eahth."

"So, actually the twentieth day of Eahth?"

"Yes, and that Bonpo must be there before the sun rises so they can leave before it gets light."

"So, before dawn on the twentieth day of Eahth."

"Right. And he should call out 'mahschlomech' so that Libni and her crew know that it's him."

"He's kind of hard to mistake, but I guess it could be more of a problem in the dark," Eluned mused.

"They will take him to the port in Seemu."

"I will see if I can send a pigeon to my aunt before then so that she will receive him," Chokhmah said.

"Do you think we can risk that?" Eluned asked.

"Risk?"

"I'm just worried that Arawn has ears everywhere."

"I take your point," Chokhmah said. "I will send a letter of introduction with Bonpo."

"You have an aunt in Favonia?" Yona asked.

"Queen Miryam," Eluned replied for her.

"I had forgotten I did not tell you that," Chokhmah said. "It is one of the reasons we are going there first."

"Plus they have one of the treasures," Eluned added. "The Coat of Padarn Red-Coat."

"We could have seven of the treasures at that point," Yona said, "if I can get my hands on Hevel's hamper."

"And we can get the phaeton and chess board. I have a feeling the latter is not going to be easy to acquire," the Princess sighed.

"We will definitely have our work cut out for us when we return to Prythew," Chokhmah agreed.

"You may want to write me a letter of introduction, as well," Yona suggested. "I may get there before you."

"That would be nice," Eluned said. "Did you tell Libni that you might have to escape from Adamah?" They had slowed their pace as they drew closer to the castle.

"Yes. We have a plan for that. She or one of my other friends, whoever is closest to Seagirt, will meet me there. They will arrange it among themselves in the meantime."

ONCE AGAIN, ROUTINE REIGNED as Eluned, each night before slipping into bed, crossed off that day on a calendar she had drawn in her journal on the seventeenth of Saitheh when Chokhmah had noted they had only thirty-nine days remaining to their stay in Arberth.

As long as she remained polite to Arawn, she and Yona were allowed, with Chokhmah as a chaperone, a fair amount of freedom. Apparently the Princess had proved herself trustworthy (enough) once again when she allowed the king to escort her around the May Day fair. Although it did trouble her a bit that the king no longer seemed particularly interested in getting to know her better.

The women spent as much time as possible riding in Avalach, but Eluned had constant doubts about the efficacy of riding with a widow and a woman who might not be considered technically "pure."

After all, unicorns showed themselves only to virgins, and she was clearly the only virgin among the three having never even been kissed. Well, she amended to herself, perhaps kissed but surely Gwrhyr and Arawn didn't count because it involved not only no desire on her part but also she had been kissed against her will.

Someday, she sighed to herself, someday (inevitably, I hope) I'll feel passion for someone who will feel equally passionate about me.

It was while she was ruminating on the possibility of this happening that the women chanced upon a woodcutter working hard (or just hurrying?) to saw a blow-down into pieces.

"Excuse me," she prompted when he didn't look up at their arrival in front of him.

He jumped as if startled. The sound of their approach had been covered by the noise of his frenetic sawing at the tree blocking the path.

"I'm the Princess Eluned," she introduced herself, "and this is King Hevel's fiancée, Yona, and my lady-in-waiting, Chokhmah." She figured he would be more respectful if he were aware of their station and connection to the king than if they were just three random women out riding in the forest. Although, she discerned rather quickly, there weren't that many people in Arberth who had the luxury of riding for recreation. It would be obvious to him that they were high born.

"How might I he'p yer, yer highness?" he asked, putting down his saw and wiping the sweat from his brow with a dirty rag. A tattered hat barely covered his head, and his clothes were nearly as bad.

Eluned realized that he was probably in the wood illegally. Bravo, she thought before saying, "It's a silly question, really, but the King was telling me that there was once a unicorn in Avalach but that it hadn't been seen for many years. Is that correct?"

"That'd be true, m'lady, I mean, yer highness. Ther's them that think Nyx fled Av'lach more'n a cent'ry ago."

"Fled?"

"Left fer another kingdom, a more peaceful place, if'n yer catch me drift."

"Avalach isn't peaceful?"

The woodcutter flushed, but stood his ground. "Durin' ther day, yes. But ther's them that say evil spirits are abroad at night."

"Evil Spirits?" Yona asked. "Why is that?"

The woodcutter looked at his feet, clearly regretting having said anything at all.

"You can trust us," Chokhmah said in the voice she used when trying to calm someone. Eluned had come to understand that the gypsy's powers weren't limited to healing potions and understanding the tarot. She, like Jabberwock (and Arawn, for that matter), seemed to have some supernatural gifts as well. And, where the king used his eyes to mesmerize, Chokhmah used her voice. "What you say will remain with us," she continued, "and never reach the ears of the King."

"Ther's them that say that the first King Arawn begun ter practice his pagan rites in these verra woods," he admitted.

"Yes, we are aware that the current king is a devotee of the sacred three," Chokhmah replied, soothingly. "Is there a specific reason the people would fear Avalach at night?"

"Folk go missin' ever' once'ter while. Young women, partic'ly."

"Virgins," Chokhmah stated.

"Yes'm."

"So, it is thought by the people of Arberth that the kings have been performing human sacrifices in this forest?"

"Yes'm. Here, and over ter Prythew."

"We suspected as much," Chokhmah stated, but her voice was grim.

Eluned felt the hairs at the back of her neck prickle, and shuddered. "So the forest is haunted by those sacrificed and those they were sacrificed to?"

"That is our'uns belief, yer highness."

"Which would definitely explain the absence of the unicorn." Eluned shuddered. "I'd leave myself. Today, if I could."

"P'raps," the woodcutter began, cheeks coloring once again, "wen yer highness is queen, yer could use yer inflerence to turn ther King back ter Omni."

"If I had that power over him," she replied in earnest, "I promise you that I would do so. Or, at least, try. In truth, I no longer believe the King intends to ask for my hand in marriage."

"Then why has he kept you in Annewven?" Yona asked, dismayed. "Surely that's why he hasn't ransomed you."

"I wish I could believe that," the Princess said, but she suddenly felt very cold, chilled to the marrow. She shivered as a cloud passed in front of the sun and a gloom fell upon the clearing where they sat their horses. No, it was slowly all becoming very clear to her. Arawn was not interested in her connection to the King of Zion and the problems marriage to her would cause that kingdom. It was actually her virginity that was attractive to the King. And not because he wished to deflower her.

Arawn was interested only in his magic, his necromancy and what his "sacred three" could offer him in the way of power, no doubt. And what would make a more suitable sacrifice than that of a virgin princess?

The summer solstice was less than a month away. Would it be possible for them to get out of Annewven with the treasures before then?

As Eluned worried about Arawn's plans for her, she debated whether or not she should express her fears to her friends. She finally decided that she would bother neither Yona nor Bonpo, both of whom were preparing to leave and might feel some responsibility in remaining behind to see she made it to Favonia safely.

She would tell Chokhmah and Jabberwock once Yona and Bonpo were safely away. Bonpo was within a couple of days of leaving. Hevel and his retinue would leave shortly thereafter for Adamah followed by Hywel and Auron, Gethin and Celyn. They would take the phaeton back to Castle Pwyll first, followed by Arawn, Eluned, Chokhmah and Jabberwock. Only the staff necessary to maintain the upkeep of Castle Emrys until the following winter would remain in Arberth.

When Eluned awakened shortly after dawn on the nineteenth day of Eahth, she found herself curiously calm. She had spent so much time worrying about Bonpo making it out of Annewven alive that she was actually surprised that she hadn't spent the night tossing and turning and fighting off nightmares. Maybe it was because the end was finally in sight: it would be the most dangerous segment of their time in Annewven, without question, but one way or another, it would soon all be over. At least, she hoped so.

Barring any unforeseen circumstances, Libni would pick up Bonpo and he would be on his way to Favonia, safe at last. The value of her vessel being a pirate ship was that should Arawn's sailors spy her, she would have a much better chance of escaping them.

At any rate, the 19th day of Eahth brought with it a certain calm. She was able to join the others for breakfast and finally be genuinely unconcerned with what would happen in less than twenty-four hours.

So, unless she heard otherwise, she would have to assume they had made it to Favonia. In the meantime, she just needed to practice looking shocked when informed that Bonpo had vanished.

IT TURNED OUT THAT ARAWN WAS MORE RELIEVED than angered that Bonpo had disappeared.

"I never quite trusted the giant," he said while apprising them of his disappearance. "King Zhang informed me that the dzu-tch left the country in disgrace after endangering the other dzu-tch by killing a man."

The Princess felt the color drain from her face. Fortunately, Arawn made a false assumption.

"See," he said almost gleefully. "You weren't aware of that, were you?"

Eluned shook her head, but in reality she was thanking Omni for the fact that she and Chokhmah and even Gwrhyr were from kingdoms in the Triquetra Alliance. The Awen Alliance was clearly evil, and she hadn't realized just how well connected he was to his allies. It seemed like pure grace that Bonpo had ended up in Zion and not Kamartha or even Adamah, Simoon or Annewven.

As if reading her mind, Hevel said, "And he didn't even try to resettle in an allied Kingdom. Zion, of all places!"

The Princess felt her cheeks burning with the anger she felt and tears welled in her eyes. They could think what they liked. She loved Bonpo.

"Or someplace neutral at a minimum," Gethin added.

"What do you think of your cook now?" Arawn asked her.

The Princess bowed her head to try and hide her tears. "I guess he wasn't to be trusted," she managed to choke out before sobbing. She stood up quickly, and making her excuses, fled to her room.

WHEN SHE GOT THERE, she found Jabberwock meeting with Chokhmah.

What is wrong, my love?" Chokhmah looked alarmed.

Eluned found herself laughing hysterically. "I'm sorry," she apologized when she finally calmed down enough to speak. "I was so angry at Arawn that I started crying, and he assumed it was because I felt betrayed by Bonpo. Once I understood that, it was easy to continue to cry and leave the room.

Jabberwock's glassy eyes glittered in merriment. "You remind me more of Fuchsia all the time, my dear. So the giant has escaped and the King doesn't care, I take it?"

"He considered him a traitor to his people," she paused, "so to speak. I guess the dzu-tch can be called people. Really big people. And they seemed to find the fact he left Dziron for Zion nearly sacrilegious."

"Interesting," he said. "Is that what made you so angry?"

"I wanted to say, 'I'm sitting right here, people. My father's kingdom!' But either they're so accustomed to my being here or they've already sacrificed me to their sacred three," she groused, forgetting she hadn't intended to tell them until Yona was gone, as well, "that . . ."

"What?" Jabb and Chokhmah interrupted simultaneously.

"Oops," she said, hiding her face in her hands.

"Why do you think they want to sacrifice you?" the Bandersnatch asked.

"It's just that Arawn doesn't seem enamored of me like he once did, and then we ran into the man in Avalach cutting wood. No doubt, surreptitiously," she looked at Chokhmah, who nodded. "And, he said, that all the kings Arawn have worshipped the sacred three. Well, he didn't say the 'sacred three' but that's what he meant. And he said they also sacrifice virgins to their gods. And we know about the woman whose earrings Yona bought me, although she wasn't a virgin. They must be more difficult to come by in Prythew. We also know he had no trouble having that vendor killed. So," and she pointed to herself. "Virgin. I'd make the perfect sacrifice, right?"

"Omni have mercy," Chokhmah murmured, hand fluttering once again to ward off the evil eye, "she has a point."

"And we were planning to leave Prythew on the solstice because the King would be preoccupied," Jabberwock said.

"Change of plans, please," the Princess said, finally taking a seat on the sofa.

"That might present other difficulties," Jabberwock groaned.

"What? What other difficulties?"

"Before we left, it was Gwrhyr's understanding that he needed to be back in Prythew by the solstice, preferably the day before. I'm not sure we can get a message to him to let him know otherwise."

"Damn it!" The Princess cried, "I don't want to die. And right when things were just starting to look up again."

PART THREE

"We travel, some of us forever,
to see other states, other lives, other souls."
-Anaïs Nin
The Diary of Anaïs Nin, Vol. 7: 1966-1974

"Sailing on the wind
In a milk white gown
Dropping circle stones on a sundial
Playing hide and seek
With the ghosts of dawn
Waiting for a smile from a sun child."
-King Crimson
Moonchild *from* In the Court of the Crimson King

1ˢᵀ Deer

If riding in the phaeton got easier each time, she hadn't noticed a difference. Once again, she had to be taken straight to her bed and administered a sleeping potion before finally waking at sunset on the evening of twenty-seventh of Eahth.

Yona and Hevel had left without much ado, three days earlier. Yona had promised she would see the Princess again in Seemu but could not begin to guess when that might be. And, of course, they'd never heard anything from either Libni or Bonpo on whether or not he had made it safely to the island. Libni was wisely staying away from Arberth, and Bonpo could not risk sending a pigeon or letter.

Only thirteen days until the solstice, twelve if she didn't count that day. This year, the solstice occurred on the thirteenth of Deer. At this point they could do nothing but wait until Gwrhyr's return. It was up to Jabberwock to arrange stealing the chessboard. He had ingratiated himself so thoroughly to the King that he pretty much had free reign of the castle. And there was absolutely no reason that Arawn would suspect a creature without opposable thumbs capable of stealing his precious treasure.

But the Bandersnatch had a plan. He would push the

board and pieces in to a bag that Chokhmah would provide him with and then carry the bag with his teeth to the phaeton. The weight of the treasure would probably force him to drag it, but he was sure it would work if he acted like he knew what he was doing, no one would know what was within the bag.

Chokhmah was in charge of securing Halelu to the phaeton when the time came to flee. They would have to leave Heiduc and Honeysuckle behind, which saddened the Princess, but neither could she choose between the two.

The first order of business for the Princess was to check on her sword. It had, she hoped, remained hidden the entire time they'd been in Arberth. She carried the desk chair over to the armoire and climbed up on it. She wasn't tall enough to see over the top (Chokhmah had done that for her), but she could reach over the extended edge and feel if the blanket wrapping Dyrnwyn was still there.

Yes, she breathed a sigh of relief. It was still on top of the chest. But was the sword hidden within that blanket? She pulled the bundle up and its heft, alone, assured her that White Hilt had remained hidden. It had been so long since she had seen it, held it in her grip that she was going to have to take it down and actually look at it. As a matter of fact, she decided, she could stand to start practicing her swordplay again. This journey was becoming more and more dangerous. Who knew when becoming competent in the use of her sword would come in handy?

FORTUNATELY, IT LOOKED as if they were going to have a lot of free time on their hands. Now that the King was back in Prythew until winter, he would have to hold court again. And when Eluned awoke the following morning feeling completely refreshed from the phaeton trip (odd, she thought, how so brief a journey could cause her to lose more time than it took), petitioners to see the king had queued up nearly all the way down the mountain and into the village, itself. Unfortunately, for his poor subjects, the King only held court until noon, didn't hold court on Deethseel, and asked the majority of his needy subjects to return on Deethyeen.

AND WHILE THE FIRST THING she and Chokhmah needed to do was establish a new routine, they ended up somewhat hindered by the weekend—Eluned was forced to spend a Yona-less Deethsadoorn afternoon and evening with the King, Gethin and Celyn, Hywel and Auron. The Princess decided afterwards that it was the King's attempt at establishing some normalcy to their return to Castle Pwyll. She only hoped that he didn't intend to appropriate all of her time. Surely, come Deethyeen, he would once again become absorbed in the routine of ruling his kingdom. At least, she prayed so.

On Deethseel, once she and Chokhmah had returned from the main service at the Cathedral in Prythew, she had to join Arawn, and what was it Yona had called them? His 'stick-in-the-muds' or 'cronies'? Anyway, she had been requested to join them for a formal lunch in the dining room. Afterwards, Eluned found herself greatly relieved to be released on her own recognizance, so to speak, until dinner that evening.

She returned to her room to work with Dyrnwyn although she found herself wishing Gwrhyr were around so she would have someone to spar with. She had only a vague memory of how to fight with a sword from the basics she'd been taught several years previously. She had no doubt that Gwrhyr would be more than happy to use that abundant knowledge of his, she thought, wryly, to make her feel like she didn't know what the hell she was doing.

After she'd exhausted herself with Dyrnwyn, and it didn't take long for that to happen as she'd forgotten how heavy the sword was, she and Chokhmah played cards until it was time for her to get dressed for dinner. They had already decided that there was absolutely no reason not to start attending daily mass in Prythew since they had established the pattern of going to the early service in Arberth. It would give them a reason to leave the castle each morning. The more time out of sight, they hoped, the more time out of mind for the King and his spies. They were sure that they were being watched, but by whom was the question, which meant they had to be extra careful.

They decided that the plan would be that once they returned to the castle and broke their fast with whomever happened to be in the dining room when they returned (it turned out they were often alone), they would change and head to the stables to see that Halelu and Honeysuckle were saddled for a morning ride. They needed to get the stable hands accustomed not only to seeing them, particularly Chokhmah, but also to their regular use of the mounts they had brought with them to Annewven. They didn't want it to seem suspicious when she came to get Halelu for the phaeton. And, more importantly, they didn't have much time to work with and so time was of essence.

But what Eluned was most interested in doing involved going back out to the gazebo and finding out where the secret tunnel led. It would have to be when Arawn was busy because she didn't know how to shut it and it would have to close on its own. She hoped only that they'd be able to reopen the doors once they had explored the tunnel and what it led to at the other end.

That meant they had to make a daily labyrinth walk part of their routine, as well. Perhaps they could arrange to have a picnic in the gazebo everyday, Chokhmah suggested. They would risk a surprise visit from Arawn but Eluned sincerely doubted that the King was interested in checking on her anymore. He would definitely not waste his time on that! She was sure he had eyes on her most of the time although she was probably being silly about thinking he wanted to use her as a sacrifice to his Sacred Three. On the other hand, both Jabb and Chokhmah seemed to be taking the threat a little more seriously now that they were back in Prythew. Unfortunately, she didn't know how she could hide from the King. Locking herself in her room wouldn't work, and she was pretty sure none of the villagers would hide her. She just had to pray that Gwrhyr would get back early enough for them to leave before the solstice.

So, after they frittered away the weekend (there wasn't much they could routinize on Deetheseel as it was an odd day every week), they jumped fully into their new schedule on Deethyeen morning.

"I AM DYING TO TRY OUT that secret doorway again," Eluned told Chokhmah during their morning ride, "but I'm afraid we'll get caught with the entrance up."

"I agree it is a risk," Chokhmah said. "Perhaps we should wait until tomorrow to try it. That way we will know if the King intends to have us interrupted when we are out there."

"Good point," she agreed, "but fortunately Arawn seems to have a very low opinion of my intelligence. Do you think he actually believes that everyone he knows, low-born to high-born, is less intelligent than he is?"

Chokhmah laughed. "It is true, but that is because men like him do not realize that they are not quite as wise as they believe themselves to be. Thus, they consistently underestimate those around them. Considering his reputation, I imagine that his people have long since discovered that it is more wise to play ignorant than to risk angering the Crimson King."

THEY REACHED THE VALLEY BELOW THE CASTLE and reined in their horses next to the River Duir in order to take a minute to admire the beauty of their surroundings. The Duir was broad at this point and flowed smoothly past the grassy bank upon which they paused. On the opposite side, a hardwood forest grew to within ten yards of the river. It should have been quite lovely. The myriad greens of the leaves were nearly luminous in the morning sunlight, but for some reason, Eluned was filled with a sense of unease. There was something about the forest that sent chills down her spine while butterflies took flight in her stomach. She put a hand on her chest trying to still her racing heart.

"What is the matter?" Chokhmah asked seeing the expression on her face.

"I'm not sure. I suddenly felt really scared. It started when I looked across the river, but I don't see anything inherently evil in a forest of oaks, rowans, ashes and the like. I don't understand."

Chokhmah contemplated the woods across the river for a full minute. "I definitely sense something not quite right."

"Perhaps it's similar to Avalach. You know, the same evil spirits."

"Ah, you mean that you believe that is the forest where Arawn performs his sacrifices?

"Perhaps. I'm not sure if it's anything that concrete or whether there's a general cloud of doom hanging over my head. It's as if it's an overcast and gloomy day, and yet I know, logically, that the sun is shining and that there isn't a cloud in the sky."

"Perhaps you are depressed," Chokhmah suggested.

"It's more than that. I just can't completely describe it."

"A feeling then?" Chokhmah said. "Or an intuition."

"Yes, kind of like both."

"Then you should pay attention to it as we sometimes sense things before we know them to be true."

"In that case," Eluned laughed, "I sense that we should return to the castle. The labyrinth is calling my name." She winked at Chokhmah to let her know that she was being silly.

ELUNED AND CHOKHMAH SAT IN THE GAZEBO sharing a lunch of cold chicken sandwiches and lemonade. The Princess felt her fingers actually tingling in their need to press the buttons that would open the door, but she took another deep breath.

Patience. She needed to be patient. So far, they hadn't been interrupted, but that didn't mean they wouldn't be. They needed to stay in the gazebo at least an hour just to make sure.

If they remained undisturbed, they could return tomorrow and open the door as soon as they arrived.

They packed the leftover food into the basket, and spent the remainder of their time in the labyrinth pavilion chatting quietly about Bonpo and Yona, and what they might be doing. The last half hour of their "watch" passed without their being spied on, at least to their knowledge. So hearts feeling a little lighter, they wound their way through the labyrinth and back to the castle. Tomorrow, they would discover where the gazebo tunnel led.

3RD DEER

Patience definitely not being one of her virtues, Eluned's anticipation for finally opening the tunnel and seeing where it led was nearly more than she could bear when she turned in for the evening. She tossed and turned all night, fidgeted all the way through morning Mass, absolutely could not stomach breakfast, and was on the verge of tears for most of their morning ride.

"Do I need to prepare you a sedative tea, my dear," Chokhmah teased. "I am under the impression that if someone were to say 'boo,' you might literally jump out of your skin. You must eat some lunch before we open the tunnel or I shall make you return to the room and take a nap."

"You wouldn't!" Eluned gasped, wide-eyed and horrified.

Chokhmah chuckled, "I just might, my love. I know you are excited, but we should be acting in a way that would be considered normal. Now, you sit here and practice some deep breathing while I go get the picnic basket."

When she returned, the Princess appeared visibly calmer. "I apologize," she said. "I don't know why I've gotten myself so worked up about this. It's just a tunnel after all."

"Well, do not chastise your self too harshly." Chokhmah's

voice was soothing, "After all, the last time you entered a tunnel you disappeared for nearly a week."

"True. And now I think I'm afraid of disappearing forever."

"Then why is it that you are so anxious to do this?"

"I'm not sure," Eluned said, pausing as they walked their way toward the center of the labyrinth, "but there is also a part of me that senses that this is important to do, and I guess I won't know why until we do it."

Chokhmah pulled a ham sandwich from the basket and handed it to Eluned. "Then you had better start eating, my dear, if we are to open the door as soon as we arrive. You have brought the code?"

The Princess patted her chest with her free hand. "Right here in my pouch."

Nodding, Chokhmah unwrapped a sandwich for herself, and then took a bite. When she had swallowed, she said, "I just thought of something."

"What's that?" Eluned asked, mouth full. With the first bite of sandwich, she realized she was quite ravenous.

"We must hide the basket before we go down the tunnel. Should someone find it there but not us . . ."

"By Omni, I'm glad you thought of that," Eluned shuddered as she contemplated what that might have meant. "I hate that there's so much to keep in mind. I'm terrified of missing something."

"Agreed. We must be ever watchful."

Chokhmah tucked the basket into the rose bushes as Eluned climbed the steps into the gazebo, pulling her pouch from beneath the blouse that had been made for her in Arberth. She had chosen a really rough-spun cotton fabric in a shade of sea green that matched her eyes and she liked it so much that she had to force herself not to wear it. The buttons were heart-shaped, iridescent glass beads.

She retrieved the vellum, and pulled something long and thin from her pocket. "This time I remembered to bring something with which to press the buttons," she told Chokhmah, holding up a porcupine quill.

"Where did you find that?" Chokhmah asked, joining her in the gazebo.

"I've had it with me all this time, actually," she explained. "They make marvelous pens. I just haven't needed to use it yet, but I thought it would work well on the buttons." She handed her the slip of vellum that contained the code.

"Nub, asem, hat," Chokhmah read as Eluned depressed the appropriate symbol. "Xomt, men, teht, and chesbet." Once again the door rose silently on its well-oiled hydraulics.

"Ready?" Eluned asked.

Chokhmah took a deep breath, peering down the hole. There was a soft light that illuminated the top of the ladder that descended into darkness and out of sight down the tube-like shaft. "We have forgotten to bring a light," she groaned. "We will just have to be very careful. Remember not to look down. Do you wish that I go first?"

"No, I'll go. I'm the one who's been so insistent about this." She swung her leg over the side (she was wearing her leather trousers because she thought it would be easier to climb up and down ladders in pants rather than in a skirt) and stepped onto the third rung. She wasn't exactly adept at maneuvering on ladders, but she was young enough that it should be fairly easy, right?

She descended a little ways, and as she reached the darkness, another light illuminated the ladder. "Oh, look," she called to Chokhmah, pausing to make sure that Chokhmah made it over the side in her somewhat voluminous skirt. But the gypsy was clearly accustomed to adapting as she had tucked her skirt in such a way as to make it more pants-like and less likely to trip her up on the way down. "There must be motion-sensitive lights here."

It felt as if they climbed downward forever. Surely, it was a good half hour before they reached the bottom. Chokhmah assured her she was exaggerating.

"A quarter of an hour, then," she finally conceded, but it had felt like a very long time. Now they had to find where the tunnel led. How long would that take? Considering the fact they were underground, everything seemed very sterile. The tunnel was lined with a light-colored tile and a diffused light filled the corridor although Eluned wasn't quite sure where it emanated from. It almost seemed to seep through the tiles themselves.

Their footsteps on the tiling sounded extraordinarily loud to her ears, and she couldn't help but cringe occasionally. Part of her really wanted to take off her boots and walk in her socks, but she didn't want to waste the time nor get caught without her boots on, so to speak.

It seemed to be just over a mile to the other end of the tunnel, where another vertical tunnel with yet another ladder lead upwards. "All right," Eluned said, "how do we open this door? Do you think there's a switch somewhere? I don't see anything that looks like it needs a code."

They fumbled around for a few minutes searching for anything that looked like it would open the door.

"Perhaps," Chokhmah suggested, "we must climb the ladder first. It may be that there is a switch closer to the top."

Sighing, Eluned began the climb to the top, which was, fortunately, much shorter this time. Once there, she began feeling around for something that might resemble a switch or a button. Finally, her fingers brushed against a small button, on the ladder itself. She would have missed it completely if she hadn't been adjusting her hand to allow herself a wider sweep of the area around the door when her finger brushed against it unintentionally. She was pretty sure it would never have occurred to her to look for a switch on the ladder.

This button felt more like a rivet than a pressure-sensitive latch, and it was very close to where the bar of the ladder attached to the wall, could in fact have been one of the bolts attaching the ladder. And, as the hydraulic door slowly whirled upwards, she breathed a deep sigh of relief. She had been sure they were going to have to walk all the way back to the other door and figure out how to get out there.

No, actually, she admitted to herself, she had already begun imagining starving to death in the tunnel, berating themselves for fools. For, after all, she had never told Bonpo, Jabb, Gwrhyr or even Yona about the mysterious tunnel. Damn it, why had she been such an idiot? Damn it, why was she worrying about something that hadn't happened?

"Eluned?"

"Sorry, I was a thousand miles away," and she climbed out of the tunnel and stepped onto a carpet of leaf litter. Oaks, rowans, ashes, birches and other hardwoods towered over her. She inhaled deeply. The forest smelt wonderful but there was something of the odor of decay underneath. And, it wasn't decaying leaves. It was worse than that. Worse even than just a dead squirrel or other small mammal rotting amidst the leaves. Putrescence. Sulfuric. She couldn't quite describe it, but it wasn't pleasant.

"Do you smell it?" she asked Chokhmah, who was now standing beside her and then she looked at her face. Yes, her nose was definitely wrinkled in distaste.

"I think we are on the other side of the river, my dear."

"Yes."

"And that feeling remains strong?"

"Absolutely."

"Yes, I can feel it as well." They were speaking quietly as if they were afraid of being overheard by someone or something.

"Well," Eluned took another deep breath, steeling herself, "there is a reason the tunnel emerges here. I think we need to find out why."

"I agree," said Chokhmah, looking around her. "Is that a path?" She was pointing to what looked like a seldom tread deer trail to her right.

"I think so," Eluned paused, studying the barely worn track for a moment. "It doesn't look as if it gets much traffic."

"But that would make sense, would it not? How often would the King travel here to worship or sacrifice? Once a month? Every other month? Not often, I would presume."

"True. Then I guess we should see where it leads."

The path wound through the hardwoods for about a quarter of a mile before ending in a clearing. In the center of the clearing was an altar not unlike the one Eluned had seen within the circle of standing stones in Ruisidho.

"Damn," the Princess breathed, swallowing hard.

"What is it?"

"That looks just like the altar in Ruisidho. At the time I thought I was being so daring climbing up on the altar. I told Gwrhyr I wanted to know what it felt like to be awaiting sacrifice."

"I imagine he was not amused."

"No, and it's probably just as well he isn't in Prythew at the moment. I think what we're doing right now would make him really angry, especially if he knew of my fear of you-know-what, " she couldn't help but whisper the latter.

Eluned studied the altar a little while longer. It was black, probably a meteorite like the other, but there were darker stains on it that she was sure were blood. Probably because it was used more regularly, she shuddered.

There was also a bizarre configuration of ash wood poles situated about the altar with one pole a few feet from the head (or foot) of the altar, and two on either side at about a foot from either end. Weird.

Eluned guessed the tunnel was a convenient way for the King to come and go from the altar in the clearing and back to the castle without being seen.

She wondered how many people participated in the not-too-secret services and sacrifices that took place in this glade and probably a similar one in Avalach.

Eluned had lost track of how long they'd been gone from the labyrinth, but she was sure it had been long enough that they ought to be heading back. She inclined her head in the direction of the tunnel and Chokhmah nodded acquiescence.

When they arrived at the hidden door, they realized that unlike the door in the gazebo, this one had been disguised to look like the earth around it; in this case, leaf litter and grasses. Therefore, there were no buttons to push. They looked around for a mechanism to open the portal. But, other than trees and more leaf litter and grass, there was nothing but a small cairn-like pile of rocks arranged within a foot of the door.

Eluned and Chokhmah began to move the rocks around in search of some sort of button. As the Princess lifted one of the rocks near the bottom of the cairn, she heard the telltale whoosh of the hydraulics and the door whirred upwards.

"Eureka!" Eluned shouted, but in a near whisper.

"Excelsior!" Chokhmah agreed quietly.

THEY FOUND THEMSELVES BACK AT THE GAZEBO ladder in a little over half an hour. Feeling a bit panicky, Eluned climbed the ladder as swiftly as possible. This time, she knew what to look for, and like the ladder that opened into the forest, this ladder also had a switch underneath the brace attached to the wall of the tube. She pressed it, the door whirred upward, and she stepped out into the gazebo, breathing a huge sigh of relief when she found it empty.

Chokhmah stepped out beside her, and then reached down to press the button to close the door. The heptagon slid back into place and once again appeared as if it were just part of the parquet floor.

Retrieving the basket from the rosebush, the women hurried back to the castle.

"You know," the Princess mused, "there has to be an easier way to get out of this labyrinth. I find it difficult to believe that Arawn walks the entire way in and out each time."

"Ah, very interesting. I had not thought of that. We shall start searching tomorrow, shall we not?"

WHEN THEY REACHED THEIR ROOM, Eluned was disgruntled to find that she had been summoned to dinner once again. She had so hoped that the pattern would change once they were back at Castle Pwyll. Why was he suddenly seeking out her presence? She was even more shocked that evening when Celyn and Auron invited her to lunch with them the following day and Arawn made it clear that he would like to see her at dinner every evening.

"And you must have a costume made," he said. "Celyn and Auron will help with that. Isn't that correct, ladies?" They assured him it was and he continued, "Because next week is the traditional masquerade ball that we hold every year in conjunction with the solstice."

"A masquerade ball?"

"Yes," Auron enthused. "And every year there is a different theme. This year it's the supernatural."

"How very interesting," Eluned was trying to hide her confusion. She had been preparing herself to avoid being sacrificed, and now it seemed that they were planning a costume party. But she had seen the altar, the blood. She was definitely flummoxed.

"Yes," Arawn practically purred, "and I should like you to go as the Lady in White."

"The Lady in White?"

"Oh yes," Celyn was enthusiastic, "she's a ghost, a wraith. She wears a wedding dress. That's perfect, your highness," she practically winked at Arawn, "I can just see the Princess as that tragic bride."

"Tragic?" Eluned gulped. She didn't like the sound of tragic.

"Some say she was betrayed and killed by her husband on her wedding night," Celyn explained.

"Others say she was betrayed by her fiancé," Auron added. "Either way, you have to wear a wedding dress."

"And a long, ghostly veil." Celyn said. She and Auron seemed more excited about her costume than she did.

"Everyone will be there," Hywel said. "King Hevel will return for the ball as will Chazak."

"Yona?" Eluned asked.

"That is not certain," Hywel explained. "King Hevel may not bring her until they are married."

The Princess was both relieved and disappointed. She missed her friend but neither did she want her caught up in this strange religion.

"King Hamartia and Queen Foehn will be present, as well," Arawn noted.

"Matraqua will join us too," added Gethin.

"So, essentially everyone who was at the first dinner party I attended?" Eluned asked.

"As well as other lords and ladies from around Annewven. It is the event of the year," Auron promised.

"This will be next Deethyai," Eluned asked, calculating that she had little more than a week to get her costume together.

"Oh, no, no," Arawn said. "The masque is never on the solstice, itself. It is always the day before."

The Princess wasn't sure she wanted to know why.

"This year's masque will be even more special," Arawn said, lifting her hand and kissing it gently.

Eluned's eyes widened in puzzlement and a little fear. "Why?" it sounded more like a croak than a word.

"Because I have a special announcement to make that evening."

"Announcement?" Eluned's heart was racing. Surely he wasn't going to pronounce their engagement?

"Ah, but you will find out next Deethmerker, my dear," the king promised.

The Princess tried to smile but it felt more like a grimace. Omni help me, she prayed, silently.

4ᵀᴴ DEER

As the Princess had to lunch with Celyn and Auron that day, Chokhmah said she would search the labyrinth for a quicker way in and out of it.

"There must be a way when you enter on the straightaway or when you exit from the center on the straightaway," Chokhmah said. They were standing at the open bedroom window looking down on the labyrinth, the gypsy pointing at the two most likely secret exits. Now that it was essentially summer, the rose bushes that surrounded the gazebo were in full bloom, a stunning array of pinks and reds and yellows.

"I wish I could go with you," Eluned sighed. "I'd almost rather be drawn and quartered than have to spend time alone with those women."

Chokhmah chuckled. "It will not be that disagreeable, I assure you."

"Hmmm," the Princess sounded dubious. "What I find most troubling is that they are going to help me have a wedding dress made. I've never thought much about a wedding dress one way or another although I will have to wear one when I wed Uriel. But wearing a wedding dress as a costume before I've even been engaged to Arawn strikes me as singularly wrong."

"Yes, it is unfortunate that he chose your costume. Who would you have preferred to dress as?"

"Cuhvetena!" Eluned laughed. "I already have the necklace." The Princess sighed again and took a deep breath, "Well, I've procrastinated as long as possible. I'm sure they're waiting for me downstairs."

"It will all be over soon enough," Chokhmah said, soothingly. "Try to enjoy it as much as possible."

As Chokhmah had predicted, lunch with Auron and Celyn had been rather enjoyable. Almost suspiciously so. It was as if they had gone out of their way to be nice to her and to make her feel like a part of their little clique. Was it because they thought the King intended to marry her, and thus they wanted to remain in her good graces?

They had even met another couple of women at the The Golden Apple, the inn where they'd dined in Prythew—the Lady Bronwen and the Lady Gwenda—whom Auron introduced as the wives of two of Arawn's dukes, both of whom ran massive estates.

Bronwen's husband, Collen, raised much of the livestock, as well as the poultry, for Prythew and the castle, itself. Gwenda's husband, Tudur, owned the vineyards that produced the wines that were the staple at Castle Pwyll. A slightly inferior wine was sold in town, Gwenda said.

Like Celyn and Auron, Bronwen and Gwenda were also relatively young and gorgeous. Bronwen had long, honey-blonde hair, huge blue eyes, a straight nose and full lips. She also looked in exquisite shape, as did Gwenda who had wavy brown hair the color of hazelnuts, large dark eyes and delicately arched eyebrows.

For some reason she couldn't quite put her finger on, she found it very disturbing that King Arawn surrounded himself with beautiful people. Now that she thought about it, she wasn't sure she had seen anyone old in either Castle Emrys or Castle Pwyll. Very odd.

All four women were very chatty and talked excitedly about the upcoming masquerade ball. The Princess had to do little more than listen and make the occasional comment as they nibbled on their salads. And much to her chagrin, not a single one of them would admit to what their costumes would be, but Celyn had no compunction informing them that Arawn had asked her to be "The Lady in White."

Afterwards, Celyn and Auron took Eluned to the seamstress they frequented to discuss possibilities for Eluned's costume. By the time they left the little shop, the Princess had agreed on a design that was both ghostly and wraith-like and very virginal. It would consist of long, filmy layers of snow-white netting with a crosshatch of netting across her chest and abdomen, before the layers fell in a cascade to the floor. Long loose sleeves and a long white veil, studded with pearls and diamonds, and which would also hide her face, completed the outfit.

"You won't even have to wear a mask," Auron practically trilled.

"Everyone will be wearing masks?" Eluned asked.

"It's a masquerade," Celyn said. "That's what makes it so fun although it's usually easy to guess who's who."

"True," agreed Auron. "I wouldn't worry about it. It's nearly impossible to not recognize the King, for example."

"His hair," Celyn said.

"Oh, I guess I can see that," Eluned said, but she still disliked the fact that everyone would immediately know who she was.

THE PRINCESS WAS GREATLY RELIEVED to return to the comfort of her room, but Chokhmah had not yet returned. Eluned looked out the window—maybe she could spot her in the labyrinth—and froze. Why had it not occurred to them? If she could look down on the labyrinth from her room and see what was going on in it, there must be other windows along this eastern wall that looked down on the labyrinth as well.

Had they been spotted opening the heptagon door? Maybe they had been allowed to be in the labyrinth alone because someone was keeping an eye on them from above. A hot flush spread downwards from Eluned's face and her heart started racing. Omni have mercy, she was thinking furiously, trying to remember all their time spent in the labyrinth and gazebo and what someone watching might have seen.

Eluned looked again and her heart began to slow its pace a bit. From this high angle, you couldn't actually see the center of the gazebo. But anyone with even a rudimentary sense of deductive reasoning would have to wonder why they hid the picnic basket in the rose bushes and then entered the gazebo before "disappearing" for an hour or so. That would be truly bizarre behavior. On the other hand, it would depend on who was watching. She really needed to find out.

The door opened behind her and she whirled around, startled.

"You look as if you have just seen a ghost," Chokhmah remarked, closing the door.

Eluned motioned her to the window. "Look." She pointed to the labyrinth.

Chokhmah studied it for a minute before admitting that she didn't see anything unusual.

"Look again. With different eyes."

"Different?" The Princess watched as understanding dawned in her eyes. "Omni have mercy," she crossed herself. "I feel like such an imbecile."

"And we've just been blithely puttering around down there as if it were our own secret world," Eluned said.

"So do you think he has someone watching us?"

"I'm sure of it. It would certainly explain why we've been given so much freedom."

Chokhmah walked over to the fireplace and collapsed into one of the armchairs. "We have no way of knowing either how many nor who his watchers are."

"But I think I know a way of finding out who's watching the labyrinth," Eluned said. "And we can do it now."

So, CHOKHMAH WENT DOWN to the kitchens and explained that they wanted to have their tea in the gazebo. She brought the basket to Eluned and then returned to the room to wait until she saw the Princess enter the labyrinth below.

ELUNED WASN'T SURPRISED TO FIND HERSELF QUESTIONED by the guard.

"All alone?" he asked in surprise.

"No, of course not," she lied. "My lady will be down shortly. I asked her to get me something from my room. She'll join me in the gazebo in a few minutes.

NEARLY A QUARTER OF AN HOUR LATER, Chokhmah was sitting with Eluned on the bench in the gazebo.

"That was not as difficult as I thought it might be," she said. "It turns out that taking on the guise of a servant has gained me entrance to places I might normally appear out-of-place. I found our little spook watching you almost adoringly, I would say, out of a window in the servants' quarters. And, so it seems, we are in luck."

"I don't understand."

"Do you recall the young page that summoned you to lunch when we were in the library before we left for Arberth?"

"The cherubic lad?"

"Rhys is his name. I had a little talk with him."

"I'm sure you did," Eluned nodded in understanding. "I imagine he will not be reporting anything to Arawn?"

"Correct. In fact, he will make it sound as if we are unimaginably boring to keep watch over. I suspect he would have done so without a little extra encouragement, but it is better to be safe than sorry."

"I agree. I will go out of my way to continue to be kind to him. Anyway," Eluned sighed, relieved that particular little problem had been handled, "you never told me if you found a way to enter and exit more quickly."

"No, I did not have a chance. I was asked to attend a meeting with the rest of the castle's servants to help plan who will be taking on what tasks for the masquerade next week."

"Well, thank Omni for small blessings. I hope they haven't given you something too tedious to do."

"I will be helping with the party favors. Making sachets for the women, which is something I will actually enjoy doing."

"It does sound apropos. I assume you'll have to go back to the market for herbs and flowers or whatever you need to make them?"

"Yes, the sooner the better. Perhaps as a part of our morning ride tomorrow?"

"Fine with me. I don't have to go back for a fitting of my costume until Deethsadoorn. Now, maybe we can look for the hidden entrances on the way out of the labyrinth."

IT WAS AS CHOKHMAH SURMISED. Part of the hedge was, in reality, a door that opened onto the next straightaway; and, at the end of it, another door leading out of the labyrinth. Too simple really. The only reason they hadn't seen it was because they hadn't been looking for it. Branches from the hedge had been stapled or nailed to the door to help disguise it but on closer inspection, Eluned could see that were dry and starting to brown.

"They must have to replace them on a regular basis," Eluned remarked.

"I imagine that it is not too difficult," Chokhmah said. "They probably do it when they trim the hedges."

"Good point."

While Chokhmah returned the basket to the kitchens, Eluned hurried back to the room in order to begin getting ready for dinner. She needed a bath. No, she thought, correcting herself as she climbed the stairs, I actually desire a bath. The day had left her feeling soiled and violated, and she still had to face Arawn and his cronies that evening. Despite how nice Auron and Celyn were being, she still didn't quite trust the somewhat drastic turnaround in their treatment of her.

IN SOME WAYS THE DAYS TUMBLED BY much more quickly than she could have imagined. The castle nearly hummed with the level of activity as the servants prepared it for the masquerade. Eluned's days were filled with Mass, horseback rides and swordplay, costume fittings and meals with the King. Before she knew it, it was Deethmarth night and she still had yet to hear from either Jabberwock or Gwrhyr.

"I'm thinking it would be wise to go ahead and pack as much as possible tonight," she told Chokhmah. "I'm not sure how much time we'll have tomorrow."

"That is true. Keep in mind that you can carry only as much as fits in your bag."

"Which means I need to decide what to leave behind," she said, opening the armoire and examining the clothes there. Because it was summer, she would leave behind the wool cloak as well as the wool sweater she'd acquired in Mjijangwa. As matter of fact, she would just leave behind all her woolen and flannel clothes. They were going to the Favonian Isles. She wouldn't need them for the time being.

On the other hand, she would keep the leather jerkin and pants. She liked them way too much to leave behind. She would also take the outfit Chokhmah had given her. She was very fond of it, as well.

But, despite their beauty, she would leave behind everything Arawn had given her (Especially the black velvet dress she felt so uncomfortable in. Good riddance to that!). Well, except for the pair of slippers made of the same creamy dupioni silk as the three-piece dress. She loved the way they shimmered and she could wear them with Chokhmah's outfit.

The jewelry would definitely go with her to Favonia, Cuhvetena's necklace, particularly. That could come in handy again. She would also take the lavender undershirt and brocade dress that had been a part of her Paschal costume. They were quite lovely. That left only the green cotton blouse, which she was currently wearing with her white cotton skirt, and the grey cotton sweater from Arberth. Those would come in handy when she wore the leather breeches.

"All right," she turned to face Chokhmah, "I know what I'm taking and leaving. I'll pack it up first thing in the morning. I just wish we'd hear something from Jabb or Gwrhyr."

There was a scratching at the door. "Speaking of the Janawar," she said, going to open the door.

"I apologize," he said, trotting into the room and plopping down in front of the now empty fireplace. "King Arawn has kept me very busy."

"Doing what?" Eluned asked, dropping into one of the armchairs. Chokhmah seated herself in the other.

"Among other things, using my knowledge of Zion and its allies to help prepare him for war."

"You didn't!" Eluned's eyes blazed with fury. She was shaking. He couldn't have betrayed her father.

"What do you think?"

"You did not," Chokhmah's amber eyes glimmered with amusement.

"You should have more faith in me, Princess," the Bandersnatch feigned hurt. "You know that I am incapable of assisting our enemies."

"Sorry," she said, biting her lip. "I should have known better. It just shocked me, and I have no idea, well, I guess I do have some idea of what Arawn is capable of, and I thought, perhaps, he had used his magic."

"You forget, my dear, that I am a much more accomplished magician than he is," he said with the crooked grin she loved so much.

"A ledgerdemainist, thaumaturge or magus?" She teased.

"Necromancer, sorcerer," he added.

"So you have been feeding him misinformation?" Chokhmah guessed.

"I am an accomplished liar," he bragged.

"Have you seen the chessboard?" Eluned asked.

"As a matter of fact, we have been playing nightly. He has been practicing his first three moves in case the board comes into play at some point."

"You mean that he might use it after he's waged war against one of his enemies?" Eluned wondered.

"Exactly, my dear. If someone won't surrender, he hopes to use it as an alternative to laying siege."

"And he is that confident that he will win." Chokhmah stated more than asked.

"Humility is not one of his virtues."

"Will you be able to appropriate the chessboard?" Eluned asked.

"Appropriate," Jabberwock smiled again. "Nice. I like it. Yes, I can easily steal the chessboard. I have full access to his chambers. I will do it as soon as he leaves for his solstice sacrifice."

"And what if I am that sacrifice?" Eluned couldn't help but ask.

"He has been hinting that he intends to announce your engagement tomorrow night at the ball," Jabberwock said.

"Will you be there?"

"I am fairly certain he doesn't wish to explain me to those who aren't yet in the know."

Eluned still felt uneasy. It just didn't feel right to her.

"Speaking of the King, I must go. Time for our chess game."

The Princess stood to open the door for him. She watched him go and then called, softly, "Wait."

Jabberwock turned to look at her.

"We're meeting at the stables first thing Deethyai morning, correct?"

"Correct you are, my dear."

This was all going much easier than she had hoped, and that scared her. If it seemed to good to be true, she scowled, then it probably wasn't.

11ᵀᴴ Deer

When the Princess awoke the following morning after a long night spent tossing and turning, it was with a sense of dread so deep that even her marrow felt cold. Eluned couldn't define her trepidation; she just knew she wanted to be in Favonia more than anything else in the world. What she wouldn't do to be heading down to the stables at that moment and not to their last service in Prythew. The Princess would be praying especially hard today for all their safety, but particularly her own.

"Oh where is Gwrhyr?" she moaned to Chokhmah, as they slid into a pew. "What if he doesn't make it back in time?"

"I am sure Gwrhyr is competent enough to fend for himself," Chokhmah tried to soothe her.

The gypsy had used her special voice, but Eluned's anxiety began to spiral into full-fledged fear despite that. 'Omni, please let him be safe,' she prayed, silently and simply but heartfelt, suddenly dropping to her knees on the pew's kneeler. 'Please let him still be alive. Please let Bonpo be alive and safe in Favonia. Please let Yona be safe and alive in Adamah. Please help us to get out of Annewven safely with the treasures and please, please, please, don't let me be tomorrow's sacrifice.'

HER FEET FELT LIKE LEAD as she trudged her way back up the hill following the service. And it was all she could do to choke down a cup of black coffee at breakfast. They couldn't go horseback riding as the stables were being readied for the guests; she couldn't read because her eyes didn't seem to want to focus on the words; and Eluned couldn't even try to transcribe her fears into her journal because the words seemed just beyond her reach.

Chokhmah finally made her some tea with which to soothe her nerves, and soon she was fast asleep. Yet even so, while she slept her muscles would occasionally twitch, and the Princess would shake her head as if in denial, and when she awoke she found that she had napped for barely half an hour.

Eluned still wasn't hungry at lunch but Chokhmah insisted she at least sip some chicken broth.

"You must have something, my dear," Chokhmah coaxed her. "There is bound to be much alcohol tonight, and you should have something in your belly."

"This day is never going to be over," she whimpered, and could only manage a few spoonfuls. The skin beneath her eyes looked bruised with fatigue, her green eyes were wide with fear. "If something terrible does happen, make sure you get Dyrnwyn to Gwrhyr," she told Chokhmah, holding the treasure in her hand one last time before packing it away. The way the blue light raced up her arm gave the Princess a bit more confidence. She wished she could take it with her to the ball. "I know," she laughed, but it sounded strained. "I'll just wear my ring, and then if something happens, I'll pull the moonstone from my pouch. How about that?"

"That sounds like a wonderful plan, my dear," Chokhmah concurred from the bathroom door.

Eluned pulled the engraved ring from her pouch and slid it onto the ring finger of her right hand where she intended it to remain. Just having it there made her feel exceptionally better not to mention stronger. She could do this! She had to put all her trust in Omni. It was the only solution.

"Your bath is ready," Chokhmah said, drying her hands on a towel. "Wash your hair. I prefer to braid it while it is still wet."

"Yes, yer highness," Eluned teased, and hugged her before ducking into the bathroom.

BY THE TIME HER HAIR WAS BRAIDED and she was slipping into her 'Lady in White' costume with the bodice fitted tightly across her chest and abdomen, and the remainder of it long and flowing, Eluned was beginning to wonder if the intense fear she had been experiencing had been supernatural. It had been nearly overwhelming in its possession of her.

"Perhaps it was like the time I was hypnotized by the barrow wight," she suggested to Chokhmah.

Now that the Princess was feeling infinitely stronger, she was even beginning to look forward to the party. Everyone else seemed to think that King Arawn was going to announce his espousal to the Princess that evening. Perchance they were right, and she was wrong. Besides, now she had a plan, she thought, patting the pouch that lay beneath her bodice, tucked between her breasts so that it couldn't be seen. It was uncomfortable, but worth it.

Her bag was packed and lying on the floor of the armoire; the sword, wrapped in a blanket (she still needed to get a scabbard), leaned against the back of the armoire hidden by the dresses she wasn't bringing. She guessed she was as ready as she was ever going to be.

THE CUSTOMARY RAP OF SMALL KNUCKLES on the door.

"And how are you tonight, my fine sir?" Eluned asked when she had opened the door.

Rhys blushed. "I'm not a 'sir,' your highness."

"Of course you are," she smiled at him and tugged one of his golden curls. "You're my 'sir.'"

He blushed again but managed to look thrilled as well. "Are you ready, your highness?"

"I am indeed, but please call me Eluned."

"I couldn't do that, Ma'am!"

The Princess sighed, pulling her veil down over her face, "I suppose not. I would hate for you to get in trouble. Shall we?" she said, taking his arm.

AS THEY PASSED THE DINING ROOM, Rhys pointed out that food would be available there for those who wished to assuage their hunger. "But," he continued, "the ballroom is in the southwest tower. And that is where the King is waiting."

Why did the final sentence cause her to shudder? "Shows you how much I've been paying attention," she murmured. She hadn't really thought about it one way or another, but she supposed it would be necessary to have a ballroom for a ball.

The Princess was announced at the door, and as she stepped onto the pearl grey marble of the dance floor, she felt, once again, that uncomfortable moment when she had to force herself not to cringe away from the turning of heads. She despised being the center of attention unless she was amongst friends.

There were already more than two-dozen masked people standing around the room, and more were rapidly arriving behind her. She stepped further in toward the center of the room, casting her eyes about as she looked for a familiar face. Why hadn't she been met at the door? Surely as the nearly affianced of the King, she would be treated better? It wasn't a comforting moment.

The circular ballroom was decorated to make it appear almost cloud-like in shades of white and silver and pearl grey. Swags of airy fabric seemed to drift against the ceiling, and a slight mist hovered above the marble floor so that the few couples that were already dancing to the waltzes being played by a pianist on the far side of the room, appeared to be dancing on air.

Celyn and Auron had been right. It was definitely hard to miss Arawn's flaming copper hair, and he was already heading in her direction with a glass of champagne in each hand. As he approached, she tried to ascertain what his costume was intended to be.

He was dressed entirely in blood red leather except for a golden armored and intricately molded breastplate that protected his chest. He also had a pair of dark grey wings attached to his back. An angel, she wondered, before realizing that was exactly what he was portraying: a fallen angel. Lucifer. How perfect, she wanted to roll her eyes. Another bad omen. But he was quite stunning as he approached, and clearly he was trying to catch her eye. Fortunately, the Princess was no longer fooled by his charisma, and she had long since perfected the art of not quite looking into his eyes, which could be quite hypnotic. Fortunately, the veil that covered her face only helped her to hide the fact she wasn't looking at him. The red leather mask that hid the upper half of his face, she noticed, did nothing to hide his mesmerizingly bronze eyes.

"My Lady-in-White," he said, handing her a glass of champagne.

"Lucifer," she said, bobbing a brief curtsey, before lifting her veil and taking a much-needed sip of the champagne, which was crisp, dry and perfect. I can do this, she told herself. I can do this.

"Our friends await," he said offering her his now free arm, and leading her over to where Hevel, Hamartia and Foehn stood holding champagne flutes of their own. Apparently Yona had not been invited to attend. And for that, she was extremely thankful.

King Hamartia and Queen Foehn were quite obviously dressed as elegant vampires down to incredibly sharp (and realistic looking, Eluned thought) incisors. Had someone informed her that they were, in actuality, vampires, she would not disbelieve. They struck her as both inordinately alive and undead at the same time. She greeted them as warmly as she was capable, and then turned to King Hevel.

He was dressed in furs and wore a long mink cape and a crown of holly. A narrow mask did little to hide his face. All in all, it looked dreadfully hot for a summer masquerade.

"I'm afraid I don't recognize your costume," she apologized.

"Hevel is Bel," Foehn informed her. "The Holly King."

"Oh, I see," Eluned said as if she understood what they were talking about. Hopefully, she could ask Chokhmah about that later. "It is truly beautiful in here," she changed the subject, turning to Arawn, whom, despite the fact she despised him, she was at least comfortable with. What a pass things had come to for that to happen, the Princess couldn't help but grimace, which caused her to be thankful, once again, for the veil that covered her face. While she could see through it quite well, the fabric made it difficult for others to see her. The only annoyance was being required to lift it every time she wanted to take a sip of champagne. "I feel as though I am walking amongst the clouds." Eluned added.

"It is rather impressive, isn't it?" Hamartia said.

"Look," said Hevel, "it's Hywel and Auron." He waved to get their attention.

Wow, Eluned thought, he still has a colossal infatuation for Hywel, and the man is so patently heterosexual. For a minute, she actually felt sympathy for the King. She couldn't say she quite blamed him. Hywel was an extraordinarily handsome man. He could literally be the god, Thor, she thought as he strode up to the group. With that long golden hair and those overly muscular arms, she was positive that women all over the ballroom were silently swooning. And, Eluned had no doubt, from the way he was looking at her as he walked up (even his mask didn't hide that), she could easily occupy his attentions for the entire evening. His eyes almost literally lit up when he saw her, but for some reason she couldn't account for, she felt nothing for him but a modicum of platonic affection. Maybe he just wasn't her type. Eluned didn't know. She only knew that she felt nothing.

Auron looked luminous as a fairy, and Eluned told her so.

"Thank you," she gushed. "Your costume turned out so well. You could actually be the Lady in White."

"She wasn't real, was she?"

"Oh, I believe she was based on someone real," Auron replied, turning away from Eluned as Celyn whispered something in her ear.

A servant took Eluned's now empty champagne flute and handed her yet another. She was going to have to be careful. She'd had so little to eat that day that the first glass was already going to her head. She supposed she ought to head to the dining room for a bit of sustenance, but the thought of doing so didn't exactly thrill her. It would mean making excuses and drawing attention to herself. The Princess decided she would just have to wait longer between sips.

Hywel asked her a question about her costume, and she had to admit she knew very little about the 'Lady in White.' "It was the king's idea," she confessed, although surely Auron had told him. Eluned guessed he was just trying to be friendly. And that was one area in which she couldn't fault him. He was the only one of the group who had been consistently kind to her even when it aggravated his wife for him to do so. "As a matter of fact, I was just asking Auron about her. She said she's based on someone real but no one seems to know who or what happened."

"I'm not familiar with that particular ghost story," Hywel said, shaking his head.

Their party was rapidly expanding. Gethin and Celyn, who looked almost too adorable as leprechauns, soon joined them. Then, Matraqua and Chazak strode up together with something a little stronger than champagne in their hands. Clearly Matraqua was supposed to be Bacchus. Grape leaves twisted in a crown about his head, and Eluned thanked Omni he'd had the decency to wrap his stocky and hirsute body in a sheet of silk. Most images of Bacchus represented him in the nude, she remembered from her lessons with the Bandersnatch.

Hywel whispered to her that Chazak was another god, Loki. The Princess was not as familiar with him. She seemed to remember he was some kind of trickster, but that was about it. She asked after the Ladies Hilya and Aviv and was informed they had remained behind.

"My wife does not really enjoy this kind of event," Matraqua told her. Eluned remembered that their names hadn't actually been mentioned, but she had assumed they would be there as well. The Princess found herself wondering if the fact that Hilya and Aviv weren't particularly attractive had anything to do with it. It was true they were all wearing masks of various degrees of coverage but everyone in attendance was physically striking in appearance. It was indubitably beginning to trouble her.

No sooner than she'd had that thought that Bronwen and Gwenda approached with their spouses.

Bronwen, attired as a mermaid, introduced her husband, Collen, dressed as Neptune, complete with trident. Gwenda, and her husband, Tudur, claimed they were Parvati and Shiva. Clearly they weren't part of the 'inner circle' as they stayed only long enough to extol everyone's costume.

"So," the King asked, "are we ready?"

"Ready?" Eluned asked Hywel, who was still standing next to her.

"We're dining privately in the King's parlor," he informed

her. That irritated her. Why hadn't she been told? Even Rhys had assumed she was to eat in the dining room. Was there some reason she was consistently kept in the dark, and then just expected to know things? But, she was famished, so she took Arawn's arm when he proffered it and helped lead the way to the parlor. So far, this masquerade ball was unlike any other dance she'd ever attended.

At home, the ballroom was more of a banquet hall with a long table set up at one end on a raised dais at which the King and his guests of honor would sit; two other long tables were set perpendicular to it against the wall for the not-quite-as-high-born. The entertainment and dancing took place between those two tables.

Once again Eluned was struck by just how much King Arawn distanced himself from most of his subjects. Her father always made a point of greeting as many people as possible. What part of the word, evil, do you not understand, she chided herself.

A servant placed a bowl of chilled strawberry and mint soup with toasted almonds in front of her and she waited impatiently, stomach growling audibly, while every one else was served. How did she always manage to get herself into a predicament where she was faint with hunger?

Her flute was once again empty, but a serving girl quickly filled it with the ubiquitous champagne. She was definitely approaching tipsy. Thank Omni she was eating something.

A salad with blueberries, Gorgonzola, walnuts and grilled chicken followed, and the Princess felt that she was finally eating something with at least a little substance to it, something to soak up all that champagne.

They finished with a raspberry ice. And even more champagne. Apparently, the plan was to eat lightly but drown themselves in alcohol, which probably meant they would return to the ballroom and dance. At this point, she just looked forward to the evening ending. The champagne was definitely going to her head and the lack of food hadn't helped that.

BUT DANCE THEY DID. Mostly waltzing for what seemed like hours on end. Eluned was having flashbacks of the time she spent with the faeries. It didn't seem like a good omen. She danced with Arawn, first, then Hevel, Hamartia, Hywel, Gethin and then Matraqua and Chazak before being handed off to King Arawn once again.

During the occasional break, Eluned was forced to quench her thirst with champagne because that was the only thing that was being handed around. What she would have done for a glass of cold water. Yet, the Princess thought, or perhaps she hoped, that she was dancing most of the alcohol out of her system. Yet when Eluned heard the tolling of the bells from the cathedral in Prythew announcing that midnight had arrived, she found that she was quite dizzy when the music stopped suddenly.

The King called for the champagne glasses to be filled 'one last time' as he had a 'very important announcement' to make.

Eluned swayed, rather bleary-eyed next to him. Yes, the champagne had definitely gone to her head. Yes, she'd had a lot, but over the course of hours, why had it affected her so much?

The Princess took a deep breath, trying to focus. This was the moment. The moment that Eluned had been dreading for what seemed an eternity. It had finally arrived, and all she wanted to do was lie down in her comfy bed upstairs and wake up on the morrow knowing it was all over. Hangover or not— just let this be in her past. But, she cautioned herself, she must wait. For she was sure, if indeed he was about to announce their engagement, and despite the fact her synapses didn't seem to be firing properly, that the Crimson King would make a great spectacle of the proclamation that they were espoused. And then she would have to act surprised and grateful, and graciously acknowledge the congratulations. The Princess would need to give a performance that Queen Fuchsia would be proud of. And then, maybe then, Eluned hoped, she could finally go to bed. That is, if the room would stop spinning first. Why wouldn't the room stop whirling around her as if she were frozen to one spot, as if she were the center of the galaxy and the room revolved in her orbit?

Something wasn't quite right. Despite the fact she could barely think, she knew that. She already knew that too much alcohol tended to make her feel weepy, and sometimes even morose. Eluned remembered crying in Gwrhyr's arms in the gypsy camp. But now she felt numb. Literally. The Princess was suddenly aware that she couldn't feel her legs although it appeared that they were still holding her up. And that was when the champagne flute slipped from her hand, and she watched in slow motion as it exploded into a thousand shimmering pieces on the marble floor. Eluned made an attempt to reach for the pouch around her neck where the moonstone lay hidden, but she found she couldn't even move her arm anymore.

The Princess felt as if she was watching herself from the clouds against the ceiling. She saw Hywel catch her as her legs folded beneath her. And she regarded the ballroom in horror as the laughter rang against the walls. Laughter at her plight. They thought it was funny! And then, mercifully, she slid back into her body and descended into nothing but silence and darkness.

12ᵀᴴ Deer

A susurration like the murmuring of leaves or the burbling of a brook eased its way into her awareness beckoning her ever so gently back towards the light and consciousness. Even before Eluned opened her eyes, she felt her wrists and ankles straining away from her body as if she were on a rack.

But she wasn't on a rack. The Princess could feel the roughness of stone against her head, her body, and that deep bone-searing cold. They were the same sensations she'd experienced in Ruisidho, an alien texture. She knew she must be bound to the altar in the woods across the river, but she wasn't yet ready to let them know she had awakened. The Princess needed to determine as much as she could of her situation before she opened her eyes.

Eluned cleared her mind of her rising panic, and tried to recall the set up of the clearing. The altar had been in the middle with a pole of ash wood stationed at the head of the altar along with an ash wood pole on each side at arm and foot level. The way her limbs felt stretched away from her body, she must be bound to them. And that's when she realized the scratchy coarseness she felt about her throat meant her head must be bound to the fifth stake. They had no intention of allowing her to escape without death, it seemed.

Omni have mercy, she prayed, gritting her teeth to distract her from the tears of self-pity that threatened to stream from the corners of her eyes. She tried to focus on the murmuring and realized it was the quiet chanting of voices. Many voices. Were they waiting for her to awaken before sacrificing her or were they waiting for the appointed time of the solstice—seven minutes after ten o'clock in the morning. Eluned had looked it up in an almanac in the castle's library.

It was morning. She could feel the warmth of the sun on her face. If she had been unconscious since shortly after midnight, that meant she'd been out at least eight hours if not closer to ten. Although she wasn't tired, hunger pains gnawed at her belly.

Someone had either lifted her veil from her face or removed it completely. She felt her curls stir in a slight breeze. Removed it entirely then. The better to see her exposed throat, no doubt. Or was she just making assumptions or 'jumping to confusions' as Jabberwock liked to say? Would they slice her throat or impale her heart with a ceremonial blade? Perhaps strangulation was the method they preferred? Although, she supposed, it was just as possible that they would employ three different methods—one for each of their sacred three.

Perhaps she would never open her eyes. She wasn't sure she actually wanted to see the people who were eagerly awaiting her death. The thought of seeing Hywel was particularly repellant to the Princess as she had trusted him the most.

On the other hand, the stronger part of her wanted to stare them defiantly in the eyes. It probably wouldn't affect them either way, but it would make her feel better.

The Princess lifted her lids until she could see a bare sliver of light. Somebody murmured something a little more loudly as if they were speaking to someone rather than chanting. She closed her eyes again as she realized they had seen her eyelids flutter. So, they were watching her very closely. Damn. Oh well, she sighed inwardly; I might as well go ahead and get this over with.

Her eyes suddenly flew open. Whoever had been standing next to altar and observing stepped backwards with a gasp. Outside the circle of the altar defined by the poles she was lashed to, numerous figures completely hooded and in white robes, stood scattered about the clearing. The worshippers continued their chant as Eluned surveyed those closest to the altar. Unfortunately, other than the holes cut for their eyes, the hoods hid their faces.

Three figures, standing to her right, were dressed in embellished robes and hoods. One of the robes was more elaborately embroidered than the other two. No doubt the 'high priest' was Arawn, flanked on either side by Hamartia and Hevel. Hamartia was on his right, she realized, as he was the taller of the two.

Arawn was watching her. His bronze eyes were cold and calculating—inhuman. Eluned was horrified to see an obvious bulge pressing his robe outwards. She felt the bile rise in her throat. The bastard was clearly enjoying her predicament. The Princess whipped her head to the left in an effort to remove that image from her mind. This time, the tears stung her eyes and it took great effort on her part to refocus through the glaze of moisture.

As she blinked away the salty film, her eyes came to rest on the hooded figure standing adjacent to the pole that held the bonds of her left hand. He was unusually tall, she noticed, and his eyes were teal and boring directly into hers. The memory of forceful lips pressed to hers rose unbidden to her mind, and her heart soared. Gwrhyr!

Tears filled her eyes once again, but she fought them back. She needed to stay focused because there was now a slim chance she might actually make it out of this situation with her life.

Gwrhyr had disguised himself as one of the worshippers, and the white hood was a godsend for disguising his face as well as making it less noticeable that he was trying to communicate to her with his eyes.

The Princess looked away for a moment so as not to draw attention to him and found herself gazing into another set of familiar eyes. His face was hidden, of course, but she was positive the tall man with the brilliant blue eyes standing next to the pole that held the rope attached to her left foot was Hywel; and to his right, Gethin. Where was the remainder of the inner circle? She cast her eyes to the right. Matraqua and Chazak stood beside the right pole; the women were in the center at the foot of the altar.

She observed them with a burgeoning feeling of animosity. They had made her summer in Arberth as uncomfortable as possible with their snide remarks and open dislike, and upon their return to Prythew, had suddenly behaved as if they were her best friends. Not that she had trusted them for an instant. Omni have mercy on their souls, she thought, because it may take me a lifetime to forgive them.

Her eyes returned to Gwrhyr who looked downward at his right leg. He made a discreet gesture, as if he was holding a sword, and she realized that he had brought Dyrnwyn with him. He looked at the rope holding her hand and made a slicing motion with his right hand.

Eluned had to turn away once more. She was terrified that Arawn would notice something although he probably couldn't see much of Gwrhyr from his position. She arched her neck to look behind herself, and the rope about her neck cinched a bit more tightly. That was the most important rope to cut. She would be strangled in an instant if someone got to it before Gwrhyr had the opportunity to sever it immediately after slicing the rope binding her left hand.

Eluned realized that she and Gwrhyr had mere seconds

to play with before the element of surprise passed, and people started reacting. And the longer they waited to act, she grew cognizant of, the more likely the others were to respond quickly. At the moment, they seemed to be waiting to see what she would do. Or, perhaps, her original guess was correct, and they were waiting for the solstice to occur.

The Princess took a deep breath, planning: she could cut her right hand free immediately, but she wouldn't be able to release her feet until Gwrhyr had severed the rope that held her neck. Once those were cut, she could quickly do her feet, but which way to jump off the altar? Toward the left, the path to the tunnel was just beyond Gwrhyr's left shoulder. That was the way they needed to run.

No time like the present as her father liked to say. She looked at Gwrhyr and nodded.

Everything happened so quickly that she had a hard time explaining it to the others later. Gwrhyr simultaneously pulled Dyrnwyn from beneath his robe with his right hand and a short sword with his left.

Severing the rope between the pole and her hand with his left hand, he tossed Dyrnwyn to Eluned with his right, praying to Omni that she caught it. As he saw her left hand slide easily around the white and gold hilt, he was already moving toward the pole at her head.

It was all transpiring so quickly that Eluned felt as if only she and Gwrhyr were moving. As her hand slid around the hilt, the blue lightning-like fire was already racing up the sword and down her arm.

Eluned heard Arawn gasp before screaming in denial. He lunged toward her as she sundered the rope holding her right hand. She had not previously seen the sacrificial dagger in his right hand, but now it was raised high and falling toward her chest. Almost without thinking, she swung Dyrnwyn upwards, slicing through the Arawn's wrist almost as easily as a warm knife slides through butter.

The Princess felt the rope around her neck loosen, and quickly sat up to slash through the ropes holding her feet. Hywel was already moving forward, a dagger in his hand. His blue eyes looked shocked. Behind her, Arawn was shrieking in pain and fury.

Glancing behind her as she jumped to her feet, Eluned saw Hamartia attempting to staunch the flow of blood gushing from the stump of the King's wrist.

Hevel was picking up the King's hand, which lay on the ground amidst the leaf litter next to the knife that had fallen from its grasp. His face was a pale shade of green, and tossing the hand away from him, he turned away from the altar and vomited into the leaves.

Hywel was now racing along the altar toward Gwrhyr. Apparently the sight of Eluned standing tall on the altar, still in costume and with the magnificent sword blazing in her hand was more daunting than Gwrhyr with his short sword.

Matraqua and Chazak were beginning to move although most of the other worshippers seemed to be moving slowly away from the tableau at the altar.

Eluned couldn't allow Hywel to reach Gwrhyr. It wasn't that she didn't think her friend could out fight Arawn's Lord High Steward because, indeed, they seemed equally matched. Rather, she knew they needed a head start to reach the tunnel before the others regained their wits and started chasing them.

The Princess did the only thing she could think of on short notice: she flung herself onto Hywel's passing back, knocking him to his knees. She scrabbled quickly off his back, whirling her sword threateningly about her, the light sparking along the blade and her arm, in an attempt to prevent anyone from trying to be brave.

Gwrhyr moved forward, pressing his sword against Hywel's throat and kicking the dagger aside. Auron cried out, and Matraqua bellowed, lunging forward with a curved blade that looked dangerously sharp. Gwrhyr shouted a warning, and Eluned turned, parrying the Chancellor's attack.

But he was quick, and she needed to take advantage of her superior reach. It was with deep regret she found herself thrusting Dyrnwyn into his chest. She pulled the blood-soaked blade free, swallowing hard as her stomach flip-flopped and saliva filled her mouth. She didn't want to think about what she had just done. They had to get out of there.

"Now!" she yelled, and then she and Gwrhyr were running through the remainder of the worshippers who had yet to disappear into the forest like the ghosts they seemed to be attired as.

When they reached the small cairn, Eluned pushed back the rock that hid the button that opened the gate, depressing it and waiting impatiently as it slid upwards. Grabbing a couple of loose boulders from the cairn, she indicated that Gwrhyr should go first.

"What are you going to do?" he asked.

"I'm going to try and jam the door," she said. "Surely someone will be coming after us. Damn, there's Hywel now," she said, as she saw him running toward them, dagger back in hand but still more than a hundred yards away.

Gwrhyr hurried down the ladder as Eluned stepped onto it, herself. She depressed the button on the ladder and waited until the door had nearly closed before jamming a rock between the door and the ground. But the door slid into place, crunching through the rock like an egg.

"Damn it!" Eluned screamed in frustration.

"Not exactly rock solid," Gwrhyr said, stepping out of the way as Eluned tossed the other rock to the ground before scrambling down the ladder.

"You think?" she said, sarcastically, punching him on the bicep, before picking up the rock. "I think it's time to run again. And I despise running."

The Princess also discovered she hated running in a long dress with two pieces of rope still flapping around her ankles. She was terrified that at some point she was going to trip and injure herself, smashing headfirst into the tiled floor. And running with a sword in one hand and a rock in the other wasn't particularly easy either. But the adrenalin was flowing and her feet seemed to skim over the white tiles.

When she heard Hywel behind them, she even managed to pick up her pace a bit. As they rapidly approached the ladder beneath the gazebo, she was willing to bet they'd made it from one end to the other in less than ten minutes.

Next came the really difficult part. It was hard enough to climb down a ladder, but it took much more effort to climb upwards, and this end of the tunnel contained the longer ladder. And to make matters more difficult, she still had her sword in one hand and rock in the other.

"Can you take this?" she asked Gwrhyr, handing him the rock.

"You're not thinking of trying to jam the door again? It's the same type of rock."

"No, but we may need to drop it on someone's head," she explained. "You go first. I'll only slow you down, and besides I may have to fend off Hywel."

"I'll fend off Hywel."

"I have the longer reach," she said, holding up Dyrnwyn.

"You have a point," he sighed in resignation, stepping onto the ladder.

"A much longer and sharper point," she giggled in near hysteria as she climbed onto the ladder just beneath him. But ascending the ladder was rapidly draining her reserves, and it wasn't long before she started falling behind Gwrhyr.

At one point, as he waited for her to catch up, they could hear the sound of Hywel (they supposed) moving up the ladder beneath them.

"Don't throw the rock," she warned Gwrhyr, her voice strained by the exertion of climbing. "Wait till we see him."

"Give me some credit, Princess," he chided her. "I'm not a complete idiot."

"Sorry," she apologized quickly. "I'm trying not to panic."

"Don't worry," he assured her. "I'm not going to let you out of my sight."

Hywel was clearly gaining on them. Between his height and muscularity, he was zooming up the ladder compared to Eluned. A cold dread tickled the edges of her sanity. She had no doubt that between the two of them, they could easily repel Hywel. No, what worried her was the fact they might have to do him great injury if not worse. If she had to choose any of the inner circle to maim or kill, Hywel would have been her last choice.

When Gwrhyr finally reached the top of the ladder, the Princess was still more than six feet beneath it. As Gwrhyr pressed the button to open the tunnel entrance, she looked down to see that Hywel was just over an arm's length below her. Another foot and he could grab one of the ropes that trailed from her ankles.

"Hurry, hurry, hurry," she prodded, her voice rising in fear, "he's right below me!"

Gwrhyr scrambled through the door and turned to offer Eluned a hand as she pushed herself upwards the last few feet. But, just as Gwrhyr's hand closed on hers, her right leg was tugged downward. Hywel had reached the rope. A second later, she felt Hywel's hand close around her right ankle. The pearl- and diamond-studded slipper she'd been wearing since the previous evening fell off her foot and tumbled into the darkness, as Hywel braced himself to pull her downwards.

"He's got my ankle," Eluned said, almost calmly, staring into Gwrhyr's eyes. "Take this," she handed him Dyrnwyn, "and give me the rock." She couldn't come to grips with how positively tranquil she felt. Hywel was still tugging her leg downward although his hand was now around her knee, but she had hooked her right arm through a rung so while it was painful she wasn't really going anywhere.

This time being short had its advantages. She was actually closer to his head than Gwrhyr would have been. Using all her force, she slammed the rock into his face. Eluned could hear the crunch as his nose shattered and blood spurted from the wound. Hywel bellowed in pain, and for the briefest of moments, let loose of her knee.

The Princess used the advantage to propel herself another few feet up the ladder, but Hywel was already grasping for the rope again. He missed, but managed to grab a handful of her dress. He was still clinging onto it as Gwrhyr pulled her out of the tunnel and onto the floor of the gazebo, ripping a large segment of the hem from her costume.

Eluned turned to depress the button on the ladder but Hywel was already at the top, his head emerging from the tunnel into the gazebo. Blood poured from his nose, staining his chin red and his eyes gleamed with fury. What had happened to the gentle man who had once been so kind to her?

With great compunction and no choice, she took Dyrnwyn from Gwrhyr. "Take another step upwards," she threatened, "and I will be forced to slit your throat." She turned to Gwrhyr, "Or do you just want to kick him in the face?"

"Your call, Princess," he answered, but there was no time to decide as Hywel was already flinging himself out of the tunnel.

"Damn," the Princess said as Gwrhyr's foot made contact with Hywel's broken nose. He screamed in pain but continued to move upwards. "This is so pointless," she said in great sorrow. "You can't possibly defeat us. Please go back down the tunnel."

"No," Hywel howled through the blood, face twisted in rage. "Never!"

"I'm sorry," the Princess said, and slid the sharp edge of Dyrnwyn's blade across his throat.

Gwrhyr pushed him, sliced carotid spraying blood, back through the tunnel door. They could now hear others on the ladder and as Hywel fell, his body collided with a number of them. They heard screams as some lost their grips and fell downward along with Hywel. They both grimaced as they heard the sound of bodies making contact with the tile floor.

Eluned reached in to the tunnel to shut the door. She had a feeling that whoever was still on the ladder would come through the tunnel door a little more circumspectly.

"Time to run again," she sighed, turning toward the gazebo's steps. "Please tell me everyone and everything else is ready to go?"

"Chokhmah and Jabberwock are supposed to have the phaeton ready," he said as they took the straightaway, which he'd neglected to close, out of the labyrinth.

As they burst out of the labyrinth, the King's Guard took one glance at Eluned's bloody sword and dress, which now had the blood of three men soaking them, and gave chase, yelling at them to halt.

"As if," Eluned gasped under her breath. The stables were on the south side, just beyond the southeast tower. Eluned continued to run but now she had a stabbing pain in her gut, and her heart felt like it was going to explode in her chest.

Remind me why we're doing this again, she would have asked Gwrhyr if she'd been able to speak.

They rounded the southeast tower and Eluned saw the phaeton, with Halelu harnessed to it, and Chokhmah and Jabberwock waiting impatiently beside it. If it hadn't been the morning after the masquerade, there would have been more activity around the stable yard. As it was, no one was about other than the guards still giving them chase.

"Get into the phaeton," Gwrhyr yelled as they ran up. "We don't have much time."

Chokhmah lifted Jabberwock up into the front seat, and climbed in after him as Gwrhyr reached the carriage, and turned around to swing Eluned up into the back seat.

Now that they were in the phaeton, Eluned was clinging to Gwrhyr for dear life. His heart was pounding as loudly as hers.

"Now everyone think Whanga Palace, Seemu together," Jabberwock said, "on the count of three. One. Two. Three."

Eluned found herself praying "Whanga Palace, Seemu" with every fiber of her being. And then the disconcerting streaming darkness descended.

12TH DEER

A gentle breeze tinged with a touch of salt and frangipani brought Eluned back to awareness. She opened her eyes to find herself tucked into bed with a dozing Bonpo sitting beside her. Someone had removed her bloody dress as well as the trailing ropes from her hands and feet and neck.

Tears welled up in her eyes and without warning great wracking sobs shook her slender frame. Bonpo jumped to his feet.

"Leened, wat da matta?" the giant's face creased with concern. "Hockma!" He called the gypsy, at a loss as to what he should do.

She appeared at the door to the room. "What is it?"

Bonpo, in consternation, pointed to Eluned who was still sobbing. Chokhmah sat on the bed and pulled the Princess into her arms, rocking her and stroking her hair.

"It is quite all right," she told Bonpo. "We have no idea what she just went through, but with the amount of blood on her dress, it must have been traumatic."

Eluned quit sobbing long enough to ask, "Gwrhyr?"

"Still asleep. He seemed to enjoy the phaeton as much as you do."

"You ok, Plincess?" Bonpo asked.

"I'll be fine," Eluned sniffed.

"I go check Gooheel," he said.

Eluned giggled. "He's never going to be able to pronounce any of our names, is he?" she remarked once he'd left the room. There was a slight edge of hysteria to her voice. She was 'Plincess' or "Leened." Chokhmah was "Hockma," and he didn't even attempt Jabberwock, sticking with the Janawar's real name, Hiurau.

Chokhmah smiled, and squeezed Eluned's hand.

"You have no idea how happy I am that we're all together again," the Princess told Chokhmah. "Is Yona here?"

The gypsy shook her head, sadly. "Miryam said they have had no word of her. We can only pray that she is still making her way here. Perhaps stealing the hamper was a lot more difficult than she anticipated."

"Well I hope she's already done it because Hevel isn't going to be too happy when he returns," and her face paled as she remembered just why that was true, and she began crying again. "I had no idea when we began this journey," she sobbed, "that I was capable of killing people. I know it was self defense, but it feels so wrong."

Bonpo and Gwrhyr appeared at the door, and Eluned indicated that Gwrhyr should sit on the side of the bed farthest from the door on the other side of her. Bonpo returned to his chair as Gwrhyr joined Chokhmah and Eluned on the bed.

"I would have done anything to prevent your having to do that," Gwrhyr said as Eluned rested her head against his shoulder. He wanted desperately to kiss away her tears, to take her in his arms and comfort her but he wasn't sure if Eluned's affection was just shared experience.

"Where's Jabberwock?" Eluned asked.

"I send word you wake," Bonpo said. "Should be heel soon." And no sooner than the yeti had spoken, the Bandersnatch was pattering into the room.

"How on earth do you do that?" Eluned wondered aloud as Jabberwock jumped up onto the bed.

"Do what?"

"Appear whenever your name is mentioned."

The Bandersnatch chortled. "I have to have some secrets."

"Apparently," she said, and then sighed again, remembering all that led up to the phaeton ride.

"You don't have to talk about it," Jabberwock said.

"I don't even want to remember it," she wailed, "but it keeps coming back to me."

"It was touch and go there a few times," Gwrhyr said.

"You know," Eluned began, "cutting Arawn's hand off doesn't bother me at all, and I can live with having killed Matraqua, but the way Hywel forced me to hurt him. Kill him," she swallowed hard, "that will be in my nightmares forever."

Chokhmah hugged her as Gwrhyr squeezed the hand she had slipped into his.

"Unfortunately," Jabberwock said solemnly, "this is only the beginning. We officially have only five of the treasures. We have yet to discover whether or not Queen Miryam will add The Coat of Padarn Red-Coat to the treasures we've already collected."

"And we don't know if Yona managed to get the hamper," Eluned added.

"That still leaves nearly half," Gwrhyr said, and the group descended into silence considering the toll of retrieving just two of the treasures. Eluned hadn't even mentioned those who had been killed by Hywel's falling body. Not that they actually knew the body count, she thought. How many people would die before all the treasures had been gathered together again? Would this quest be worth the cost?

"Well," Chokhmah said, breaking into the silence, "we might want to get ready for our audience with Queen Miryam. Once she knows what we are doing, she may be more inclined to aid us in our quest."

WHEN THEY WERE READY, they walked together to the Queen's throne room where Miryam waited with the rest of her family. Prince Mauri and his wife, Elili, were there with their twin daughters, Leleua and Talei, and their son, Irirangi.

Eluned felt her knees go weak as she was introduced to Irirangi. He was gorgeous despite the unusual tattoos on his face—tall and muscular with long black hair and flashing brown eyes. And the way he smiled at her! She felt her heart thump painfully as her stomach somersaulted.

The Princess found she couldn't even pay attention to what was being said during their time with the Queen. Her eyes kept wandering back to Irirangi, who stood next to his sisters. And she was thrilled to see him sliding glances in her direction as well.

Eluned was so consumed with making eye contact with the exotic looking young prince that she completely missed Gwrhyr's reaction to the flirtation. His jaws and hands were clenched as he wrestled with what he felt was betrayal on the part of the Princess. He had just saved her life. Had that meant nothing to her?

Chokhmah had not missed his reaction, though. She sidled over to him and patted his back in commiseration. It did not take her gypsy skills to foretell that this was bound to happen at some point during the quest. Eluded's question on the night of her tarot reading revealed just how desperate she was to fall in love; and not just to experience love but to find it at *first sight*.

And while she was confident that Eluned would soon itch to return to the quest once more despite what had just transpired, the question Chokhmah had no answer to was just how quickly. When she had spoken to Gwrhyr earlier, she had discovered that he was already calculating just how long they needed to stay on the island, but this new development could seriously change the dynamics of the group. She found it highly unlikely that Gwrhyr would be amenable to asking Irirangi to join the quest. Not only would he rebel at having him along, but she felt sure that both Jabberwock and Bonpo would admit to feeling strongly that her nephew's son was not meant to be a part of the journey.

Glancing at her friends, she could see that Gwrhyr was trying in vain not to look as hurt, angry and extremely jealous as he felt; the ever-cheerful Bonpo was frowning; and even Jabberwock had lost the usual glint of amusement in his eyes.

Eluned, on the other hand, was oblivious to the by-play going on amongst her fellow travellers. Her face glowed with the blush that only infatuation can bring to the cheeks. Finally she knew the excitement of love at first sight, and he is even a prince, she smiled to herself. She finally had a face to put to her imaginings, and she was contemplating just how much coming to Favonia had already changed her life. Perhaps Irirangi could join them on their quest, she thought, biting her lip in anticipation. Wouldn't that be exciting? But that would be some time from now, right? She was finally on the island of her dreams and she wanted nothing more than to bask in Irirangi's attentions and the warmth of the sun far, far from the cold stone altar she had just been bound to. Surely she deserved a break after what she'd just experienced? Besides, Yona had yet to arrive. There was plenty of time.

Part III continues in
Book II of the Hallowed Treasures Saga: In Lonely Exile

You will find an excerpt from *In Lonely Exile*
at the back of this edition of *The Path to Misery*.

The Thirteen Kingdoms

The Triquetra Alliance

I. The Kingdom of Zion
Sigil: Golden Gryphon on Black

Ruled by: King Seraphim and Queen Ceridwen

Children: 1 daughter—the Princess Eluned

Capitol: Castle Mykerinos is located in Goshen

The River Musk flows southward through Zion and Castle Mykerinos is located on a plateau above the river. Other towns and landmarks include Roodspire and Muskroe, the Mountains of Misericord and the Misrule Pass.

II. The Kingdom of Aden

Sigil:
Scarlet Phoenix on Gold

Ruled by:
King Uriel (son of King Gavreel
and Queen Angharad, both deceased)

Children:
Not married but betrothed to Princess Eluned of Zion

Capitol:
Castle Bennu is located in Ponike,
which is a harbor town on the Gulf of Eudaemon

Other towns and landmarks include Batum.

III. The Kingdom of Sheba

Sigil:
Red Hawk on Green

Ruled by:
King Adeyemi and Queen Yobachi

Children:
Three sons—Daud, Paul, and Uwem;
Two daughters—Nala and Prisce

Capitol: Salama Palace is located in Mwezi-barafu

Sheba is bordered to the east by the River Mab. Other towns and landmarks include the Desert of Serket, and Baharimoto, a port town at the River Mab delta into the Anoon Ocean.

IV. The Kingdom of Favonia

Sigil:
Copper Sea Turtle on Blue

Ruled by:
Queen Miryam (King Rangatira is deceased)

Children:
Prince Mauri. He is married to Princess Elili,
and they have three children—one son, Prince Irirangi,
and twin daughters, Leleua and Talei

Capitol:
Whanga Palace is located in Seemu on the island of Favonia.

The other Favonian Islands include Hakinaipo, Hemamoku, Tapurora and Paliaina. Vailima is the main town on Paliaina, which is the smallest and most remote of the islands.

V. The Kingdom of Dyfed

Sigil:
Silver Unicorn on Purple

Ruled by:
King Cian and Queen Chelli

Children:
Eldest child a daughter, Gittan, and a younger son, Bryan.

Capitol:
Castle Abbert is located in Portuma on the Anoon Ocean

The River Leprican flows out of The Seven Sisters, a mountain range in the west of Dyfed and into Hardaigh Forest. The harbor town of Thírnagall is just west of Adamah's western border. Bogaine is a small village to the northwest of Thírnagall.

THE AWEN ALLIANCE

VI. The Kingdom of Annewven

Sigil: Crimson Dragon on White

Ruled by:
King Arawn (aka The Crimson King)

Children:
King Arawn is not married although he does
have a number of illegitimate children

Capitol:
Castle Pwyll is located in Prythew; King Arawn winters at
Castle Emrys in Arberth on the Anoon Ocean

The River Mab forms the western border of Annewven, and the River Duir flows through the Prythew valley. Ruisidho is a village near the western border of Annewven that is home to Standing Stones atop a hillock. Avalach Forest, near Arberth, was once home to the unicorn, Nyx.

VII. The Kingdom of Simoon

Sigil:
Grey Wolf on Forest Green

Ruled by:
King Hamartia and Queen Foehn

Children:
4 sons: Kaiser, Jarvis, Bemot and Raynor

Capitol:
Castle Rodolf is located in Sigwald

The River Duir flows southward through Simoon and into Annewven before reaching the Anoon.

VIII. The Kingdom of Adamah

Sigil:
Gold Lion rampant on Silver

Ruled by:
King Hevel

Children:
King Hevel is betrothed to Yona

Capitol:
Castle Lavieven is in Stonehelm

The mountain range of Panavhadesh runs through the center of the kingdom, north to south. It towers over Adam's Way, a trade route running from Hashirim southward to Markhesh-van. Other towns on Adam's Way include Tobermory and Hagafen. The major port of Seagirt is located on Adamah's eastern border on the Anoon Ocean.

IX. The Kingdom of Kamartha

Sigil:
Black Satyr on Pale Blue

Ruled by:
King Janak and Queen Lakshmi

Children:
3 sons: Amit, Baldev, Chetan;
4 daughters: Amala, Bala, Chandra, Divya;
Amit and Amala are twins

Capitol:
Lamaxana Palace is located in Kaumari

Queen Fuchsia, the Princess Eluned of Zion's great grand-mother, is from Kamartha and grew up in the Wilds of Discord near the Kingdom's southern border with the lost Kingdom of Pelf. Later, she returned to Kamartha to become an actress on The Masala, the theater district in Kaumari.

X. The Kingdom of Dziron

Sigil:
Golden Dragon on Crimson

Ruled by:
King Zhang and Queen Ling

Children:
3 sons: Qiang, Chao and Huang.
One daughter: Xiang. Princess Xiang, who is 16, is betrothed to Prince Aahil of Tarshish who is 22 years her elder.

Capitol:
Tsering Palace is in Jungnay

The Vale Vixen in the Peaks of Vulpecula was once home to the Janawar. The Peaks of Vulpecula is home to the Yeti.

The Neutral Kingdoms

XI. The Kingdom of Naphtali

Sigil:
White Winged Horse on Red

Ruled by:
Queen Njima

Children:
She is single, having broken her betrothal
to Prince Aahil of Tarshish.

Capitol:
Castle Indalo is located in Jazeel on the
western side of the Pegasus River.

The former capitol—Shamash Palace in Kamea on the Djed Sea—was deserted after the events that caused the Devastation of Pelf and formed the Sea of Blood.

XII. The Kingdom of Tarshish

Sigil:
Black Cobra on Tan

Ruled by:
King Dodi and Queen Chahindra

Children:
2 sons—Boutros (the eldest) and Aahil (the youngest child)
and one daughter, Huda

Capitol:
Iqbal Palace is in Tartessos, a port town
on the western border with the Anoon Ocean.

Tarshish is the southernmost kingdom. Smuggler's Bay is located to the east, and is a favorite hiding place for pirates.

XIII. The Kingdom of Pelf *aka* The Devastation of Pelf

Sigil:
Black Kraken on Red

Ruled by: No current rulers.
King Alborz and Queen Jazmin ruled before the Devastation.

Children:
2 sons—Alborz and Gaspar;
1 daughter—Parisa. Only Alborz survived.

Capitol:
Zhaleh Palace was located in Buta on Pelf's southern border
with the Anoon Ocean.

Currently the Devastation of Pelf is inhabited by what are
known as the Aberrations.

PRONUNCIATION GUIDE

Princess Eluned: E-leen-ed
Gwrhyr: Goor-heer
Chokhmah: (ch as in loch) Hock-mah
King Arawn: Aroun as in around
Queen Foehn: Fern
Captain Bleddyn: Blethin (th as in the)
Lord High Steward Hywel: Hoo-well
Lady Celyn: Kay-lin

Animals

Heiduc: Hi-duke

Other

Prythew: Prith-yew
Dyrnwyn: Doorn-win
Castle Pwyl: Poo-ull

DAYS OF THE WEEK

Monday: Deethyeen
Tuesday: Deethmarth
Wednesday: Deethmerker
Thursday: Deethyai
Friday: Deethgwener
Saturday: Deethsadoorn
Sunday: Deethseel

MONTHS

Beth (December 24 to January 20)
Luees (January 21 to February 17)

Neeon (February 18 to March 17)
Feharn (March 18 to April 14)
Saitheh (April 15 to May 12)
Eeahth (May 13 to June 9)
Deer (June 10 to July 7)
Teeneh (July 8 to August 4)
Colth (August 5 to September 1)
Meen (September 2 to September 29)
Gort (September 30 to October 27)
Hetal (October 28 to November 24)
Rees (November 25 to December 22)

Read an excerpt from

In Lonely Exile
Book Two of the Hallowed Treasures Saga

12th Deer

As the first of the bells began to chime out the hour, Yona slipped out of her room and padded, as silently as she could, down the grand stairwell. She would have preferred to use one of the smaller stairways, but this one led directly to the foyer where the wicker basket was displayed in its glass case. 'You're a shadow,' she tried to convince herself, hugging the wall, 'no one can see you.' Fortunately, it was relatively dim with just a few flickering torches lighting the way.

When she reached the main entrance hall, she peered from the shadows of the staircase. Not only was the foyer blessedly empty, it was dark as well. She slipped a vial of oil, the glasscutter, her hairbrush, and a rag from the hamper. The oil, according to her research, made it easier to cut the glass; the rag would hopefully muffle the noise when she used the brush to tap the glass. She placed the rag and brush at her feet to keep her hands free for the oil and glasscutter.

Slowly, heart thundering in her chest, she opened the vial containing some olive oil, all she could lay her hands on, and smeared it in a circle around the ancient lock. She then anointed the cutting wheel, as well, just to be safe before pressing the wheel into the glass, defining, as best she could, a circle through the oil. She stopped, listening for the approach of the guards. Silence. She picked up the rag, and covering the lock with it, she rapped the end of the cutter against the circle. A faint crack, but the glass didn't move. She put the glasscutter on the floor and picked up the brush, which was wider and made of tortoise shell.

Biting her lip and taking a deep breath, she struck the glass forcefully. It was pretty thick. The glass tilted inward, lock still attached to the outside of the case. She returned the brush and glasscutter to the hamper, and using the rag, physically twisted the glass and lock until they snapped beneath the pressure.

Still no sound of guards. Were they taking advantage of the King's absence by making their rounds less often? Or not at all? She swung the door of the display case open and removed the hamper, transferring, as quickly as possible, her belongings from the replacement hamper, which she then put in the display case.

She stood back to observe her handiwork. It was pretty damn obvious that it was a different hamper and that there was a gaping hole in the glass, but she didn't actually have much choice. She hoped the guards were sleeping it off somewhere and wouldn't reappear until morning. As added insurance, though, she removed the two nearest torches. There, she nodded to herself, the display case was now hidden in the shadows.

Grasping her treasure firmly by its wicker handle, she made her way to the servants' entrance. From there she would be allowed to leave the castle without much notice; just another nun leaving after praying with an ill child or dying parent.

Bowing her head, she made her way down the cobbled streets of Stonehelm. The city was silent but for the occasional skitter of a rat or yowl of a cat. Even the dogs seemed voiceless this morning.

Yona kept moving. Dawn was only a couple of hours away,

and she wanted to be as far from Stonehelm as possible when the sun rose.

5TH DEER

As luck would have it, stealing the hamper, the treasure belonging to the Kingdom of Adamah, was turning out to be significantly more difficult than Yona had imagined. While she and her fiancé, King Hevel, had left Arberth on the coast of Annewven for Hevel's kingdom of Adamah before her friends had returned with King Arawn to his capital of Prythew, it had taken them more than four days by sea to get to Seagirt.

She had easily arranged to go with the king straight to his castle in Stonehelm using as her excuse the fact that she wanted to avoid her parents for a little longer. "They're so strict," she told him. "I'll be stuck in the house until I come visit you again. Despite my age, they treat me like a child. Please let me stay until Teeneh. That's not that much longer." As Hevel actually didn't care one way or another, he readily acquiesced.

But from Seagirt, it was more than a two-day trip by horseback to get to Stonehelm and Castle Lavieven. By then Yona had been so exhausted it had taken her an entire day to recuperate before she could start looking into the logistics of stealing the hamper.

And, it didn't take her much time at all to ascertain the essential problem was something she'd never even considered. She had already suspected that the treasure, which was made even more special by the fact it was one of the Thirteen Hallowed Treasures, was not guarded twenty-four hours a day. Yona had quickly discovered that the King had it guarded during the day only when there were more of his subjects on the premises. At night, on the other hand, the regular guards checked it only during their rounds—a problem easy enough to maneuver around.

No, the real quandary was now that Castle Lavieven had its King back in residence, the number of people loitering about, day and night, was astounding. Servants, stewards, knights, pages, you name it—there were folks everywhere—all essential castle staff, but a preponderance of people nonetheless! Yona was truly flummoxed.

Perhaps things would calm down again once Hevel left for the Summer Solstice Masquerade in Annewven. She wasn't invited because she was still Hevel's fiancée, but once they were married she'd be expected to attend. Her new friend, the Princess Eluned felt sure the event included a religious ceremony involving human sacrifice, and Yona wasn't sure she was wrong. Eluned, along with her other friends were supposed to steal Annewven's two treasures while she stole the hamper.

Like the rest of her friends, she would have to wait until Hevel (or, in their case, King Arawn) was otherwise occupied before she attempted to steal the treasure. Unfortunately, she scowled, that meant she could not even begin the journey to meet her friends in Favonia until they were on their way to Favonia.

She felt her stomach drop. It had just occurred to her if she had to travel after King Arawn's treasures had been stolen, her journey would become much more perilous. Hevel wouldn't have even suspected her of the theft (at least, at first), if she had been able to steal the hamper before the chariot and chessboard were taken from Annewven.

Afterwards, though, both Annewven and Adamah would be on alert because they would know she had taken the treasure. How could they not? She had spent so much time with Eluned there wouldn't be any doubt. Even if Eluned, Chokhmah, Gwrhyr and Jabberwock weren't successful, they would still search for her. They would also realize she had no intention of marrying Hevel.

Her father, who held command over Hevel's navy, would

be patrolling the coast continuously. She had to come up with a new plan. There was no going back to Seagirt now, because, despite everything, she still intended to steal the hamper and make it to Favonia.

Later in the afternoon, she made her way to Hevel's library to pour over his maps. She needed to know her options. There were so many things to take into account, but only one option seemed the most possible after she had considered everything. She would have to make her way along the trade route that twisted and curved beneath the mountains of Panavhadesh to the village of Markheshvan, which sat at the base of the mountains near the border between Adamah and Tarshish.

There she could hire a guide to lead her across the mountains through the Hatseetz Pass, which was the easiest gap to travel through, undetected, because it was the most difficult to reach. Should she reach Markheshvan and maneuver the Hatseetz Pass successfully, she could make her way to Smuggler's Bay on the coast of Tarshish, or, as her pirate lover, Libni, referred to it, "Abandon Hope". The horseshoe-shaped bay had a narrow entrance, which was easy to guard from the sea and sheer cliffs dropping straight into the bay that made it difficult to approach from behind.

But, smugglers are ingenious, even cunning, when it comes to protecting themselves and there was, naturally, a secret path down the cliffs. Libni had told her about it once when Yona was sixteen and they'd shared everything. Although that had been nearly five years ago, she was sure the path still existed.

The other obstacle was her appearance. She was a stunning young woman and she was betrothed to the King. Someone was sure to recognize her along some part of the journey to Tarshish. How could she change her appearance enough to make her unrecognizable to those she came in contact with? She needed to blend into background, so to speak. She needed to be someone who no one would give more than a passing glance.

Trying to disguise herself as a male was out of the question; her figure was just too feminine to pull it off. Besides, she'd missed her chance to pick up some male clothes while she was in Arberth because she'd opted to spend the day with Libni instead. There'd be too many questions if she tried to acquire trousers and a tunic in Stonehelm.

Her eyes brightened as the perfect answer dawned on her. Fortunately, no one else was in the library to catch her grinning like a fool. A Sister of Holy Supplication—that was the answer. No one yet knew she wouldn't be attending the masquerade nor did they know the theme of the celebration was the "supernatural". Of course, she couldn't help but snigger, considering their beliefs, the kings and their cronies would actually get a good laugh if she showed up in that particular costume!

Regardless, she could have one of the seamstresses create the nun's costume for her without any questions being asked. She hurried from the room. She had no time to waste.

A Sister could travel anywhere in Hevel's kingdom, she thought as she raced along the hallway to the staircase, and not only travel anywhere, but travel anywhere unmolested. She bit her lip, trying to hide her smile, as she dashed down the stairs to the first floor below ground where the seamstresses stitched away all day.

Theirs was a dreary life and she felt not a little guilt requesting the costume. The Princess had done wonders in opening her eyes to the plight of servants. Yet, hers was a much higher commission—bringing the treasures together once again for the benefit of humankind. Surely her God, Omni, would bless the woman who made her costume.

The seamstress promised Yona she would have the habit finished before she and the King left for Prythew the following week. King Arawn had been kind enough to offer to send Hevel the magic phaeton on Tuesday with a servant in order that he and Chazak, his chancellor, could get there more quickly. So, while she hated being deceitful about the costume, she was also determined to remain single-minded in her goal of removing the hamper from the Kingdom of Adamah.

Now to figure out just how she was going to remove that particular object from the glass case in which it was displayed. For example, where was the key to open the case? She was going to have to ask Hevel some pointed questions without it arousing his suspicions.

Fortunately, she was dining with him this evening. She'd make sure to tell his wine steward to bring out a bottle of the ancient vine as it was the most potent. She stopped by the wine cellar on the way back to her room. She needed to make sure she looked good this evening. Despite his indifference to her as a woman, he actually felt great pride when she played up her "attractiveness", which, she found herself smirking, was Hevel's way of saying cleavage.

YONA WAS BRUSHING HER HAIR OUT after her bath, long auburn waves tumbling half way down her back, when she realized she would have to cut it if she were going to play the part of a Sister of Holy Supplication. If for some reason she were caught with her veils off, she needed to look as close to the real thing as possible. She felt a brief stab of regret. Her hair was beautiful. Yet, there was also something a bit exciting, something nearly taboo about cutting it because while men often wore their hair long, she'd never known a woman to wear her hair short other than the nuns.

She pulled it away from her face. Not bad, she thought, I might actually like short hair. But she was getting distracted. She turned to the armoire where what few dresses she had with her were hanging. She chose the scarlet silk. It was cut the lowest and was snug across her ribs, as well, emphasizing her not insignificant cleavage. The things we do, she thought, shaking her head as she pulled it from the hanger.

"So," YONA SAID, as she poured Hevel some more wine, "I was looking at the Hamper today because I've never actually looked at it before. I know it's one of the thirteen treasures, but I am not really familiar with why it's a treasure, or rather, what its special magic is."

"It's a simple magic," he explained after taking a sip of wine, "one need only put within it a meal for one man, and a meal for one hundred men can be withdrawn from the hamper."

"Nice," she said. "Very impressive. Do you use it often?"

"Use it? Heavens no!" Hevel looked shocked. "I don't think it has been removed from its case in more than a century. The key has long since been lost at any rate."

Yona nodded her head in understanding while thinking, 'Damn, now I'm going to have to break the glass. How do I do that quietly?' "Have you decided on your costume for the masquerade?" she asked, changing the subject.

The interrogation had gone much easier than she'd anticipated, but the news about the lost key left her nearly frantic. Originally, she thought it might take them a while to notice the hamper she had planned to replace the actual picnic basket with wasn't the authentic treasure. People were so used to it being there, after all. But, if she had to break the glass, they would notice right away—possibly the night she stole it. Too bad she'd never learned to pick locks.

She knew one or two people in Seagirt who could probably help her out that way, but not here in Stonehelm though doubtless the town boasted a lock picker or two. Unfortunately, she neither had the time to find one nor earn his or her trust. And though gold could open a lot of doors, she just couldn't take the risk that she would be discovered before she stole the hamper. Why was nothing ever simple?

So, it was back to the library the following day. She had heard that diamonds cut glass, but after a bit of research browsing through books on everything from jewels to cut glass, she discovered that despite the fact she had a beautiful diamond sparkling on the ring finger of her left hand, she was going to need something a little more complicated. If she wanted to cut the glass on the display case, she would need a glasscutter. And that meant she would have to find one. Mentally she walked through Stonehelm and decided her best chance would be with someone who cut glass for windows and that type of thing. For small panes, they might just have a glasscutter around.

If she could get a glasscutter, the sound of the case breaking might not be as loud. She would just need a towel to mute the sound of her tapping (or hammering, if that's what it took) the scored line. Or what if she scored a circle around the lock itself? Could she tap the lock loose? Would that be less obvious? She would just have to try it and if it didn't work she'd go for the smash and grab. But that meant she would have to be ready to flee the palace as soon as she'd retrieved the hamper from the case. And, she needed to keep in mind what Libni had told her more than once, "As long as you look like you know what you're doing, no one will bother you."

Now she had to come up with an excuse to visit a glass company. She was quite adept at pocketing small items, a skill she had honed when she first started hanging out on the docks with her pirate and smuggler pals. Once she had the glasscutter, she need only wait for Hevel to leave. She would bring very little with her, essentially what would fit in the hamper, which should reduce her possessions to need rather than desire. Although, she thought, opening the slim volume that Eluned had bought for her in the market in Prythew, the poetry of Schlomo might be the exception.

WHILE ATTENDING MASS IN THE CASTLE'S SMALL CHAPEL on Deethseel, she had a flash of inspiration. She had given herself a headache trying to come up with a reason to need a sheet of glass. But, what if she didn't need glass but rather wanted to commission a piece of stained glass for the small chapel in memoriam of her grandmother? She had been very close to her mother's mother who had passed away two years ago. Obviously, it would have to be something from Scripture, but what? Perchance a representation of The Amma, the mother? That could work. Yes, she liked it.

On Deethyeen, she picked up her costume, no one yet the wiser to her plans, and stashed it in her room away from the prying eyes of her maidservants. She then told Hevel about her plans for a window dedicated to her grandmother, which, of course, he was fine with. It wasn't his religion anyway, and as far as Yona was concerned, the less he had to think about her the better. He was too busy immersed in last minute plans for the Summer Solstice.

The trip to the stained glass artist she had chosen happened without a hitch. It was easy to pick up one of the many glasscutters that littered the worktables. So, the following day, after saying her farewells to Hevel and his Chancellor, Chazak, she returned to her room, intending to hide out the remainder of her time in the castle. She feigned sickness and sent her ladies away after they had procured for her the bread, wine and cheese she would need to make it through the following day.

That night she chopped off her long hair using a pair of shears she'd slipped up her sleeve while in the quarters of the seamstresses. It looked a bit ragged, but she thought it quite becoming, nonetheless. She bundled the shorn hair into a sack and hid it in the back of her armoire. Hopefully, she would have a significant head start before they realized she was missing. And once they discovered the hair, she would have already "disappeared."

She packed what little she could bring into the faux hamper, including a couple of apples, a loaf of bread, a flask of wine and a flask of water, and a wedge of hard cheese. After all, she prayed, if Omni were good, this little bit of food would last her all the way to Smuggler's Bay, if necessary.

The sun eventually set on the appointed day, and she put on her costume, carefully arranging the veils to show as little of her face as possible. And then, she waited. Patiently, at first. But, as the hours slowly crept by (she was waiting for the bells to toll three o'clock in the morning), she found herself pacing her room in an attempt to keep her rising panic at bay.

Finally, the first of the bells began to ring the hour, and Yona began her journey.

Acknowledgements

A special thanks goes to Griffin, Frank and Laura for reading through *The Path to Misery* when it was still *Thirteen Treasures* and offering me helpful criticism. And to Lois and Ginger from my Writers' Group for helping me refine the prologue.